CAGED REFLECTIONS

THE REFLECTION SERIES
BOOK TWO

SK PRYNTZ

Author's Note:

I adore you all so much. When I became an author, I never dreamed that I would find such loving and truly amazing people that I am honored to now call my friends. You are the blood and bones of these pages of love. Thank you.

Please regard the trigger warnings.

TRIGGER WARNING LIST

To My Readers: This is your Trigger Warning List.

Above all, mental health matters, and I want to be extremely clear: this tale is a horror romance. There is no small amount of triggering content in this book, including but not limited to:
   -Rape (MMC Experiences in detail)
   -Murder
   -Gore
   -Sexual Assault
   -Sexual Assault of minors (This book is about the sex trade, and there are minors depicted.)
   -Sex Trade Depictions
   -Vomiting
   -Torture
   -Sodomy
   -Kidnapping
   -Whipping
   -Unconventional Views of Law Enforcement
   -Slanderous Name Usage

-Profanity

-Detailed PTSD

-Descriptive Death Scenes

-Cow Prods on Humans

-Serial Killing

-Body Mutilation

-Forced Auto-cannibalism

-Orbital Injury and Death

-Pyromania

-Death by Fire

-Child Death

-Gaslighting

-Binding

-Attempted Abortion

-Mental Health Depictions

-Desecration of Corpse

-Beheading

-Loss of Parent

-Buried Alive

-Drug Overdose

-Comatose Depictions

-Forced Drug Use

-Waterboarding

-Entrapment

-Funeral

-Hospital Scenes

-Explicit Sexual Encounters

-Self-Mutilation

-Suicide Attempt

CHAPTER PLAYLIST

AVAILABLE ON SPOTIFY

- Dedication – "Sound of Freedom" by Justin Jesso
- Chapter 1 – "The Grace" by Never Ending White Lights
- Chapter 2 – "Wild Horses" by Bishop Briggs
- Chapter 3 – "My Song Know What You Did in the Dark" by Fallout Boy
- Chapter 4 – "Yummy" by Justin Bieber
- Chapter 5 – "Paper Hearts" by Tori Kelly
- Chapter 6 – "Before You Go" by No Resolve ft. Katey x Krista (Cover)
- Chapter 7 – "To The Boy" by Kylie Muse
- Chapter 8 – "Unholy" by Our Last Night (Cover)
- Chapter 9 – "Please" by Omido x Ex Habit
- Chapter 10 – "Cravin' " by Stiletto x Kendyle Paige
- Chapter 11 – "Torch" by Black Veil Brides
- Chapter 12 – "Forever" by Papa Roach
- Chapter 13 – "Pretend My Pain Away" by Citizen Solider
- Chapter 14 – "Truth or Dare" by Bad Wolves

BONUS TRACK LIST

"Down" by Jason Walker

"Rebirthing" by Skillet

"Cursed" by Ari Abdul

"Colors" by Elvis Drew

"All This Time" by Tobby Mai

"Whispers in the Dark" by Skillet

"Iris" by The Goo Goo Dolls

"With Me" by Sum 41

"Pyre" by Elle Chante

"Justify" by The Red Jumpsuit Apparatus

"Wake Up" by Coheed and Cambria

"In The End" by Black Veil Brides

"Watch The World Burn" by Falling In Reverse

"I Will Not Bow" by Breaking Benjamin

"Tangled Up In You" by Staind

"Chasing Cars" by Snow Patrol

"Elastic Heart" by Written By Wolves (Cover)

"Coming Undone" by Korn

"Running Up That Hill" by Loveless (Cover)

"Comatose" by Skillet

"Dare You To Move" by Switchfoot (Alt. Version)

BLURB

Eilizaveta (Ivy):

In more ways than one, Ivy has lived her entire life caged. She may have been rescued from her prison, but the monsters still haunt her dreams, never being truly free. Her body bears the marks left by her past. Her mind is tormented with the echo of those never rescued. Ivy is on a mission to free those souls that were taken by destroying the ones who claimed them, but The Masks organization is not the only foe she faces. Her knight in shining armor and the undeniable allure she feels for him will be the biggest challenge. He, too, is looking for a monster to slay. He just doesn't realize that the monster is her.

Micah:

Tormented by a past that has always led his future, Micah is always the diligent soldier, the perfect man for his job as a Detective. He has uncovered so many secrets, and every day, he gets closer to finding the target he's been tracking, closer to finally slaying the monster who has been ripping the city apart. Micah has found himself conflicted for the first time with his position. He wants to protect his Little Ghost from the past that haunts her. Ivy has a secret that Micah can't quite figure out. His allure and passion for her are blinding, and he only wants to see her demons slain. How can he protect someone who never stays in one place? How can he truly save a ghost?

His job is to bring justice. Her mission is to bring pain. What will happen when the reflections of the past and future collide? Will the love of the tortured souls be enough to free them both of their pain? Or will they both forever remain caged?

Micah Quinn

Chapter 1

Passing by my bathroom mirror one more time, I ensured my tie's knot was done correctly. I didn't like wearing penguin suits now any more than I did as a child. Honestly, I only wore them when my mother's nagging voice annoyed me enough to give in. My parents always wanted me to be the prized show pony, the good son, the diligent soldier. My little sister, Penelope, was the only person who didn't expect anything from me. She just wanted me to fit in and be loved by our cruel family.

A sigh of shame echoed around me at the thought of Penn and her dainty little hands scolding me when she'd shoo my fumbling fingers out of the way to fix my tie for me. She'd always had the grace and etiquette of our mother but also the sass and rebellion of our father.

"I miss you, Penn," I whispered to the air.

1

The charged room felt warmer with the thoughts of her spirit. The usual anger and shame burned my cheeks when I said her name, but the anger at myself and the guilt that I didn't protect her when she needed me...was still too much to handle.

When she disappeared from our home that night, my entire family changed. It was as if we all became a different version of ourselves, the grief too much to bear, too hard to accept. My sister was the light of our home, the reason my parents ever truly smiled.

When that light was extinguished, when the words of a blank-faced cop snuffed out the glimmer of hope...we all felt as if we had disappeared with her. Our true essence was buried alongside the empty casket.

Her body was never found.

The police managed to find the bones of a teenager, but there was nothing concrete to bury. The name scribbled on her headstone was the only defining evidence that it was Penelope's empty grave.

Even after the burial, it took years of my mother shoving posters of Penn's face into everyone's hands with no results and my father barking orders to police officers with no resolution to help us accept the truth. She was gone.

Admitting to myself that I took part in extinguishing her light simply by being complicit made it nearly impossible for me. I joined the army after graduating college, escaping my family's suffocating memories. It wasn't until years of failed attempts to die honorably as a soldier that I left to try to do real justice for my sister.

Becoming a police officer to find her and take down the monsters that stole her from us was the only way I could help fix what we'd lost, but somewhere along the way...I literally lost my damn mind. My father may be a lawyer with every rich fuck in his pocket, but the forced time the lawyers created for me at Hospital Twelve didn't erase my past completely.

I was no saner than the inmates I had cared for while there. Hospital Twelve was just as much a piece of me as all the others within its confined walls. I suppose my father gave me a new lease on life by releasing me after a year of wallowing in my self-pity at the asylum.

My friends became enemies.

My enemies became friends.

I found a purpose beyond the pain and self-loathing, a way to quiet the nightmares that plagued my mind, even if it was just a moment of peace.

I became justice.

I was justice.

I saved people.

Whether running down a thief to retrieve an old lady's purse or catching serial killers, I was justice. The one thing that kept me going in this world was thinking of all of their names—every life saved and every dragon slayed.

The department came up with the stupid name for me ever since they thought I took down the Snow White killer. The truth was that their 'dragon slayer' was a fraud. I'd arrived that night only to find a smoldering barn, a massacre of men, and my very dead chief.

It was easier for people to believe that I single-handedly took down a serial killer who was putting Rochester into a mass hysteria for years than to admit things didn't add up. That wasn't the first time the bigwigs in law decided things were better left unsaid, and it wouldn't be the last.

Adjusting my tie, I looked at the folded paper on my desk. If there was one person worth saving in this world, it was Ivy. I found her in that cage six weeks ago, her body so frail, beaten, and abused. She was so strung out on whatever drugs they forced into her that I couldn't even see the beautiful color of her eyes until recently.

From the moment I'd saved that breathtaking woman, I'd refused to leave her side. She was scared, timid, and unsure of the world around her. She reminded me of myself. I didn't bear the scars she had on her body, but my mind was covered with them.

She was strong-willed, stubborn, and vibrant. I'd known the day I'd carried her in my arms out of that hell that she would survive. Ivy was a goddamn miracle and one I admired. She was resilient and moving on, whereas I felt stagnant, like I was continuing to live but only in a corporeal form.

My phone rang on the dresser table, jarring me from my thoughts.

"Quinn speaking," I said.

The dainty sigh at the end of the line made me soften. My shoulders visibly sagged as I let out a breath of my own. "Ivy?"

She was being released from the hospital today, which was the whole reason for my 'suit and jacket get up.' I was taking her to the Harold. After all she'd been through, she deserved to be wined and dined more than anyone. I was so damn proud of her. I probably wasn't worthy of having that honor, but I wasn't going to complain about fate's choices today.

"Yes. It is me." Her lilted accent was soft but noticeable. "Hello, Detective."

I shook my head, tsking at her. "Call me Micah. I insist. Today, I am officially coming to you as a friend, not a detective."

The phone was silent for a minute. I almost thought she'd hung up or I'd lost the call until she spoke again. "Okay, Micah."

Giddiness ran through my veins when she said my first name. It made me blush. I swear that girl made me a horny teenager all over again. It was not just because of her breathtaking beauty—her long, wavy black hair, so black it looked blue, eyes the color of molten gold, or a body that was so petite and defined...no. My reaction was more because of who she was. She had a shyness to her that reminded me of Penn.

She was kind, curious, and beyond sassy when she didn't get her way. Her interactions at the hospital revealed how spunky she was. The nurses were constantly bothering her with requests. Urine and bloodwork samples had become an everyday occurrence.

She often refused.

This caused the staff to give me an ear full as if I had any control over her choices. My chief scolded me once as well. It was the day Ivy took her refusals a bit too far. She poured apple juice into one of the urine sample cups and drank from it when the charge nurse came by to grab it. I still laughed, thinking about the look on the nurse's face. It was priceless.

Ivy loved creating little pranks like that.

It became our game, sleuthing out the hidden surprises she wanted me to find. Her favorite prank was to wrap the faucet in plastic and secure it with elastic bands, waiting with a big smile on her face until I unknowingly turned it on and drenched myself.

It wasn't until I pushed a little prank on her that things changed the dynamic between us. A friendly banter became... something unexplainable.

I WALKED INTO THE HOSPITAL ROOM, MY EYES ALREADY PEELED FOR MY Little Ghost's prank of the day. She was sitting on the bed. Her robe hugged around her body, and that devious smile...she didn't even bother to hide.

"What is it today, Little Ghost?"I carefully stepped over a blanket on the ground and moved it away with my foot.

She didn't speak but smiled wider. I narrowed my eyes, using my mighty detective skills near the back wall. There weren't any bananas hiding or toothpaste caps ready to explode in my face. This prank was sneakier than her usual form of attack.

"Dare I say, you are improving in your wicked ways." I winked at her. She blushed and hopped off the bed.

Her enthusiasm always gave her away. I wouldn't actually find her tricks as easy as I did if I didn't follow her mischievous gaze of where she wanted me.

I eyed the faucet and knew without a doubt what was waiting for me. Even so, I feigned stupidity for her enjoyment.

"Little Ghost," I warned, a playful growl in my tone. "You know it's a crime to prank a cop."

She snorted, her eyebrow raised. "I do not think that is true."

I laughed at her expression and watched her walk over to me. She came up to my chest, and I enjoyed looking down at her.

"Your hands are dirty, Porthos," she said, unable to stifle her evil laughter entirely.

I raised a brow at her but decided to play her little game.

"You know Ivy..." I said, my voice unintentionally low, my body leaning toward her. "What will you do if one of these days you're the one getting wet?"

She blushed, her breath catching in her throat as she looked up at me.

Her playfulness was replaced by...intrigue?

Unexpected heat spread throughout my chest, and my heart rate picked up. I reached for the faucet, my innocent words playing in my mind. Even more so, I realized I meant them.

My distracted brain omitted the fact that the faucet was rigged and water sprayed out of the contraption like a hose. It soaked me from head to toe, bouncing off my body and getting Ivy just the same.

I looked at her, her black hair resembling a drowned cat, and I laughed my ass off. She stared at me, daggers in her expression at first, but then she laughed, too. We laughed nonstop until the water collected under us like a puddle.

I tried to guide Ivy back to the bed, but I slipped on the damn floor and all but threw her on the mattress before I toppled onto her. She felt *too good underneath me. It made me forget I was a detective there to keep her safe. With Ivy, I was simply a man.*

THAT STORY AND THE OTHERS THAT FOLLOWED WERE ALL COMING TO a close. Today, she was leaving the confines of the hospital for good. Tapping the speaker button on the cell phone, I set it down on my bed to continue talking hands-free.

"Are you excited to get back to your life?" I said, stupidly not thinking that her life before the hospital was full of daily beatings and abuse.

Way to go, Quinn...

To my surprise, she giggled at my silent curse, the sound musical and light. How I wish I could see that smile now.

"I am looking happy to be in a new chapter." Her accent wasn't as thick as it had been, but her English was still a little hard to understand at times.

I had been teaching her English for well over six weeks, ever since she got admitted to the hospital. The tutoring sessions I'd completed with her had gone well, and I could see daily progress in her speech.

"You're looking forward to a new chapter," I corrected. "That's amazing, Ivy. I am very excited for you."

She made the adorable 'hmmph' sound she always used when she fucked up a word and repeated my corrected sentence during our lessons.

Her frustrated growls or the way she'd shake her fist at the papers when we were practicing her grammar made me smile. When these moments occurred, I knew for certain there was nothing I could do that would withstand her wrath. She had called me all kinds of words in Russian when I would tutor her. I was beginning to learn a few of them.

7

The latest word was 'asshole,' which I guess I deserved.

"Yes, Micah. I am looking forward to new chapters in my life. I will see you soon?" Her beautiful voice came through the phone's speaker, filling my room.

She was improving, but the Russian and American English languages were so different that she sometimes struggled to understand certain phrases and idioms.

"Yes, soon." I grinned so big that my cheeks hurt.

"Goodbye, Detective. We will talk about my chapters later."

The phone call ended, and I was still smiling, recalling the memory of our last session.

"TRY TO BE SPECIFIC, IVY," I OFFERED, WATCHING HER SILENTLY STEW.

Her beautiful desert-colored eyes could bore a hole in the sheet of paper in front of her.

"Detective." She huffed her hair out of her face. "In Russia, you say specific, you call dumb." Her irritable tone was adorable. "You call dumb to me, Zasranets?"

My eyes widened, and I couldn't help but laugh. I had been telling her to be specific in what she was saying for weeks, and she always looked at me like she wanted to smack me upside the head. Now, I knew why.

"Uh...w-well..." I stammered, fidgeting with the paper in front of me.

Her stare was intense. It was one of the things I loved about her. Goddamn, who was I kidding? I loved a lot about her.

"I'm sorry. I didn't know that, beautiful." I reached over and brushed my hand over hers.

Her blush at my affection made her fair skin glow. She responded to my touch differently ever since that day with the faucet incident. I wondered what she would look like, laid out on this table, breathless, open, and gasping underneath me. Would her ivory skin have that blush all over her gorgeous body?

I adjusted my fucking hard-on under the table. I swear...this woman constantly tested my professionalism. Anytime I was around her, I popped a tent like a damn teenager.

I was tempting fate, but I gripped the bulge in my pants, watching her eyes follow my action with an unreadable expression on her face. It was like she was a witch sent to return me to the age of a pubescent human who couldn't control his body.

I could hear her repeating the sentence, but my eyes followed her naturally full lips as she spoke.

"I am looking forward to a new chapter..."

She watched my eyes, then lowered hers when I glanced up.

"I am sorry, too, Detective," she said slowly, her eyes not leaving my hand.

My body was being pulled toward her by some force I couldn't explain. At least, that was what it felt like. She wasn't leaning toward me but wasn't pulling away, either. My badge attached to the front of my shirt lay flat on the table as I leaned over the surface more and more.

She was so close yet so far.

The papers fell off the oak table top, but neither of us took our eyes off one another.

"Svin'ya," she whispered when I was a breath's distance away from her lips.

God...to kiss her...I swallowed hard, not remembering even how to pucker my fucking lips. She made me nervous, and the fact that she was here right now and waiting for me...

I searched her eyes and then her lips over and over.

"I want to kiss you," I warned her, my heart pounding so hard in my chest that I worried she could hear it.

She gasped, and I caught the sound, pressing my lips to hers.

Her lips were too sweet. She wasn't moving, so I was careful, teaching her slow, steady movements while tasting her.

I was addicted. Goddamn, I was absolutely addicted to her.

She was healing from horrific imprisonment, and here I was, stealing kisses. The thought sobered me up, and I pulled back from her. She was breathless, even with the kiss being light and tender.

"I'm sorry," she said, and I frowned, not understanding.

Had I upset her?

I reached my hand forward to offer comfort and an apology, opening my mouth to ask, but she smiled playfully.

"I called you an asshole."

Bewildered and completely smitten with this woman, I laughed.

Who would have ever dreamed being called an asshole would make me the happiest I had ever felt in my life.

SMILING SHEEPISHLY AT THE MEMORY, I GLANCED DOWN AT MY socks. One was white and one blue. I had done this for good luck since I played football in high school and college.

It had never failed me back then, so I hoped my luck was still with me tonight.

Ivy was not the typical type for 'mismatched socks.'

My 'luck with the ladies' back then probably had nothing to do with socks at all and more to do with me having no censor on my dick, but I could pretend my magical socks still held some luck in them. Ivy didn't have a single quality like the girls of my past. She was more like the sweet, shy soul I'd been with when I lost my virginity. Ironically, I felt as stupidly nervous with Ivy as that night with Maggie Cline.

I scrubbed my hand down my face, and with a self-quick pep talk, I stuck the little box in my suit jacket and walked out the door.

I ARRIVED AT THE HOSPITAL, GETTING ALL KINDS OF LOOKS AT MY formal attire from the johnny-wearing residents. The hospital doors opened for Ivy, and my breath caught in my throat. Her stunning black hair was coiled on top of her head, and her glittery blue gown had a slit in the material drawn up to her thighs. The sight of her made my mouth water.

I didn't know where she got the dress but damn.

The bodice magnified her slim waist and hugged her small breasts. She looked rejuvenated and different, but still, the sight of her knocked me on my ass. I had come to know her so well that I loved watching new puzzle pieces of her unravel before my eyes. Her beautiful walls were coming down one by one to show who she really was.

The nurse walked beside her and laughed when she saw my reaction, following my gaze to the gorgeous woman before me.

"Easy, boy. She's healed a lot, but she can't get too crazy tonight."

The warning was obvious, and Ivy blushed, looking away. I offered my arm to her, ignoring the nurse.

I didn't know what the fuck was going to happen tonight, but a nosy-ass nurse surely wasn't going to be the deciding factor for whatever was in store.

"I'll be as gentle as I can manage, but with you looking like that..." My words trailed off, and Ivy met my eyes.

"Oh, Svin'ya. You have walked such a silly path for me."

I smiled tightly. Her little nickname of calling me a pig had made me laugh my ass off in the beginning. She knew it was an insult to the police, much less to the detectives, but her smug smile every time she teased me by saying it made me want her even more. However, I preferred it when she called me 'Porthos.' It meant 'heaven.'

This time, when she spoke the name I had grown to love, it was like she was offering...a goodbye.

Her amber eyes looked sad, unshed tears brimming underneath her inky lashes.

I didn't understand. My thoughts were racing while I tried to maintain a steady composure of control. Trying to ease my discomfort, I tucked her arm under mine, trying to feel as close as possible.

We walked to the car, an awkward silence stretching into the air around us.

"Your apartment will be to your liking. I stopped by earlier today to ensure all your favorites were there. I had a buddy of mine make copies of some classic American movies. I figured...I don't know. Maybe we can watch them together while you're studying your English."

Ivy looked up at me, a little gasp escaping her. "You broke your movie law?"

I snorted and wiggled my eyebrows at her, realizing she meant the copied material.

"What can I say? Some rules are fun to break."

She shook her head at me, lightly whacking my arm with her small hand. It was quiet again, and the walk to my motorcycle felt more and more tense. I let the silence continue, trying to give her the space she seemed to need.

When she spotted my Ducati, she balked.

"I may not know English good, Micah," she said. "But I know the word die!"

I couldn't help but laugh. "C'mon scaredy cat."

I hopped on the motorcycle, started it up, and extended the helmet to her.

"I will not ride that! It kills me, Micah."

I rolled my eyes. "No, but if we miss the reservation at the Harold, the friend I bribed to get us that table, there, surely will."

She looked uncertain. I sighed and reached over, shoving the helmet onto her head.

"I haunt you when this kills me," she warned, finally sliding onto the back.

I snorted again, reaching back and wrapping her hands around my body. Damn, she felt good.

"Well, you are my Little Ghost," I said. "You are free to haunt me anytime. Hold on tight, baby girl. I got you."

―――――

WHEN WE REACHED THE RESTAURANT, THE DOOR TO THE FANCY-ASS place was heavy. Just like the way she said my name back in the parking lot. Why did the weight of this door feel like a metaphor for how tonight was going to go? I plastered on a smile and gestured her forward, her beautiful form walking with minimal expression.

Once we were seated and the waiter explained the special dish of the evening, we stared at the menus given to us. The silence was palpable.

"Gotten used to American food yet?" I watched her closely.

Ordering fries in this place was hard enough because they acted like requesting fried food was a mortal sin. I ordered onion rings, too, to piss off their prissy asses more.

"I think so?" She scrunched her face. "I am just trying to learn food again."

Internally slapping myself, I noted once more that I needed to remember that the beautiful woman sitting before me was recovering from traumas I could only begin to imagine.

I had refused to look at her file. That night, after talking with my traitorous partner, Ella, I had filed away that knowledge from everyone's eyes, including mine. All Ivy wanted was to be viewed as a human being, not the drug-addicted, abused shell we found. There had been weeks of sitting in her hospital room, waiting and hoping she would wake up.

She always seemed so surprised to see me there, but eventually, she knew I wouldn't hurt her. She had no family or friends come to claim her when the newspaper got wind of her rescue, which made me feel even more protective of her.

Would my parents have bothered to claim Penn after seeing her so broken? Maybe...or maybe not.

The past was well and truly dead, and thinking about it would only bring pain to the living.

"I...uh, got you something," I said, fiddling with the damn bulky box in my suit jacket.

Ivy's cool amber eyes were always wide, but now they bugged out of her head.

I laughed, grabbing the box. "Close your eyes?"

She blinked rapidly but finally closed her eyes, those lashes shadowing her cheeks in the dim light.

I got up from the booth, awkwardly scooting around the deep red material of the seat. Being careful not to startle her, I brushed her hair from her face, clipping into her hair the gold barrette.

The snapping sound made her eyes pop open. In the close proximity, I found myself leaning over her head. My hands were still in her hair, and I had to take a deep breath. Her eyes were so captivating and curious. Her lips were wet, open, and a deep, luscious red.

God, I was going to fucking mount her on the table if I didn't back the fuck up.

Probably not the smartest thing to do with my Little Ghost.

I sat my ass back down like the idiot I was, using the menu to hide my cock that decided now was a great time to make an appearance. Her delicate fingers tracing over the gift didn't help to stop my desire to slam her luscious body on the table or curb the urge to bite her pale skin.

"What?" she said, turning around to use the reflection of the glass behind her to look at her gift.

"It's uh...a bird cage. It's a clip thing for your hair. You are too beautiful to hide behind that lovely black shadow your hair sometimes creates."

Her mouth was open now, her little gasp making me bite my lip to stop my groan. I was thankful she couldn't see how absolutely feral I felt for her. My favorite deep blush on her cheeks was creeping up her neck. I had to reach her, touch her. Leaning forward, I gripped her wrist and pulled her toward me until my lips were a whisper away from hers.

"You are free, Ivy. Fly free."

It was the one thing I wanted her to remember from tonight.

It wasn't until we left the restaurant, and I turned to her in that alley, that I realized her expressions from before—every look, every smile hadn't met her eyes.

My heart shattered.

"You're running. Aren't you, Little Ghost?"

She wasn't cowardly enough to deny it. No, Ivy had never intended to go to the apartment the bureau had set up for her.

She'd never intended to help locate her captors.

She'd never intended to stay...with me.

"I am sorry, Micah."

Unshed tears were now loose, streaming down her cheeks. Oddly, I looked at the clip in her hair. The cage trapping her black waves enslaved her tresses just like she had caged me without even knowing. Without her, I would be the one trapped eternally, a bird unable to fly.

"Why?" I said, the weight on my chest heavier than expected.

She was leaving me, too, just like my sister, friends, and parents.

She stared into my eyes, looking as though she were memorizing every feature of my face. Her hands came out and roamed around my chest as a light rain sprinkled over us.

"What about your new chapters?" I pressed, trying to hold the bite of pain back from my voice.

Her touch was electric, and it felt like lightning running around my skin as she traced lines on my shirt.

The rain was pouring down now, her dress turning nearly as black as her hair from the storm. She looked alarmingly beautiful yet nearly transparent from her heartache...my Little Ghost.

"Our books do not belong together," she cried, hugging my chest tightly.

I frowned and tipped her chin up to me. Leaning down, I crushed my lips to hers. The feeling instantly caused a shockwave through my body. This connection wasn't like the time we'd kissed in our study session. This kiss was rough and unforgiving. I showed her my anger, my lust, my pain...my love.

She stiffened, but as I deepened the kiss, she softened to me, her lips opening, allowing me to explore, to taste her.

To remember her.

I was so high off her kiss, intoxicated by the warmth, her spicy perfume, and her breathy moans as she molded her body to mine that I never heard anything. I hadn't thought to keep an eye on my surroundings, which was ridiculous. I had been trained my whole life to be aware.

From the time I was a kid, I checked the halls before walking into them, making sure it was safe from my bitchy mother and asshole father. I always kept one eye open for danger.

That was until I was struck over the head. The last thing I saw was Ivy's rain-soaked wavy hair whipping around her face as she ran from me toward my bike, leaving me on the concrete ground.

Ivy

Chapter 2

One Year Later

My idiot brother and his girlfriend were going to be the death of me. If anyone matched Lucius and his unhinged nature, it was Phoenix. I didn't mind her. It was a little trippy to find out she had dissociative identity disorder. I had actually met one of her alter egos before I knew "knew" her. The alter ego had popped out when she was with Micah when they saved me.

Micah.

Ugh, my memories were constantly attacking me. My brain would never let me live peacefully without the image of his bright blue eyes staring into mine before he kissed me in the rain that night.

I did what I had to do.

My life and my mission were not for Micah Quinn. I made that decision before him. It had become a cemented plan the last time a monster's beady dark eyes stared into mine, and his rough, demanding hands forced me to do his bidding.

All their faces, features, and voices—they'd all blended together, and there was only one word for those men—monsters.

Shaking my head from my thoughts, I smoothed my hair, clipping my bird cage clasp into the twirled bun.

A knock sounded on my door, and the duo popped in to check on me.

"Hey, *sestra*," Lucius said, petting my head like a dog. I dodged him.

Swatting at his hand playfully, I slid to the side. Phoenix was beside him, her beautiful pale blonde hair looking nearly white. It still made me giggle that she was once called Snow White.

"You look beautiful, Eili." Phoenix smoothed my hair back to normal and adjusted the clip.

"Lucius, you have something to tell your beautiful sister, don't you?." I furrowed my brow at my brother.

His black hair hid his eyes.

"Tell me, Lucius."

Lucius and Phoenix shared a look I couldn't read.

Finally, Lucius sighed. "Fine, okay."

Phoenix pinched Lucius on his nipple and giggled. Typically, their antics were okay, but important information was in the balance.

"We found one of the men who..." His words trailed off, looking to his partner for guidance.

"Purchased your services?" Phoenix continued for him.

I grimaced. Ah. That would explain my brother's antsy nature in the matter. He rarely danced over things.

"But don't worry, Eili." Lucius twirled a curl of my hair in his fingertips and placed a kiss on my forehead.

"We're going to make him pay for what he did to you, *sestra*."

Phoenix pulled me into an embrace, and I mechanically returned the gesture. I stared into the eyes of my worried brother.

"Yes, we promise," Phoenix said close to my ear, pulling back to look at me.

She yanked me forward again to hug me once more, but I stepped out of her grip.

"That's really unnecessary." I patted her arm lovingly.

To avoid the stares of my well-meaning family's eyes, I picked up the edge of my dress lying across my bed, brushing the lint away from the corners.

Lucius stepped forward, his expression determined. "The fuck it isn't!"

"Fuck that!" Phoenix said at the same time.

The couple was of the same mind sometimes and said things in such a union that it was eerie. I pushed my brother away gently, trying again to de-escalate the situation.

"I know you can bring him justice and pain," I said, grabbing a different outfit from the closet.

"Both of you...but..." I continued. "Killing one man of thousands isn't going to erase the scars."

I couldn't let them know my plans, my actions, or my means of hiding the pain of my past. Lucius and Phoenix finally looked somewhat placated, but their bodies were still swaying with mild uncertainty.

"I honestly just want my life to be separate from those monsters. Please. I beg you both. Do not shed any more kotva, Brother."

Because it was mine to spill.

Waiting for Lucius and Phoenix to go to sleep and stop fornicating was a grueling task. However, when their snores filled Hank and Gertie's house, I snuck into my brother's office and rifled through papers until I found the address and the name I recognized.

God, my brother's handwriting was barely legible. Squinting to read what Lucius had written, I tried to copy it down on a new scrap of paper.

Lucius had managed to blend into American culture seamlessly over the years unless he was angry, but writing in English was still his kryptonite. I couldn't say much about that because I could finally speak English well enough to make my way around America. However, most noticed my accent as soon as I opened my mouth.

It was well into early morning when I returned to Rochester, the high-rise apartment complex gleaming because the sun was beginning to rise. It was a twisted irony that this building was the apartment complex Micah and the Bureau had chosen for me to live in last year.

Reaching into my duffle bag, I grabbed the gadget I had sought and jiggled the doorknob until the click sounded. As I opened the now unlocked door, there were no squeaks or loud sounds. I wasn't sure how many lock picks I had broken off into the metal lock slots before perfecting my timing, but I was clocking this job's time as exceptional.

The maid's station was where I began my hunt. Once I'd located the white garb the staff wore, I quickly changed into it, stashed my jeans and T-shirt in my bag, and stuffed it into one of the open lockers. Throwing on the ridiculous hat that completed the degrading uniform, I made my way to the front desk.

A man, about fifty or so, had his back turned, watching a football game on the lounge television. His 'hoots and boos' were audible in the otherwise subdued space.

Trying to be quiet, I slipped my small frame behind the counter, avoiding his greasy figure and flipping the book's pages on the desk labeled 'Tenant Residential Information.'

Swallowing my 'A-ha,' I closed the book and returned to the counter, but the man grabbed my wrist, freezing me into place. His gaze instantly went to my imaginary cleavage and then roved down my body. His touch and stare felt like bugs on my skin. I closed my eyes briefly to center myself.

"Good evening. I need to bring a towel to a client," I said, snatching a piece of linen from a shelf.

But the man continued to hold my wrist, eyeing me more like a steak by the minute.

"You new? You must be because I'd remember your sweet ass," he said, licking his hairy-lined lips.

"Let my hand go now, please." I smiled with sweetness as the venom inside me began to grow. "I won't ask again."

The man chuckled at my request. His gaze turned suspicious, but the sport's game on the television roared with a new win, and his attention averted long enough for me to duck around him and head to the stairwell.

I couldn't help but walk by and inspect the apartment room meant for me. Wasting a lock pick was silly, but I had to practice. The door unlocked with a click, and I carefully went inside.

I had never been brave enough to come here. The entire year of building myself into something strong also included letting go of what made me soft—Micah.

I entered the room, and everything was still working, including the lights and TV. It was like a frozen moment in time, just waiting for me to return like I hadn't left. I ran my fingertips over the old movies, daydreaming about what it would have been like to have cuddled into my detective, watching them all.

He didn't like popcorn. We would've eaten some kind of candy instead. He had a sweet tooth, although I could never recall his favorites. The name was hard for me—some red-looking fish that tasted like rubber.

Tears filled my eyes, but I swallowed hard, holding them back.

My inability to let go of the part of my past needed in order to move forward with my plans had been harder than I thought.

However, it was necessary to achieve the level of numb oblivion I would need to move forward with my intended purpose.

I leaned against the wall, my eyes closing while the memories of Micah ran wild in my mind.

A masculine grunt echoed throughout the space, and I froze. The sound was coming from further into the apartment, behind a closed bathroom door.

I swallowed hard, my instincts and training kicking in over my fear.

Silently walking over to the door, I pushed down the handle. Steam billowed out from the small, opened crack of space, and the sounds grew louder. Slowly peeking around the door, I spied a tall man inside the shower. He was turned away from me, his big muscular back bunched as he leaned over, holding onto the wall.

"Mmm, fuck. My Little Ghost."

At those words, my stomach knotted, and I stood, stock still. My Micah only called me that name, but why was he here? My eyes widened as he turned around slightly.

Why was he...oooh.

His eyes were closed, his mouth and his tattooed hand was gripping his very large penis. Covering my mouth, I tried to resist choking on my tongue. Micah was here...masturbating in my shower and saying my name?

"You can't run from me, Ivy," he groaned, his muscled arm bulging as he stroked faster.

The steam around the room created a cloud around us, and I sunk down into it to hide. I couldn't look away. I couldn't stop listening to my name come out of his sinful mouth.

This was wrong.

I was wrong.

I needed to leave.

"Please. Fuck, I need you."

Micah's words might be spoken to an image of me in his mind, but they controlled my tangible form as much as my imagined one. I stopped trying to escape but made sure that I would be out of sight when he opened his eyes.

I watched him from the mirror of the bathroom, his abdominals tightening...the muscles contracting with each pull of his member.

He was like a piece of art.

One I was coveting.

I caught myself subconsciously reaching for my clip, fingertips playing along the smooth metal surface.

"Micah," I breathed softly.

The detective's body jolted as his pleasure took over. His blonde hair dripped into his face, saturated by the shower head spray. I wanted to see his eyes so badly. I missed those pools of vibrant blue. I never watched someone come like this. I never saw beauty in the way they saw pleasure. It had always been about pain and torment, but with Micah, it was...enticing.

A warm, weird sensation began to overwhelm me.

I wanted to stay. I wanted to walk into the shower, hold him, kiss him, and tell him I heard him call for me.

But I couldn't.

He wasn't mine. I had a job to do that didn't include watching a painfully beautiful man orgasm in the home meant for me.

I slipped away, out of the apartment, and down the stairs. My anger at myself for running yet again weighed heavy on my shoulders. I hid behind a trashcan outside, watching as he walked away and locked the door behind him. I imagined what his face would resemble if he saw my motorcycle. The one I 'borrowed' from him the night I ran away. The image made me laugh, but it didn't quell the strange heat in my stomach.

After a while, when I knew it was safe and the halls had quieted, I made my way back up the staircase. It was eight flights of steps until I found the room I needed, slipping a hazing liquid on all the cameras surrounding the place before I picked the lock to the door.

Feeling my way around in the dark, I followed the small bit of moonlight to a closed bedroom door, the sound of snores abrading my ears from the other side. Moving back around to another closed door, I listened for a sound. I heard a small voice, and it was crying. Not wasting any more time, I picked the lock and made my way inside.

Micah Quinn

Chapter 3

"*Get down!*" a scream warned.

Boom!

Men...Men were screaming.

The bomb that just went off had my ears ringing. I had to stay down on the ground, pretend I was dead, or I would be. I could hear the recruit. He was only eighteen. His name was John.

I hadn't spoken to him much, but his booming laughter was contagious. It showed his youth and his lively personality. Now, all I could hear through the ringing of the horrible sounds of war and crashing thunder was the boy's screams.

He was dying.

I chanced a look over the mound of wet earth I crouched in. John was lying in the middle of the field. He had shrapnel from the bomb embedded in his torso and legs. He was bleeding out slowly, the metal pieces creating a sickening tourniquet. He wouldn't die for hours.

The screams were likely to lead the enemy right to our doorstep. Or worse, a civilian tried to help him, getting caught in the crossfire. I could see the snipers lining silhouettes in the trees. Their guns poised over John and his agony-filled shrieks. If anyone dared to try and help Johnny Boy, they were doomed. I couldn't see anyone else.

My helmet was melded shut with thick mud, acting like a block of concrete as it dried and got wet all over again from the rain. I aimed my weapon toward the center field, sticking the long muzzle out and pulling the trigger.

The pop pop pop of the gun ended the cries, the screams turning to gurgles and the gurgles turning to a thick silence. I used the reflective pool of water to view the trees. Those shadowed eyes stared back at me.

I JOLTED UPRIGHT, MY HEART POUNDING LIKE A FREIGHT ENGINE. The screams of death and rattling sounds of those men from my past were still an echo in my ears. I hadn't been back home very long, and I'd slept even less. It was pouring rain, and I covered my ears with my pillow, trying to drown out the thunder and lightning pounding at my house made of glass.

Glancing over at my alarm clock, I realized I'd missed the meeting with the new kid set for today. Dammit—so much of a cop that I missed the welcome training for a new rookie.

Sighing at my lack of responsibility, I scrubbed my hand back and forth across my face and pulled my blankets back over my head. The image of Ivy's beautiful eyes calmed me. Those golden pools reminded me so much of the desert sands I'd nearly died on.

Maybe I would have faired better if I'd died there. When Ivy left me, I may as well have been killed that night because I became a shell of a person. Sex and anything close to a flirty conversation immediately turned cold or into something I needed to do purely for work. I only jacked off rarely to quiet the aching need, but nothing was ever enough, and every fantasy revolved around her.

Before I left work last night, I looked into the folder that had been haunting me on my desk—"The Cinder Killer" case. This unsub was quickly becoming a problem for the department and me. The trouble was that the victims popping up weren't exactly scholars. I had made an oath long ago that justice would be met for even the biggest monsters, but I had to admit that some of these killers were doing our jobs for us. As long as innocent lives weren't taken, I wouldn't shed tears for those lost to the unique power structure playing out around us.

The last "victim" was a survivor. His rap sheet was longer than a damn Bible, including rape, assault, theft, and domestics. He claimed a woman about five foot two in a blue jumpsuit attacked him randomly. With the smug look in this man's eyes and the fear in the eyes of the alleged victims, I could say for certain this man didn't 'happen upon' the supposed unsub on accident.

He'd been drinking and had way too high of a blood alcohol level even to be driving, and only a block away from the back of a strip joint known as Gya.

My years of work screamed that he got handy with a dancer there, and either that dancer or a loyal customer decided to teach him a lesson.

Buzz, buzz, buzz.

Who was calling me now? Yawning, I opened my phone, the number unfamiliar, and the time reading 4:45 AM.

"This is Quinn."

"Is this really a cop like the angel said?" The small sound on the other end of the line sobered me up like a bucket of ice water.

"I'm a detective. Detective Micah Quinn. Who am I speaking to?" I said in a soft voice.

The little girl was quiet, her body making shifting noises.

"The angel said I'm safe. The monster is gone. She said you will come get me now. The dragon slayer…."

I ran a hand through my hair, willing my brain to work with the action. Reaching for a pen and some paper, I readjusted the phone.

"Uh. Do you know where you're—?"

I stopped speaking as a small folded paper fell from my desk. I quickly picked it up off the carpet. It was folded into the shape of a heart. Confused, I opened it to see an address written on the inside. This place was located in the city at the high-rise apartment…Ivy's apartment. I frowned but read off the address to the girl, and the little one squealed in happiness. Amazed, I repeated the information to her.

"Is that where you are, little one?"

"Yes! The angel didn't lie to me." The little girl had a smile in her voice as she said, "I am really saved."

LANA ARRIVED AT THE STATION ABOUT THE SAME TIME I DID. FROM what I could tell, she was clearly tired, but her appearance didn't suffer.

"Hi, Quinny!" she said, beaming at me.

"Hey, Lana. Let's roll."

"Feeling' eager today, I see?"

Trying hard not to roll my eyes, we jumped into the undercover car and headed out. As soon as we arrived, I smelled smoke even before opening the car door.

"I'll call this in," I said, and Lana nodded.

It didn't help, though, because as soon as we received the 'all-clear' to enter, I realized it was...

"The Cinder Killer. Looks like they struck again."

The Cinder Killer was officially a serial killer. Their kills extended to five different victims. The man smoldering in the living room was the fifth.

"I'm going to assume he's missing his winky, too," Lana said as she grimaced at the corpse, who was still smoking, literally.

The Cinder Killer got their name because each kill was the same. After removing the penis from the victim, they would make them digest it. Only after that did they make them swallow gasoline. The victims' bodies melted from the inside out from fire and chemicals. It created an eerie effect of each victim's remains looking like a deflating human balloon. Features were hard to distinguish, and identification relied solely on dental records. Luckily, Ally very rarely couldn't crack a case.

"Why does the killer flambé these guys?" Lana said, but I ignored her, making my way toward the back hallway where a little girl was wrapped in a maid's uniform.

Could the killer have been from the staff? Or, more likely, stolen a uniform.

"Hi, there," I said, kneeling down to her level. She couldn't have been older than ten or so. "We are here to get you out of this place, little one."

She smiled, the gruesome scene of the melted man not phasing her one bit, which made me shudder at the horrors she must have witnessed.

"What's your name?" I said, seeing Lana walking over to join me.

"Marcie," she said, eyeing Lana suspiciously.

"It's okay," I assured her, giving Lana a thumbs up. "She's with me. This is Svetlana Perez."

Lana gave an awkward smile, giving her best child-like greeting.

"Awe, you poor thing," Lana crooned. "I'll take her to the station, Quinn. You got it here?"

I shook my head, the folded heart burning a hole in my pocket.

"Actually, if you don't mind, I'm gonna take her in. I got some stuff to file there anyway."

Lana shrugged and gave Marcie a fist bump before walking back to continue the investigation. Marcie seemed amazed at the lights from the city as we drove back to the station, her excitement growing when I allowed her to flip on my undercover police lights.

When we finally arrived, I had Marcie greeted by a number of people before the social worker, Dana, came by to collect her.

I felt strangely protective about letting her go, but I knew this was for the best. Hopefully, she'd find her family, and if not, she'd be given a new one. With a bit of luck, Marcie would be placed with someone who could erase all the horrific scars and memories that sweet little one had endured.

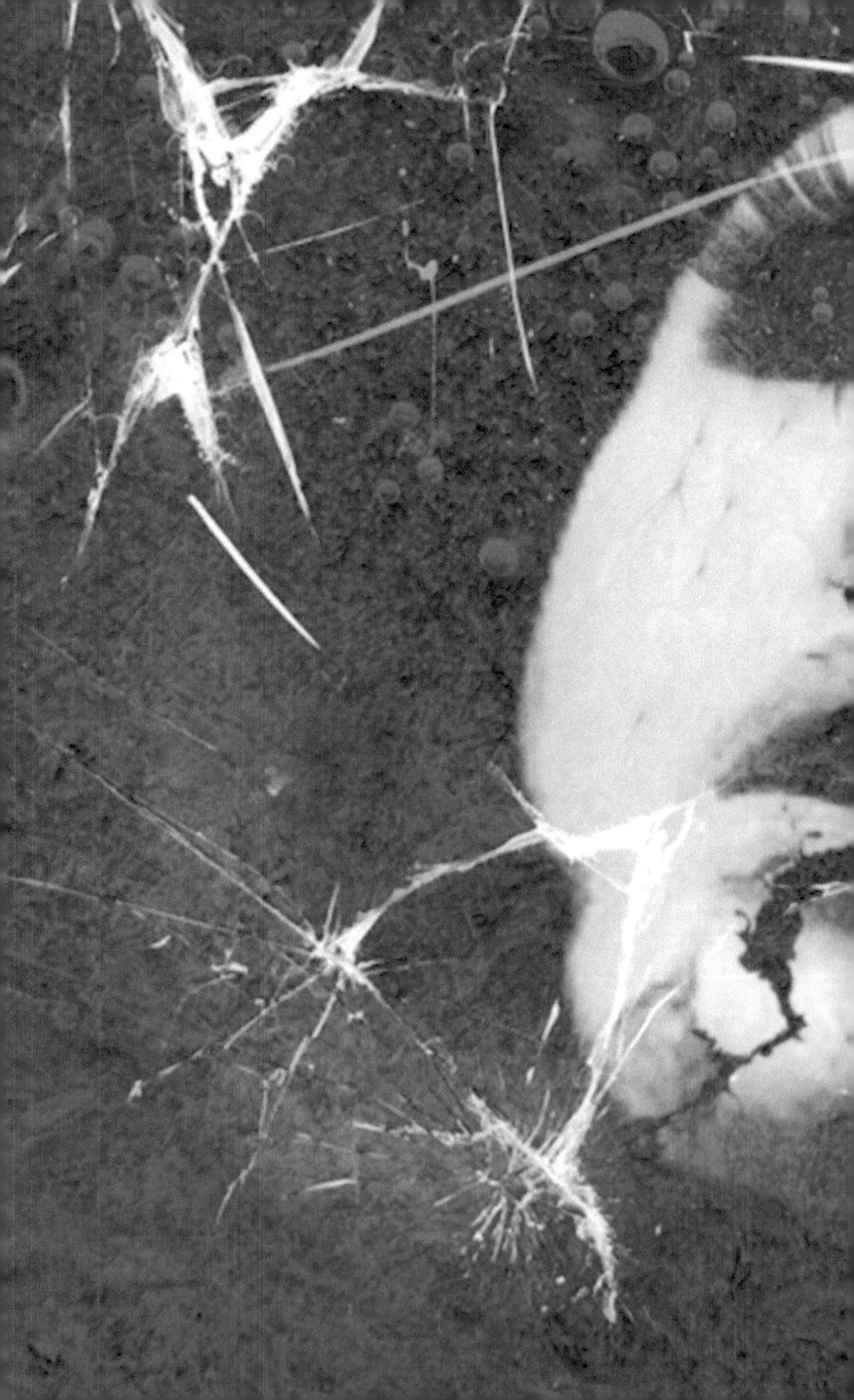

No One

Chapter 4

The sniveling brat was fussed over by pretty much the entire precinct, showing her expensive face-off to all the law enforcement. I suppose I wouldn't be able to flip my purchase after all.

That old fat fuck Pete was a melted pile of goo on his apartment floor now. Frustrated that I hadn't been able to get to the scene and snatch the investment before the fucking precious Micah Quinn hauled her off, I sighed.

I'd have to replace her now. It was old-fashioned, but enough people left their little princesses' windows unlocked at night. It wouldn't take long to find one suitable enough for The Masks Organization to take in.

It really was a bitch to train up a new girl, though.

I think I'll get an older one this time. They cry less and sell faster.

My phone vibrated in my pocket, and I cursed when I saw the name lighting up the screen.

Fucking perfect.

"Hi, You. You didn't have to call little ole me. Fancy a chat?"

He wasn't amused, though he never had been. His accented, gruff tone was about as cuddly as a hedgehog. Except there was no fuzzy underbelly.

He had fucked me enough times—figuratively and literally—that I was certain there was zero remorse or soul to that man. Just mechanical need, greed, and money.

"I hear there are problems occurring with our investments," he barked.

I cringed because what I had to say next wasn't fixable, so I righted my blouse. The need to correct...something was too strong.

"Sir, there has been a need for a few replacement purchases."

"If you did your fucking job, you cow, there wouldn't be a need for replacements." His tone soured even more. "If you don't find who the fuck is messing with my investments and put an end to this theft, *you're* the one who will be replaced next. Am I clear?"

I swallowed, trying to infuse my tone with the confidence I didn't feel at all.

"Of course, boss. Understood. I will correct the issue." I said nothing else because he grunted with his disapproval and hung up.

He sure knew how to make someone feel like they weren't good enough even to exist.

All of this had me shaking in my boots about my personal investments. Would this Cinder Killer come for them next?

Ivy

Chapter 5

*P*eering into the window of Quinn's apartment, I watched as he kicked off his shoes, undid his suspenders, slid them off his arms, and unbuttoned his white shirt.

He'd taken special care when waiting with Marcie. He only let go of her little hand when the DCFS worker physically rubbed his shoulder and told him she would be okay.

That wasn't fair to Marcie.

To say the words "She would be okay" was cruel. That woman knew nothing of the strife this child had endured. Marcie was stolen from a mall from her mother's cart at the age of three.

She was ten now.

Her mind and body were so broken from the years of abuse that it was hard to believe she'd be able to live a normal, everyday life.

Jenika said that Marcie was one of the five we'd recently

rescued that belonged to The Mask—a sex trade organization that branched out so far it was part of multiple states and perhaps even countries. She'd agreed to meet me at Gya when I was finished with...whatever the hell it was that I was doing here at Micah's place.

I had been studying my enemies for a year and training myself to become stronger so that I could return the pain to each person who'd used my body for their messed up form of "pleasure."

I'd succeeded in delivering that pain to five of those men so far. I'd even kept a smile on my face.

My methods were a bit messy, I could admit, but every time their disgusting bodies invaded mine, I always felt like I was burning from the inside out.

So that was how they would die.

Jenika said the media was hysterical about 'The Cinder Killer.'

I mean, really, what was it with Americans naming ruthless murderers after fairy tale princesses?

Focusing back on Quinn, I was entranced by the way his body moved as he grabbed a beer. The refrigerator light illuminated his features, causing my breath to catch in my throat.

I'd watched him for a year. There was nothing like the apartment, yet every action he made increased my heart rate.

At the same time, I'd rebuilt myself into the monster I needed to be. I knew Quinn would hate me if he could see me for what I'd become.

But the draw to him was so potent that I couldn't help myself.

Perhaps it was selfish of me, but I needed to see his face, be on his balcony, and smell his husky cologne in the air.

I pressed myself into a planted bush, hiding from his line of sight as he walked out onto the balcony.

Looking out into the dark sky, he sighed and ran a hand through his hair.

I waited for him to talk to his sister's spirit like usual. Instead, I was shocked to hear my name on his lips again.

Oh, how his moans were still so potent in my mind.

"Why did you leave, Ivy? Why did you leave me?"

I froze, unable to form a thought pattern.

Did he see me? Was he thinking out loud? Should I come out and admit my presence...or should I stay hidden?

The wind picked up, and his eyes closed, breathing deeply and inhaling the scent.

"I swear. Even your memory torments me. I can almost smell your perfume. That spicy sage fits your personality. Sassy yet fragile."

A tear slipped down my cheek. The pain in his voice laced around mine like a vise on my heart.

It was always raining in Rochester. A light drizzle started to come down, reminding me of that kiss in the rain. A thick fog slowly crept up and hid the night sky, and I traced my lips with my fingertips.

Quinn looked up at the rain and touched his lips, mirroring my action.

I WAITED AND LET THE RAIN MEET MY TEARS UNTIL THE SOFT SNORES inside filled my ears.

Walking inside, I slipped off my heels and padded silently on the smooth surface. Wringing out my hair and warming myself by the fireplace, I watched the crackling sparks of the embers and the flames, letting my hand rest above it and the water drip down.

It was so crazy how a simple spark could create an inferno, yet a droplet of water and the ember died forever.

Making my way to the bedroom, I told myself to leave, that I had no right to be this close, that I was too selfish, too careless. But I didn't care.

Quinn's naked chest rose and fell, his features contorting into a frown as he fidgeted on the bed.

The rain was pouring now, the sounds of thunder rolling through the building. His loft made me feel like I was walking on glass.

All the walls were too sheer, and the entire city was visible from every room except the bathrooms.

It was a glass house, a place that could easily shatter, yet Micah loved its beauty, and I had the feeling he felt like his home—open and breakable.

Sliding my fingernails lightly along the bed, I stopped when I reached his head—that dark blonde hair looking like gold fighting with coal. There were so many strands of each that it was hard to tell.

His beard was longer now. The usual tapered look had grown into an actual fuzzy texture.

I dared let my fingers touch his face, letting the rough beard hair tickle my palm. His lips parted, and I traced my fingers over the edges, remembering how sweet and strong he tasted.

My mind was caught in the memories, and I wasn't aware he had shifted until his eyes sprung open. Staring right into mine, he grabbed my arms and flipped me underneath him while locking my wrists above my head in a single instant.

I began panting and feeling dizzy because I wasn't breathing right, and I was underneath his very naked body.

After a few deep breaths and several heartbeats, I peered up at him.

The way the moonlight shone down on his beautiful face and the weight of his large, muscled frame oddly helped me breathe again.

"Hi, Micah."

Micah Quinn

Chapter 6

*I*vy was here...underneath me, staring up into my eyes with her inky black hair spilling on my white bed sheets.

I was dreaming. I had to be.

She felt so real, smelled so intensely tangible. That spicy sage was so rich and raw.

She wasn't moving. Her body was firmly locked under mine, her wrists caged in my grip, and I could feel her erratic heartbeat under my palm.

"Ivy?" I said again stupidly.

This was the girl I had been sick over finding for a year. Three hundred and sixty-five days—all of which I'd yelled, screamed, used a million police resources illegally, and yes, I even cried.

Now, my dream girl who betrayed me, stole my motorcycle, and ran from my arms was in my bed underneath me.

Her golden eyes swirled with warmth and surprise at the feel of
my cock pressing into her belly. Her arousal of her scent and touch
amplified my lust for her. I growled, shifting and grinding into her
pelvis, my naked body feeling singed in her heat.

I was definitely dreaming, but couldn't I have some peace in a
dream?

Pulling one of my hands free, I locked it onto her throat, her
gasp so delicious it felt like it bounced off the glass around us.
Letting myself grind harder between her thighs, her dress falling
to her sides, I captured her mouth and sucked on her bottom lip.

She mewled and whimpered my name—such a delicious
dream. I didn't want it to end.

"That's right, baby. Beg me. If you want me, you're gonna have
to earn it."

She whimpered again, grinding her hips into me and rolling
forward when I pulled back.

The head of my dick was rubbing her soaked panties right on
her slit. I deepened the kiss, gliding my hand down her slender
stomach over the top of the little piece of fabric covering her
pussy. It was drenched.

I moaned, feeling the slick heat of her so close to me, just a
barrier away.

Nearly roaring, I ripped it off her. She squeaked in surprise and
softened again when I kissed her once more, letting my tongue
explore her.

Taste her.

Claim her.

"Ivy, you're a dangerous woman."

Grabbing the ripped fabric, I twirled it around my finger,
shoving the material deep into her pussy. She was confused but
started to follow my movements when I pushed the panties in and
out of her, adding another finger to stretch her around me.

"Oh. Please. More Micah. I need to feel you."

She was open to me. So ready and waiting, I could take her right here, right now. This woman had run from me and made me absolutely mad looking for her all this time. Dreaming or not, I realized my pain and the betrayal of her was all too real, and the heat of arousal started to fade.

Taking the panties off my finger, I shoved them inside her pussy, blocking her sweet honey from me. Caging myself from her as she had done to me in reality.

Her cry was confused, needy, and hurt. "Micah?"

I ignored her, willing the dream to fade and whatever hell was coming forth next.

The dream didn't fade enough because I started to smell the salty scent of tears before I opened my eyes and found myself alone...again.

WAKING UP, I GOT A CALL FROM LANA REGARDING A SIGHTING OF A prostitute I had put an APB out on last week. Jenika Ryan.

She had allegedly been in contact with a potential spot for trafficking known as The Mask. Her affiliation was unknown, but she was thought to have been a survivor, so her cooperation was imperative.

After I had found that my partner in the homicide department was a double-crossing psychopath, I moved up to the special victims unit. I hadn't seen Ella since the day she stole my fugitive, and it never made any sense. The betrayal from her was one that cut deep. She had been as close as a little sister like Penn, and when she betrayed me, it felt like a knife to the heart.

"What do you think she knows?" Lana was antsy around people.

She seemed to do best with the actual investigative work, but speaking with confidential informants was part of the job. Lana was cute in that way.

Her dorky nature reminded me of some famous person, but it didn't fit her look at all. She was a knock-out blonde with a fitness body and a voice like velvet. Our undercover work always went over like butter. No one ever dreamed Lana was anything but whatever that husky tone promised.

"I don't know. Bleu has had her sitting for a bit now. I think we can go in."

Lana was at my heels as I opened the door to the interrogation room and walked over to the fiery redhead who looked like a punk version of Ariel.

"Good evening, Miss Ryan," I greeted, reaching out my hand to her.

She ignored the gesture and grimaced at my greeting. "Look, doll face, my junkie mom was Ms. Ryan. I'm Nika. And I don't know what the hell you want with me, but I ain't telling anyone shit with your clown suits and big words."

I looked over to Lana, who looked down discreetly at her attire and smoothed her skirt.

"I do not want information, Jenika," I said, causing her to raise an eyebrow. "I want you to join my team and gain new information. Not have you re-living your past."

She looked skeptical, chewing her gum and biting her black nails.

"We want to help those that may be next," I continued. "If we have information about The Mask, we can intercept them, find their hideouts where they are keeping prisoners, and rescue them."

"Yeah? Of course, you do. Shiny Prince Charming swooping in and saving all the princesses. Look, dude. We are whores. We are happy. Just leave us alone."

I sighed and went to plan B. "I think you may want to reconsider my offer."

"You think so, pretty boy? What's in it for me?"

I reached into my pocket, tossing a pile of cards on the table: fake IDs, passports, business cards, and more.

"We will turn our head to what these may have been linked to, for starters, and we'll trust that you are not affiliated with the enemy."

Lana was silent, studying the girl and watching her contemplate her actions.

Snatching the cards from the table, the girl smiled and popped a bubble with her gum. "Well, copper, it looks like you got yourself a new spy."

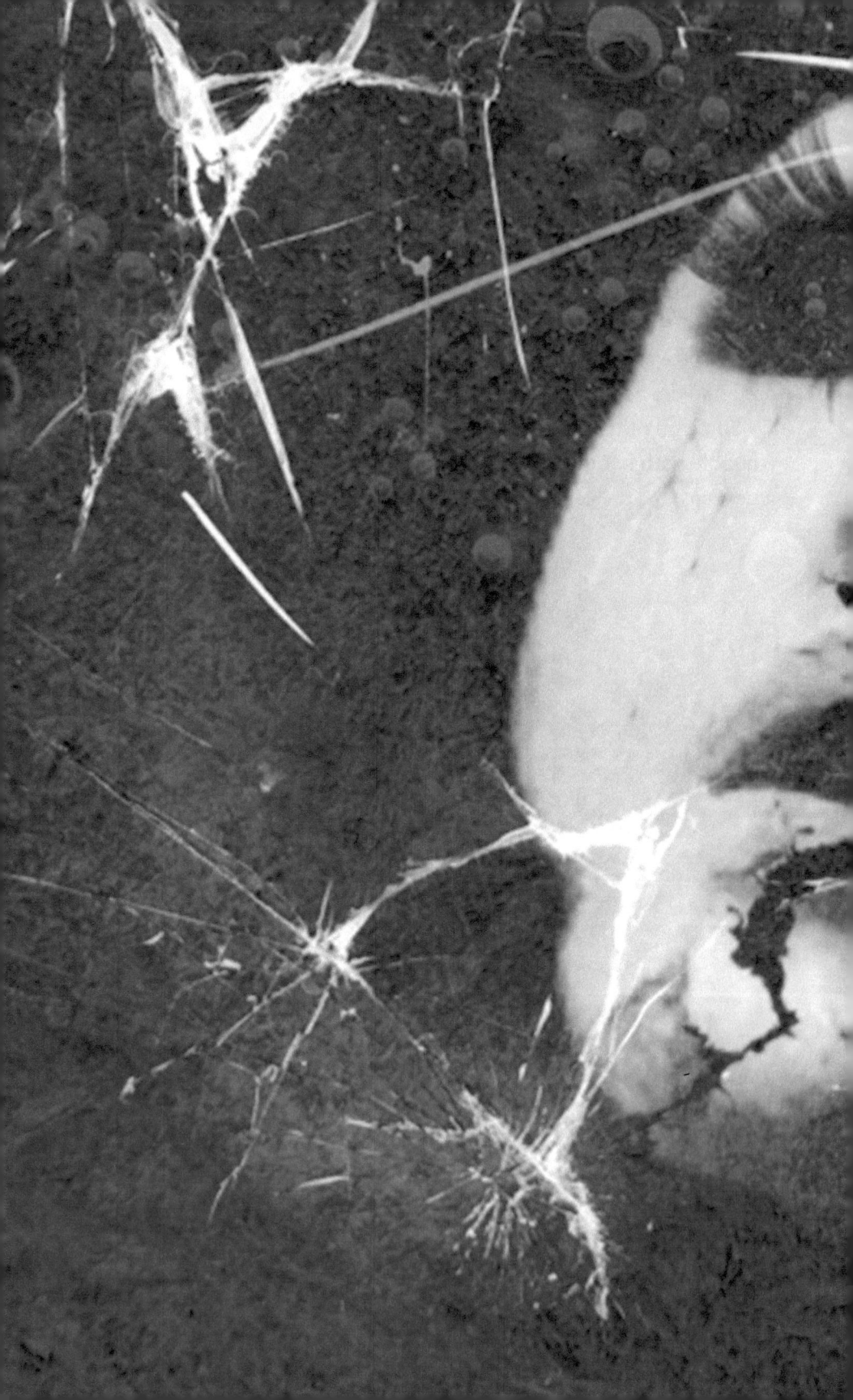

No One

Chapter 7

 picked up the remote, flipping to a station.

A reporter caught my attention: "Mass hysteria of all parents is rising as five young girls have been taken from their homes in the middle of the night. Ages have ranged from seven to fifteen, and with the murder count of 'The Cinder Killer' rising, it's every parent's worst fear that their child may be next."

Laughing, I popped the top of a beer bottle, tipping it back and taking a swig. It tasted like piss, but it matched the ambiance of the run-down hotel we were stacked in. Five girls shook in the corners of the place, their sobs increasing when they heard the news from the TV.

"Stop whining. It's unbecoming of your status."

These girls were handpicked by 'yours truly' in the most ritzy, well-to-do areas. I had to aim high in order to keep the boss off my back. He seemed pleased with the new investments. A quick phone call with Kristiyan assured me that my personal purchases were safe and well.

I had no leads on who this bitch the Cinder Killer was other than them being a coward and a messy one at that. They were clearly inexperienced, and I'd use that to my advantage.

"Please. Just let us go home. Our parents will pay whatever you want," the oldest of the girls, Melanie, said.

They were all wearing their pajamas still. Their training hadn't begun because I was too tired after their abductions, and I needed some time to recoup.

Ignoring the defiant rich girl, I flipped my screen to the security cameras at Mister Perfects. My nails dug into the sides of the shitty couch as a fucking woman appeared on his screen. Her dark hair was splayed out on his pillows, and he was straddling her body…and kissing her!

Was this a joke?

Some of the girls looked away from the images they could see, their innocence about sex was undeniable, but I didn't give a shit. I was, however, absolutely fuming at the sight of my golden boy kissing another woman.

Who did he think he was?

I didn't have sound on the cameras, and I cursed at being unable to hear their conversation before she stormed off barefoot and he fell back asleep. It was a strange encounter, and I had the feeling he may not have been fully aware she was there.

Did he think he was dreaming?

Well, for his mistake, he just made sure I wasn't going to be his dream girl right now, but instead his living nightmare.

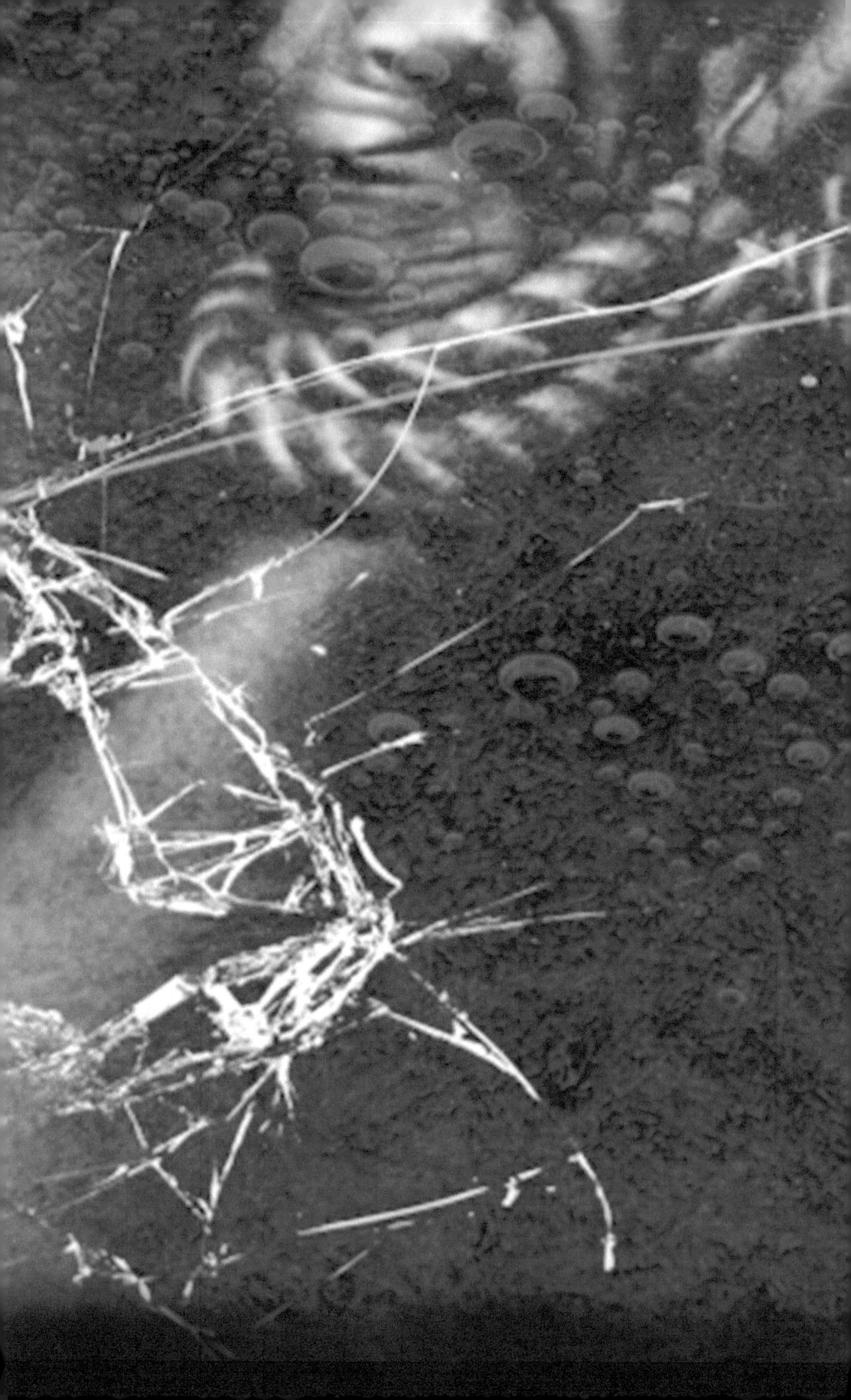

Ivy

Chapter 8

"*H*e did...what?"

The john cringed at my voice, startled by the outburst as my nails tightened on the back of the chair. I feigned a sensual smile and continued dancing on this rando guy while focusing on Aurora.

"Yeah, babes. Your detective nabbed Jen out back when she was selling one of the coyotes a fake ID. That was yesterday. Where have you even been?"

I ignored her, putting more pressure on the man's lap, drowning out the thoughts of the other night and Micah's unexpected cruelty.

After that night, I returned to base and enveloped myself in Gertrude's pancakes and the motherly love I missed so much. It hadn't been easy avoiding Phoenix and my brother, but I managed.

"So much is going on, Cindy. There's a serial killer now! And kids are popping up missing all over the place."

I snorted at my alias name and the fact that Aurora, of all people, was the one to tell me. The irony was not lost on me. The children going missing, however, really set me off.

I had tracked down one man by the club, sniffing around the girls. He didn't tell me anything. Unfortunately, he was too much for me. He was too strong, and he ran from me before I could make the kill.

I had been cursing myself for three days now, wallowing in my hatred.

"Cin?" she stated again.

My attention was completely averted when the door to the club jingled—the reflection of one of the mirrors showing the devil himself. Micah Quinn walked into the club, looking awkwardly around at the tables and scantily dressed girls.

Aurora and I were hidden behind the sheer black curtain while we did our show. The two men beneath us didn't give a shit about anything but their five minutes. It was easy to chat freely with Aurora. She was so much like me.

The timer dinged on the side of the wall. A slight tinkling sound meant to be sexy to Americans, I'm sure, but to me, it was mostly sounding like a mortal combat scene.

The guy beneath me started to groan about being poor.

Quinn's form was laughing with another man. This one was tattooed and muscular with long, straight blonde hair. He was taller than Quinn, but only by a few inches. His gruff voice flowed through the space to us like reverb on a music track.

"Thanks, man, for coming. I know this isn't your scene, but Lisa will have the baby any day now, and I really needed this for old-time's sake. Hell, she gave me her blessings and told me to take pics of the hottest ones."

I froze, listening to the men speak, but the grumbling fool

inside the room with us started getting up and reaching for the curtain.

"No!" I shouted involuntarily, feeling like an idiot. He had frozen, but the look he gave me was that of an alien or very unstable individual. "I mean, come get another dance, handsome."

Aurora looked through the sheer curtains, her pretty blue eyes landing on Quinn and his friend and then back to me with a look of curiosity.

I pleaded to her with my eyes, an unsaid message loud and clear.

She sighed but shoved the guy down and started dancing again. I fell in tune with her, our bodies swaying with the beat outside the room. I turned around, dancing with my ass to the handsy pervert, but my field of vision was clear to Micah.

The bartender, Barbara, poured them some gin and made small talk. Their conversation was not close enough for me to hear.

I looked at my friend. Her wig was gray and beautiful, glossy and transforming.

"How much you love me?"

She laughed and blew me a kiss.

"Enough to switch places tonight?" I asked, full of hope.

Her manicured brows furrowed, and she touched the hair.

"Why?" she said hesitantly, goading me.

But she knew exactly why. I sighed and glared heatedly at my detective. She snorted

"Girl, you're a crazy thing, but go on, babe. Put on a show!"

Micah Quinn

Chapter 9

I tried to avert my gaze from all the dancers on stage. Their beautiful bodies made me uncomfortable. I guess I felt more exposed than they did.

Psy, my amazing college friend from home and military buddy, was celebrating. I would not be the cause for him losing his natural high from the festivities.

"So, have you and Lisa picked out any names?" I took a sip of my water.

Psy frowned, his hand reaching up to fuss with his mane of blond hair.

"Lisa doesn't seem to like my ideas too much." He laughed. "I guess Zeus and Poseidon are frowned upon."

Psy and Lisa were high school sweethearts. That woman was the light of his life, and she was always there for him whenever we returned from deployment. The love they had was that sickening mushy shit that made me want to cry and puke at the same time. I'd known they struggled for years with fertility. Lisa went through a battlefield of her own to get that plus sign on her pregnancy test.

It took a significant toll on their lives, and seeing Psy smiling again after surviving his personal war made me happy. Now, after those years of saying goodbye to unborn little ones or not being able to achieve a pregnancy without stabbing her in the ass with medicine, he wanted to name his kid after a god. The war didn't kill my friend, but his wife certainly would.

It was just like Psy to name his unborn baby after a god. To be fair, the man looked like something from Greek mythology. He had better hair than more than half the women in here.

"She likes Lila for a girl. And Kojec for a boy."

I racked my brain, trying to remember where I'd heard those names. Maybe some animated movie?

Psy pointed to his wavy locks. "It's my mane. Always reminded Lis of a lion since high school. She threatened to blender my balls if I ever cut it."

"Do you like the names?"

He shifted in his seat a bit. His discomfort was visible.

"I mean, I don't mind Lila...but I don't want our son to be named after something of me. He deserves better, not living in the shadow of his jaded old man."

I looked my friend over. His tatted-up, biker-bar-owning exterior was not quite able to hide the pain he kept inside. We both knew the pain of living through a military-forced war.

Along with the fertility shit I couldn't begin to understand, Psy was also afflicted with the dreams every soldier had when they finally came home. Everyone dealt with those nightmares in their own way. I had tried therapy and joining fucking book clubs.

Ultimately, I came to the conclusion that I was nothing but a trained assassin. It wasn't like I could get a fucking job as a librarian after the shit I saw overseas.

So, the only logical choice was for me to continue down the path of being a paid officer who hunted killers. Sure, being a police officer was a bit different, but it was close enough. The most brutal battle by far for any soldier would always be our inner demons. Psy's addiction nearly drowned him. Hell, sometimes I still thought that Lisa and their soon-to-be-here baby were what kept my dear friend alive.

"Don't think like that, man." I clapped him on the shoulder, squeezing it. "Your son will be lucky to have you as his dad."

Psy was a big-ass dude. His burly, muscled-up body looked like a tank most days, so it could bring me to my knees to see the man get misty-eyed.

"Thank you, brother," he said, wiping quickly under his eyes.

The number of dancers tapered off, new music began playing, and the lights in the club dimmed. The floor lights on the stage in front of me were the only thing visible.

I turned my attention toward the entrance of a little curtain. A salacious little lady popped out of it and walked down the stage straight to where I was seated.

The lights were blinding, and I couldn't make out much. Her hair was long and gray. Her body was an insatiable, curvy, short-framed dream.

There was something familiar about her. I couldn't put my finger on it, but as she swayed gracefully around the stage, captivating everyone's gaze, including my own, I kept feeling a warmth spread throughout my body.

Psy laughed, nudging me with his arm. "Ya know that's frowned upon, my brother?"

He broke my trance with the girl, and I looked at Psy. His grin and shake of his head confused me.

I started to ask what, but he nodded toward my lap. I had a damn raging hard-on.

Blushing like a fucking schoolgirl, I took off my jacket and laid it over my offending dumbass appendage.

Psy laughed again and took a swig of his drink, motioning for one of the bartenders to come over. Guto was a nice Brazilian man. I didn't know the other one, but I had worked a case a little over a year ago just outback by the dumpsters, and Guto was always "helpful" with what he'd known, which was jack shit. He was a kind kid, especially staying here after that spineless fuck club owner left this place high and dry.

I didn't know shit about Gya. I hadn't been back here since that investigation. The whole situation didn't hold great memories for me.

"Nice to see you, man," Guto said.

Now, the club was owned by someone else. I wasn't sure who, but the club was doing much better under the new ownership.

"Who's the dancer on stage?" I motioned to the gray-haired beauty.

Guto waggled his eyebrows at me. "Her name's Dazzle."

I rolled my eyes, annoyed at the obvious alias. "Look, man, you know I'm a detective. Give me her real name, yeah?"

Guto looked uncertain, looking at the girl curiously before turning back to me. "Her name is Aurora. Why?"

I didn't know anyone named Aurora. However, my dick seemed to disagree.

Psy chuckled next to me, his baritone voice booming. "My boys got a crush on her. Mind asking her to give him a private dance? It's on me."

My mouth dropped open. "Nah, man. No. I don't—"

"I insist, Mic." Psy stopped me in my place.

The lights were turned back on. It took my eyes a minute to adjust, but when I did, I stood. I swung my head from the left to the right, but it didn't matter. The girl on the stage was gone.

My protests were met with laughter as I was all but shoved into a small side room near the back. A curtain clicked into place, a strange perfume scent made my nose wrinkle, and the intensity of the situation amplified.

Over in a corner, I spied the woman with beautiful gray hair. She turned around and walked toward me, but I didn't feel the same way. There was no sense of familiarity. This girl's body was beautiful. But it wasn't the same as the one on stage.

The dancer came closer as she swayed with the beat of the thumping music outside.

"Excuse me, Miss. Please forgive my candor, but I think there's been a mistake."

The woman smiled, her pretty blue eyes sparkling with a mischievous glint to them. I felt like this was some kind of joke I wasn't a part of, or maybe I was the joke…

"You asked for the magic of Dazzle's dances, pretty boy," she stated, giggling and coming closer to me.

"No, I think there has been a mistake." I tried to sit up from the chair. "Forgive me, but you are Aurora?"

She didn't seem phased by the use of her real name…odd.

"Yes, detective. That's me," she purred.

Her smile was as wide as a Cheshire Cat, and she felt dangerous though she was a beautiful girl. I definitely wasn't aware of her inside knowledge of me.

How did she even know I was a detective? Did I say something? I must have.

"Were you expecting perhaps…" She leaned closer still, my body pressed firmly to the chair, trying to avoid contact out of respect. My attempts at dodging clearly weren't going well. I looked around the room, the sudden scent of spicy sage catching in my nose through the haze of a million strong perfumes when the girl said. "Someone else?"

Micah Quinn

Chapter 10

Not even twenty-four hours later, the call of the spicy sage smell had pulled me back to the club. Yes, Psy had a great time last night, and it had been nice to support my friend, but now I needed to know why my body reacted the way it had.

Women, young and old, were moving about the space, and I felt unbelievably stupid sneaking in here like this. I would hide behind these poofy-looking exterior walls if possible. I didn't have on my uniform, and I was a grown-ass man, yet here I was, blushing at the beautiful women shooting smiles my way as I stood behind the desk.

This year, without Ivy, I'd pretty much forgotten how sex even felt. My dick had gone into a sort of hibernation with my refusal to use it.

Those nights in her apartment were the only time I felt safe enough to give in to my desire. I kept that place running, buying off the department when they tried to sell it off. I wasn't moving a single movie out of place. Her pillows and little prank book would stay there as long as I was alive. Maybe…she would come back to it someday.

"Hi there, sir. You asked for a private dance?"

The girl speaking to me looked too young even to be here. She was barely eighteen, if I had to guess, and I could only imagine her "daddy issues" with getting a job at this place.

"Uh, yes." My voice cracked, sounding like a damn teenager myself. I cleared my throat and tried again. "Yes, thank you. A room in the back, please."

It felt dirty getting 'atta boy' looks from the horndog men around me. Half of me wanted to pull out my badge and arrest them all for clear solicitation, but the other half…I had to see her.

If I shut this place down for the obvious violations, I would miss my chance to hide behind a curtain and watch the silver-haired beauty from afar.

The eighteen-year-old startled me when her hand linked around my forearm, and I couldn't mistake the hurt in her pale eyes when I pulled away.

"Um. This is your room, sir…enjoy your show."

The feeling of embarrassment was painting my face and neck. My German heritage didn't negate my mother's Polish blood, which caused this embarrassing conundrum.

Fucking red ass cheeks.

Great, I was about to get a fucking lap dance, and I was thinking of my mother.

Way to go, Quinn.

I sat down in the leather chair that looked as fancy as the rest of this place.

"You fucking idiot," I said aloud to myself.

I coughed out my words when a mesmerizing beauty walked

into the room. This wasn't the woman I had requested. The blue-eyed girl from the other day who knew I was a detective and likely wouldn't try anything funny...

Wait, this *was* the woman I'd been trying to view in private under the hidden guise of the one-way viewable curtains!

Her eyes flashed when she saw me, the color dimmed with bright blue contacts. Her hair was silver, just like on the dance floor last night. Her body was made up of those lithe curves, small breasts, toned muscles, and one hell of an ass.

Her ivory-colored skin looked delectable.

Goddammit! Why did this woman make me feel so ravenous? I had not so much as twitched in a year, and now, all of a sudden, this woman gave me a full hard-on?

I coughed again, trying to cross my legs to hide my offending moronic dick.

The woman was standing beside the curtain. Her provocative leather outfit was hidden behind a silky black sheer robe, making me breathe harder.

The woman didn't speak, but the expression on her face said it all—she was surprised. Maybe she recognized me as the one ogling her on the stage? She swayed on her blue high heels, seeming to wait for an instruction.

I sat back in the chair. The woman walked closer to me, fidgeting with her robe's tie. A sultry type of music began playing, and the lights dimmed down, which I welcomed because I was sweating.

The pole I hadn't noticed before was lit up in a square around the bottom with red LED lights, and the woman stepped up onto the platform, her robe falling off her slender shoulders to the floor.

The way this woman moved, my god. Her body swayed around that pole in the dim light, the red light highlighting her every curve and making her wig look like it was glowing like fire.

A devil in disguise.

The way she danced was so expertly sinful. It was the polar opposite of how she acted standing beside the curtains.

Which personality was real—the devil or the angel?

Maybe a combination of both.

I certainly felt like I was a mixture of both. My past made me into the man I was—the time I spent in the services molded my playboy nature into a respectable man. But that raw part of me was always clawing to come out in moments like these.

A growl left my throat, and the girl stopped her dance, startled by it.

She walked toward me with a curious, toying smile lit by the lights. She gripped my tie and pulled it free of my neck.

I exhaled, not realizing I had been holding my breath.

Her body leaned over me, that leather inches from my eyes with her perfect breasts. I didn't care about large knockers that could suffocate me. I loved that she was so muscled, and her pebbled nipples poked out from under the leather bikini top she wore.

I tried to see her outfit, uncovered like this. I was so close, but she was blocking out the light of the club with her body. The only light available was the glow of the pole behind her, haloing her body in that delicious, blood-red color.

Breathing heavily, I watched her hands, dangerously aware of every move she made.

She wrapped my tie around my eyes, the light of the pole the only source of illumination I could kind of see.

I grunted, hesitating, but then I relaxed when her hands slowly wandered up my body. She grabbed my hands and placed them on her hourglass hips.

"Fuck…" I breathed, my voice unfamiliar to my ears.

She was breathing so smoothly, and I was panting like a damn dog.

"I-I'm sorry, miss," I said.

God, the stupid sounds falling out of my mouth wouldn't stop. I tried again to catch my breath, crossing my legs to smother my fucking erection. She laughed. The sound was breathy and so damn sexy that I nearly came in my pants.

How pathetic was that?

I started to pull off the tie, pulling my hands free of her damning body.

She stopped me, reaching into my pocket, pushing my hands above my head onto the iron-looking bar attached to the big pole in the center. I hadn't known what the hell the bar was used for, but now I was starting to see the picture.

A concession of clicks startled me, and I gasped, pulling my hand, which was now attached to the bar above my head.

"What? Miss? What is this?" I shook my hands, my own handcuffs wringing in the darkness.

She was silent, but I could feel her heat.

"What are you doing?" I asked, feeling a bit self-conscious. Was this something that all dancers did? Using a client's handcuffs to restrain them? Did she know I was a detective, too?

"I am not here to cause trouble," I assured her.

She started unbuttoning my pants. I wiggled on the chair, the chains preventing me from getting too far. Her soft giggle made me pause.

Was she enjoying this?

"Hardy har. You got me. Now, can you let me out?" I said. I was getting slightly annoyed.

The little minx laughed at me again, her dainty hands fumbling with the buttons of my dress shirt. The cool metal of my dog tags chilled my exposed chest. I could see a small slit of space around me at the bottom of the blindfold. Her hands came into view. She was looking at my name printed on the metal.

"I served two tours overseas," I said, trying to answer her unspoken questions.

Her hands moved lower from the tags. My breath caught in my throat, and I watched the buttons of my pants pop open.

Shit, did I pay for...

"I-I...you don't have to do that, ma'am. I just...I just wanted to watch the um dancers. Not have a..." I sounded like a bumbling idiot.

But it didn't matter because she was ignoring me, working through the zipper and finding my erection easily as it pushed against the pocket of my underwear.

I was rendered completely silent when her hands gripped me. I couldn't help but hiss at the warmth of her exploring fists.

She was touching me like she was memorizing every inch of me. It was erotic as fuck.

"I-I..." I stammered, my body tightening on its own accord. "If you don't stop touching me, I will get that pretty face very messy."

I was losing control, the beast emerging like the horny bitch he was.

"I'm sorry," I said, trying to get a handle on my emotions.

She stroked my cock faster. My abdominals completely contracted with the strength I used to stop myself from coming all over her.

"Please," I begged through gritted teeth.

The woman leaned down, her hair tickling my face. A whisper of her lips trailed across mine, and I lost it.

My come coated her just like I had warned. My mind cleared from the pleasurable haze, and I tried apologizing, but her heat was already gone.

All I could see was darkness and a bit of faded light around the edges of the fabric on my face.

I tried to wiggle my head to knock off the makeshift blindfold. It slid halfway off my eyebrow, and I continued the ridiculous action until one of my eyes was free.

Sure enough, I was alone in the dimmed room, the pole empty, and the red light lighting up only my shame. My seed stuck on my stomach and chest.

But something was different.

My nose had been half covered when the dancer was up close to my face, but now I could smell that faint scent...of spicy sage.

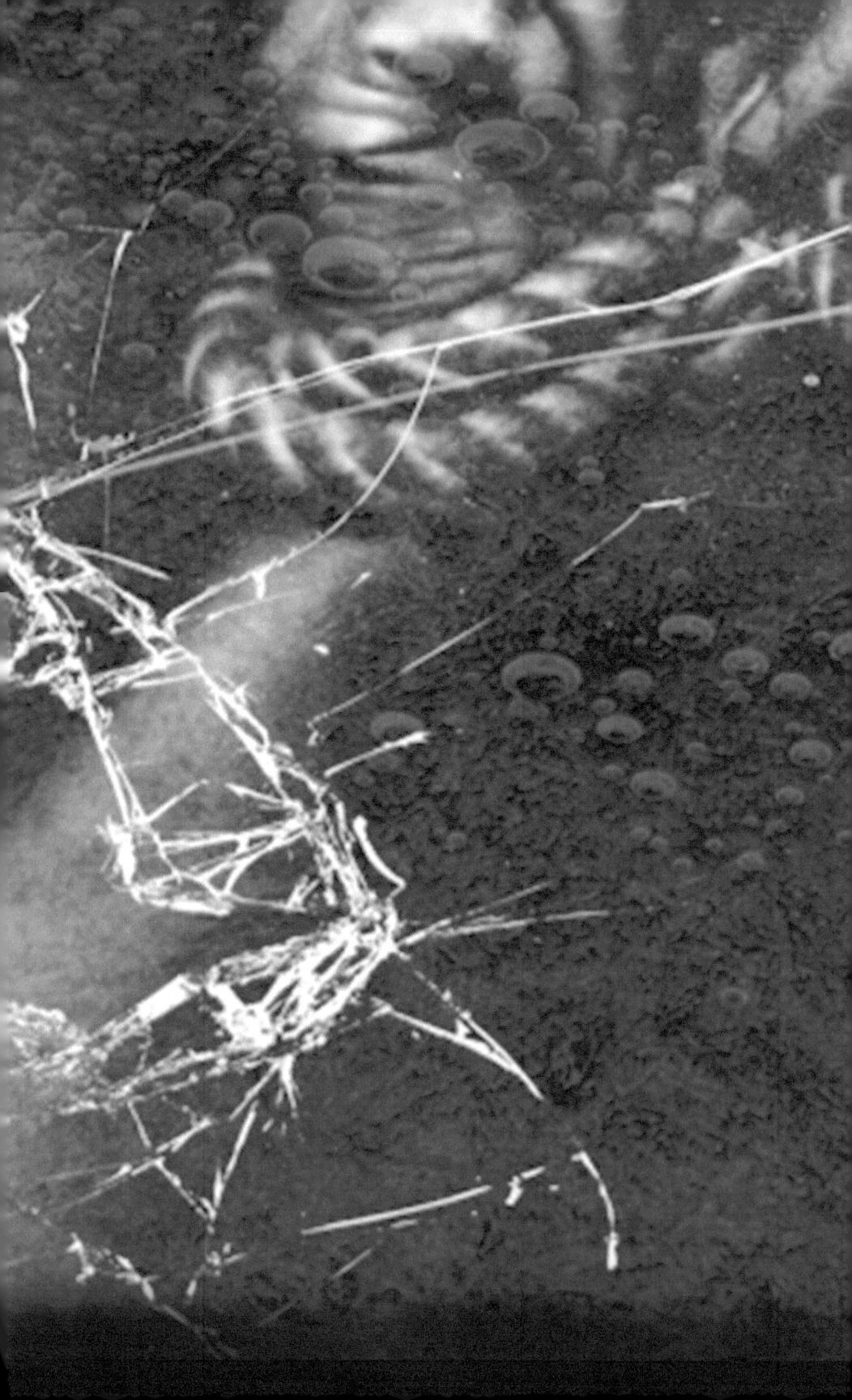

Ivy

Chapter 11

Speeding down the highway in my Micah 'borrowed' Ducati, I had to blink so rapidly that my vision stopped blurring. It was that rage that was fueling my moxie to do what I had to do.

The police station wasn't far, and it was right about shift-change time. Most people at the bottom of the department, who weren't fancy big men in suits, were actually pretty dumb when it came down to women waltzing in having a damsel-in-distress attitude.

I'd learned that it was insanely easy to manipulate the male species over the past year of my training. It was one of the reasons why I even got a job at Gya—to understand what it meant to manipulate men for my gain.

My brother would lose his head if he knew I worked at a gentleman's club, much less one created on the bones of his precious nightclub. But honestly, I think I would throw his favorite word back to him at this point.

"Fuck you."

It was interesting that words held power, especially from the ones who spoke them. I seemed to get quite a rise out of people when I said things like that.

I really wanted to shout them in Micah's face right about now. I wondered who his friend was. Micah was always friendly with everyone. I hadn't met a single person to hate the man, but this particular guy, Psy…they seemed really close.

Maybe there was history there?

I couldn't shake the memory of Micah's dog tags. They showed he was a soldier. He fought for his country and survived. That metal had bounced off his chest with the way he moved. We were both survivors in our own way.

I didn't know why I even did that. It wasn't my right to do. I just…I wanted to feel his cock. It was so warm, so freaking huge. Nothing like I had ever experienced. His moans brought me to the night in the apartment, a front-row view just for me of his amazing power and beautiful orgasms. The vibration of the motorcycle on my pussy wasn't helping to cool off my sinful thoughts. That was only a few days ago. I had to find Jenika. She didn't deserve to be a pawn in the justice game.

ARRIVING AT THE PRECINCT, I SLIPPED INSIDE THE BASEMENT entrance. It wasn't crowded with random people looking to report their issues.

My small frame was perfect for squeezing behind the big pipe extending from the wall and allowing my entrance into the main electrical area.

Reaching into my pocket, I fished out my translator book and located the words I wanted: "Interrogation Center." I felt guilty knowing my actions would free some well and true criminals, but I hoped that Quinn's team would realize my schemes soon—just after I was finished.

Clicking off each switch linked to my route, I cringed at the echoes and machines whirring in the large industrial-smelling area. Taking a deep breath, I flipped the main switch that plunged all into darkness.

The screams of the frightened crowd upstairs surrounded me, only cementing my earlier guilt, as some children were part of that crowd. I hated putting kids in any discomfort, much less complete darkness with criminals.

Centering myself, I blocked out the noise and continued forward, walking through the doors easily as the mechanisms for the locks were all turned off now.

The darkness didn't bother me at all. I had lived so long in that cage. The darkness was my friend. It was the light that had brought with it pain and foreign hands invading my body until they were content. When I was in the dark, I was alone.

What would the darkness bring me with my freedom?

I entered the door that I recalled from my blueprint maps as the interrogation room. I wasn't sure what Nika had said, but she didn't deserve to be a prisoner to the uniformed assholes all because she had survived a brutal crime ring of skin traders.

"Nika?" I whispered, bumping into cabinets and tables, unsure of my surroundings.

There was still chatter going around about the blackout, and I could hear the click in the distance of the generator powering on.

Dammit, I wasn't fast enough.

Now, I was locked in.

I heard noises and saw a light bouncing around the area. I cursed and tried to duck under the table. I was too late. The bright light froze me into place. I stood, my back turned, and I reached above my head with my hands.

"YOU'VE GOT TO BE FUCKING KIDDING ME."

I spun around at the masculine voice—the flashlight aimed at my head and the glint of a silver gun poised in my direction.

"*Ivy?* What are you doing here?"

I couldn't answer.

Nothing I could think of sounded remotely sane. That was probably because my scars had left more damage in my mind than my body.

"Micah," I stated, looking over to use his flashlight to confirm the area we were in.

He just stared at me like he was looking at a ghost. Had he realized I wasn't a dream? I had left my shoes at his house. I couldn't be a dream and leave behind pieces of myself.

"Ivy," he said again, shaking himself and walking up toward me. Inhaling deeply, he closed his eyes. "That's what I thought. I'd know you're spicy sage anywhere, baby. Why did you run from me?"

I chewed my lip, unable to give him an answer. My non-answer was just as much the confirmation he needed, however.

"How long have you been back? And why did you...." Now, he seemed hurt.

His blue eyes swirled with the pain and loneliness I knew he felt. I had watched him from that balcony for so many nights. I knew the countless hours he'd spent searching for me.

"I never left," I admitted. However, it wasn't fully true. I have lived with Gertie and Hank for some time now. They had become my home. Rochester had been where I'd worked right under his nose this entire time, though. "You have been closer to me than you realize, Porthos."

"What do you mean?" His brows furrowed. "I have looked for you everywhere, my Little Ghost. How could you be here without me being able to find you?"

I studied him, allowing myself to look at his truly beautiful face. He still hadn't shaved, and I was starting to like his new rugged appearance. It differed so much from the clean-cut soldier I had spent many hours learning from.

"You cannot find someone you aren't looking for, Micah."

That confused him more, and I felt badly as his expression showed his struggle to comprehend what I meant.

You do not know me, so I cannot be found.

His phone went off, and he cleared his throat, lifting a finger in the air, demanding I stay put. "This is Quinn."

I strained my ears to hear but couldn't make out anything except "Guy...Attempted..." and "Asking for you."

"I see. Send him to room six. The generators should return online shortly. I will be there in a few minutes," he said into the receiver. "And Morgan, check on room eight. Make sure the CI is contained."

CI? That room would be worth a look.

Micah closed the phone and turned back to me. "We aren't done, Little Ghost. I don't know why you're here or why you ran... but Ivy?"

I stared into his blue eyes as he got a breath's distance from me, his strong hands trailing the edge of my jacket and twirling the ends of my black curls.

"I'm not the teddy bear you walked out on...it's only a matter of time until I catch you."

Swallowing, I whispered, "What do you plan to do if you can, Porthos?"

I felt his smile against my skin before I felt the sharp lash to my bottom.

"I'm going to take my time punishing you."

I inhaled a breath and pushed him off me. He made me feel dizzy in such close proximity. His moans still echoed in my ears, those coveted sounds I'd protect with my life.

"You stole something from me." I accused.

He furrowed a brow, a lazy grin appearing on his face.

"I suppose we're even then, Little Ghost. You stole my motorcycle."

I scoffed, and Micah leaned against me, his hands linking around my back onto the desk. I was too caught up in his beauty to notice the clicking sound until it was too late. My mouth dropped open. Anger mixed with shock raced through my body.

"Micah Quinn. You did not handcuff me!"

Micah chuckled, checking his work, ensuring my wrist was secured in the metal bracelets linked to the desk's metal extension. This wouldn't hold me long.

He leaned down to my ear, a dangerous husky warning coming from deep within his throat. "You think you are the only one who can play with handcuffs, baby?"

I blinked, and the realization that he knew sank in. Somehow, he knew I was the one to leave him chained to that chair at Gya.

Was this his punishment?

I rattled my chains and reached my free hand forward to smack him.

He caught my hand with little effort, bringing it up to his lips and placing a kiss on my palm.

I shivered.

"See you soon, Little Ghost."

Micah Quinn

Chapter 12

I t took everything I had to walk away from my Little Ghost, knowing she would disappear again and wondering if she was ever even there in the first place. I pulled my jacket to my nose, inhaling her spicy perfume. It clung to me, and I had to believe my mind wouldn't be that cruel.

That begged the question, though…

Why was Ivy here?

She looked so shocked when I left her. Her pouty red lips parted, her golden eyes wide. I knew her little ass was stinging from my hand, and my body vibrated at the knowledge. She looked like absolute perfection in my handcuffs, so helpless and at my mercy.

Shaking my head from her tight little body and willing my stupid appendage to behave, I pushed open the door and greeted Morgan.

"Hey man, what is this about? I was…in the middle of a missing person's case."

Brent Morgan smirked, his arrogance oozing from every dumbass pore on the man's body.

"Of course, oh mighty Special Detective Micah Quinn. How rude of me to interrupt your important work."

I rolled my eyes so the cocky shit could continue. Maybe I despised him the way I did because he reminded me of my old partner, Goliath. That man was a walking disaster, but really, Brent was a version of my younger self.

"The man in there is the one that says The Cinder Killer attacked him."

Now, that got my attention.

I looked back in the direction of the office, knowing she was chained to the desk and wasn't going anywhere.

Well, Little Ghost, it looks like you'll have to wait for that punishment...

THE MAN WALKED AROUND THE TABLE IN THE INTERROGATION ROOM. His constant raging was fogging up the two-way mirror and burning a hole in the sleek epoxy of the floor. I stood, arms crossed by the door, leaning against the wall and waiting for the man to speak.

In the past, I had found these types of men were best left alone until they decided you were doing them a favor and opened up. I went over the file in my head as I continued to watch him pace around the wooden desk in the center. Malachai Biggs was known on the streets as Cassanova. He was alleged to have more than a few hundred of the local prostitutes under his order.

His nickname was clearly created by himself as he looked like the perverted mechanic on 8th street where I grew up back home.

His hair was thin, balding, and frayed as if he'd tried to make out with an electrical outlet. He smelled about as clean as the homeless community under the King's Bridge. That was where he had been found. Bleu picked him up as he ran at him, claiming he was attacked from behind, and woke up to a figure covered head to toe in blue leather.

I had to give these criminals credit. They had stepped up their game lately in the disguise department. I couldn't be sure this was The Cinder Killer. However, until I could get more details from this flake, that was the assumption I'd have to keep. It left a pit in my stomach to know this creep, who had a massive list of crimes, would soon be back on the streets.

Huh? Maybe I was stalling because I knew that about him.

"Mr. Biggs." I walked toward him.

He stopped and stared at me. He was on some hard-core drugs, and it killed me to say, but at times like these, I missed the Snow White Killer era. There were still so many puzzles left unsolved with that case, and it was only growing colder as the days stretched on in the piles of files of so many others.

I joined the police department to solve those crimes and dole out the justice those low-life murderers got away with for too many years. My sister's murder was now one of the coldest files in those piles.

Ten years.

Ten years, I had failed to bring her killers to justice. For ten years, she lay decomposing in god knows what conditions. Her grave was empty, apart from the severed bottom half of the bones.

The coroner's report flashed in my mind, the blinding light and buzzing in my ears sounding like a bomb going off in my head.

Raped, broken limbs, burned, acid residue on skin tissue, and blood clotting shows torture postmortem.

Rage boiled in my blood because it wasn't enough for these evil humans to break my sister's body and only grant her death as a final mercy. No. They had to defile her corpse as well.

"Whoa…aren't you a cop? I'm the victim here, but you look like you're about to cap my ass!"

Glancing down, I was horrified at the hand placed on my glock.

I opened my mouth to apologize, but Lana entered the room. She moved until she stood between us. Anger radiated from her, but the tight smile plastered on her face told me I was right. She had been watching through the one-sided glass. The pimp looked at her, uncertainty and curiosity in his eyes.

"What are—"

"Okay, Quinn, you are needed in the filing room for case number eight one six. I think I can take it from here, yeah?"

I winced at the code name. 'Get the fuck out.'

"Sure. File eight one six. Got it."

I needed to get ahold of my anger and find out what this fucking moron knew.

"I'll get right on it, Officer Perez, but I am in the middle of an interrogation right now."

I looked pointedly at Lana, holding her gaze and pleading with her for my sanity.

"Micah," she said. "That file really needs filing. I think I'm capable of handling this interrogation."

I am not letting this go. I'll be damned if another serial killer is going to pull a fast one on me, and at five victims, this may be an early chance to get some answers on The Cinder Killer.

The suspect was eyeing Lana. His gaze was raking down her from her blonde curled hair to her pointy stiletto heels. She avoided his gaze, smoothing her suit jacket and tapping her nails on her thigh irritably.

"Don't I know you?" the man said to Lana, swaggering as he approached her.

She snorted, pushing him off her.

"You wish," she said to him and turned to me. She walked toward me and put her dainty hand between the straps of my suspenders.

I swallowed at the action, not expecting such a forward touch from my partner. I blinked down at her, zeroing in on her hand. Her eyes were like onyx. So black you could fall into the abyss and not return. I always knew that, but this close, I could see flecks of a silver color swirling in that abyss.

The suspect coughed, breaking the spell of her gaze, and I stepped to the side.

Did I imagine that look?

"You guys need a room or something? I mean, if you're gonna fuck, at least give me the footage for my business. I'm uh…a photographer."

I locked my jaw, disgusted at the pimp, and frustrated at myself for that strange moment. The last time I let myself get close to my partner, he turned into a betraying psycho and ran off with one of the most notorious killers without a reason. I would never be so blind as I was with Ella. My ineptitude got a good cop killed. Lana may be beautiful, but she needed to keep her distance from me, or she would end up like Emily.

"Officer Perez, please escort this gentleman to room two. I will return after…filing."

I didn't wait for Lana to respond or listen to the jeers of the asshole ogling her. I simply nodded my head in professional courtesy and walked out of the room.

My goal was to get some information from the new informant, but when I got to the office where she was being held for questioning, I found it was empty. All that was left in place was a folded paper heart.

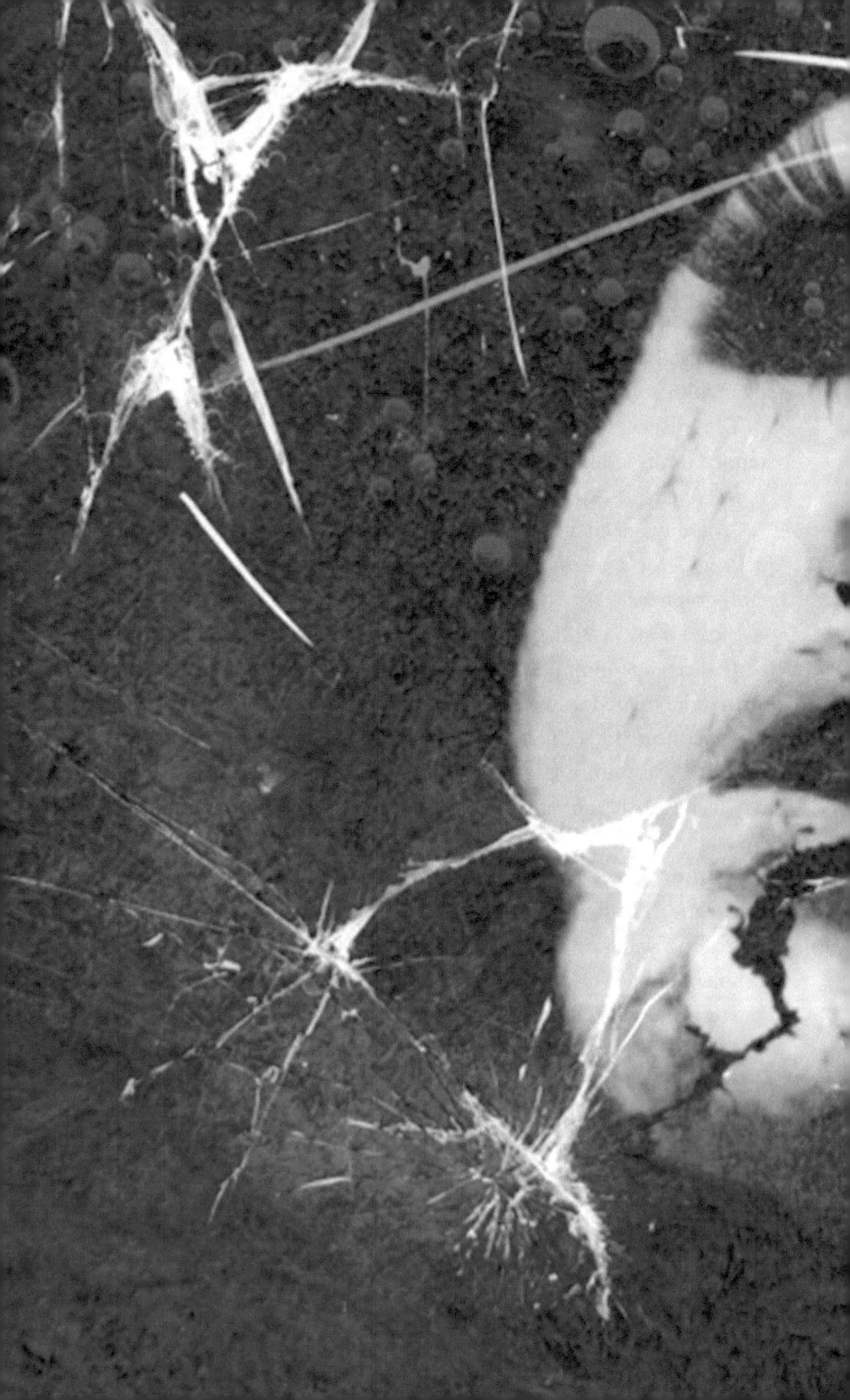

No One

Chapter 13

"Get up, girls!" The teenagers groaned and swatted their hands over their eyes at the blinding sun rays streaming inside the hotel window. Some cowered against the wall, and others returned my glare.

I was being too lazy with this bunch. I needed to get them trained and out of my fucking hair.

Fucking Micah Quinn. That man had me chasing my tail lately. I hadn't even been able to investigate his loft for whatever bitch had left her shoes. My CCTV showed him pacing in his high rise, swinging that pale blue shoe on his finger over and over. I wanted to burn it, burn him, and burn the damn glass to boil him in the liquid it left.

He broke my heart from what I watched. Kissing that fucking black-haired whore. Had it not been for my duties here with these snots, I'd have followed that cunt and made her eat her fucking shoe.

"Madame. It's too early. Please let us sleep."

I rolled my eyes at the youngest of the girls and her whining.

"No. You have a visitor coming today to show you what is expected of you. If you don't please him, you will be replaced."

The girl's haunted eyes grew wary, my meaning of replacement clear.

"Please, just let us go."

This was growing tedious, and I had enough of the bitching and pandering to get back to their pampered, perfect lives. "Go get changed now, girls, or you will be punished."

As the girls mumbled and moved around, preparing themselves, I thought about watching my pretty boy all but tear apart one of the interrogation rooms of the police station. What was he looking for? My thoughts were cut off when Biggs, aka Cassanova, traipsed into the room. The girls plastered themselves against the wall.

I silently bit my tongue until I tasted blood. I knew the lessons would start soon.

This always brought me back to my pathetic past of being the girl on that wall. The fear in their eyes showed in their reflections, memories I could still taste from one of those nights. The funny thing was, eventually, you stopped seeing reflections, and everything just became a blur. The person's image of who you once were became caged behind the glass of the person you had to evolve into to survive.

"Why, hello, ladies," Cassanova purred, running his hand across the cheeks of the girls lined along that damn shit wallpaper.

All of them cringed away, except for Melanie, of course. Her spunk and resilience to this forced lifestyle may give her a shot at surviving life once she was sold. That, or it would make sure she suffered a fate worse than death.

"Please..." It was a whispered echo falling on deaf ears, and after Cassanova twirled the girls and assessed their bodies for his pleasure, the echo faded.

"Now, ladies...your first lesson begins."

I felt my back bow, my heart picking up as I bit down harder on my tongue. The pain in my mouth would pale in comparison.

I walked stoically toward the greasy, ugly man, waiting for him to give me the command.

"When you are in the presence of a man, he is your leader, ruler, and master," I said, reciting the lesson from my blackened heart. "You are beneath him."

I felt the sting as the asshole in front of me shoved me to my knees.

"You will bow to your master, Pets. Your life and purpose are to ensure your master is satiated."

I reached into my skirt pocket, opened a candy bar, and reached my hand upward. I swallowed bile as the fucking shit stain took a bite, and the crumbs fell into my hair.

"In hunger..." I stated robotically, ignoring the gawking stares of the horrified girls as they watched me.

The bile continued to rise as I watched my hands unlatch his belt. This time, I forced myself to meet the girls' gaze, ensuring they knew this was their future. If they wanted to survive, they had better learn fast.

"And?" Biggs demanded, punishing me further and latching his dirty hands in my hair. I watched some strands fall to the ground.

"And?" I repeated, swallowing one more time before pulling his pathetic dick out of his pants. "In sex."

"Yes, that's right, my whore," he crooned, rubbing his vile flesh on my face. His sweat clung to my skin. "Open that whore mouth and show daddy who is your master."

Forcing my mouth open, I let the tears fall down my cheeks as he filled my mouth. Some of the girls shielded their gaze, and Melanie was consoling another as I was gagged again and again.

What I didn't expect was Melanie to walk forward and intervene. "Stop. She can't breathe. You are going to kill her!"

Good, just let me finally die.

Cassanova laughed and plowed into my mouth harder, black spots twinkling in my vision. Finally, it was time to sleep.

"Remember, girls, if you can't take it like this pathetic bitch, then we'll just use other parts of you until we are done."

I felt my body being dropped to the ground, the crash barely registering from the lack of oxygen in my fucking brain. It was all just tugging and ripping.

Cassanova pointed to my CCTV screen where Micah unknowingly looked past the hidden camera, even he was to bear witness to my shame. As the cloud of black finally took me, I could hear his taunts.

"Now everyone is watching, even lover boy. Wouldn't want to let him down, would you?"

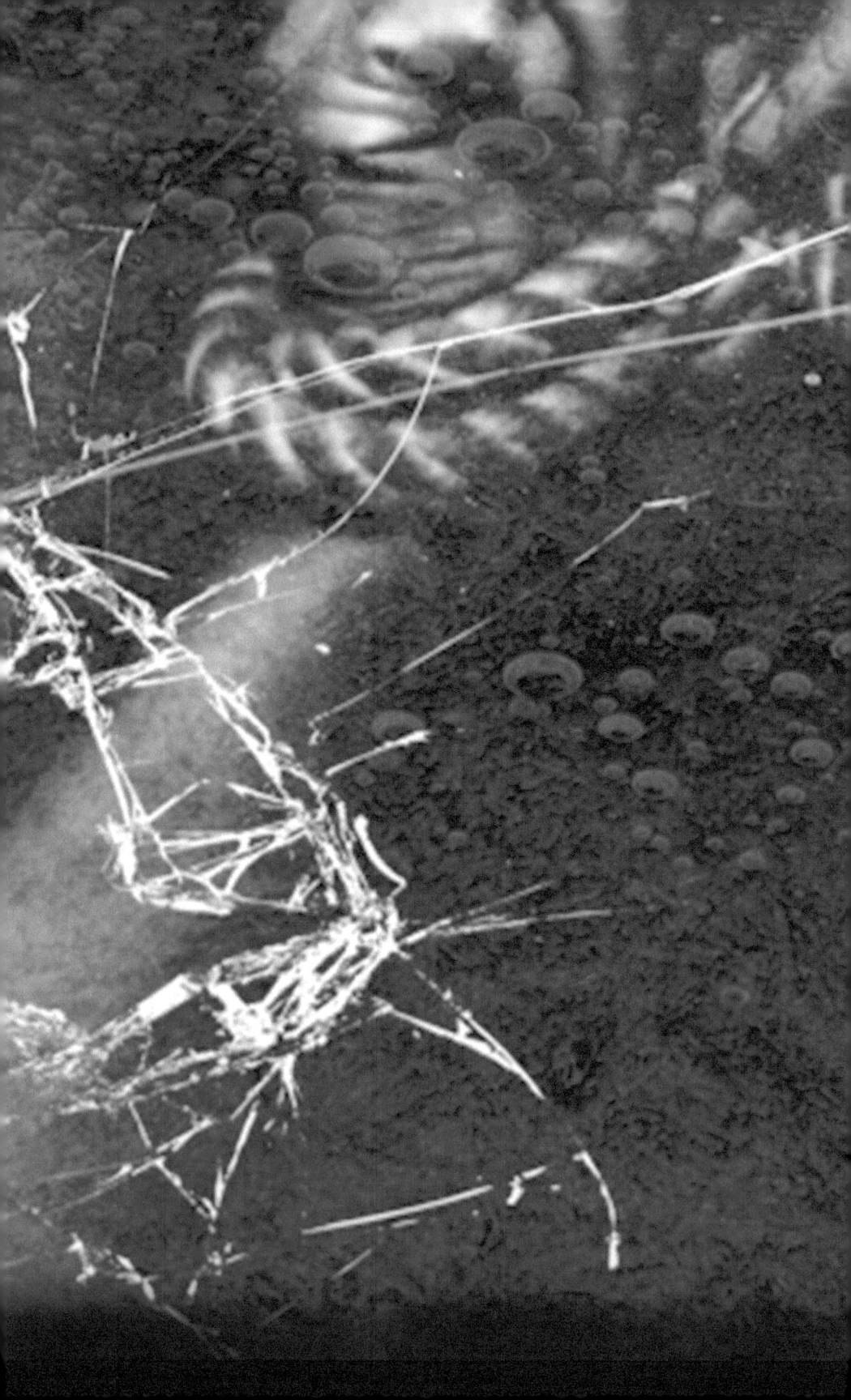

Ivy

Chapter 14

"Ivy, you are insane!" I ignored Aurora and pushed inside the door. My heart was pumping out of my chest, and I couldn't get it to relax.

"What the fuck is happening, baby girl?" She was yawning, and the natural curl to her hair was evident as she sleepily twirled it between her fingers.

"I just need to stay here for a bit. That's it."

She didn't seem convinced, so her manicured eyebrow was raised high.

"I love you, and you could live here if you wanted to, but doll, I need to know the nitty-gritty details of this gossip, or your beautiful exotic ass is sleeping on my floor."

I laughed and rolled my eyes. "Ugh, come on, Aurora. Can you let this one slide? You, of all people, should understand."

"No, I most certainly cannot," she chastised, pushing me toward a rug.

Frowning, I threw my hands up. "Fine, it looks comfortable, so you are the joke."

"You know it's 'the jokes on you' miss. Russian princess. You have been studying English too long now to pull that shit with me."

I smirked and shrugged my shoulders, slipping off my camisole and primly sitting on the fluffy white rug. It looked so much like those bears in Iceland.

"Does this happen to have something to do with that goddamn dreamboat of a detective?"

The image of Micah and his stern blue eyes clouded my focus. I could practically feel my skin tingle where his hand left its mark. I rubbed my wrists, my irritation at his trapping me, growing my lust.

Aurora gasped dramatically and clapped her hands. "I knew it! What did that pig do this time?"

I smiled sheepishly. "Actually..."

Interest piqued, she leaned on the kitchen island. "Go on."

"I stole Nika back," I admitted, smiling to myself.

"Girl. Are you nuts?" she exclaimed. "He's going to come knocking down my door eventually, you know. You can't hide forever."

I couldn't hide forever. That was true. Micah even told me he would catch me, but I could make the time I had worthwhile. That was why my heart was beating out of my chest. I had tracked the criminal I had made the mistake of letting loose tonight after dropping off Nika back home. He had just left a hotel in the city. His pants were covered in blood, and my stomach flipped at the knowledge of what that meant—he had raped someone.

"I just need to take a quick nap for a cat."

"A cat nap," Aurora annoyingly corrected me. "And what do you plan on doing, exactly?"

I chewed my lip, not at all about to tell the truth about going back to that barn and torturing that rapist for information on who he hurt, even if it was Aurora. "I am really tired. Can you scold me tomorrow?"

Aurora, of course, did not look at all convinced, but she grumbled something and left me to sleep in peace. "Yeah, okay, baby doll, just remember there are monsters in the dark. That shit isn't fairy tales."

It was a good thing then that I could be one of those monsters.

I WOKE UP WITH A BAG ON MY HEAD. IT SMELLED LIKE A SEWER, AND it was too cold.

Oh god, had someone captured me? Where was I?

Stirring and fighting with the bag, I ripped it off my head, jerking my hands out and swinging at whatever may be near me.

"No Ivy. You always play dead until you find out who your attackers are and if you can get out safely."

I blinked in the darkness, the voice so familiar to me, yet I was completely alone.

"What the fuck?"

"You cannot see you are unarmed, and you don't know if you're in a dangerous environment. An opponent would have killed you already."

I spun around, searching for the voice. Dizzy at the awful odor around me, I was chilled by what smelled like a river nearby.

"When I found out about you, I knew I needed to help you, but you aren't ready yet."

"Who's there?" I swiped my arms in the shadows.

"Let's try again another time, Ivy. Remember what I taught you."

Confused, I turned fully around, but it was too late. A fist made contact with my head, and my vision went black.

Micah Quinn

Chapter 15

*C*rash!

    I jolted awake, my hand on my Glock, ready to blow the intruder to bits. Raking my hand down my face, I tried to sober up.

    Fucking hell, why did I choose to down that malt liquor?

    "Who the f-fuck is there?" I slurred, sleep and alcohol still fighting to surface.

    Stumbling into my kitchen, the lightning from outside lit up the area. I looked down and realized I was as naked as the day I was born.

    Dammit Quinn. How are you going to protect yourself?

    My eyes widened as another crack of thunder sounded, illuminating the shivering, soaked figure across from me. What I didn't expect to see was my Little Ghost shaking so hard that her teeth were chattering, covered head to toe in rainwater and mud.

"Ivy?" She looked so defeated.

What happened to her?

I ran my hand along her body, assessing for harm. She didn't move during the examination. She just kept her eyes on the floor.

I picked up her small form into my arms. "I got you, baby. It's okay, I am here."

A dam inside her burst then, and she broke into sobs. I kept soothing her hair as I walked us upstairs to my main bathroom. Refusing to set her down, I maneuvered her in my arms to switch on the spray while carefully stripping off the grimy layers of her clothing.

I bit my lip and prayed my dick would respect her by staying the hell down for once. She was breathtaking, and watching the water slowly bring her skin back to her beautiful ivory-white color...she was flawless.

"I am failing," she stated against my shoulder. I barely heard the defeated whisper.

"Failing what, baby?"

"Who am I kidding, Micah? I should have perished in that cage along with the other girls. It is what you call dumb luck that I stand today."

I frowned and pulled her face up to me, using my thumb to wipe the mud from her cheeks.

"Listen to me, you stubborn Russian beauty. Luck is not why you are here. You fought. You're strong, and you knew I would find you one day."

Her sobs picked up, and she gave me a sad little smile.

"This is not a storybook, Porthos. Shiny princes are not real."

Determined, I set her down, grabbing her hand and bringing it to my face.

"Do I feel fake, Ivy?" Her breath caught as she held my face, trailing her fingertips over my lips. Electricity buzzed within my body at her touch.

I slowly moved her hand down to my chest, placing it over my heart. "Does my heart not beat under your hand?"

She closed her eyes and brought her other hand to my pectorals and abs, exploring the ridges under her fingertips. I swallowed and tried to calm myself, but it was no use.

She gasped and looked down, my offending hard-on stabbing her plush little breasts.

I shook my head. "You know that is very real, Ivy."

I grabbed the soap, sudsing my chest and her arms. I jolted, letting out a hiss when her small hands wrapped around the base of my cock. Her touch burned me.

"Fuck," I breathed out in a harsh whisper.

She looked scared but fascinated as she experimented with my heavy weight in her hands. Was this how she looked when I was blindfolded in front of her before, too?

"I have never seen one...so big."

My masculine pride swelled even more.

Don't get a big head? Yeah...too late.

"Little Ghost..." I warned, my control fraying with each curious caress.

"Do you not like this?" she asked uncertainly, painting her pretty features. She tried to pull her hands free, but I locked them around me.

"Quite the opposite," I managed to groan.

"My body feels strange," she said, clenching her thighs together. That did nothing to help my self-control. Growling, I thrust forward in her hand.

"That's because you are soaking wet for me, Little Ghost."

She looked at the shower head, confused, and shook her head. "No. I feel...warm. Micah, I feel..."

She was so close I pulsated in her grip, my balls drawing up.

"Not the water, baby girl. You are dripping from your pussy because you're turned on."

She looked into my eyes. Shy and lustful. Her eyes were like molten gold.

"I want...to taste you, Micah."

I came undone at her voice. Her sultry accented tone whispered against my chest.

"Oh, fuuuck. Yes, Little Ghost. Taste me."

Pushing her down to her knees, I was trying to keep the control I had left, but her whimpering was breaking me into a dangerous part of myself. I had to be careful with her. I had to show her the kindness she had never known. I didn't even know why she ended up in my house or how, for that matter, I couldn't scare this beautiful, broken woman. If she wanted to taste my cock, I had to let her have the control to do so, not manhandle her like the fuckable little doll she looked like.

"You're so big, Porthos. How can I put you in my mouth?"

I smirked down at her. "Open that pretty little mouth wide. I will help you. I will *teach* you."

Following my instructions, she kneeled before me, pouty red lips opened wide, her piercing gaze threatening me to lose myself.

Control Micah. Let her have control...

I swallowed the lump in my mouth and stepped forward, gripping my cock, and pushed into her mouth.

Feeling her tongue snapped the last few threads of restraint I had. I fucked her mouth hard, stretching her cheeks with each thrust of my hips.

"Oh, my fucking god, Ivy," I moaned. "Yes, fuck yes."

She was swallowing my dick, using her hands to follow her mouth, her lips sliding up and down.

She was wicked.

I didn't see the meek Russian woman I had known throughout those months of her healing. I didn't see an innocent, shy victim of trauma and abuse. I saw a strong, confident woman determined to make me lose my goddamn mind.

"Mmm, Micah," she moaned, the vibration along my cock making my knees shake.

"You take me so fucking well. Holy fuck. You're such a good fucking girl, Little Ghost." My Little Ghost liked praise.

Her speed picked up, and I couldn't help but pant at the expert way she sucked me.

I wasn't going to last much longer. Fuck, this woman was going to be the death of me.

Grabbing her around her middle, I flipped her upside down. My arm wrapped snuggly around her waist, her delicious pussy glistening in my face. She squeaked in surprise and leaned her head to watch me.

I grinned at her, feeling her inky hair tickle my thighs.

"I'm going to fucking devour you, baby girl." She gasped and gripped my thighs with her spiky nails. "Better hold on tight."

She gripped harder, leaving bloody pinpoints, as I dove into her sweet heaven.

She tasted like honey. Her spicy sage was clinging around her and making me feel absolutely high. My head was still foggy from the alcohol, and I knew in the back of my mind that I wasn't being gentle at all with her like I had intended, but god...I needed her.

"Oh, fuck," she screamed, my tongue making circles on her little clit.

Smiling, I increased my speed, dragging my tongue down her center.

"Micah? Oh wow. I feel...much pressure."

So my Little Ghost was a squirter?

"Fuck yes, baby girl, that's right. Spill that sweet liquid all over my tongue. Let me drink you."

She squirmed, trying to pull away.

Using her hair gripped in my hands, I flipped her up and pressed her body against the shower wall. Her pussy was beautifully close, pulsating with need in my mouth. Anchoring her there, I locked her hands above her head, sucking harder on that perfect clit.

She gasped and whimpered. "No! I am going to pee on you!"

I laughed, looking up so she could see my eyes. With a wicked grin of my own, I said, "No, Ivy. You are going to soak my face with your fucking come."

But she continued to shake her head. Growling now, I moved my hand and smacked her dripping pussy. Startled, she whimpered again.

"If you don't stop squirming, I am going to handcuff you to my bed and lick you all fucking night."

Her eyes grew wide, but her pleasure finally got the best of her, and she ground into my mouth.

Slipping in a finger, I massaged her inner walls. "This is a preview of what my fucking cock will do to you. When you are ready for me. Whatever that day is."

Moaning, she finally toppled over the edge, her pleasure racing through her. Her body was possessed, shaking and screaming my name. Hearing my name on her pretty mouth as she came all over my face made me spill my release all over the shower floor.

A while later, I wasn't surprised when I woke up to find my Little Ghost gone again. But this time, it hurt. She had fallen asleep in my arms. Her sage perfume scent was cloying to me, but now it was fading.

I looked over at the fireplace. The blue leather shoe still lay there, lit up by the fire's light.

Walking over, I picked it up. "You can't run forever, Little Ghost. I will always find you."

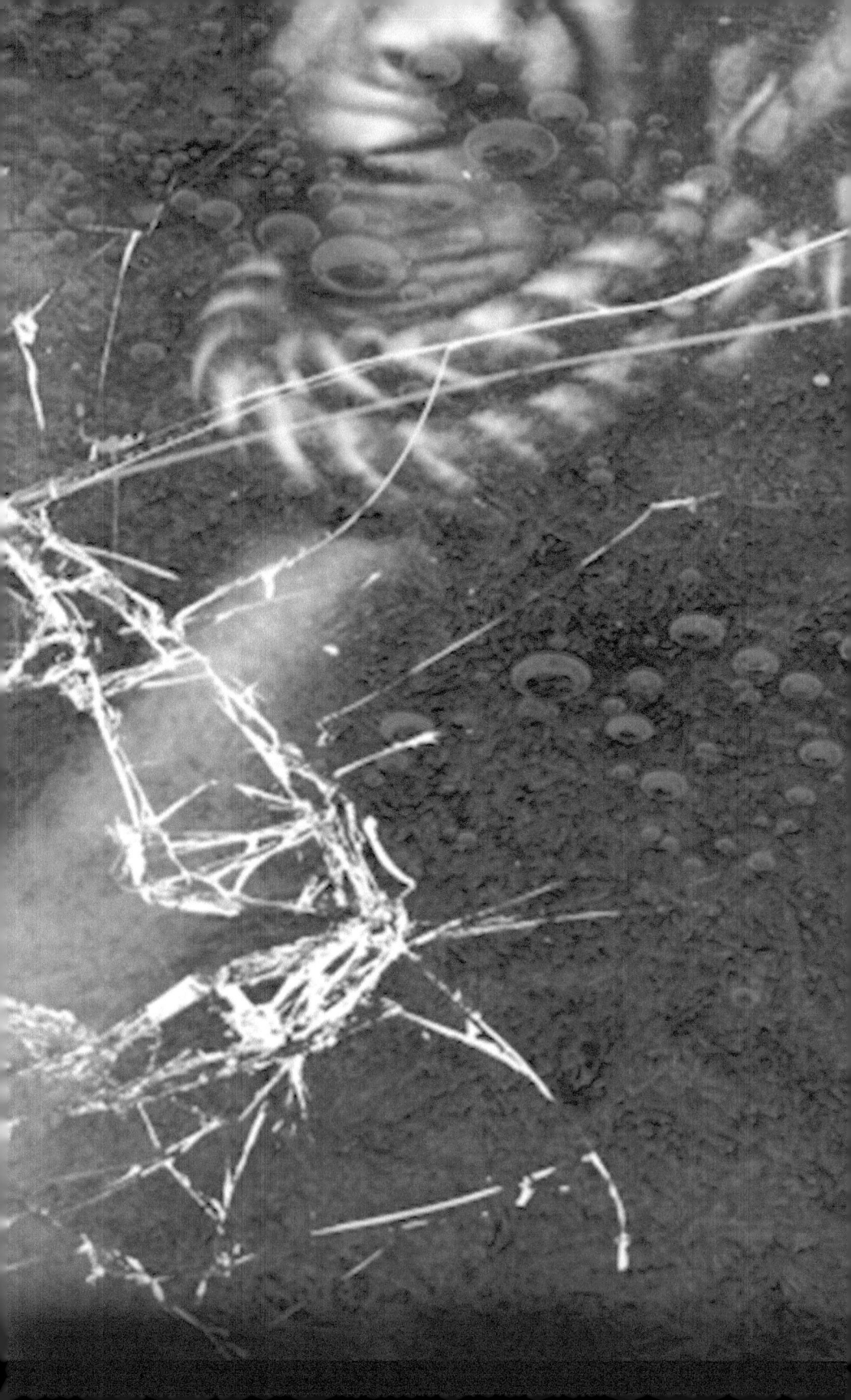

Ivy

Chapter 16

"You can do this." I pushed open the door.

The man's screams were echoing off the barn's walls. It didn't matter how far I had dragged this rapist after his death. His voice would surely haunt me.

Pulling my mask over my face, ensuring my blue leather outfit was covering every part of me, I snapped on my gloves and stepped inside.

"What the fuck? You fucking cunt! I will kill you for this. You won't live, you whore."

I let his insults slide off my back. He could call me what he wanted.

The whore comment stung, but I guess it was fair as I had gotten this creep by luring him with the promise of sex. Why he hadn't questioned driving well past the city to an abandoned barn was beyond me…maybe he intended to make sure it wasn't consensual.

"Would you shut up, *chudovishche?*"

I walked over to the dusty table, eyeing the tools littered on the wood. Weighing in my hands, the closest weapons I recognized were a mallet and a cow prod.

Was this barn once used to butcher animals?

Squinting into the darkness that the limited light allowed, I could make out furs and hide draped over one of the empty horse stalls.

It was so damn dark in here.

I slid out my lighter from my pocket and created a small flame. The crackling thunder outside the barn made me shiver, memories of Quinn's tongue flashing in my mind with the strips lighting up the sky from the windows.

"Pet, come on. You don't want to hurt me," the man purred.

I felt myself smile, making me wonder how far down this path I'd gone. I called these men 'monsters.' But what was I becoming by disposing of them? I could feel a darkness taking over me, and Quinn's memory deteriorated along with my light. All I could think of was hands and mouths taking and hurting me again and again. This man had blood on his pants. Even now, the pathetic rapist wore those stained jeans.

Was he proud? Was this to flaunt that person's pain?

That rage started crawling or building, licking up my skin like poison. I grabbed the cow prod, holding the flame of my lighter onto the end.

The man's eyes reflected in the orange glow at the end. His fear was palpable. My darkness craved this.

"What are you doing with that…Pet?" The uncertainty in his voice was rising.

I ignored him, mesmerized by the bright orange glow in my

hand. The lightning flashed behind me, and the man squeaked in surprise at my closeness.

"What's wrong...Pet?" I said, almost chuckling.

Throwing his degrading name back at him now felt good. I was in control here. This snake would not get away from me again. My failure with losing him before was why that blood on his jeans taunted me.

Angry at myself and him, I slashed the hot iron down his jeans, the fabric catching the flame at the contact and extinguishing it with a crispy black smoke. Now, the smell of cooking meat hung in the air.

The man screamed. His body was sufficiently hooked to the beam with my chains. They rattled as he cringed and tried to pull away from the fire. Those blood stains were gone, charred black and crisping at the edges.

His groin was exposed now. His pubic hair singed slightly, and his thigh flesh sizzled. His eyes tracked my gaze, and he vehemently shook his head.

"No! No. Come on, anything but that. Please."

I tilted my head at him. "Did they beg?"

He grimaced at my voice, little sparks still dancing on his skin.

"What?" He panted, confused, biting his lip at the pain of his burning flesh.

"Your pets?" I said, bringing the molten tip closer to his prized flesh. "Did they beg you, too?"

He looked away, not wanting to give me the answer I already knew. Hearing the haunted screams of all the women who had been killed after their brutal rape and torture, I let the rod drop to its mark.

His screams blended with theirs. My reality and my past collided. Sometimes, I wondered if I would eventually be trapped in a world that only I could see—reliving my pain and the monsters within it forever.

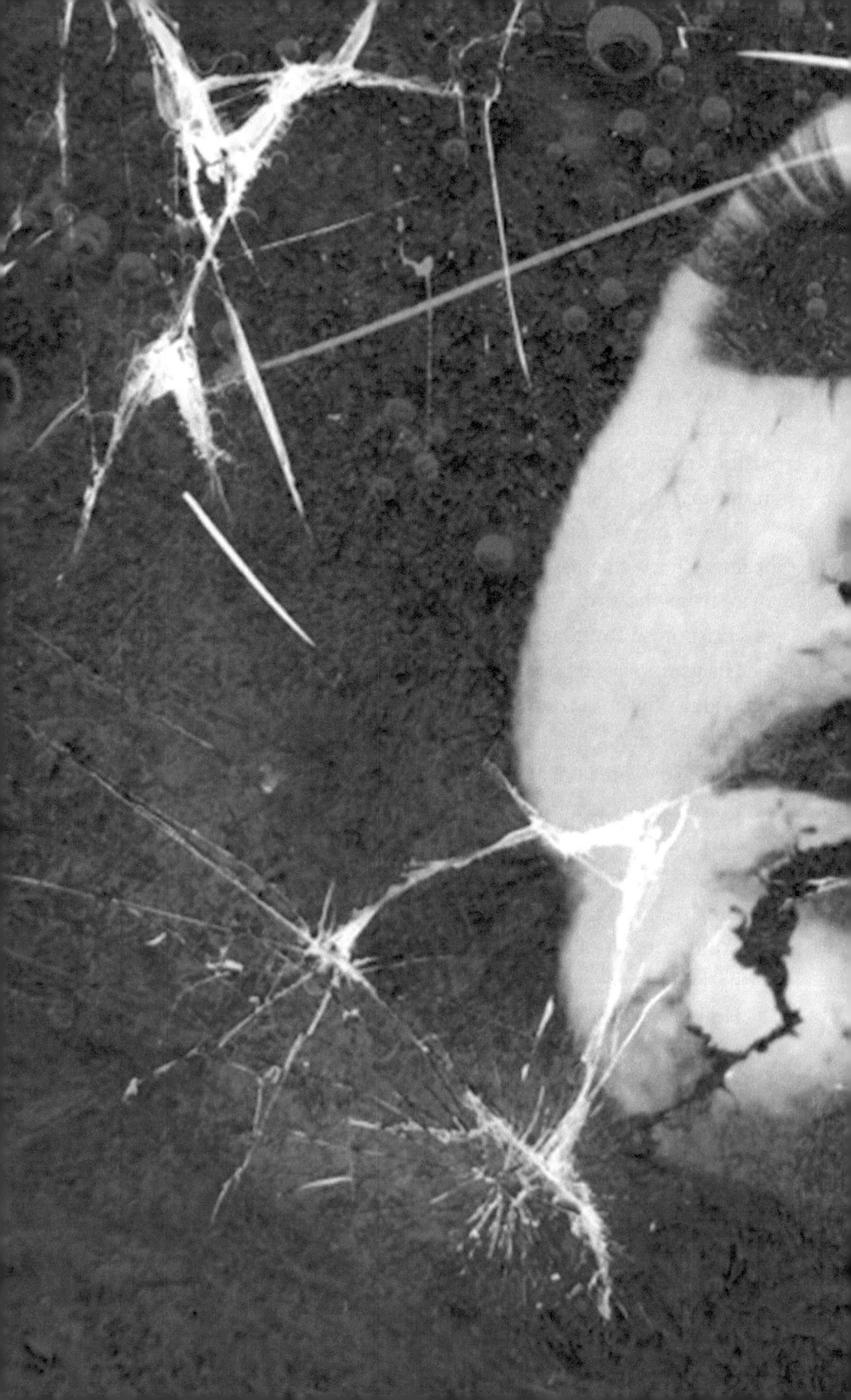

No One

Chapter 17

I rechecked my watch.

That fucking prick wasn't coming.

"Madame?"

I glared over at the girl. Her shrill voice gave me a headache. God, my throat hurt, the pain a never-ending burn every time I swallowed. That paled in comparison to my body. I was ripped to shreds in so many places that I still couldn't stand up. My core felt the worst. Blood kept seeping through my skirts.

Melanie didn't get the hint and decided to walk over to my broken, useless body. I couldn't even get out of bed.

God, I was pathetic.

"What do you want, dime?" I always called the girls dimes. Their titles, names, parents, houses, and backgrounds were never anything less than perfect.

"Madame, you're very hurt...I really think you need a doctor," the child said stubbornly.

It was her birthday today. The stubborn girl turned sixteen today. Was this a ploy?

"Silly girl. I am fine." Swinging my leg over the bed, I winced as the tear in my skin reopened yet again.

"Please...look, my mom is a doctor. I have seen people in your shape, and after what..." She paused. It was apparent that she was unable to speak the truth of my brutal punishment. The grimacing look on her face told me it was too much for her. "Uhm, what happened to you."

I laughed, the pain making me dizzy at my bruised abdomen. Delirium was surely setting in.

Where was that lowlife pimp?

"Melanie. Just leave me in peace. Your lessons are rescheduled for now, so go do something besides mother me."

She looked stunned by my use of her name.

"But—" she argued, but I held up my hand. "Go parent the rugrats. That will be most helpful. Do not harass me."

She looked hesitant, but my wavering tone and exhaustion must have resonated with her because she smiled weakly and left.

Laying back down on the bed, I let my tears fall freely. This pain was suffocating. The ceiling danced with stars, and I pleaded with whatever cosmic puppeteer there was.

Just let me die...please.

Micah Quinn

Chapter 18

" *H* i, Quinny! Family's a bitch, so I'm out, but guess who has new rookies."

I flinched at the sing-song nature of the voicemail from Lana. She had called out for a family emergency or something of the sort, and her last little jab was letting me know that I was going to be followed around by a clueless puppy today.

Sure enough, as I hung up the phone and walked into the conference area, a traditionally blue uniformed freshman was sitting on the table across from Bleu with about four other new students.

Upon seeing me, they all stood up and turned toward me, all except a young black man with kinky black short braids. He kept his attention on Bleu and all but pretended I didn't exist.

Bleu cleared his throat in an expectant manner. "Ah, yes. This is the dragon slayer, aka Detective Micah Quinn. You all probably have heard that he took down the notorious Snow White Killer last year. He is the head of the special victims unit now."

I refrained from snorting and walked away at the mention. I still felt like the world's biggest fraud. I hadn't captured shit. The department just wanted me as the figurehead for their fuck up, and that wouldn't be the first time the force had used me to clean up their mess.

The killings had stopped after that night here in Rochester, but I had been keeping tabs on other locations. A few times, there had been suspicious activity in Boston of drug dealers gone missing. That wasn't my jurisdiction, of course, but one of these days, I would be making a house call.

"Detective Quinn, what an honor. Good morning, Sir."

I forced a smile and shook the hands of the eager beavers. They had their sparkly new badges from a school that didn't teach them shit about how heavy and blood-stained that badge could become.

"Good morning, cadets," I greeted, noticing the man still sitting in his seat was only looking at Bleu.

Directing my gaze to him, I walked into his personal space and looked down at him in his plastic seat. I was sure he could feel my eyes on him. Sure enough, he looked up and met my stare. It wasn't contempt on his face but a look that said, 'I know you're not a hero.'

The look vanished as his fellow classmates watched him, replaced with a kind, classic soldier smile. A smile I knew well as I wore it as much as my armor.

"Pleasure to meet you, Detective."

Shaking his hand firmly, I sized him up. He was a decent-looking guy. I was sure he didn't have any issues with the ladies. His chocolate eyes and mocha complexion captivated the attention of the female officers. They were ducking their heads behind the computer screens on their desks or peering not so discretely through the glass as they walked by the conference room.

Had I done something to earn that look he had given me before?

At any rate, it was refreshing to see someone who didn't treat me like a god.

"The name is Quinn," I said. "And yours?"

Maybe I knew this kid. He looked vaguely familiar, but then again, I had encountered thousands of people while living in Rochester. It wasn't like my hometown in Texas. All the faces started to blur together, and my mind told me everyone was familiar and a threat.

"King," he said, holding my gaze. That challenge sparked in his eyes again, the irises swallowing the brown to make his eyes appear as if they were a vortex of black. "Randall King."

As the cadets were given their marching orders, I stepped back and waited to see what puppy would be mine for the day.

"King," the sergeant barked. "You are with Quinn."

I was pretty sure our faces replicated the same displeasure. He collected his shit, and I sighed, reading over the agenda for the day.

"Congratulations on graduating from the academy," I said conversationally.

He ignored me, and Bleu chuckled. It took all of two seconds to realize that he wasn't a talker. I turned to my friend.

"How's the baby girl doing?" Bleu started to speak, but Rookie turned on us.

"Look, *sir*..." this kid said the word like a fucking insult. "I know you seem to like getting into people's business, but I don't have a fucking life. So back off me."

I was speechless. Bleu and I exchanged a look before shrugging and walking the rest of the way to the squad car.

Bleu was getting off on this.

The quiet stretched as the hum of the engine purred underneath us—the perplexing rookie in my passenger seat. Bleu said the newbie's area of study was the serials.

That was ultimately why this man was in my car driving to the scene with me. With Lana being absent, I was stuck playing babysitter. Maybe my sergeant just knew this dude hated me and wanted to make my day extra fun.

"So, how was your time at the academy?" I said, trying one more time to make small talk in the quiet space.

Randall stared out the window. Talking was not this kid's forte. He'd maybe said two words this whole drive, and any amount of conversation I tried to start was met with one-word answers.

Sure enough, he shrugged, not even answering with words this time. Taking the hint, I shut my dumbass mouth and drove the rest of the way in silence. My phone buzzed, and I put it through the speaker of the car.

"Quinn speaking."

I could hear beeping and shuffling in the background.

"Good evening, this is Miranda Franklin. I am a doctor at Strong Memorial. I am calling regarding Miss Svetlana Perez. You are listed as her emergency contact. She has been involved in a car accident."

I nearly swerved off the road.

"Shit. Is Lana okay?" Oh god, my bullshit façade was cracking.

"She is badly injured, sir. There are multiple signs of trauma, including broken ribs and a head injury."

"I don't understand," I mumbled stupidly. "I thought she was up North in Canada with her family. How was she in Rochester?"

The doctor didn't answer my rhetorical question. Instead, she continued, "Sir, I recommend you come to the hospital and await her surgery. That is the only real way to assess her damage properly. She's being brought to the operating room now."

I shook my head to clear my dumbfounded thoughts.

Looking over at my quiet rookie, I gave him a sympathetic look. I slammed on the brakes, taking a side road and barely missing the curb. The big-ass squad SUV swerved into a big U-turn.

"Whoa, Hollywood! Are you trying to kill us?"

Note to self: drag racing made quiet rookies quite talkative. I would have laughed had I not felt the intense urgency take over, and my foot slowly increased weight on the peddle.

"Buckle up, passenger princess," I warned, pressing my foot down hard and flipping on the siren.

Now, he decided to talk, but it was just a stream of curses.

Why would Lana lie?

The sound of the trilling siren was all I could hear to drown my thoughts of what could be going on with Lana...and why, yet again, I found myself not knowing a damn thing about my partner.

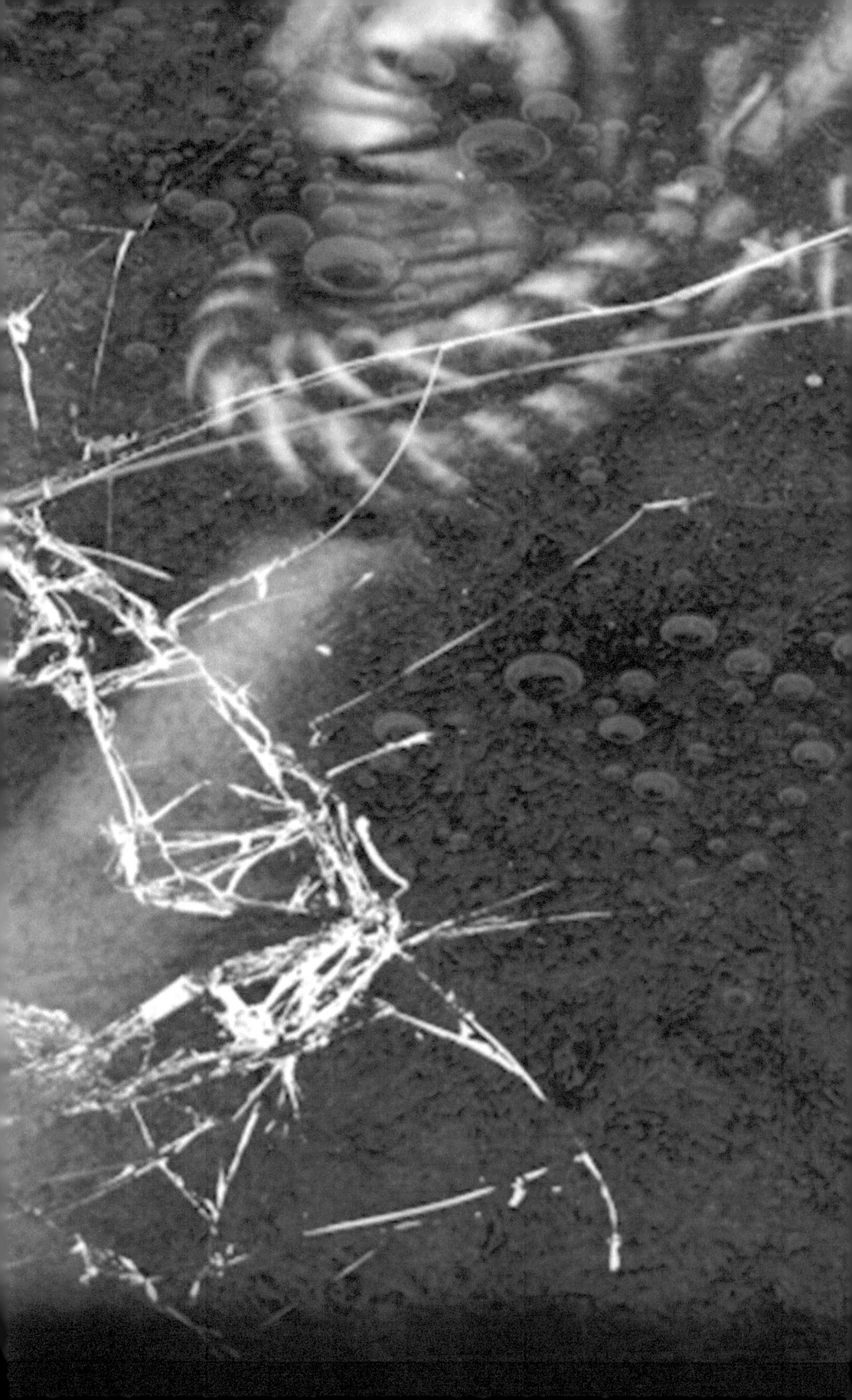

Ivy

Chapter 19

"Why the long face, little one?" I tried to smile at Hank. He had become the father I never had.

"I am just tired from working. That is all."

He walked over and patted my hand. "Just remember, sweet girl, that you need to rest sometime while being the amazing woman you are."

I smiled at him because the lie was beautiful.

Lucius strolled through the kitchen. Averting my gaze, I stared down at my hands, unable to look at my brother.

What would my brother think if he knew what I was? What have I done?

Lucius had destroyed Markus. Ripped him to pieces for what he'd done to me. My brother's hands were always covered in the blood of his enemies. He didn't kill without a purpose, and it certainly wasn't for his petty revenge.

Phoenix didn't kill innocents. The dangerous duo was a force to be reckoned with. Lethal on their own, and since being attached at the hip to one another, I was sure there wasn't a soul to withstand their wrath and live to tell the tale.

Hank clapped Lucius on the shoulder as he stuffed his face with some pastries.

"How you doin' *sestra?*" Lucius said after Hank hobbled away.

I bit my lip. My brother knew something was up. Of all the things I have hidden from him, what did he think he knew?

"Work mostly, what about you, *Brät?*" I met his wondering gaze and regretted it immediately.

"You know, when we were little, I came across one of the sorry ass 'associates' of Papa," he said, twirling an apple in his hand.

"That man was beaten and bloodied. You and I were playing hide and seek, and I had chosen to hide in the basement."

I waited for him to continue, unsure where exactly he was going with this story.

"That was the first time I had seen a man die, Eili. He pled for me to free him, but Papa came down the stairs, and I hid behind the water heater. I watched his eyes when he was killed."

I shifted on the barstool, my discomfort obvious.

"The light turned off inside those eyes. He just stared at me blankly. Papa never saw me, and I went back upstairs to make sure you stayed away from the basement." Lucius walked over to me and reached into his pocket. His finger looped around my barrette.

Instinctively, I reached up to my head.

"This," he said, lifting the metal up in the air. "Was not where it belongs."

I swallowed and snatched it back. "Why tell me this, brother?"

He stared at me, his green eyes hard and dark.

"Because Eilizaveta, I have lived my life with blood on my hands, so you didn't dirty yours."

I gasped. His meaning was clear.

"Phi and I found this yesterday. Funny story, actually. See, we were following a police radio call lead about The Cinder Killer."

I stiffened.

"Know anything about that, sestra? Know who this person is that is making rapist murderers linked to sex trade affiliations turn into a mutilated pile of skin?"

I shook my head.

"Wonder how your jewelry—" He pushed his chest into my space. "That you never take off was found in a pool of the blood of a dead man!"

He was shouting at me now.

"Do you really mean to act innocent of bloodshed, Lucius?" I shouted back.

He snorted in exasperation. "I never pretended to be innocent, Ivy. Can you say the same, dear sister?"

The chill in his tone made me bristle. I opened my mouth to speak up, but Phoenix strolled in, skipping to the beat in her head. She realized pretty quickly that the tension was palpable.

"Uhh, brother-sister squabble?" she said, walking to her mate.

I couldn't even look at Lucius. I plastered on a fake smile for Phi because I really liked her, and if Lucius screwed that up, I'd murder him.

"Something like that. How is your morning, Phoenix?"

Her grey eyes showed something as she eyed my hand with my barrette. "Where did you get that little trinket anyway, Eili?" she said.

I sighed, slipping it back into my hair.

"A man that set me free," I said. "In more ways than one."

Phoenix circled around me like a cat, my brother unaware while he shoved his face full of Gertie's sweets from the fridge.

"Interesting."

I eyed her curiously as she continued to move around me.

My breath caught in my throat when she suddenly stepped

right in front of me, the back of her hand running down my cheek. "Maybe it's time to play dead before someone else takes you in the middle of the night, Princess. Your brother is annoying, but god help me. I love him with my entire soul, and if he lost you..."

I DRAGGED PHOENIX INTO THE OTHER ROOM, AND IT WAS HARD TO keep my voice down.

"You? *You* were the one to kidnap me?"

Phoenix did not look at all apologetic, but she didn't look like she would lie to me either, so I appreciated that.

"Yes," she said flatly. "You need to learn if you're going to go after monsters, baby girl."

I blinked at her nonchalant attitude.

She shrugged.

"I know your big bad brother can be a brute, but trust me, he loves you. He just may spank me for this, so even more reason to do so, but I'm going to teach you how to slay your dragons."

I balked at her as her phone went off.

"Hey, girl! Thank you so much for giving me a callback," she said in a professional tone. "Yes, San Diego is great! Did you get the file I asked for, Maggie?"

Giving me a wink, she plopped down on the chair in the hallway and booted up the dinosaur computer in the corner. It made an awful screeching noise and hummed while dust flew off it, but otherwise, it was resurrected enough for Phi to pull up an email with a long list of addresses and names.

"Your boyfriend didn't rat me out. I told everyone at the office that I moved to a department in San Diego," she said while clacking away the keyboard.

I chose to ignore her calling Quinn my boyfriend...and the warmth that spread through me along with it.

"This file is a list of names that have alleged connection to The Masks."

Unable to help myself, I scoured the list, trying to memorize each location and name from the blinking square monitor.

"Easy there, eager beaver," Phoenix chided. "Don't go running off half-cocked. Remember what I said? You play dead until you know your surroundings and your opponents' weaknesses."

I bit my lip, irritated that I was so new and stupid to this. I marveled at Phoenix and her ability to be so effective as a killer.

"This man..." she said, tapping the screen with her green-painted fingernail. "A local to Boston. Get dressed, Ivy. You are going to learn how to hunt your prey and lead them into your trap. It's less messy than your previous methods of capture. Be the spider, not the fly."

I scrunched my face. "Be the spider...."

Lucius came into the hallway and hoarded some more of those pastries in his pockets and hands.

"What are you up to, babe?" he asked his love, kissing the top of her head. She switched the screens to a ballroom, and the flashy lights for the advertisement made the screen dance.

"Nothing much," she said, returning the kiss to her lips and stealing a scone from his pocket while he was distracted.

"Just a little girl's night."

I took a deep breath, watching the two of them fawn over one another. It made me miss my annoying detective.

Girls night out? I could do this...couldn't I?

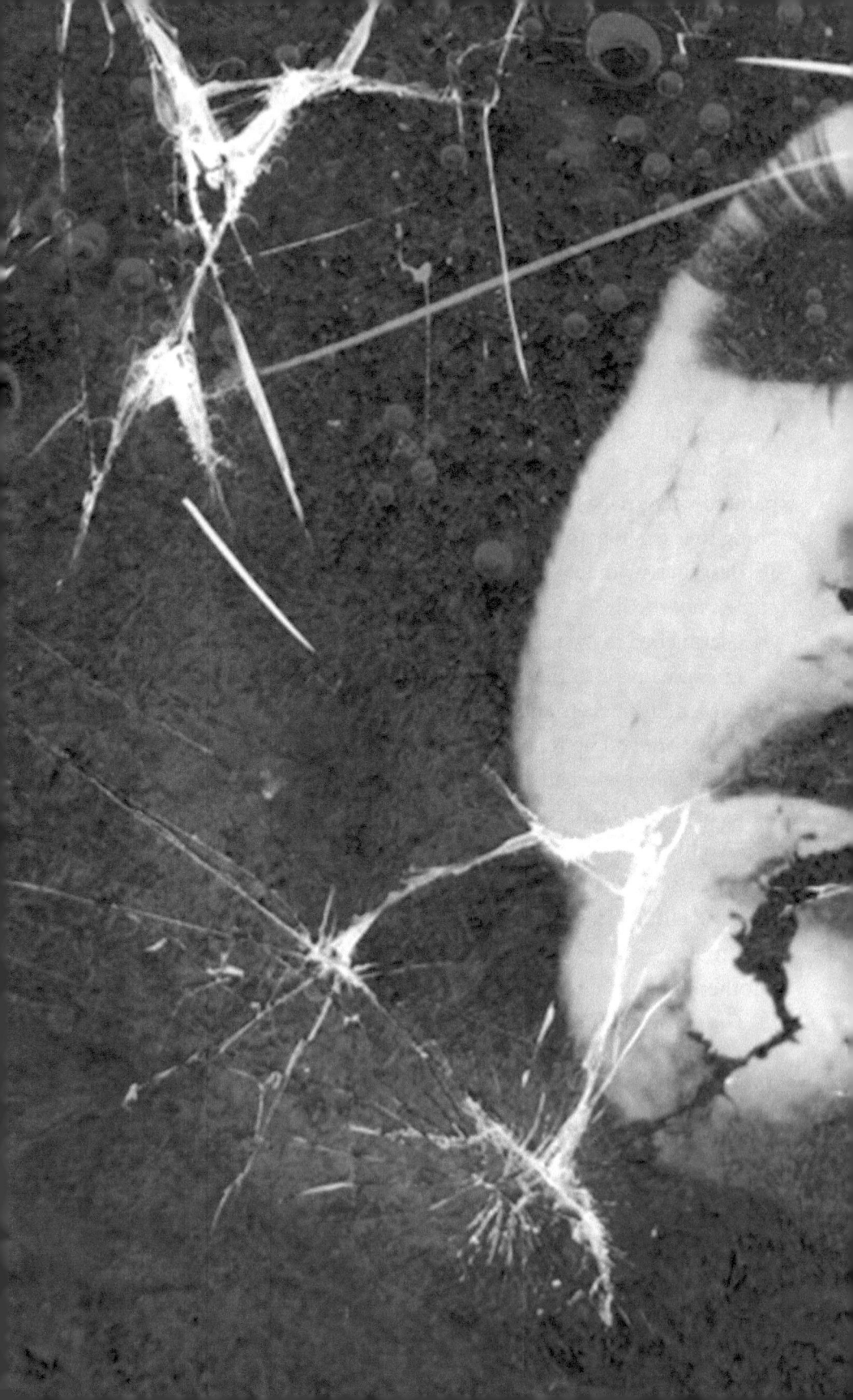

No One

Chapter 20

I took in a breath. My lungs felt like I was inhaling shards of glass with each pull of oxygen. There was darkness around me, a pull that threatened to swallow me if I let it. There were soft, trilling sounds, and my arm squeezed like someone was holding me roughly. Then it released, and a beep sounded.

The smell in the room was cold, a scent of disinfectant and old people.

What the fuck?

"Madame?" a soft voice whispered by my side.

My eyes felt like they were crusted over from misuse, and I wondered how long I'd been asleep. I opened my eyes to a glaring light above my head and quickly shut them again. Little painted clouds sparkled around it.

Where was I?

I certainly didn't remember sparkly clouds in the hotel.

A loudspeaker went off, and I heard the words blaring around me.

"Code blue! Dr. Nitre to Psych."

Oh fucking hell...

Now I recognized the smell, and the beeping and booping made sense. I was in a fucking hospital. My heart raced, and I began to panic, feeling like a prisoner in my own body. Despite how hard I tried, I couldn't lift my arms.

A rustling sound made its way to my ears, and I guessed it was a door. My hand was being held, and a low voice was speaking to me.

"Oh my god, what have you done to yourself?" I couldn't comprehend that he was here. I couldn't focus on what I was hearing.

"What happened to her?" the voice said, gruff but kind.

Who was he speaking to?

"I..." the small voice responded, uncertainty heavy in their tone.

The voice was Melanie. She was going to tell him I kidnapped her. The girls, wherever they were, would all be given back to their parents. Parents that only wanted them for the publicity they brought.

I knew the people who threw them into the world. I had been born in the same cesspool, dressed up like a damn show pony, expected to spin around in oversized dresses and marry some pompous ass.

That was before I was kidnapped. After I had been taken and used, my body and soul lost all value to my parents.

Even after I escaped The Masks and found my way home, I was already a tarnished product to them. It wasn't like I ever fit their perfect mold in the first place, but the papers filled with my name and the "generous" donation for my return had made their lives as showcased as they always wanted to be.

So when their ruffled, broken daughter returned to them, and they knew the fame would end, they shut me out. They slammed the door in my face and told me I was a liar. My name—my real name still flooded the local papers all these years later. The mourning family was looking for their beloved daughter.

The night that door hit me in the face, I made a deal with the devil. Alyosha sent a man to kill me and tracked my steps the minute I was freed. His words still echoed in my ears from all those years ago…

"Silly princess. Your crown was gone the moment we took you. Now you'll be whatever the fuck your master deems you to be, understood? Or you will lay to rest with the rest of the royals who thought themselves above the true king."

I fell backward onto the cemented ground, my dress ripping with my soul.

"Wait!" I screamed, shielding my face from his beautifully cruel face.

Monsters should be ugly, wart-filled, and obese. This man was breathtaking. The devil could destroy the world if he chose. I needed him to see me.

"I can be so much more than another man's whore. If you let me."

He paused, his golden green eyes calculating.

"What do you possibly think to offer me?"

I swallowed all the bile in my throat. I knew I looked like shit. My hair was a mess from running from the masked captor. The asphalt from my falls had ruined my gown. My makeup was smeared from all the tears and sweat dripping down my face.

Hearing my mother's voice in my head, I swallowed the pride and fear and got up to stand before the monster.

"I can teach them," I said with a confidence I couldn't feel. "I can train the others to be the best for their masters. I have been trained my whole life to be obedient. I know I could make them into the perfect ladies."

He scoffed, looking at me distastefully.

I swallowed while he walked around me, circling me like the predator I knew he was.

"You are not obedient. How do you expect me to believe you can teach someone something you don't know yourself?"

I ground my teeth together in frustration and bowed before him. My knees hit the hard, unforgiving ground. I looked pleadingly into his eyes. He smiled, a dangerous, chilling smile that resembled a cat ready to pounce.

"Good girl, little one. You may be useful yet." He ran his fingertips across my cheek, down my neck, and the foreign touch made me stall. No man had touched me like that.

My school had a million girls sucking faces with the senior boys who snuck into the facility, but I didn't. I wouldn't even touch the freshman boys.

There was only one man I even wanted to talk to, but Penelope's brother was such a womanizer that I doubted he even saw me. He always left her to fend for herself when their dumb parents went off. Maybe they would return to see that their sparkly little light was...gone.

Penn was such a perfect debutant—everything I wasn't.

"There is the matter of your replacement. You were going to be a very prized client of mine."

I bit my lip hard enough to taste the blood and feel the pain of the words I was about to say.

"I know where you can find your replacement."

Micah Quinn

Chapter 21

I looked at the girl standing beside Lana.

Was she family?

She looked familiar, but I couldn't place where I had seen her.

"My name is Quinn," I said, matching her soft tone. "Micah, Quinn. What's your name, sweetheart?"

She looked like a scared doe, and I was shifting from one foot to another.

"I…I'm Melanie."

"How do you know Lana?" I was genuinely curious.

She was silent, looking at the blonde in the bed, studying her closely.

"She's…my teacher."

I thought that was strange. I didn't know Lana was a teacher, but I guess it made sense. She had weeks off, and the grapevine gossip said it was some secret job. Nothing wrong with being a teacher.

"You need a ride back home?"

The girl's already wide eyes practically bugged out of her head.

"H-home?" I tried to school my features at her strange response.

"Yeah. Don't you have to be home soon?"

Tears fell from her big blue eyes, and I became alarmed.

"Hey, it's okay," I assured her, reaching for the teen and patting her shoulder.

"Yes..." she said tentatively. "Home."

I had Bleu stay at the hospital to keep an eye on Lana, and then I took off to the parking lot with my rookie and the girl.

THE SKITTISH GIRL SAT IN MY SQUAD SUV. I MADE THE ROOKIE TAKE the backseat, but he allowed it without fuss. I made a mental note of that. The rookie was good at taking unexpected punches to the day, which earned my respect.

After getting the address from the girl, we rode in silence until the massive gates appeared. The familiar wrought iron gates made me nauseous to drive through. My upbringing of expected perfection was a nagging memory that persisted with each passing mansion.

This gated community was a mirror of my childhood home and all the polished men and women who probably lived behind these kinds of cell walls. Memories of my parents and growing up like this were almost hauntingly similar to this place.

I drove past a redhead, her updo and sparkling dress bringing a pang to my heart. Teenagers making a quick buck to mow others' lawns, and high-class women with their noses so high to the sky they barely watched the dogs attached the leashes around their hands.

"I'll let Lana know I took you home when she—"

"No!" the teen bellowed, pounding her hands onto the dashboard.

"Fuck!"

Instinctively, I hit the brakes, and the car jerked to a halt. All of us slammed forward with the arresting stop. Randall groused about being thrown into the bars in the back of the car, but I was staring at the girl.

What caused her outburst?

"Are you okay?" My eyes still focused on her in the passenger seat.

She'd begun breathing so fast as tears welled. Worry and adrenaline were coursing through my veins.

Something was way off because her physical symptoms continued, and she was now paler than a ghost. This kid was going to vomit or pass out or both. Driving the few feet left, I parked the car and got out. I waited for the teenager to exit the vehicle, and Randall stayed back, giving me a nod before I shut the door and walked to the house.

As expected, the spacious home could be on a postcard. Knocking on the door, I realized my detective get-up and badge were on full display, and I hoped I did not alarm the girl's parents.

The door opened to a distraught woman. Her face was sunken in and tear-stained. She looked blankly into my eyes.

"Uh, good evening, ma'am. I apologize for the disturbance. I just wanted to bring—"

The woman gasped, and I realized she saw the girl peeking out from behind me. The duo looked at each other like long-lost strangers, and a sickening feeling settled into my gut.

I suddenly recognized where I had seen this child. She was on all the newspapers and fliers in the station. She had been missing. My mouth dropped open, the shock stalling my movements.

The woman ran and dove for the young teen. She wrapped her in an embrace, and they both began sobbing uncontrollably.

It had to be a coincidence.

Lana couldn't have known this sixteen-year-old girl was missing...right? Maybe she was taking her to the station when they got into a car accident?

Truly observing Melanie, she looked a bit malnourished and dirty, but there were zero marks on her. There was nothing to signify she'd been in an accident.

Was she somehow related to Lana?

What the fuck?

I had to return to Lana and figure out what the fuck was going on. I waved for King to follow us and walked into the house.

The mom and daughter were crying and hugging each other nonstop. Randall walked into the house, and I handed him my pad and pen. "King, This is yours. Record their formal statement while I call this in."

My rookie looked at me with uncertainty in his dark eyes but grabbed the pad and pen.

"Uh. Good evening, ma'am. My name is Officer King. I need to collect a statement from your daughter."

I watched the scared girl cling to her mother as Randall showed compassion and asked her a series of questions. She didn't know anything. There were others, but she never knew where they were.

The rookie wrote down the details she could recall of the room and the descriptions of the other girls there.

"There was a man," she said with a hesitant tone. "C-Cassanova."

My eyes widened. That was the victim we found killed in a barn far outside of town not long ago.

"Cassanova?" I questioned. "Did he—" The mother flinched, making me rethink my wording. "Were you hurt, little one?"

The girl shook her head. "No...but the madame was."

Her voice was so soft and sad, as if she were reliving the memories of that occurrence.

"What happened?" Randall started. "It's okay, sweet girl. You are safe."

Randall was strangely good with kids, maybe it was because he was pretty much still a kid himself. His file said he was twenty. He was the youngest graduate this year of the academy, but his record was exceptional despite his lack of experience. The man had street smarts, like someone who must have lived on them.

"The madame...she, uhm...she fell asleep, but the Cassanova man didn't stop...hu-hurting her."

My stomach twisted at hearing those words from such a young girl. She and a bunch of other little girls were forced to watch that leper rape an unconscious woman. Tears were streaming down her cheeks, but a blank stare was on her face.

Reaching forward, I squeezed Randall's shoulder.

"Okay, darling. I have one more question, and then we will leave you to be with your mama, I promise."

The girl looked at me, her face showing relief. She was most likely happy to put this behind her.

"The 'madame,'" I said slowly, afraid of her answer. "Was that the blond-haired woman in the hospital?"

She swallowed, looking to her mom for encouragement. Her mother was crying but held her daughter and rubbed her arm for courage.

"The man...finished and took her away. I ran out and hid in the backseat of his car. He didn't see me. He dropped the madame onto the sidewalk near the hospital, and I snuck out of his car."

Clearing her throat, she continued, "The madame was going to die, I could see the building, and I heard the sounds. I ran to the hospital's ambulances, and I told them the madame was on the sidewalk. They brought her into the hospital, and I went with her."

She paused, shaking her head. "I just...waited. I should have run, but I was afraid she was going to die...then you guys came."

The pieces of the puzzle were clicking into place.

"Was Lana the madame who took you?"

The little girl looked into my eyes. "Yes, Detective. She was the madame."

I cursed and walked over to the corner of the room, pulling out my phone and dialing Bleu's number.

He answered after a few rings.

"Quinn. Man...I am sorry." His voice sounded pained.

"What happened?" Panic raced through me.

"Lana. She fucking hit me and ran off. I can't reach her."

"Fuck!" I yelled and then looked over to see Randall's scolding look.

"Damn, Bleu." I said softer, "Lana is...." I couldn't even say it. "Lana is now the top suspect in the Cinder Killer case. She was the goddamn madame of the association. She kidnapped those kids!"

"Fucking hell, man!" Bleu swore. "I need to go get my girls. I will call this in. You and King take care of that little one."

"No Bleu...Just tell them the description from the girl's statement of the place where she was held. I have an idea before you out, Lana."

"Quinn, you sure?" I was shaking. How many goddamn partners needed to betray me before I got the fucking message? "Yeah. Trust me. I am going to handle this."

Unlike Ella...Lana wasn't getting away with this.

I would find her and earn my ridiculous nickname at the precinct for real, even if it meant I was slaying my friend in the process.

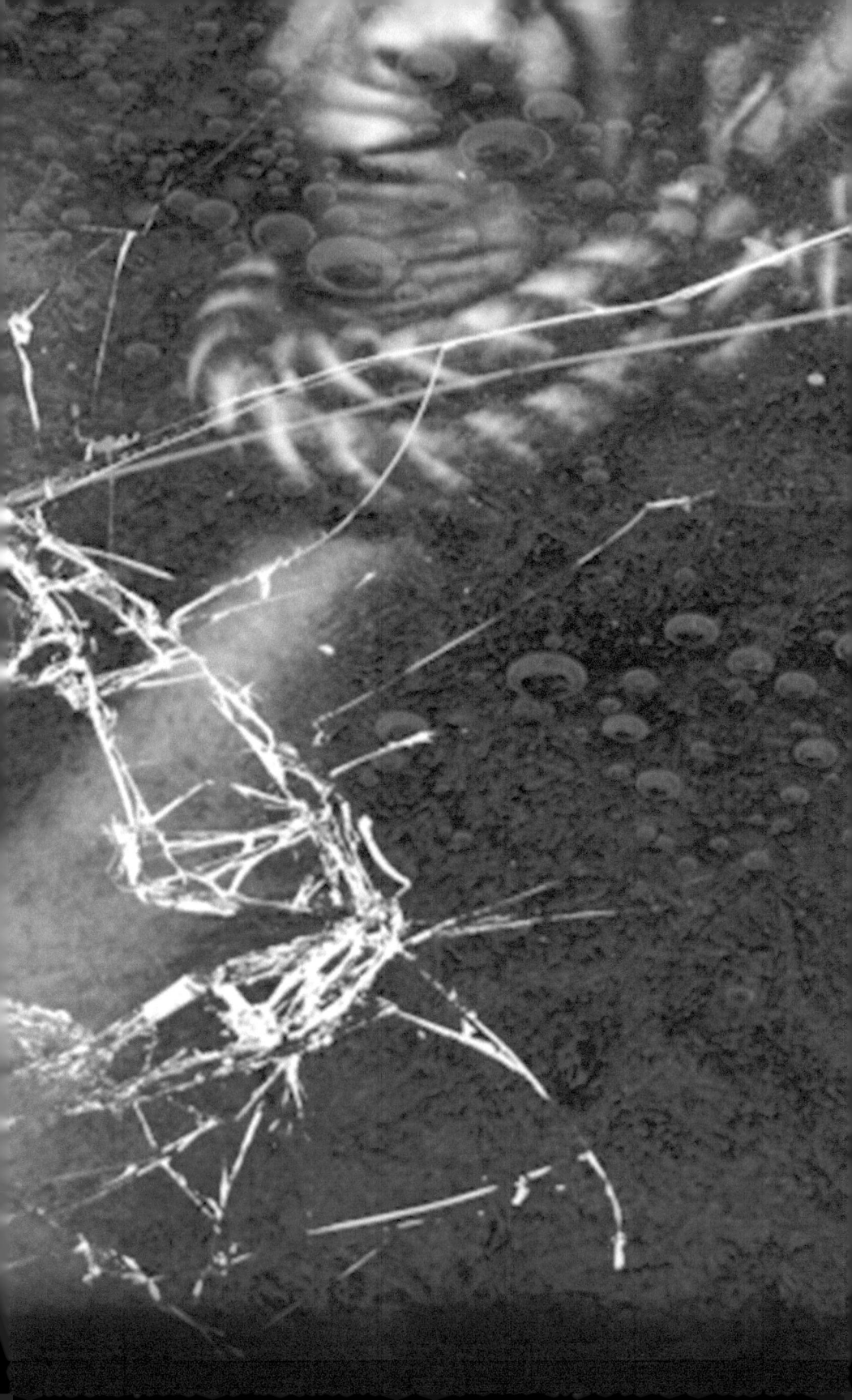

Ivy

Chapter 22

"*H*ey there," Phoenix said, walking in the light, her voice a melodic husky promise.

I almost felt bad for the man in her trap. She was truly masterful, a poison that was too potent to refuse.

"Hey there, gorgeous. What is a little thing like you doing out here so late?"

The man said, his voice kind, but the danger was present, just like it always was. These men couldn't resist but taunt what they saw as prey.

"Oh, ya know. Just taking a nice walk."

She was graceful, and I could see she glowed even from the shadows.

"Aren't you afraid of the boogeyman coming to steal your beautiful self away?" The man was circling her, but Phi tracked his movements.

"Oh, I think the boogeyman should be scared of me," she sang.

The man looked humored and dangerous as he looked around for anyone nearby. He thought they were alone, and his confidence rose.

"Oh?" he challenged, facing toward her, walking her backward toward the alley.

She smiled wide. "Yes."

Now holding a curious look on his face, the man stopped his stalking for a minute to study her.

"Why is that?" he finally asked.

Giving me a direct look in the shadows, Phi got closer to the man's face. I drew closer, too, the darkness concealing me as I made my way to her side.

"Because the boogeyman..." she whispered to the monster. "Is alone."

His eyes widened as they met mine, just in time to see a syringe with some pale liquid plunge into his chest.

PHOENIX WAS BOUNCING IN EXCITEMENT. HER EXPRESSION KEPT switching from ecstasy to a reserved calm. Her two past lives were battling, and it was almost eerie to watch.

"Okay, Eili. Your turn." She was fidgeting, watching me weigh the dagger in my hand.

Her dagger was breathtaking. It was intricate metal carved with a royal pattern within the blade itself, and the red jewel at the end gleamed, thirsty for its enemies' blood.

"I gave him a paralytic. He can speak, blink, and wiggle his head a bit, but he can't move enough to hurt you."

I watched the man fight uselessly on the ground. There were a ton of twitches and angry growls.

Swallowing, I focused on the man—the feeling of the darkness taking control of me.

"Where are the girls located?"

He laughed and spat in my face.

"You don't know what you are getting yourself into, little girl," he mocked.

My blood chilled.

Being called a little girl spiked memories of hands and mouths and forbidden places.

They always called me little, like I was an easy plaything that meant nothing.

Well, now he was my toy to play with.

"You don't know me монстр."

You don't know me, Monster.

Phoenix watched me silently. I could feel her gaze, but my prey enraptured me. I let the beautiful blade fall to the ground and reached into my pocket for my lighter. The orange flame mesmerized me once more. The man's eyes reflected in the flame as I brought it up to his face.

"Where. Are. The. Girls?"

His breath fogged the metal.

"Bite me, bitch."

Narrowing my eyes, I found a pulsing spot on his neck and bit so hard I felt the flesh tear under my teeth—a splash of iron coating my mouth.

Fear sat in his eyes as his blood dripped from my mouth onto his face. The red droplets looked like tears. So many tears were shed in that nightmare of walls—tears of the girls mingled with their blood in their deaths.

The darkness grew inside me, a film of rage coming over my eyes and my body tingling with a particular numbness.

"Look, I don't know!"

The hum of his voice droned on, canceling out his pleas. And the beautiful blood was running down his chest, his eyes looked faded.

"Did they beg?" I said.

"Wh-what?"

The red was growing into a small stream.

"I didn't do nothing to you!" he screamed, my fire licking his skin.

"The guys did. Not me! You got the wrong dude!"

His eyes were bouncing around widely. Eyes that watched the tears. The pain. The blood.

"You like to watch монстр?" A sick look washed over him, and his pants rose. He was aroused at the memories of what he witnessed. I looked at his waistband. A knife protruded from his pocket.

Calmly pulling it free, I let my flame heat the metal, switching the level of the flame higher, making the glow of the metal stronger and brighter.

"You watched them. Fantasized about their innocence being stripped from them. Watched the devils claim their souls." My voice sounded foreign to me as I brought a smoldering knife above his face and let the molten liquid drip into his eyes.

He screamed as I began to speak close to his ear. "Now, you will see only the darkness of your sins."

"You're a fascinating murderous little thing."

I rolled my eyes and waved away Phoenix.

"My brother would not be so proud of my blood lust *sestra*."

She snorted, and somehow, even that made her look beautiful.

"Meh, can't please them all. And Eilizaveta, you truly have a gift. Those girls are lucky to have you to avenge them."

Looking down at the smoldering flesh, I knew for certain she was right.

I would avenge each and every lost soul.

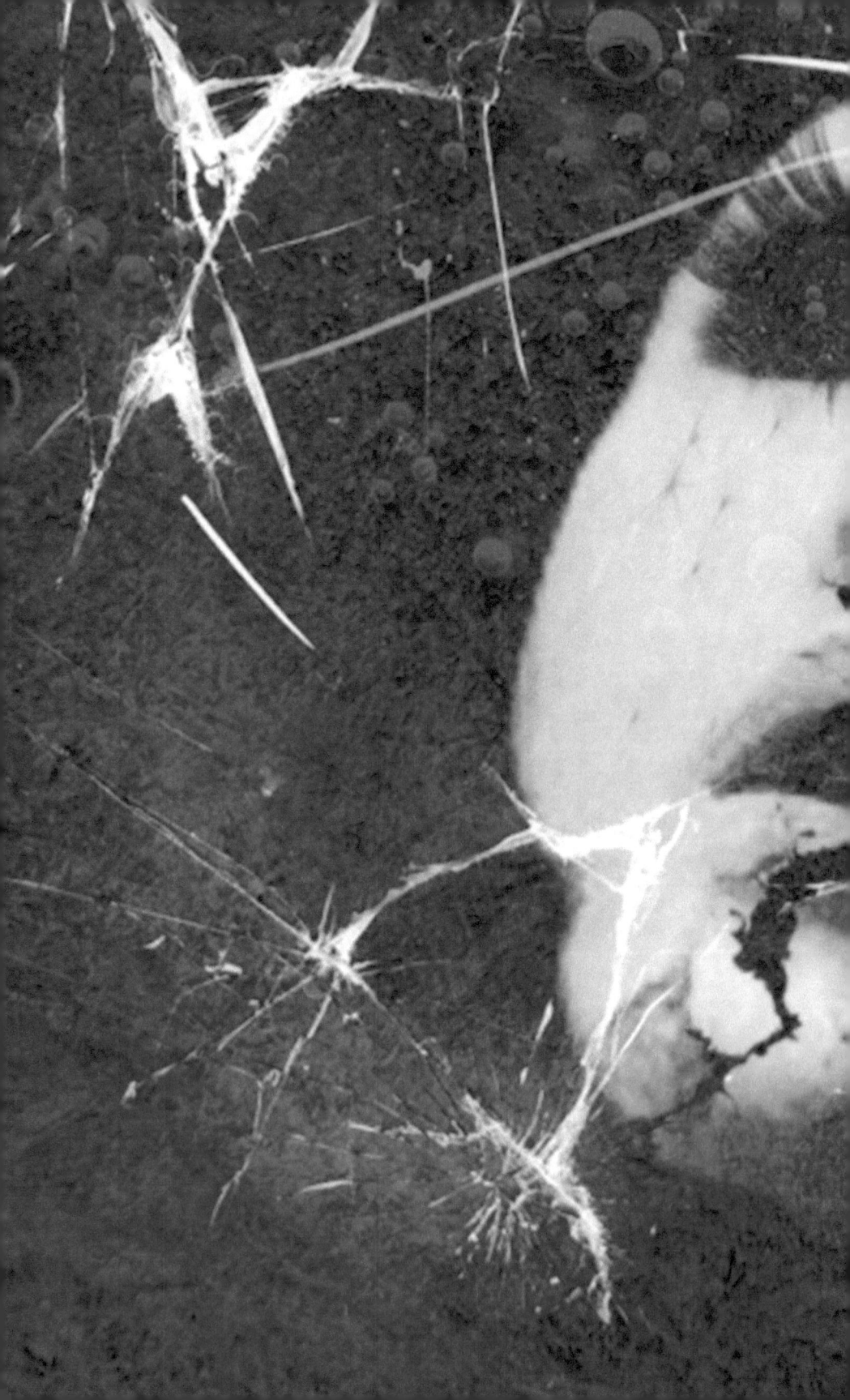

No One

Chapter 23

"Room for one, please," I said with the bitter taste in my mouth.

My body hurt like fucking hell, and it was only luck that I managed to leave the damn hospital before the pigs went hunting for me. Bleu wasn't a bad dude, and I felt guilty for clocking him.

"How many days will that be, and will any other guests be arriving...perhaps later?"

The nosy dickhead behind the counter gave me instant creep vibes, and I pulled the hoodie higher over my neck for fear he may have been one of our regulars.

Everyone started to blend at one point, and I just started to suspect everyone was a creep looking for little girls.

I shook my head, afraid my husky voice may tip him off to my identity in some way.

"Okay, beautiful, here's your key."

It was a risk to stay at this old school motel that reminded me of something out of a Henry Howard Holmes book, but as I stared at the brass intricately carved key, I realized I didn't have much of a choice.

Stupid fucking Quinn, for the one-hundredth time now, this sole man has fucked my brain and life to hell.

Closing the door behind me, I let my broken body collapse on the bed, a pillow by my head. I rolled over and screamed every ounce of air from my broken lungs.

Would that old creepy bag hear me?

Oh, who the fuck cared.

What was I going to do about the girls? They were inside that damn hotel, and if I didn't get the fuck off the police's radar as a broken 'Jane doe,' I was in hot water...I couldn't let them starve to death.

My phone chimed, and I looked at the screen.

> Quinn: Lana? Where the fuck are you? There's some shit going down with those missing persons cases. In the hospital, one of the kidnapped girls was hanging in your hospital room!

OH FUCK...I WAS SO SCREWED. DID HE KNOW MY PART IN THIS?

> Lana: Oh wow, that is crazy business! Do they know who dunnit?

> Quinn: No, but they are questioning the girl they found. Where are you?

> Lana: I had a little car accident. How old is the girl they found? What about the others?

If it were the little ones, most wouldn't even speak, but if it was Melanie...

> Quinn: Sixteen. They are still looking for the others. The teen hasn't said a word to anyone except saying thank you to me...I took her home, not realizing she was one of the kidnapped girls.

Of course, a perfect little knight would fucking save her...

> Lana: Oh wow! That is absolutely amazing, Quinny! You are such a hero, sorry to hear about the other girls missing. I hope they get found soon!

By me...

DAMN, LITTLE GIRLS...THIS WAS WHY I NEVER WANTED FUCKING children. My stomach dropped when a new name popped up on the screen.

"Good evening, sir. It's a lovely night out, isn't it?"

The growl on the other end of the line made me feel even sicker than I had this whole damn time.

"Svetlana. Kindly explain to me why the fuck our asset is blasted all over the media?"

It would take a doctor to remove my heart from my asshole upon hearing my name on those dangerous lips.

"Oh sir...I did not know that uhm..."

"You have caused a most inconvenient mess that I now have to come to America to clean up."

"But what about your son, sir?"

The huff told me I was definitely overstepping, but I needed to know.

"I will deal with my family. They are of no concern to you. Now, I expect a hotel room to be booked for my arrival, Svetlana."

I audibly swallowed the lump that refused to go down.

"Yes, sir?"

Ты потерял для меня свою пользу—You have lost your use to me.

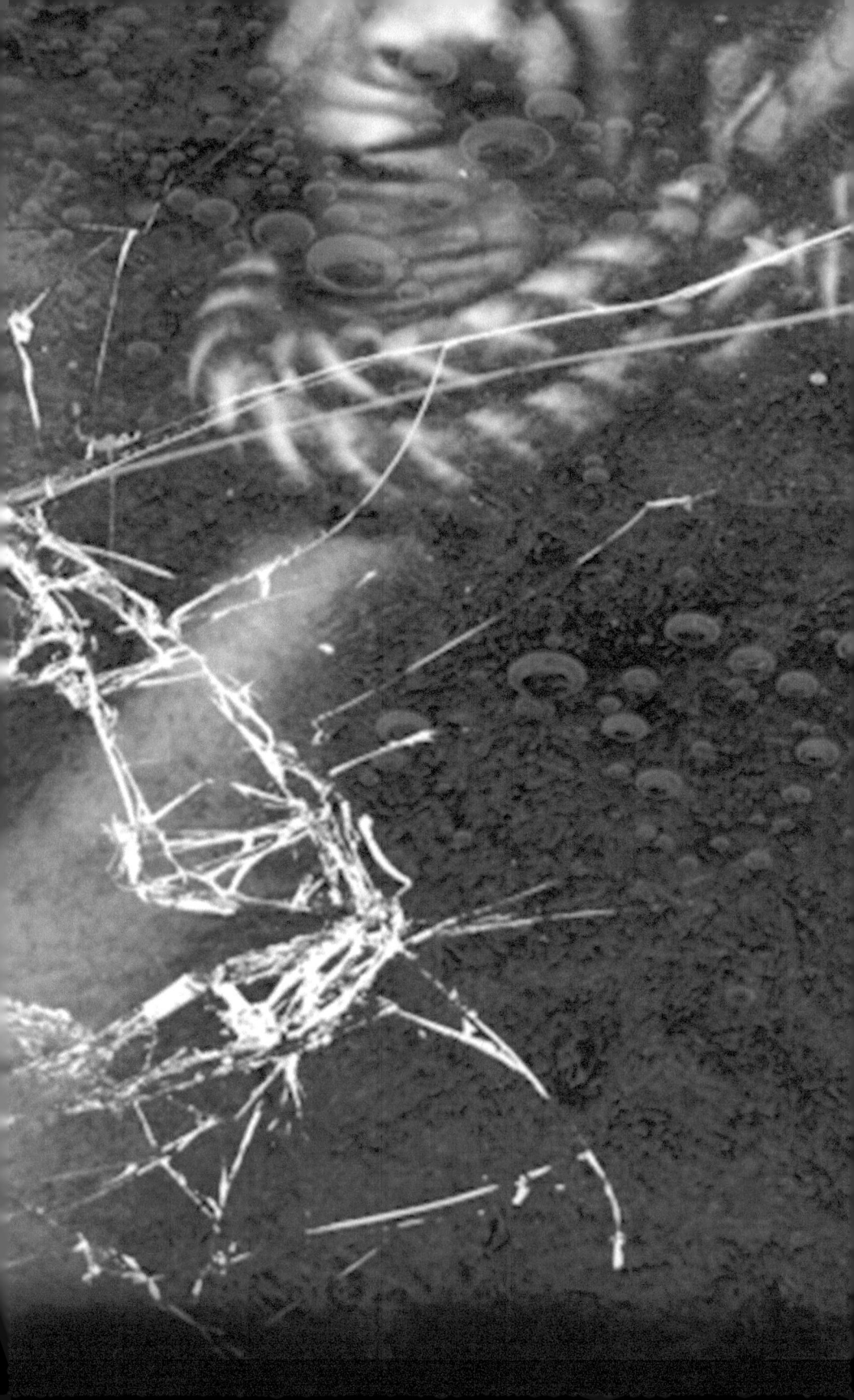

Ivy

Chapter 24

*T*he frigid air reminded me of Russia.

"Where are you going *sestra?*" I spun around, Lucius standing at the door of the barn.

"Do you remember when you told me that you tried to keep father's affairs from my eyes?" I said, not allowing myself to look at my brother.

"That little girl you shielded from bloodshed, Lucius, is not who you see now. I was not blind to our father's cruel hand then, and I am not blind to it now. I was taken from my bed at our home, thrown into a cage for an entire year of my life, grabbed, touched, made to do disgusting things, and forced to endure worse."

I could hear his sniffles behind me, so I finally turned to meet his unyielding, pained green eyes.

"I failed you, Eilizaveta. I ran from our father and my responsibility, and because of that, you were punished."

His sobs grew. The strong man before me broke. I ran to him, holding him in my arms and trying to show with my embrace that I loved him. That I forgave his cowardice.

"I look up to you, ya know?" he continued in a ghostly, vacant tone now.

"I see you fighting a battle that was not meant for you. I see you spilling the blood for those who had theirs wrongfully spilled. I admire your bravery, your strength, and your heart. I am selfish, so I fear for you if you continue on this path. It will only lead to pain and death. I cannot forgive you if the price for vengeance is your life."

My tears fell now as my mother's words circled in my ears.

'Be strong, darling. A princess doesn't cry, and if you must, use those tears to build a river to drown the ones who made you shed them.'

"Phi says you're ready, ya know," he continued, jarring me from my thoughts. "She said you are a royal, a lethal princess taking back her crown. It's yours, Eili. It always has been. And I won't be like our father who stood in your way. I will cheer you on as you take back what is yours."

I smiled wide, not believing my ears that my brother was finally allowing me to have my revenge.

"But..." he countered, making my smile fall. "You will not be alone. Every princess has her army."

"Hello?" I felt sheepish calling Nika. I had left her to fend for herself once I dropped her off, not so much as bothering to ask if she was okay. "Nika? I am so glad you made it out."

Her snort on the other line made me hesitate.

"Yeah, well, how about more than a love tap next time?"

I laughed. "Deal. Want to meet me at Pontillo's? I'll have your pork wraps waiting for you."

I knew my friend and knew she couldn't deny meat.

"Better come with pot stickers too."

Later, after arriving at Pontillo's, I found a table and ordered the usual, waiting for Nika. She arrived and eyed me.

"So you are real?" She jibed. "Here, I thought you were an illusion, baby cakes." I winced at that. She wasn't the only one to call me an illusion. Quinn had always said I was a ghost. "Nika, my love. How was your chit-chat with the cops?"

She laughed and brushed off the frostiness. "You wanna know how your boy is doing? Just ask the goofball."

I smiled sheepishly.

"He's still sickeningly perfect, Princess. When are you going to give in and have your happily ever after?"

I ignored her. "What did he talk to you about?"

Nika sighed. "He was asking me about The Masks Organization. He wants to find the trafficked girls and shut down their rings from the inside."

I'd thought about that. Why wouldn't he ask me to go back? I could take them down from their own home.

"Because you'd get hurt again. You think your prince charming would let that happen? He wouldn't even send me back there, and I am a stranger." Nika answered the question I couldn't even ask. I felt stupid. "While you stew over your man not being a demon, I'm gonna go piss."

Nika left, and I stared at my menu in silence. I about fell out of my chair when I saw a golden blonde head and a couple approaching.

Flipping the menu up to hide my face, I sunk down into the chair and peeked through the small cut-out in the fold of the lining. A plastic coating surrounded the menu, so my view was blurred, but I could see Quinn, his long-haired friend, and a beautiful, pregnant woman sitting down at a table not far from mine.

"Psy, I think you and Lisa need to leave," Quinn said, tousling his wavey hair nervously.

"What do you mean? Why? Lisa is gonna pop any day, so we were gonna just stay here and wait and try all the labor-inducing tricks."

The woman rubbed her belly fondly, a secret smile as she watched her partner speak.

"I know, but shit here is weird. Something is going on with my current case that isn't adding up. My partner is AWOL, which is a mess all of its own. There are missing little girls that the whole city is trying to find! Texas is much safer."

The man named Psy raised an eyebrow. "Uh-huh, that's why the loony bin magically vanished, and a whole new one was created within a few months."

Quinn looked visibly uncomfortable at the mention of the mental hospital his friend spoke about.

"Look, I know it was weird then, but my boy back home is in charge now, so everything on that front is normal as far as I'm concerned."

"Isn't shit always weird when you're a cop?" the woman, Lisa, interjected. "I mean, you know all about the secrets that the government doesn't want us measly civilians to know, right?"

Quinn sighed. "I guess, but this is dangerous. I can't speak on confidential matters, but..."

"Ignorance is bliss, right bro? I mean c'mon. You expect me to lug Lisa all the way back to Texas when she's so close to having this baby? For what? An unseen threat? I will take my chances here."

Now Quinn let out a frustrated sigh.

"Fine, if you're insistent on having your child here, I am at least putting some safety measures for you both into place until I can figure out more about this 'unseen threat.' "

Psy clapped him on the shoulder and eye-waggled to his wife. "Looks like we're getting a VIP-baby treatment."

I jumped when a waitress yanked the menu from my grip and asked if I was okay. Her words slid over me like water.

Quinn's gaze snapped in my direction, and his mouth opened wide.

"Uh, I changed my mind. I don't have an order, thank you," I said hastily, getting up from my seat and looking for the exit in the outside lounging area.

Micah was hot on my heels, dodging his friends' questions and politely moving through the crowd behind me.

Losing sight of him, I breathed a sigh of relief and continued outside, returning to that little underground hideout I had seen before under the bridge. It smelled awful, and it was so dim, but I allowed myself to catch my breath. I was drenched in sweat, and my mind was racing.

What unseen threat had Micah meant?

Me?

Resting against a pole by the docks where the water was roaring its melody to me, I closed my eyes.

That's when I heard a click.

Startled, I opened my eyes, and Micah stood before me.

He was soaked with sweat and was displaying all forms of being enraged. On further inspection, I realized the clicking sound was coming from my hands. I looked down, shock and anger making my face flush. My detective had handcuffed my hands to the water pole behind me.

Outraged, I shrieked at his smirking face.

"What do you think you are doing, Porthos? Is this some kind of fetish of pigs? Let me go now!"

His smile made him look different than the man I knew. This

man raged, his breathing ragged and erratic, his eyes wild and foreign to me. His close proximity warmed my overheated body, causing me to sweat even more.

He was so close I could taste the salt on his skin. His blazer was shrugged off, and his white button-up shirt and vee-neck T-shirt were molded to his body from the heat. He looked so out of place in his fancy suit pants and overwhelmingly good-smelling cologne.

"Not this time," he said, pushing his body into mine.

That wild smile was still on his mouth as he got closer to my face, running his lips down the side of my neck.

"Try to escape me now, Little Ghost."

Micah Quinn

Chapter 25

I stared down at the beautiful woman in front of me, her eyes wide with fear.

Why do I love that look so much?

"Porthos." Her words were filled with venom, but something else was there, too. God, the sound of her voice, which was so husky, it made me throb.

"You have run enough, Little Ghost," I said, unbuttoning my shirt and pulling my tie free.

Her eyes were wide, watching me as I undressed. Each article I removed made her sink further down against the wall like it was the only thing holding her up.

"*Porthos,*" she said again.

This time, her accent was stronger, her control was breaking, and her anger was melting away.

"I told you I would punish you," I warned her, fully naked now, my body still dripping with sweat.

"By touching me? Using your baton?" she questioned, rattling the cuffs, testing their limits.

I smiled wide. The beast inside me loving my little beauty caged.

"I won't," I said. "Unless you beg me, baby."

With my words, she gasped in shock and outrage, making her language colorful. A flurry of Russian flowed from her. Nothing I knew, but I could guess it wasn't kind, loving words she spoke from her tone.

I lowered my hand down to my bobbing cock. The heat of her gaze and the pressure of my palm made me pant. She was so ethereally beautiful. Her black hair and eyes, the color of sunflowers, made me fucking lose myself.

Moaning and tugging hard on my member, I walked closer to her. She could feel the warmth radiating off my body, and I could feel hers.

"Micah," she said, undulating to get closer to me.

I stayed just out of reach.

The anger I felt inside me swelled. It was aimed at her, my job, my "partner," and my friends. Everything. Anger and fire. There was so much wrong, and I couldn't control anything. All I could do was enjoy the ravenous look in my Little Ghost's eyes at the sight of me.

"Why do you run from me, Ivy? You could have this." I moaned, stroking faster, precome beading on my tip. "You could have all of me."

A tear slipped free from her beautiful eyes, dripping onto her thighs. I could see the wetness soaking into her pants. I knew how that delicious cunt tasted, and god help me...I wanted to devour her and drown myself with her come.

"We have different stories, *Porthos*. We don't fit."

I growled at the statement she used so long ago. The words she told me before she ripped out my heart and betrayed me, running away for an entire year.

It didn't matter how far I went. Even having gone back to Texas and dealing with my demons, I still couldn't shake this infuriating woman before me out of my head.

I needed to leave.

I needed to get away from her, leave her be as she said.

But why? Why the fuck didn't our stories fit? Why was she so different from me?

"Are you not the author of your own story?" I taunted, smashing my hands beside her. Her flinch made me feel bad, but the anger I felt rolling within my blood was too much to care about her fear.

"You *choose* your own path. You choose who you are. What you do..." I continued, realizing my vision was blurring with tears.

"Not as simple as you say!" she yelled back at me.

"Do you want me?" I pressed my naked body against her, letting her feel my heart beating so fast, the shakiness of my limbs, my hard-as-rock cock throbbing with need.

"Do you want this?" I stroked myself rougher, letting out all my anger and pain by torturing my dick, rubbing it raw until the pain matched what was inside me.

I couldn't stop, couldn't stop seeking the only pleasure I could have from her...I couldn't stop pressing myself into her delicious body.

"All you have to do is say you want me baby." The trails of biting kisses I left on her shoulders and stomach made her hiss through her teeth.

"You tell me you want me, and I am yours."

How ironic my words felt when I knew the truth. I was hers already. Irrevocably, entirely, and wholly.

She didn't speak. Tears were streaming down her face, but she wouldn't fucking open her mouth and say a damn word.

"I love you."

I felt like a dumbass. Confessing something I didn't even know how to handle, I still gave it to a woman who clearly didn't feel the same. But it didn't matter because here I was, crying my eyes out, jerking myself off, and roaring like an unhinged beast in front of her. Maybe I belonged back in the asylum with Goliath and the others.

She gasped as I ripped her shirt in two. The beautiful fabric fell from her body and, with it, her resolve.

She pulled on her cuffs again, standing on her tippy toes to press her chest into my cock.

"Fuck, Little Ghost." I moaned. "Please. You can't do that if you don't want me to break."

She hesitated for a moment and then pressed herself harder into my cock. Her breasts cushioned my painfully hard cock between them. She never wore a bra, and her perky little nipples constantly tormented me. Now, feeling them roll onto the head of my sensitive skin, I barely held onto my restraint. I desperately wanted to rip her off the pipe and fuck her on the hard ground.

I reached down and roughly yanked off her pants, leaving her tantalizing and nearly naked, tied up before me.

"I am not a strong man, Ivy," I warned, memorizing every detail of her gorgeous body.

"Eilizaveta," she said, making me pause.

"What?" I was so damn close to covering her with my come.

"My name. My real name," she moaned, her thighs were drenched.

"Oh, my Little Ghost. My Little Eilizaveta. You are my undoing." I pressed my knee into her core, her mewling growing louder as I rubbed my cock harder between her breasts.

"Micaiah..." I told her. My full name was something only my mother said, and not lovingly.

"Micaiah? My Micah. My Porthos. Mmm yes. Mine..."

Hearing those words.

That ownership of me.

To belong...

I felt my body release, coating the front of her chest. Her breathy moans and my name over and over—I couldn't stop. I couldn't pull away. Line after line of the most intimate part of me, painted her breasts, dripping down her body to her soaked cunt.

"I love you too, Micah. I should not, but every part of my soul loves you, too."

Her confession and her release would be a brand on my soul for the rest of my life. This beautiful woman who has been owned and caged by so many before was willingly giving me her love?

I tried to catch my breath, reaching into the pocket of my shirt on the floor.

I couldn't trap her. I couldn't take away her freedom. She deserved more. Sighing, I unlocked her cuffs, the metal falling to the ground.

Wiping myself off her with a handkerchief from my pants, I wrapped her still body in my button-down and moved out of her way.

"I won't be like them, Little Ghost," I said, those damn tears welling up again at the thought of losing her. "I won't keep you caged."

She stood there staring at me. The fire of lust and the pain of sadness contorted her features.

"I do love you, Porthos."

I tried to believe that. I really did. Closing my eyes, I leaned against the wall, knowing she would be gone again when I opened them.

I pulled her into an embrace. I just needed to hold her and feel that she was real. Her spicy sage had become such a painful and yet beautiful memory. She wrapped her arms around me. Her need to hold me close made the tears fall onto the top of her hair.

"Why?" I couldn't help but ask the question. The answer felt as important as my next breath.

Ivy was silent, just holding onto me like a lifeline, her sniffles audible in the quiet space.

"I am sorry, Micah," she said softly.

I was listening to the sound of the water crashing into the concrete, the metaphor heavy on my soul, when Ivy's petite hands moved down my chest and landed on my cock.

My eyes widened, and the unexpected action caught me completely off guard.

"Little Ghost?" I asked, slightly pulling her away from me to study her face. "What are you—"

My words were cut off by a groan I was unable to stifle as her hands became firm, a decision cementing within the lightness of her golden eyes.

"I can not do a lot of things, Porthos," she said, those damn hands getting more and more steady. "But I will do what I want."

I tried to focus on what she was saying. I may have just lost myself to her, but this fucking woman would make me lose myself a million times before I was done.

I never had much of a refraction period, and if my Little Ghost didn't stop these teasing touches, she would soon find that out.

"Fuck, Ivy," I barked, thrusting into her hand involuntarily.

She wasn't talking. She was just focusing on her task. Using my moans as her guide, she continued to stroke me.

"That's right," I encouraged her, wrapping her hands in my own. "You are doing such a good job, baby girl. Don't stop."

Her eyes lit up, and her determination and excitement at hearing my words made her braver. She tested the boundaries of my body, reaching underneath my balls and exploring that area.

I growled in response, gyrating harder.

"You are so beautiful," she praised.

I choked on a laugh. This woman who was beyond breathtaking, choosing a moment like this to call me beautiful, just attested to how blind she was to her beauty.

"You..." I groaned, Lifting her head up to me and kissing her lips. "Are fucking enchanting."

She smiled shyly, but I kept her lips on mine, deepening the kiss and claiming her as my own.

"I love you," I said again, letting my hands graze her body softly.

She whimpered when I teased her clit, her sounds caught in my mouth, and my unwillingness to let her go was evident in every grind and groan coming from me.

I started to feel close to the edge, and I cursed myself at being too damn easy to explode for this woman.

She stopped stroking me, her fear replacing her pleasure when I pulled away from her.

"I-I am sorry," she said, her hand covering her mouth.

I smiled at her, trying to calm myself down.

"No, baby. You did everything right." I had to laugh because she didn't know how right she was.

I stared down at my pulsing cock. "Look what you did to me."

She followed my gaze, and her smile returned. A little pride sparked in her eyes.

"I told you to stop because If I lose it again, I won't be able to give you what *I* want, Little Ghost."

She was quiet, waiting for me to calm my breathing enough to continue.

"I need you, Little Ghost," I said, getting on my knees in front of her. "I fucking need you. Please."

She stood in front of me, her mouth open in shock, the fabric falling to the ground from her shoulders. I laid her down on my shirt on the floor, trying my best to make the area comfortable.

"Be still, baby. This may hurt, but if you push me off, I will stop immediately."

Ivy was quiet, her body lying on the clothes and her legs slowly falling to the side. I took a breath, being careful as I slid off her panties, leaving kisses on every spot the fabric touched.

She moaned, opening her legs further for me. I did a quick measurement of myself. I didn't care about my size with my past partners. I honestly liked the feeling of stretching them, and I enjoyed making them work for it.

But Ivy...

I didn't want to hurt my Little Ghost.

"Take a deep breath, baby," I told her, laying in between her legs and preparing her pussy to take me.

She undulated off the ground with the softest of stroking. I teased her clit with my head, using her wetness to push inside her barrier. I kept up with this push-and-pull motion.

She was whimpering, and I was sweating so badly from the pure exertion of resisting plowing into her warmth.

"God, fucking help me go slow," I said, a prayer spoken out loud.

"Porthos." She groaned, pushing her body harder onto mine, my cock pushing a little deeper than I had gone.

We both gasped, and I froze.

Her face was pure bliss. She didn't look upset or scared. She looked beautiful and...ready.

"I love you," I said and finally slid myself inside her.

Her walls clenched around me, and I lost myself to the rhythmic contractions. I moaned, a fear creeping in with the realization that I wasn't going to be able to stop.

Please don't tell me to stop.

"Mmm...Micah. You feel so good. It only hurts a little, but you feel amazing. Please don't stop."

I growled, thrusting harder and faster.

Her sweet whimpers drove me forward, my release so close I could feel my balls drawing up, so I started to pull out of her. My Little Ghost wrapped her legs around me, shocking the holy hell out of me, her dangerous mouth in a determined look as she held my face in her hands.

"No," she said. "Please. Let me feel you, Micah. If this is all I ever get, I need to feel you."

I couldn't stop myself. I completely lost it, spilling every ounce of come inside her until it was like I was devoid of all liquids. I collapsed into her, only moving to the side of her head at the last second to prevent crushing her.

"I love you," I said breathlessly, my exhaustion taking over my body as sure as if she hit me in the head with a hammer.

I heard her laugh, the sound so light and free.

"Sweet dreams, Porthos...I love you."

I tried to ignore the sadness in her voice as she said those words.

She loved me, and I needed to remember that so when I woke up with her gone, it wouldn't completely destroy what was left of me.

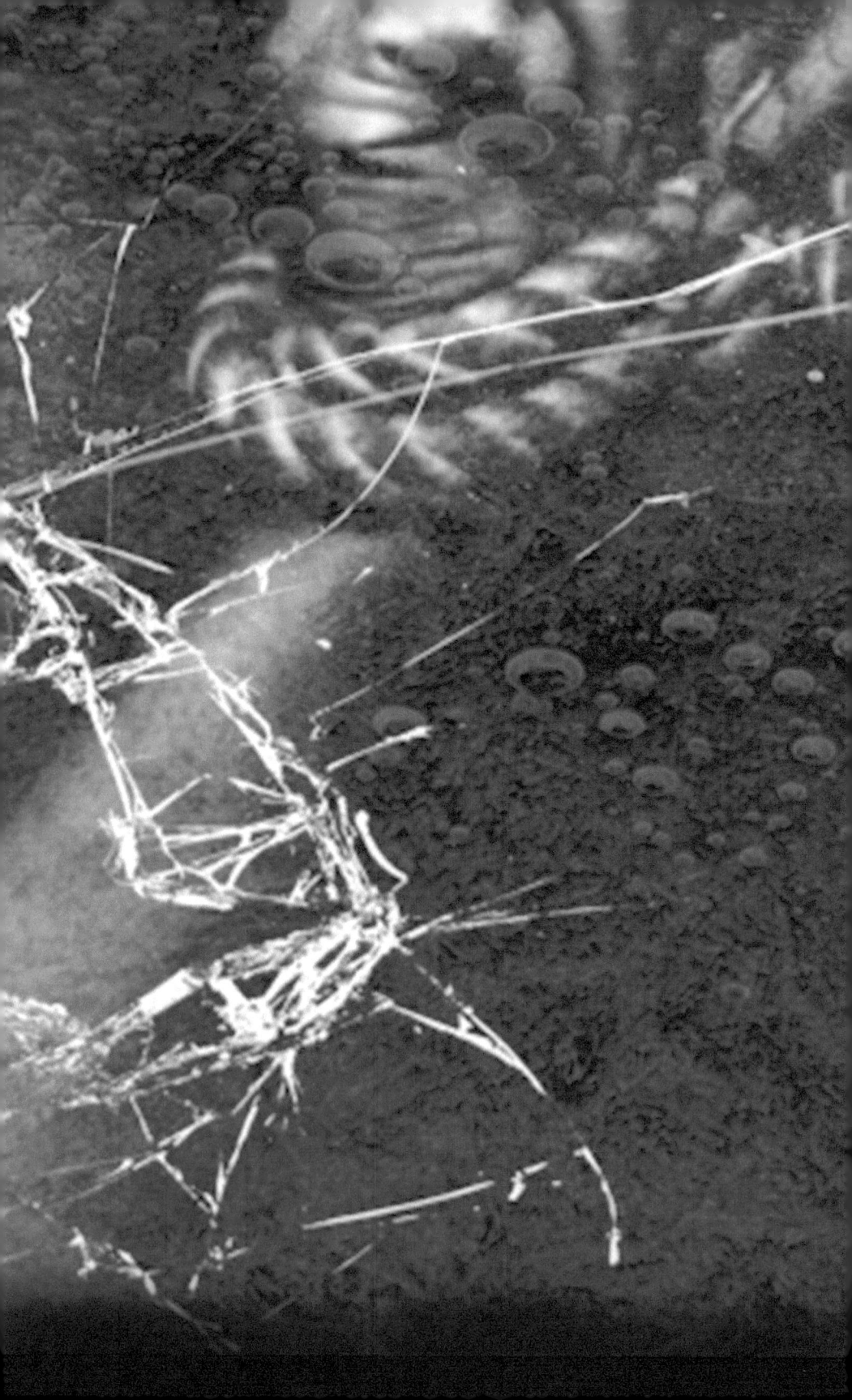

Ivy

Chapter 26

I tried to see through my tears as I watched Micah cry alone from the shadows after he woke up and saw that I was gone. Worse yet, he didn't seem surprised. I was horrible. The man of my dreams told me he loved me and gave me a choice to be free when no one else had, and here I was, running away again.

Smelling his shirt, I pulled the material tighter around me.

I had to complete my mission. I had to save the girls and kill every one of these monsters. It was all I could do for Micah. He was a detective. His job was to stop me. I had to leave him.

Wiping my face from the tears, I tried to create some distance.

"Well, well, well. Look what we found. The little princess herself is knocking off Daddy's men?"

I froze. These tunnels under the bridge were a maze. The voice echoed, and I couldn't see from what tunnel it had originated.

"Never thought you made it out of Markus's little butcher shop, princess. Guess you're stronger than even your Daddy knows. Wanna use that strength on me?"

I swallowed the bile in my throat at the mention of that monster, trying to remember the way he suffered at my hand in the end. I could hear running, an echoing clacking of shoes in the dark of the never-ending tunnels.

Swinging out my fist with the sound, I made an impact, throwing my whole body onto the unknown threat. His body went down to the cement with a crack to his head. I couldn't see anything in the dim light, but I could smell blood.

"Little Ghost?" My body froze, and the sound of Micah was close behind me.

I didn't pay attention, and my attacker got the upper hand, slamming his fist into my face and knocking me off him.

"Ahhhh..." I cried out. The pain of his knuckles crushing into my cheek was almost too much. Quickly, I tried to scramble off the ground before a foot could meet my head.

"Ivy? Is that you?" Quinn didn't sound too far away. He was getting closer by the second.

My father's man laughed, a taunting mock in his voice. "Does the princess have a little prince coming to her rescue?"

I launched myself at the man, our bodies rolling on the unforgiving ground as we fought for control.

A clinking sound tittered across the cavern ground, and I remembered that key Micah used to free me. Reaching for it in the darkness, I luckily found the item and slashed toward his neck with the sharp metal poking out of my grip as hard as I could. A shrill scream deafened me momentarily as a warm, slick pool began to coat my chest and face.

Not taking time to confirm if he was dead, I stabbed the man again, his shrieks increasing until a garbled gasp was all that remained. Trying to catch my breath, I stood up and searched for the exit of these labyrinth tunnels.

Spinning around, I was suddenly bathed in a bright light. My body was dripping with blood, and a man lay dead in front of me with the key protruding from his jugular. But it was me that Micah Quinn was looking at in horror.

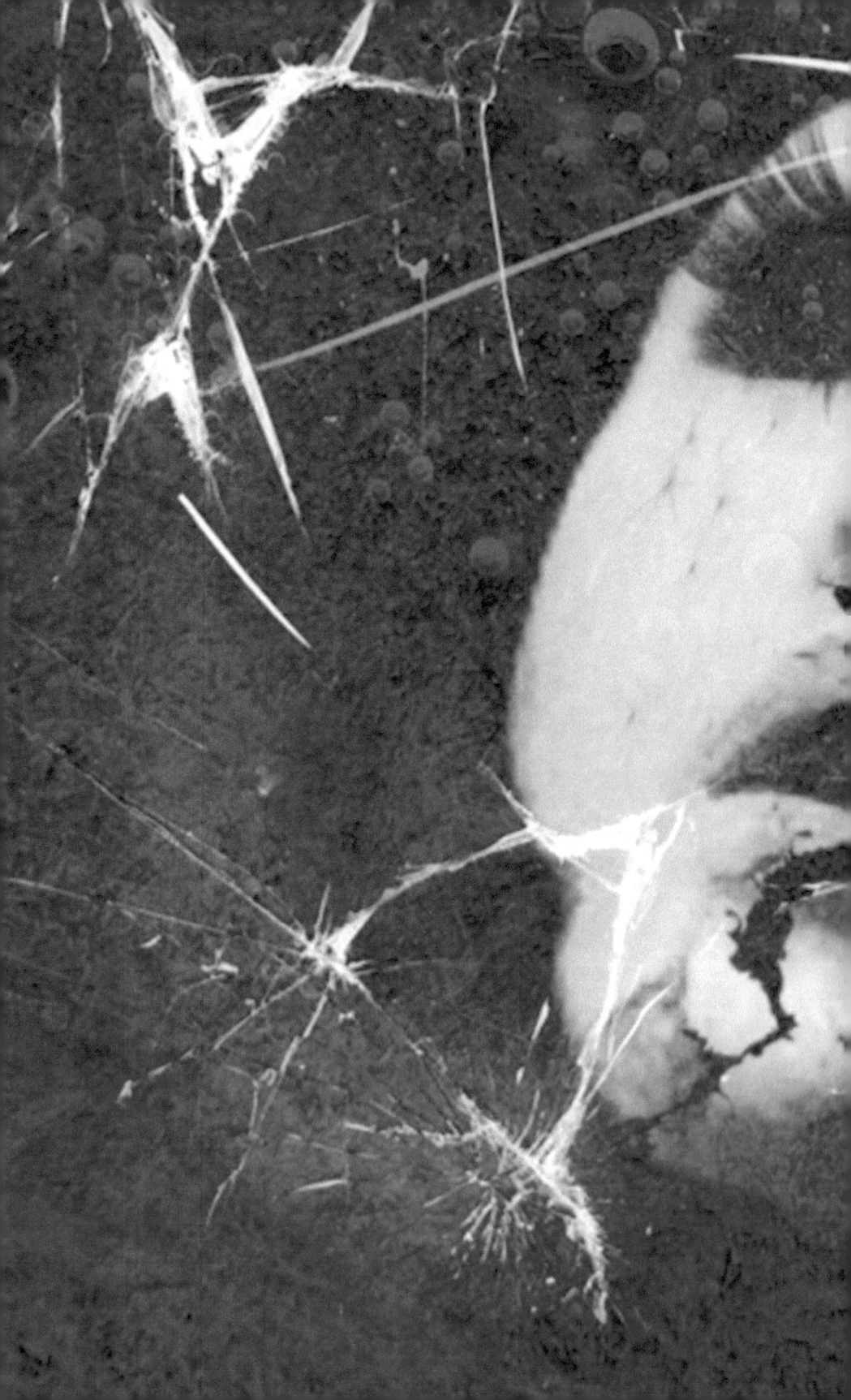

No One

Chapter 27

"Sir. How was your travel?"

The man didn't speak to me. Didn't acknowledge my existence, really.

"Uh, so your hotel room is really nice. It's at—"

"Is the area secure?" He cut me off.

I contemplated my answer. "There is no one around, sir. The guest list said there are four parties on the first floor, but no other vacancy."

He cracked his fingers, pulling his gloves onto his hands.

"Hansel, take us to this hotel. Would you please?"

The ride was too quiet. I could feel my heart beating out of my chest. We arrived in silence at the hotel, and the car stopped. True to my word, there were four cars, and the owners were present at the lot, but no one else.

"Sir?" I asked when he pulled out a rectangular case from underneath his seat.

"If you don't want to join these fine folks, I suggest you stop your incessant pestering dear Svetlana, hmm?"

I swallowed. My name on this monster's lips was never a good thing.

It wasn't until we got to the reception that I realized what that box was holding. The creepy pervert asked what name to add to the guest list, and the smile of my boss was all too beautiful as it was cruel.

"Alyosha Puriya."

I mouthed a silent apology to the man as his eyes widened, and the bullet went into his brain. Alyosha walked the hallways, his button-down sprayed with the red blood of the downed hotel owner.

Anyone he saw, he culled them like cattle, a single bullet dropping the civilians to the ground, a sickening smell of iron and death coating the walls.

The massacre continued, and my ears rang with the gun's punishment. I'd done this. I'd chosen this hotel. The people's vacant open eyes, lying in their own blood, was my fault.

"Now then. Where are the girls?"

I swallowed the vomit, threatening to come up, trying to remain as still by his side as I could, knowing I would end up on the ground like these people eventually.

Inhaling a breath to speak the damning words that would seal the fate of those little girls, I stopped when a chime of a cell phone went off. Alyosha cursed and picked up the line, using his pinky finger to press the speaker phone, smudging blood onto his screen.

"Yes? What is it, Aleksia?"

I watched the man. His beauty was so breathtaking, and his cruelty was equally as overpowering. His face contorted in rage at the words spoken from the phone.

"Boss. We searched for the missing girls as you ordered but found something else you'll want to know about."

Alyosha rarely showed anything but hate and amusement at one's pain, but curiosity painted his features now.

"And what is that?"

It was silent on the line for a while. The tick in Alyosha's jaw was increasing. I thought he'd break his teeth, but then Aleksia spoke up. "It is your daughter, boss."

Anger poured into Alyosha's face like a poison that tainted every beautiful inch of him.

"What about her?" he snapped in return. "What do I care of her corpse?"

He cracked his knuckles as if hesitation lingered around his words."Speak or lose your fucking tongue, you mutt."

"Your daughter isn't dead, sir, and she's…the killer everyone has been talking about—the one killing The Masks' members. Eilizaveta is alive," the man said.

Micah Quinn

Chapter 28

I stared at my beautiful Little Ghost in disbelief. My eyes refused to see what the light of my phone was telling me.

Ivy stood over a dead man with my handcuff key jabbed into his neck. Blood was dripping from her black hair, covering my shirt, her body, and the ground. Everywhere.

My Little Ghost couldn't be the monster I have been trying to slay…she couldn't be.

"Ivy…" I said stupidly, blinking over and over, willing my vision to change and for this to go away. It didn't.

The image was more and more clear. The pieces falling together that I had ignored for so long—the shoe. The blue shoe was left at my house. It was the same color as the descriptions of The Cinder Killer.

The men dying were part of the organization that trapped

and kept her caged all that time. Eilizaveta. Her name. Her *Russian* name. She was from Russia, and I couldn't deny how much she looked like that man my partner Ella betrayed me with.

"Lucius Vasiliev," I spat. My anger was growing. "What is he to you?"

Lucius was a snake, the son of the monster Aloysha Puriya. The leader of the fucking Moya Kotva.

"He is...my brother," she admitted, hanging her head.

I felt like such a fucking dumbass. Of course. Of course, my Little Ghost was related to that man, and she was the goddamn mafia princess.

Her body still had my come inside her. The woman I loved, the woman I gave everything I had to...was the sister and daughter to my enemy?

Why would she kill her father's men? Why was she in that cage a year ago?

"No," I said, my body shaking from the betrayal and confusion. "No," I repeated, smashing my head in my hands, praying I would awake from this nightmare.

"I am so sorry, Porthos," she whispered.

Her tears mingled with blood on her face.

"You are a monster?" I questioned, running my hand through my hair. "You killed all those people! Why Ivy? Why? Don't you feel at all sorry for murdering people?"

She was silent, her head hung low, and her sobs echoing in the tunnels around us. "Why should I apologize for becoming a monster? They never apologized for making me one!"

I shook my head. "Alyosha Puriya?"

She winced at the name.

"Your father. You're doing this for him?"

Now she looked angry. Her tears coated her cheeks, washing the blood free.

"My father..." she said, acid in her tone. "Is who had me locked in a cage, raped and tortured."

I blinked at that news. Who could do that to their own daughter?

"I was to be killed when they were done playing with me and making their money off the dethroned Princess," she continued, that anger growing. "You stopped them when you found me. They left me there to die. Drugged me with something, turned off the lights, and left."

She was shaking.

"I could hear the screams of the girls as they were killed. The sound of chainsaws...and the sounds afterward." She was lost in memories as she spoke. "Their deaths weren't enough to stop the men from...using their bodies again."

My stomach lurched at the images plaguing my mind. How much Ivy had endured during all those months in that cage...my heart couldn't handle it.

Could Ella really have been part of that? Lana? How? I knew Lucius was fucked in the head, but could someone I treated like my little sister for years really had known what was going on?

"Was my partner in on it?" That deception still hurt burning a hole through my heart. "Was Ella part of the scheme? Was I a pawn?"

She laughed without humor. "My brother fell in love with your partner. Nobody knew she was two people. Not even him."

I scrunched my face in confusion. Two people?

"The Snow White Killer," she finished.

My jaw dropped in realization. I had been credited for uncovering the Snow White Killer. My old chief was dead on that field, along with so many other men.

The department found the drugs on him, that unique concoction that only the Snow White Killer would use on her victims. It was easiest to claim the chief was the culprit and ended his misery with suicide…but I knew the truth. It never added up—the beheading, the dead bodies, and the burned barn. There was more to the story. More players.

"What do you mean two people? You're saying Ella was the Snow White Killer?" Ivy huffed with annoyance. "Ella and the Snow White Killer were different. But the same people? She didn't know she had split personalities!"

I thought back to the case. Cassie. Ella's sister. She had been killed…

"Ella killed her own sister?" I couldn't wrap my head around it. "Why?"

Ivy shook her head. "It's not my story to tell. Ask her."

My eyes widened. "She's alive?"

I knew from the look on her face that I wasn't getting any more answers. I couldn't even look at her: a liar, a murderer, a daughter, and sister of my enemy. The Princess to the Russian Mafia.

"I told you our stories did not fit, svin'ya," she said softly, her voice sounding too small.

I knew svin'ya meant pig in her native language, and now the irony of her pet name rang in my ears like a gun going off. Pig. Cop. A murderer didn't belong to a cop. Was her love a lie, too?

I scoffed. "I never dreamed you would be talking about a—"

My words were cut off when a loud blast threw me backward, a white light blinding me.

Coughing from the debris falling from the ceiling of the caverns, I called out for my Little Ghost. Despite my anger and confusion, I couldn't let her get hurt anymore. If nothing else, she deserved that. There was a deafening ringing in my ears, and I opened my mouth, trying to pop my ears. I needed that awful sound to stop.

"Ivy?" My phone broke with my fall, and now darkness surrounded me.

I could hear a scream in the distance and raced forward to

follow the noise, tripping on the crags of rock in the cave and dizzy from the blast.

"Ivy! Where are you?" I coughed, trying to cover my mouth from the dust choking me.

"Run, Porthos. Run!"

Laughter echoed in the tunnels, a ringing slowly fading and that laughter growing clearer in my ears. A group of men surrounded the area from which Ivy's voice came. I couldn't think about anything but her. It didn't matter what she had done, she was in trouble.

"I'm coming, Little Ghost. Just hang on!" Blindly moving forward, I ran toward the sound, my lungs burning while inhaling the dust, my ears still ringing from the device that had gone off beside us.

I could hear Ivy scream, pain laced in her voice. 'No!'

"Get back, you bastards!" I warned, stumbling over and over from fallen rock and erosion in the cavern.

That laughter echoed back. Closer now.

"Awe! Look, it's little Prince Charming coming to save our dear princess here." One cackled.

"Yes, how romantic! Come get her, lover boy. Wouldn't want to miss the show, would you?"

I cringed at the sound of her pain. She was strong. That much was evident by the dead man behind us, but she was caught off guard, and by the sounds of it…there were at least four assailants.

"Leave him alone, *Mänstər*!" More laughter. "Go get him, Aleksia. I am sure her Daddy wants to meet her lover boy."

I coughed, trying to expel the dust from my lungs. It felt like I was drowning. My damn gun was back in that boat dock. Why had I left it behind?

Because you didn't want to shoot, Ivy.

A large shadow slammed into my body, knocking my flashlight from my hands. It spun around on the ground, lighting up the faces of men, and that's when I realized it was too late. It was multiple men coming right at me.

A sharp pain smashed across my head, making me dizzy. Stars bounced around my vision as I continued to swing blindly at the men around me.

My ribs were kicked again and again, and inhaling became incredibly painful. I was pulling the debris deeper into my lungs.

Coughing, I searched for the light on the ground, looking for a weapon.

Ivy's cries grew in terror with each passing moment, but the light shadowed her face. She was held down by one of the men, and I could see she wanted to fight back, but the fear in her eyes wasn't for herself but for me.

I reached out for the light, their kicks resounding a cracking sound in my ears. One of the men 'tsked' at me on the ground and stomped onto the bulb of the flashlight. I blinked, but I couldn't see anything now but the darkness.

"Awe, don't cry, princess. Maybe your father will let him fuck you one last time before we blow out his pretty brains."

"*Poshel na khuy!*" she spat.

A man laughed.

"Oh baby, I would love to, but I value my dick too much for it to get ripped off when your ever-grumpy dad finds out."

My head throbbed as I struggled to get up. Each time I made a move, my ribs and back were smashed again with cruel boots and fists. A new kind of darkness was taking over my vision, and I fought against it, trying to shield my head from their abuse.

"Hey Princess, I have an idea, won't it be fun to watch this time? All that time, we had you on your knees for us, but you never got a chance to see what we did to you."

A sickening feeling entered my gut as I felt my belt being ripped away from me. One of the men used the leather to wrap around my throat, anchoring my head in the direction of Ivy. I could hear voices through the laughter around us. She was crying and fighting the man holding her down.

My anger and fear consumed me.

"No!" My voice echoed off the walls. "You can't hurt her. You know Alyosha will kill you...just take me. Use me. Leave her alone."

There was a moment of silence, likely the men thinking about the repercussions, and my Little Ghost was silent from her fear.

"Micah, no..." she screamed, her voice cut off by a smacking sound in the darkness.

"Stop," I said again, more firmly. I knew what I had to do.

"I...I won't fight you," I continued, letting my body lay flat.

I put my hands on my chest, trying to control my breathing for what was about to happen.

The men conversed in Russian, but a light appeared in one of their pockets at the end of the conversation. A light now lit up my body, and I tried to focus on my Little Ghost's face and not the men circling around my body like the fucking predators they were.

"Look at my eyes, Little Ghost. Don't look at them. Look at me."

She fought the man beside her, and he smashed her against the wall with little effort. Her body was wracked with sobs.

She cried harder, dropping to her knees and curling up against the rock wall.

"Micah...I love you. I love you. I am so sorry."

I held onto her voice and thought about her hands, her mouth, and her heat as my pants were ripped off of me.

I thought about her smile, the light in her eyes.

"Stop it!" She sounded so close yet so far away. "Please, I am begging you."

I thought about her little hands, how they explored my body so carefully, so softly every time, nothing like the rough skin of the hands that pulled and tore at my body now.

I coughed, trying again to get up, to go to her, her anguish too much for me to bear. But as I turned my head, a boot came straight at me, brutally ramming into my flesh again and again until I fell back down.

At least my body was numb from the pain as their voices taunted, laughed, grunted, and moaned. I focused on my Little Ghost, her body still as she watched me, tears streaming down her face in waves. Her face looked as numb as my body felt. She was lost in her memories of all the times these monsters had taken from her like this.

I curled onto my side, trying to block some of her view, doing my best to mouth the same words I could to her.

"I love you."

Her face contorted into rage when my body was unable to stop shaking, my voice unable to quiet as the pain engulfed me. Her sobs and pleads were becoming more torturous with every passing second.

Still, I didn't fight them.

They were all on me, flipping me onto my stomach. If they did this to me...they would leave her alone. She needed to run. My body was jarred back and forth. The gravel underneath me scratched my stomach raw. I gritted my teeth, trying to hold on past the burning inside my body. I held Ivy's gaze, my words a pained whisper lost in the moans and hard slamming of the men.

"Run."

"Oh, Porthos. I am so sorry," she cried her words into my ringing ears like a lullaby.

"I love you," she said, and I replayed that in my head as my body shook with the force of their weight, the unending abuse as they took turns slamming into me.

"I love you."

Over and over, her words comforted me, their silky melody a contrast to the harsh grunting in my ears.

I thought of my sister and what she must have endured in those last moments.

Oh, god, was it like this?

I let a tear fall for my sister and allowed more to fall for Ivy and what she had endured. And finally, I let my tears fall for...me. The pain of this hell, the mocking laughter, and the violent hands forced my body to betray me, spilling free all my shame, pain, and humanity.

"That's a good little prince," they mocked, covering me in their release, my blood, and then walking away.

I welcomed the cold—the quiet. I craved sleep.

"C'mon, pretty thing. I am sure Alyosha will have fun selling you off to the highest bidder."

Numb.

I was numb as two different pairs of hands picked my body up. My eyes were closing despite how hard I fought to keep them open. How hard I searched for my Little Ghost. She was fighting the guys as they dragged her by the hair away from my eyesight.

The tunnels were never-ending, the light flickering in from the streets above through the cracks in the passageway's walls. The ringleader of the monsters extinguished the light around me.

Finally, I caught a glimpse of Ivy.

They carried her like a sack over another man's arm. She didn't look away from me. Her face contorted in horror and pain.

"I love you." I tried, but only a croak of sounds fell out.

"I love you, Porthos. I love you. I am so sorry."

Her words and that love wrapped around me as my eyes finally closed.

Day two

They finally let me shower

Not like I have much dignity left anyways

I scrubbed my body until I bled

It didn't help I can still feel them

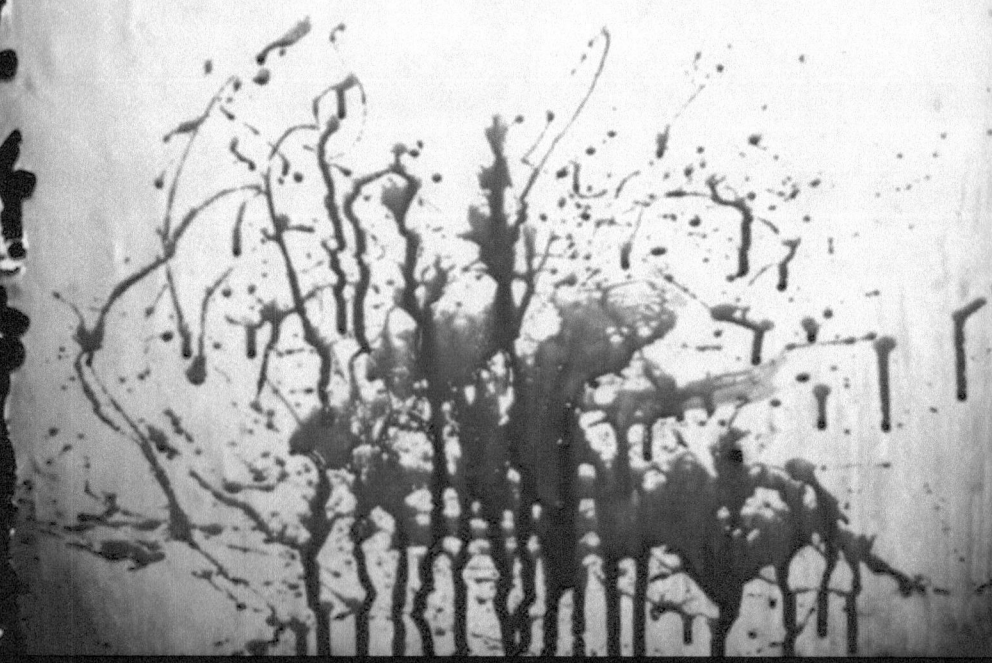

Day seven

Still no sign of my little Ghost

Every second I fear what they've done to her

Is she even alive Was my sacrifice in vain

I can not eat My thoughts worse than the pain

Day twelve

The boys enjoy breaking me
They let Vana put me back together
Just so they can break me again

Day Fifteen
When will this end

I'M

SO

Tired

Day Seventeen

Why havn't they killed me
Maybe the water boarding will do it
Maybe I will stop healing
I know my mind won t heal

Little Ghost

Day twenty two

Little Ghost

Little Ghost

Little Ghost

Little Ghost

Little Ghost

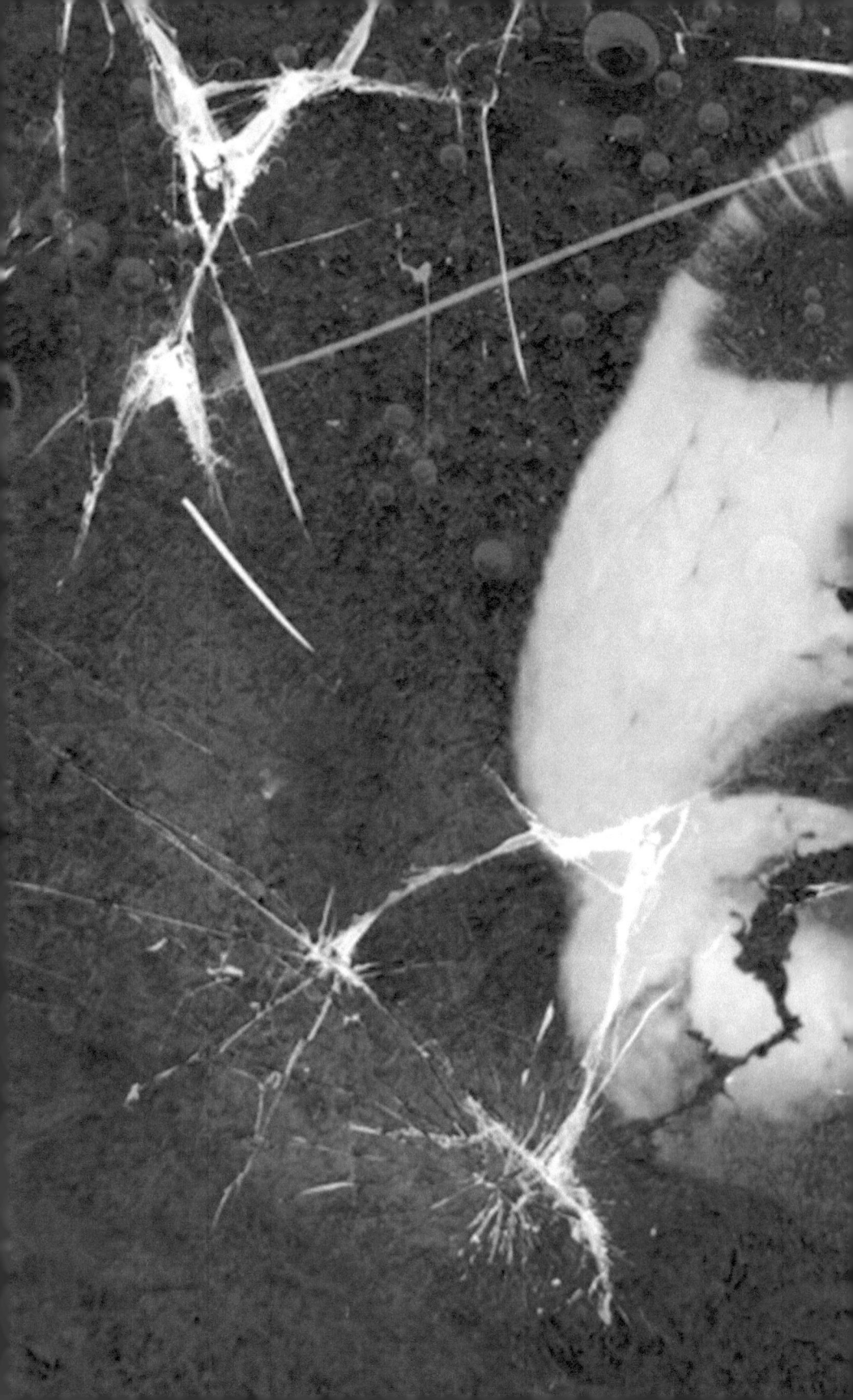

Lana

Chapter 29

"**W**hat do you mean you cannot teach the girls today?"

I held back my nausea, the feeling a constant for the past few months now.

Fidgeting in the doorway, I ran my hands through my hair. "I am ill."

There wasn't emotion in my words, but from the year I had been here, I understood Alyosha couldn't show much of anything.

"Very well, Svetlana. Penelope can fill in for you today, but there will be consequences if your duties continue to be ignored—"

The small amount of food I'd been able to eat, I purged. My body was unable to stop until there was nothing left to empty.

"Disgusting child!" My master spat, smacking me across the face and down into my vomit. "You will clean this mess."

I heaved on the ground, tears falling freely down my cheeks. I didn't know how long I cried, but I could hear Penn's sickly, sweet voice come up beside me. My anger welled in my stomach even more than this unrelenting illness.

"Oh my god, Svetlana, are you okay?" Of course, the perfect princess didn't feel shame or embarrassment, so cleaning up my puke was nothing to her.

I glared at her through my hair, swiped the rag she was using from her hand and started cleaning my own filth.

"Are you okay?" she asked again when I didn't bother looking at her.

"I am fine, Penelope. Go teach the girls their lesson. Leave me to this." I could feel her hesitate, her goody nature, her unwillingness to leave me alone.

"Please," I groused. "If you don't teach the girls, Master will punish me."

That caught her attention, her eyes drawing to my bruised arms that went so much farther down than that.

"Okay...I am sorry, Lana."

Having the annoying, doting girl gone gave me a minute to think about this.

My mother was really sick like this once...but that would mean...

I swallowed hard, pushing the thought from my mind. Did Alyosha use those protection things? When was my last bleed?

That nausea rolled in my gut again, and a new puddle replaced the one I had cleaned earlier.

"Girls, today's lesson is privacy." That voice gnawed on my nerves even more.

I pushed through the doors and made my way to my room. At least if or when I puked here, it wouldn't be for all to see. I pulled my feet up to my chest as I lay on my cot, trying to drown out the lesson. These girls were stupid. Penelope and I were the oldest people here.

There was an entire other section of the mansion designated for older girls, and my mouth was the reason I was stuck here with the three to ten-year-olds instead of where I belonged, which was with the ten to fifteen-year-olds.

They were learning so much more. They could be an asset and, best yet, sold out of this hell hole to some other master. I knew Alyosha was never letting me go. I was his personal play toy. I'd made sure through the years to become and stay his favorite.

If I lost his favor, I would be nothing more than all the others. I told Alyosha about Penn. She was my ticket into being madame one day. She was my proof that I could be more than some stupid slave used only for their bodies and never allowed to speak.

"What do you do when your master…"

I put my hands over my ears, that stupid grating voice so loud I could hear it through the small curtains. I didn't sleep here most of the time. Alyosha called for me, but lately, with my puke breath, he hadn't wanted anything to do with me.

"Please, no," I whispered to myself.

Knowing that if I were, in fact, carrying a child from him, he would throw me away to the pigs. It wasn't the first time that evil man had let nature do his dirty work, and I knew it wouldn't be the last.

I knew more than the others. I knew about his twins. And his wife. The only "thing" he seemed to love. If what I felt was true… would he love it, too? Maybe he would love me like Ana.

Or he would kill me to hide his secrets, bury me and his bastard as deep as the ground allowed. Stupid Ana. She wouldn't love him if she knew who he really was and if she knew about the organization. I gave him more than she ever could.

I had to get to madame status. I could be the best there was,

Alyosha would fall in love with me, and I could finally get my Micah Quinn.

I thought about him often. His beautiful blue eyes were so contrasting to Alyosha's golden ones. Sometimes, I could picture him instead. Pretending he was saying my name in passion. I had his precious sister, and the first thing I would do when the 'Madame title' was given to me was kill that girl.

Micah would give me all the love he lost and needed when his sweet, innocent little sister was murdered.

I would be there for him to cry to and hold. He was going to the police academy soon. I would be there, and I would be the Queen of the Moya Kotva. Madame wouldn't be my only goal. I would take my handsome prince and slay the king.

What better way to dethrone the King?

Then, watch his fall by killing his Queen.

I scrubbed the blood from the floor. The stench made me gag. I never did well with blood. Not since that night...

Present Day

"Are you alright, Lana..." Quinn asked, grimacing. "Or whatever your name is?"

I couldn't bear to look at Quinn. His broken, naked body on this slab was too much. I held my breath. My cowardice at what I had become all these years later was God's joke on me.

He coughed, more blood spilling from his mouth. Cursing myself, I got off the cold, marbled floor, rinsing the bloody rag in the sink and bringing it to his lips.

"If I asked, why would you tell me?" he said, his humor trying to shine through in his dimmed eyes.

I blinked back my tears, continuing to wipe away the remnants of his latest beating. He looked so broken, yet his strength never seemed to falter.

"There is too much to tell Micah," I whispered, and his smile fell.

"Is she okay?" he asked for the hundredth time.

This was always what he wanted to know. Of course, he didn't really care about me. It was just a way to get back to his little princess.

I bit my tongue, letting the taste of blood fill my mouth to dull the pain in my heart. Micah was never going to be mine, was he?

I moved the rag down to his raw wrists, still in the restraints. I didn't understand why Alyosha strapped him onto this board. The blood and water always around made me not want to ask too many questions.

"Please...it's been weeks. Just tell me if she is okay, Lana." Those eyes had unshed tears swimming in the ocean of blue within them. "I don't even know if she's gone..." he said, hanging his head, letting gravity pull his blonde blood-matted hair toward the ground.

I thought about his princess, his Ivy.

She wasn't dead, of course.

Alyosha was taking his time to make sure she suffered by watching her little boy-toy's daily torture sessions. If only Quinn knew Ivy's only view was his suffering. Every time she accepted a drink of water or ate some food, her lover was paying the price with his blood and pain. The worst punishment was denying the drug. Alyosha wanted his princess to be controllable again.

Bitch!

She would probably still eat a five-course meal. She had run from Micah many times when she had the chance to be with him. She'd squandered any amount of remorse I could feel for her.

She didn't have a single scratch on her, yet here, Micah was strapped to a plastic board, hanging forward, his arms drawn above his head in metal cuffs.

They'd tortured him.

His body was so broken. He couldn't move even if he tried, and every day, it just got worse.

"Lana...does he have something on you? Someone you love?"

Always the questions. Poor Quinn couldn't help but try and figure out the puzzle when there was one. If he only knew...

I finished his antiseptic and bandage needs in silence. His eyes searched for mine every chance he could.

"I can help you, Lana. If you are in trouble, I can help you be free from him. I won't let you end up like my sister."

The thoughts of Penelope swam into my mind. Every day, I wondered if I made the right choices regarding Penn. I let Quinn see my eyes for a minute, leaning on my tippy toes to question his memory.

How can he still not know it is me?

I was his sister's best friend, constantly at the Quinn's mansion. I knew his mother, Nancy, and his father, Bradford.

I knew he loved potato grillers and hated ketchup. I knew he had a golden retriever named Rosie, who was buried in the backyard, and I was there the day he planted that rosebush to put on her grave.

How can he still not recognize me?

He was always partying or drinking, with girls hanging on his arm anytime I was around, but I knew he had to have seen me. Had he even realized when I went missing, or had he only cared when his sister joined me later?

He looked at me like I was a stranger, a deranged stranger who he could maybe con his way to freedom. Not at all, like a friend who sent him roses after his dog died. I was 'a nothing' to him then, and I was 'a nothing' to him now.

"Be well, Quinn," I said with a sigh, dropping back down to my feet and tossing the rag in the sink.

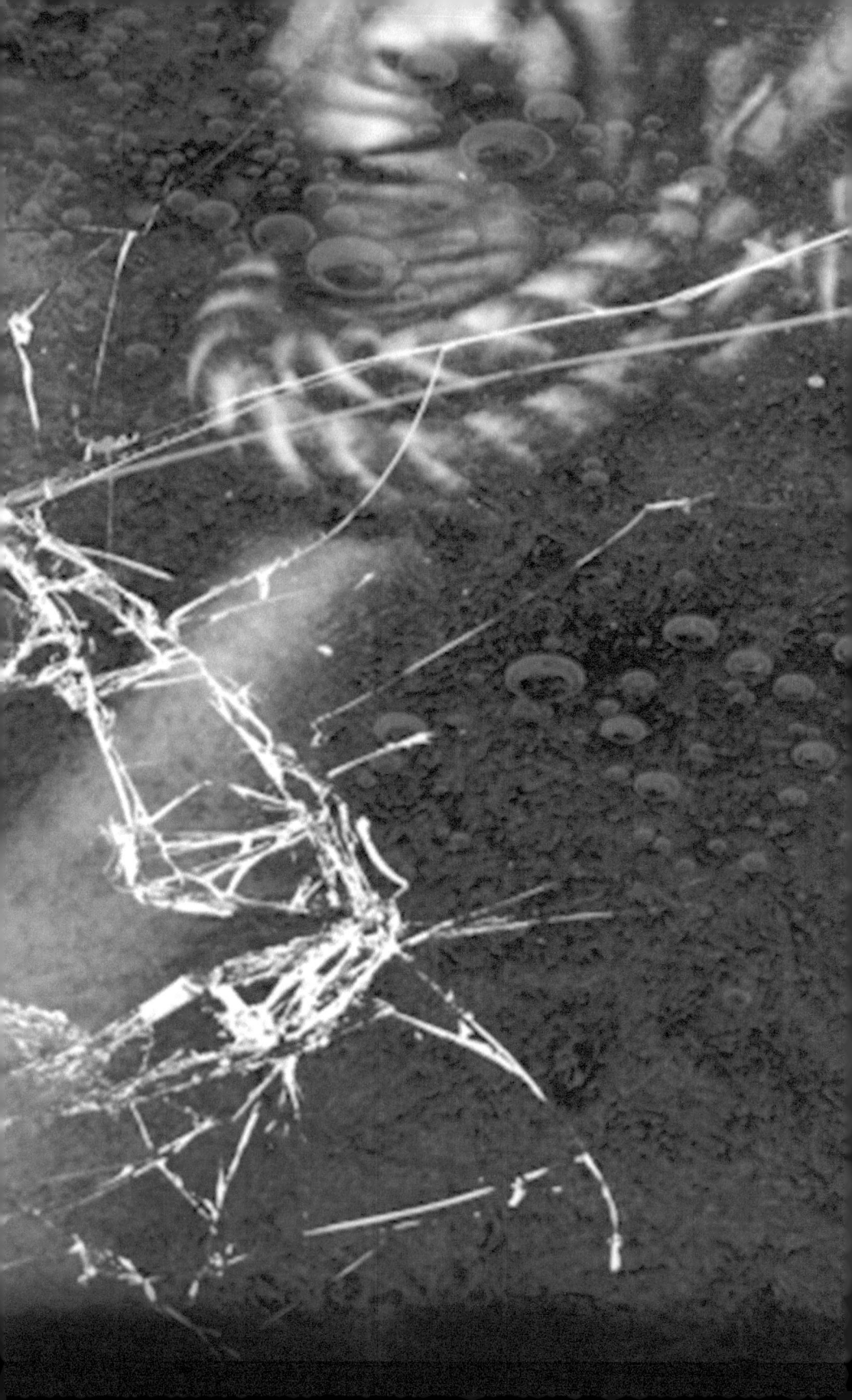

Ivy

Chapter 30

Quinn's image illuminated again on the other side of the wall. His beautiful face was so confused, so beaten. My stomach felt sick, and I held my mouth to curb my nausea.

I had beaten that glass so many times, screamed until my voice was hoarse. It was no use then, and doing it again would only tire me further. The only interaction I had was with my father. Satan himself would've given me a kinder greeting.

The door cracked open, and my father strolled inside. He had on a bloody outfit, and I didn't want to know whose blood it was.

"Good evening, daughter," he said, finding a place in this cell that looked like a room to sit down.

He chose a recliner at the far corner, bending and adjusting with his discomfort. I remained silent like always, looking through the glass at my Porthos.

"Have you decided to take me up on my delicious arrangement, dear?" I gritted my teeth.

How he could call 'teaching little girls to sell their souls' a 'delicious arrangement' made me sick. He said he needed a replacement soon, and with my acceptance, he would free Micah.

I didn't think there was any truth to his words for a second. The snake could weave a tale, but not without poison. Sure, he would release Micah, but I knew he would be killed before any true freedom was given.

"You have responsibilities as my heir. I cannot tolerate my blood being so…reckless. With your talents, you should be doing more for this family."

I bit my tongue, trying to hold back the cruel laughter bubbling in my throat at his usage of family. We had not been family since Mama died. Lucius had been smart enough to flee to America, but even after I snuck away to see him at times all those years, I never felt like I had family at all. Just broken pieces of a puzzle that no longer fit.

"I have been made aware of your means of culling my associates, Eilizaveta. You know that I was not the one to cause you harm years ago. That was Markus."

I couldn't keep silent at that, and I cursed in my native tongue. "A slave follows the order of their master's tongue."

My father smiled, his white teeth gleaming, and his eyes mirrored mine.

"Dear Pet, I was not aware of the strength you had to utilize. Lucius was always the one to show promise. You were a means to an end. I needed him to be in control of the operations. Ana birthed you first in that hour. Thus, your bloodline gave you the power of an army. I simply couldn't have that, you understand."

"I never wanted anything from you," I spat, my anger rolling off my body in waves. "Much less your army of monsters."

He twirled the rings on his fingers, the onyx stone catching the light and bouncing it off the walls. "Ah, yes, but a tiger does not choose to have stripes, Dear."

I looked back at Quinn, his beautiful blond hair hanging in his face as that awful board rotated again and again. How many times could dipping Micah into the tub of water occur before he...he...I couldn't even think straight.

"How is your brother? I never got to finish my conversation with him."

I wasn't sure what my father meant, but hearing pride in his voice only grew my anger.

"Dead," I said coldly.

Alyosha stood, his height towering over me as he walked to my side. He moved like a snake, careful movements, slow and calculated. When he stood in front of me, he captured my hair in his hand, yanking my head backward at a painful angle to look up at him.

"Dear child, you lie. If you wish to wield poison..." His calm tone disgusted me. He took a vial out of his pocket, gagging me with the contents. I choked, scratching and trying to get out of his iron hold. "You must learn of its essence."

The dark purple liquid was burning my throat and traveling down into my body.

"First, be able to withstand the one who created it." His voice was fading.

The initial onset of the drug was making my body feel hazy and numb. A beautiful peace flowed over me, a familiar heaven floating in the air.

"To wield poison, my heir, you have...to....embrace its..." My father's image darkened until all I could see was black. "Venom."

Micah Quinn

Chapter 31

The device stopped spinning. The metallic clang of the door made me cough from the water up my nose, stinging my eyes and making me weak and cold.

"Who's there?" I said, trying to swivel my head to see the intruder. "Lana, is that you again?"

The silence drew on, the only sound of water dripping from my naked body onto the puddles of water below me.

The door closed, and I waited for the device to start spinning again. My head throbbed, and my breathing was uneven from my shivering. The device didn't move. I was nearly upside down, turned toward the wall, but I could see a shadow moving around on the wall's surface. Someone was in the room with me.

"Lana?" I tried again. Maybe it was Aleksia...my memories assaulted my mind, the vomit nearly spewing from my mouth. "Who's there?"

My heart stilled when I heard a small, familiar voice. Something was off. It sounded like a monitor, a warped movie playing, eerie and quiet. "To wield the poison, you must withstand the venom."

"Ivy? Is that you, baby girl?" I didn't know whether to feel happy or not. It barely sounded like her, her voice a lulled robotic tone.

"To wield the poison, you must withstand the venom," she repeated.

I scrunched my eyebrows in confusion, smashing my head back to try and swing backward enough to see if it was really her or if this was some sick trick.

"Little Ghost?" The movement made my head throb, but finally, I was making headway.

The machine was tilted, turning me completely upside down now, which wasn't good, but at least I could see the beautiful dark-haired woman in the room.

She looked odd. Her stare was blank, and those golden eyes looked dim and unfocused.

"Ivy?" I tried again, a little louder.

Her attention snapped to me, and her movements were all wrong. She didn't have her usual grace and finesse. She walked to me like a living corpse, her arms flopping around with no use until she arrived by my head.

She stood there, and I tried to look up at her even though my blood was rushing into my skull at this angle. Her eyes were rimmed red, and her face and beautiful ivory complexion were an ashen gray.

"What did that monster do to you, baby?" I whispered, a tear slipping free.

She watched the droplet with a fixation, intrigue growing as it slid down my forehead and off into the tub of water mere inches from my hair. If I kept swinging forward, I would drown.

"If you want to wield the poison, you must withstand the venom," she said again, that raspy monotone sound leaving her lips.

"What poison? What did they do to you?" She snapped her body up, the jerky movements making me wince.

She looked completely strung out. Drugs were the only possible conclusion because I had never seen anything like this. I had seen all kinds of drugs while on the force and all kinds of reactions, but this...was unlike anything I'd seen. She was acting like a zombie, like a puppet.

She walked over to the table of instruments Alyosha used on me daily. The clinging of metal made my body wince at the memory. What was she doing?

She walked back over to me with a long, serrated knife and tilted her head. Her expression looked like she was fighting some kind of thought or command. God, could she see me?

"Eilizaveta," I said, that battle in her eyes still raging. "It's me. It's Micah. Please, my love. Come back to me."

Her brow furrowed, and she stared down at the knife in her hand, her body visibly shaking.

"If you want to wield the poison..." she said, the battle of wills jarring her words. "You must..."

I gasped in horror as my Little Ghost stabbed that blade into her side. Her cries were mixed with awful laughter as she twisted that knife over and over.

"Withstand..."

Straining, jerking, and shifting my body, I struggled with everything I had to get free. I had to get out to get to her. She would kill herself if she didn't stop.

Fuck!

There was no telling how much damage she had already done.

"The..." Her words were becoming weaker.

Her body sagged down onto the ground in front of me, her

blood turning the pools of water a crimson red. I whipped my head again, the board moving in the wrong direction. Wrenching my body harder, I felt the skin on my wrists and ankles rip open, desperate to see her fully.

"Poi...son," she finished, barely making a sound.

No...

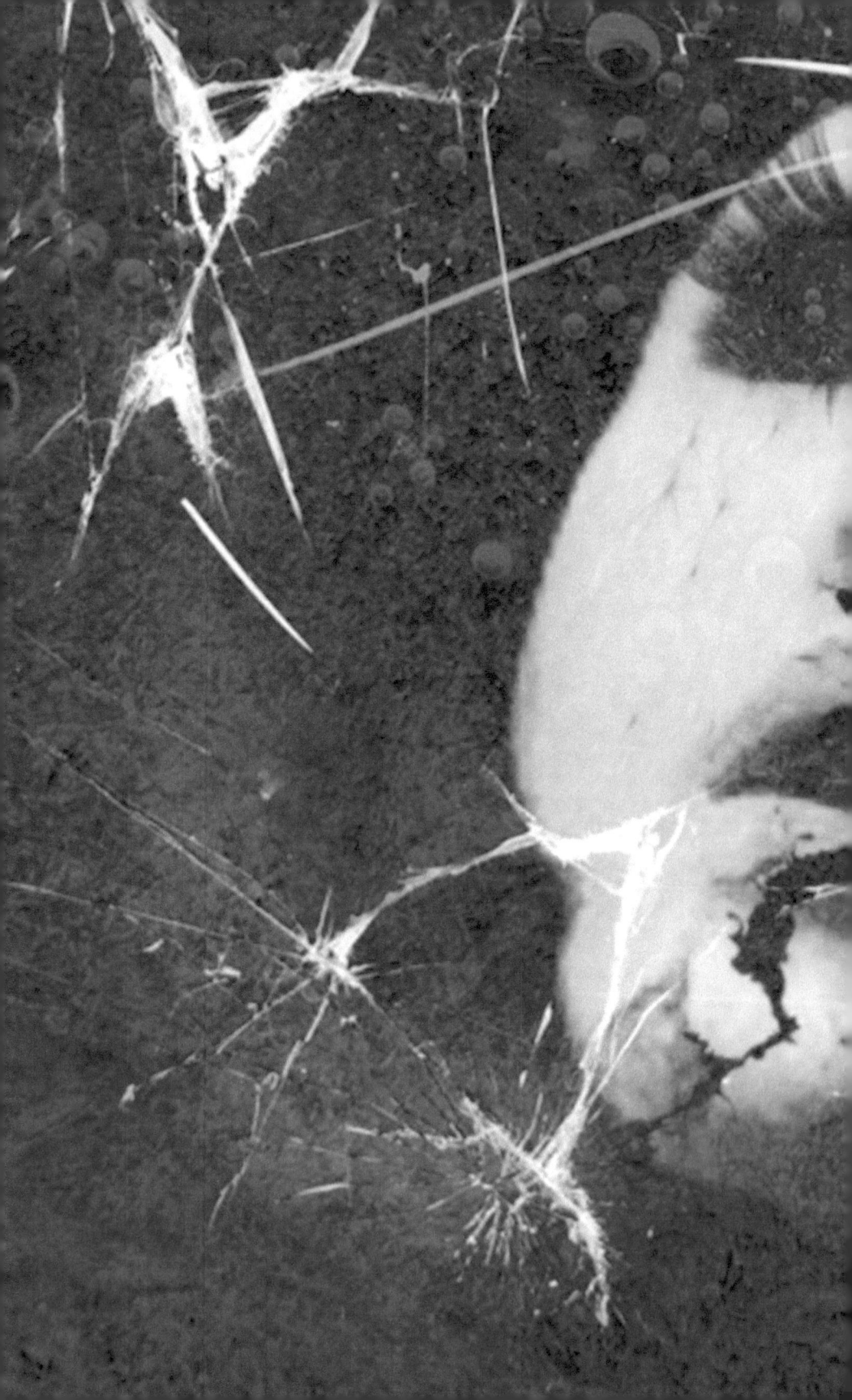

Lana

Chapter 32

"*V*ot der'mo…"

I stared down at my shaking hands. My eyes refused to see the truth. The older girl was staring at me, too. Her accent was thick, and I couldn't understand some of the language. The older girls worked in the streets, bringing in money from customers there.

They had access to the outside world, and Morgana bought me one of these plastic things. She didn't want or care to know why I asked. I felt that nausea bloom again and hovered over the window to get some fresh air to my face.

"Girl. You look green."

I tried to smile to make myself look okay, but she scrutinized the plastic stick in my hands.

"Client do that?" She nodded toward my shaking palms.

I couldn't form words because it made it too real. I had not been with any client. The only man to take my body in that way was Alyosha. I couldn't tell a soul about this. I needed to figure out a way to get rid of this problem before I was killed. Alyosha couldn't know. He would never accept a baby into his life. He kept too much from Ana.

"There is medicine you eat to help that," she said, trying to comfort me.

She was so much older than me. I barely had started my monthly bleeding last year, and now this?

"Can you get me the medicine?" I was pleading, trying to still my hands.

She shook her head. "We can't buy. Just ask the boss. He gets for girls."

My heart sank.

Alyosha was the only one who could get the medicine? But...

"Don't be scared." Morgana tried to comfort me.

Her clad leather outfit squeaked when she reached to rub my arm. "I'll tell the boss for me and give you, okay?"

Tears sprang to my eyes. The feeling I now had because this girl wanted to help someone like me was overwhelming. I had been here for years, yet not once had I received any amount of kindness from the other girls. They always treated me differently.

"Hey, Lana. What's up?"

I dropped the test on the floor in the hallway, the sound ringing in my ears like a jolt from the quiet before. I felt frozen, unable to move as Penelope Quinn walked up and grabbed the test from the ground in front of me.

Her eyes widened, and she gasped. "Oh my god, Lana, are you—"

"Oh, you should really go get the medicine for yourself, Morgana. You don't want to wait on that." I pleaded with my eyes that Morgana understood, and after some shuffling of her feet, she smiled awkwardly and left the hallway.

Penn was always the curious type and never let anything go.

"Morgana is pregnant?" she asked studiously, her gaze following Morgana's hesitant exit.

"Guess so." I couldn't meet her knowing gaze.

"Lana, they give the street girls birth control. How could she be pregnant?"

I forced out a laugh. "I don't know, maybe she didn't take it? How the hell would I know, Penn?"

Penelope had her brother's deep blue eyes. Her hair looked like someone burned it, an orangey-red color that brought out her freckles, but her eyes were always hard to look at because I really missed Micah.

Thinking of me as nothing but his little sister's best friend was as far as his feelings would go, but he was the only man I would ever love.

"Are you okay?" Her question caught me off guard. "You've been really sick for weeks."

She knew. God help me, she knew.

I swallowed the bile in my throat, stepping backward without thinking about it. Penelope was the kindest soul there was. She wouldn't tell...but her knowing at all was something that could get me killed. What if she found out I was the reason she had been kidnapped? Would she use this secret against me to steal away my title? Steal Alyosha's affection? I couldn't take that chance.

Maybe she would think this was a dream. If I could hit her in the head with something, would she wake up and not remember seeing the stupid test? I looked around the room, searching for anything I could use in the hallway. There was just a stupid candle on a hook.

She startled me from my thoughts when suddenly her arms wrapped around me, pulling me into an embrace. "It's going to be okay, Lana. We will figure this out."

I felt tears slip free from my eyes, seeing her shadow on the wall behind me.

Me...or her. She knew, and If she found out how she was kidnapped, she would tell Alyosha about the baby.

"I'm sorry, Penelope. I wish things were different."

She pulled back from me, those blue eyes swimming with confusion before I used all my strength and pushed her. I stepped back, watching as if I were in slow motion. She fell backward, smashing into the candle, knocking it over, trying to grab for anything, and pulling the curtain halfway down off of the window.

Her head smashed into the hard wall with a sickening crack.

"Penn?" I walked forward, but she wasn't moving.

Her legs were at an awkward angle, and she sagged against the wall. My nose burned with a strong scent of iron, and I saw blood on the wall behind her head.

Oh God!

Pushing myself to move toward her, I stopped when a cloud of black smoke rose not too far from her. The candle's flame had fallen onto the downed drapes, and fire quickly spread from the material to the bookshelves beside me. I coughed, frozen in terror, my eyes locked on my unmoving friend.

I could hear shouting. Alyosha and his men were coming here. They would kill me if they knew I'd done this. I knew there were locks on all the doors, some reinforced beyond this room.

I stared down at the sharp, metal pricket that had held the candle. It was on the ground. Picking it up and smashing it with all my might through the window, I ducked as shards of glass exploded around me, and my body was becoming more scraped and marked from the glass fragmented fray.

The voices were closer now, and so was the fire. It had engulfed the entire bookshelf area, the rugs, and the furniture. Thick black clouds choked me from the drugs that piled around them as I pushed my body out of the window and gasped for breath.

Screams surrounded me, so many screams of the girls trapped inside. Our corridors were on the other side of the hallway with the books. I puked on the grass beside me, rain pouring down on my head.

It was a wave of fire. I could see the girls beating on the window of my corridor. They could see me. I ran toward the area, grabbing a rock from the ground, and—

Boom!

My body went airborne, and I was thrown backward onto the ground, my body thudding so hard it ricocheted up my spine. The window I had been running to...was gone.

All the sounds were...gone.

It was quiet, and with every passing second, I heard nothing but crackling embers and wood burning. My fear and anger grew. I felt so cold. So alone.

I...was a killer.

An hour later, I could still hear police sirens wailing loudly in the distance, and the cloud of smoke hung in the sky like a gauntlet of death over my head.

What could I do now? I had no money. No family. No friends. Nothing. I couldn't go to the police because I was responsible for this. I ended all those lives. I walked in the streets, the night blanketing me and my tears.

There was leftover food in some trash cans by fancy restaurants, and I managed to keep some of it down.

What was I going to do?

A passerby bumped into me, their face showing concern. "Are you okay, sweetie? It's a bit cold to be without a jacket. Where is your home?"

I ignored the old lady, brushing my face off with my singed

sleeves. I needed to find some clothes.

"Can I have some money to buy a jacket? I lost mine."

Now, she looked at me like I was some scum peddler.

"Oh, you are one of those call girls for that asshole, Markus, aren't you?"

Who was Markus? I knew many names Alyosha controlled, but Markus wasn't one of them.

The old lady scoffed and clutched her bag tighter against her chest. "Go back to the Gallows where you belong, girl."

From what I could remember, the gallows were the flood zone area on Child Street.

People avoided that area because anytime it rained, the mud turned into a tar base that made you sink to your death and drown. There were always dead animals littering that area, and I couldn't imagine anyone running a business there.

I looked down at my stomach, the little bulge in my shirt making me think of a plan. Alyosha was probably killed in that fire. His heir was my baby, meaning they had the right to Moya Kotva and The Masks Organization.

If this guy, Markus, were smart, maybe he would make a deal with me. I could share my throne. The only thing in the way was Alyosha's damn family. Technically, those twins had the rights... but not for long.

Present Day

THE MEMORIES FROM SO LONG AGO STUNG AS IF THEY'D HAPPENED yesterday. I stared into the window of Quinn's cell. Ivy would go again to look for those girls, and Quinn would be the one who was punished.

I couldn't take it. I couldn't watch him suffer anymore. This was my fault. I had to free him. Even knowing it meant I would die, I didn't want to live without him. He was never going to look at me the way he stared at his fucking princess.

His love for her made me sick, but I couldn't keep something that didn't belong to me. I had learned the hard way many times, yet I held on to him. Micah was my one light at the end of the tunnel unless...I could kill Ivy.

I could finish the fucking job those morons failed to do so long ago, but that would just make Quinn hate me even more.

I'd already taken his sister from him. I couldn't take his princess, too. Maybe I was meant to die by Alyosha's hand all along. That fire had killed so many innocents, yet the devil lived through the flames.

I had been used so many times. By Alyosha, by Markus. No one wanted me. Nobody cared for me.

I was no one.

I was a tool. Maybe this way, I could ensure the one thing I was meant for in this fucking world was to do right by Micah and give him the life he always deserved but never had.

I'd done the only thing I could back then because the asylum had been the safest place for him. At the time, it was the only place where no one would look for my secrets, but now, it was only a matter of time until the demons in my closet would come to bury me.

I stared at the paper, the writing clear and damning. There would be no going back when Quinn's addled brain woke up and read the words written...I didn't know if Ivy could recover from the drug's influence.

This was what was used to placate her before. Her mind recognized the poison. It was obvious. Her eyes screamed with the battle that she was unable to fight.

It didn't matter.

My fate was sealed in the flames of that fire regardless, and now the reaper was finally catching up to me.

Ivy

Chapter 33

I woke up on a bed. My side throbbed like a fire in my blood. A blonde woman was washing off blood from my arm roughly and looked really angry.

What the hell happened?

"Stupid girl. You really are the dullest person I have ever known, Eilizaveta."

I blinked in surprise, not understanding who this person was, much less why they seemed to hate me so much. Was this someone from my father's operation? I tried to sit up, but the pain was too great, and the dizziness that overtook me slammed me back down on the bed.

"Do I know you?" I studied the woman.

She had long blonde hair and pretty eyes. She wasn't in any weird uniform.

Where could I have met someone like this?

"You and your imbecile twin ruin everything." she spat, and I furrowed my brows. *Lucius did something to this woman?*

"You know my brother?"

An eerie smile masked her beautiful face, making her look cruel as she spoke. "You have no idea, little princess."

With that, she reached into her pocket and pulled out some vial of liquid.

"What is that?" I said, eyeing the vial suspiciously.

"Go to sleep, princess. You have a job to do."

A flicker of memory flashed in my mind: a board, a knife, blood, and darkness. The image assaulted my consciousness, the vial opening with the sweetest smell I had ever known.

"Drink up, princess. Go be the mindless killer you hate. Those girls won't find themselves after all."

I couldn't comprehend anything but that sweet smell in the bottle. I needed it and yearned to embrace its perfection. The curious woman watched me spill the contents down my throat, a warmth settling into my body and cooling my blood like ice.

"Go give Prince Charming his now." I blinked, taking the vial from her palm and trying to drink it.

"No. You had yours. Give this to Micah Quinn."

"Micah Quinn…." I repeated, my body beginning to drift in a haze of euphoria.

"Yes." She sighed irritably and opened the door for me.

I walked through the door, that mist allowing me to float.

"Micah Quinn," I repeated, walking forward to a sleeping male on a board. It was spinning. It looked like fun. I wanted to spin—round and round like a merry-go-round.

"Ivy?" the male said, his gaze wide and sad.

Why was he sad? I was blissful. He needed the vial. He, too, would feel happy then.

"Micah Quinn," I said once more, pulling the vial free from my pants pocket.

The man pulled away from me, eyeing the vial and shaking his head. "No Ivy. That stuff makes you insane. Stop it. Throw that away, Little Ghost."

Little Ghost?

Images of this man on top of me flashed in my mind. His moans and mouth were everywhere, his fingers teasing my body, his large member pumping inside my mouth. I blinked, stumbling backward, the misty bliss swirling with a dark cloud. I didn't want the floating to stop.

Frowning, I walked forward again, opening the vial and resisting the temptation to drink every drop.

"This is for Micah Quinn," I said, aiming the liquid over the man's mouth.

He locked his lips closed, shaking his head viciously. Turning his head away from me, he spoke. "Ivy. Stop this. No."

"Micah Quinn must have the vial," I said, my anger brewing.

The mist grew, chasing away the dark cloud, and my feeling of bliss returned to me. The man still wouldn't open his mouth.

A knife was on the ground under the board he spun on. A red color crusted onto it.

"Must give to Micah Quinn...." I chanted, reaching down to the knife and stabbing down onto the slab.

A masculine scream sounded in my ears, and his mouth opened wide. Smiling, I tipped the vial into his mouth. His scream turned to gargling chokes as he swallowed.

"Find the girls," I said. "Bring them here."

His face relaxed, the look of pain fading with the blissful cloud swimming in his veins. I reached down and unlatched the straps. His big body fell forward and smashed onto the ground. His weight knocked me over, and we laughed as we went down to the floor.

The door creaked open in our fit of laughter, and the woman came through. She looked worried. Her face was painted with anger and sadness.

"Be happy, Lana. So happy," Micah Quinn said, patting the woman on the head.

She swerved away from his movement and brought a bandage and liquid over to him. His hand was bleeding from the knife, the red dripping down like a pool. I liked swimming. Pools were fun.

"You big fucking buffoon. Why did it have to be this way? Is she worth it?" she said, tears streaming down her face as she bandaged the cut on his palm.

Micah reached for her face, wiping her tears with his pointer finger.

"Find the girls, Lana. I will find the girls."

Lana finished being a nurse to Quinn and pulled his body up from the floor. I watched them from the ground. They looked like giants.

"Find the girls," I parroted. My voice sounded weird to my ears.

Lana scribbled something down, wrapped it into a cloth, and shoved it into Quinn's pants. She pushed me over by a corner. "Micah reads this when he wakes up."

I frowned. "Find the girls."

The woman growled and rubbed her hand down her face, walking back over to Quinn. "Please read the letter. I am sorry, Micah."

"Read the letter," Quinn repeated, patting his pants pocket.

Wiping more tears, Lana opened a different door. This one was set into the wall. Inside the walls were many paths. Small walkways.

"We're inside the wall, Micah Quinn." I giggled, continuing to walk forward.

Micah stumbled behind me. His legs were all messed up. Too slow.

"Find the girls," I sang, coming to the end of a doorway where light shone through. The light made my eyes water, but the blissful cloud made me numb.

"Find the girls," Micah Quinn repeated.

Micah Quinn

Chapter 34

A strange fog was clouding my mind. The influence to obey was so strong.

"Find the girls," I repeated, my words feeling foreign on my tongue.

This drug was fading, but my Little Ghost was still under the cloud. I tested my control by flexing my fingers and moving my feet away from the coordinates spoken to me. My eyes were glued to the ground, the influence of the drug and my mind battling for control. Ivy walked on, her eyes a clouded haze.

"Find the girls," she said, turning to look at my frozen form. "Micah Quinn, find the girls."

I opened my mouth, struggling with the haze—my influence repeating like a domino falling in sync with the last one.

"Find the…n-no."

Focusing on my breath, pushing the haze away from my mind, I pulled my foot forward. Blinking at the realization that I had broken this fucking curse over my control. I focused again on my breathing. Feeling the pulsing of my heart, the warmth in my blood.

"I-Ivy...St-stop," I didn't know if my midnight-haired beauty would fight this.

This drug had been inflicted on her too many times. The high the vial produced was extremely potent. My entire body still thrummed like it had been shocked with electricity.

"St...stop Ivy," I said again, fighting to walk to her.

She stopped when I reached out. My hand did not feel her touch. All I could feel was the humming vibration in my blood.

She halted, turning her body unnaturally. Her eyes were wide and unblinking. "Girls. Micah Quinn. Find the girls."

I shook my head, the stiffness leaving my muscles little by little, second by second.

"No, Ivy...fight this."

She stared but not at me. Her eyes pierced through me. The more my body fought the drug, the more I could clearly see how deeply Ivy was consumed by its effects.

"Little Ghost. Please."

Again, she stared through me. Her eyes were unfocused.

"Find the girls?" she said, a question in her voice as she blinked.

A sharp cry from the distance startled me, my hand releasing Ivy. I could smell smoke. When I walked forward, pushing off the haze with my pumping adrenaline, I could see a building in this alley coated with billowing black clouds.

"Hello?" I yelled, my body feeling numb again, this time with fear.

A window opened, and small hands stuck out, waving in the direction of the smoke. Finally, my adrenaline was pumping hard enough to gain full control of my body. Running forward, I hoisted myself on a dumpster against the building. The plastic lid cracked under my feet, and I had to jump to stop myself from falling through the top.

I held onto the last metal rung of the fire escape for the apartments, using my arms to pull myself up onto the small balcony. I was ten feet up, and I could hear them now.

"Help! Oh my god, please help!" These screams were coming from someone young.

Trying to go underneath the clouds of smoke, I reached the small window. Blurry images of running, screaming forms were on the other side of the window, but the frame was almost too damn small for my body. I could hear sirens, but the people inside weren't running anymore. The silence was more painful than the screams.

I pulled off my shirt. Wrapping my fist around the material, I smashed the glass and the siding around the metal. The interior had weakened from the fire. Knowing I only had a few minutes, I dove into the space created by the broken window and missing siding, shoving my way through.

Bodies of...children.

"No!" I roared, reaching two girls and throwing them over my shoulder, searching blindly for others.

Two more girls.

They were younger and very still. When they came into my view in the black clouds, I willed them to move...but they were like sleeping cherubs.

"Please..." I called on my god to help me.

But what I received was one of his angels. As Ivy's lithe body moved like a spirit grabbing three tiny forms, I thought about the little girl named Marcie.

'The angel was right! You've saved me.'

Angel...

Had Ivy saved girls from The Mask's organization? Were her kills–No, the Cinder Killer kills. Could it have been linked to rescuing the kidnapped children?

Had Ivy fought the fog of the drug? Or was this...the task we were meant to complete?

Ivy and I coughed, jumping from the window and smashing on the plastic dumpster lid.

My body caged the girl's safely inside, mirroring Ivy's protective curl.

The distance made me feel the throbs of the fall, plastic forks and debris sticking me in the back.

A blurred swarm of images rushed us. Hands grabbing for the girls. An array of red and blue lights danced in the cloud of black, leaking into the sky.

My vision was foggy, and my lungs felt like charred flesh while breathing in glass. I looked over at Ivy. Her eyes were glassy, that same eerie expression as she whispered under her breath in the chaos of noise around us.

I tried to get her attention as my body was being strapped to a gurney. Paramedics poking and prodding me with needles and medical tools.

"Stop. No..." I mumbled, but my voice made no audible sounds —more of a wheezing that ended in a cough.

"It's okay, Detective. We have you. You did your best. Let us take it from here."

I fought the arms, the poking, the pulling. So many sounds, so many machines. The little girls were being poked and prodded as well. For some, I could faintly hear their rasped breathing, and for others, a small white sheet lay over their bodies.

I was too late.

Those sweet girls...Fuck the fucking world that would let the black clouds consume those souls.

I had to think about the ones that made it out, the lives that would go back to their waiting families…and the lives I would personally see ending by throwing them in the flames.

"Ivy…" I tried again to speak, pushing against the roaming hands.

I couldn't see her. There were too many faces and too many blurred images racing around.

"Get some rest, Detective. You have done well."

I didn't understand that, but as a sharp sting entered my arm, the burn made me feel dizzy.

I couldn't fight it, the void finally claiming me.

"Ivy?" I OPENED MY EYES.

A blaring white light was making my head throb with its intensity. I heard a rattling, and when I regained focus, I could see my arms in handcuffs—the railing of the bed its anchor.

Anger and rage melded into my blood, fueling me.

Who thought they could cage me? Where was my Little Ghost? Was I back with Alyosha? Was this a dream?

"Ivy…"

A white curtain drew sideways, some overwhelmingly cheery nurse waltzing over to me.

"Well, good morning there, handsome. Glad to see you finally join the land of the living!"

The intensity of her voice made me instinctively cover my ears.

Grimacing at my action, the nurse covered her mouth, sneaking over to me and checking all the buttons and wires attached to my body.

"Why?" I asked, rattling the chains around my wrists.

"Well, sugar, you are quite feisty, and after about the tenth man you clocked, they decided this may be best for you."

I pondered that, admitting to myself that my training and protocol would have me doing the same.

"Where...Where is the woman that was with me?" I asked, trying to rub my eyes, realizing I was locked to the bed again.

The annoyingly chipper nurse gave me a crude look, waggling her eyebrows and walking over to another fucking curtain.

"This woman sure is a lucky girl. You have been saying her name even in your dreams."

Ignoring her words, I zeroed in on her hand. The mystery behind the game was not one I wanted to play.

"What are you guys?"

I was starting to feel impatient, and my usual filter was very lagged. I opened my mouth, starting to say something I would probably regret, but then she spoke again.

"Is she a prisoner? Were you transporting her? Whatever drug is in her system, she isn't responding to many of our medications. I am sorry, Detective."

Feeling a pit in my stomach, I watched her pull the curtain to the side. My beautiful Little Ghost lay motionless in the bed. The only movement I could see was the slow up-and-down motion of her chest as she took in slow breaths.

"Ivy?" I pulled at the restraints again, growling and shaking the damn chains. I glared at the nurse. "Get me the fuck out of these."

She chewed her lip a moment but then reached into a cabinet, brought a key over to my wrists, and unlocked the chains from my arms.

I did not bother giving the woman a response and instead hobbled with the cords attached to me over to my Little Ghost.

"Ivy? Baby?" She wasn't moving. Her breathing was steady, and the machine beside her showed a continuous rhythm of green peaks, rising and falling like her breaths.

"Sweetheart?" I tried again, trying to see past my blurred vision. "What is wrong with her?"

The nurse joined us, grabbing the chart at the bottom of her bed and sliding through a bunch of papers.

"We don't know, doll. Honestly, it is very weird. She is stable according to all our tests, but it's like her mind is not. Her brain wave patterns are all over. That drug in her system has created a separation of her body and mind."

Like a ghost, my Ivy had been caged her entire life, and now she was caged by her mind?

The injustice of it all made me feel weak, and I fell to my knees at her bedside, the rough floor unforgiving on my already bruised body.

"How...How long will she be like that?" I forced myself to ask.

The nurse did the worst thing she could possibly do. We were forced into constant training, the basic need as humans to conserve humility by showing respect to the dead, a toddler knowing love, and even more so disturbances in the world...

She looked away from me, her chatty nature and flirty voice. It all changed.

Walking over and laying the paperwork down on the table by the beds, she took a deep breath and seemed to stare at the wall behind me, not meeting my gaze.

"I am so sorry, Detective. There really is no way of knowing when a patient will leave a coma. If they do."

I felt the tears fall down my cheeks, not giving a damn that they were there.

"And when she does wake up?" I asked cautiously, trying again to catch her gaze.

"If she were to wake up...there is no way of knowing who exactly she will be when someone's brain is fighting like this. It's just a game of patience. And then, if she wakes, who comes out after."

I swallowed hard, running my hand gently over her ivory skin. She felt abnormally cold and so off.

"What do you mean who comes out?"

I didn't listen to the answer. My Little Ghost had always been two people, hadn't she? The beautiful, intelligent, confident woman I knew...or The Cinder Killer.

When those golden eyes opened, which person would I be staring at? The love of my life? Or her darkness?

Micah Quinn

Chapter 35

"What the fuck did you do to my sister, puppy?"

I tried to ignore the temper tantrum from Lucius fucking Vasiliev. I knew he was scared, and I had cried for weeks now, sitting at my Little Ghost's bedside, begging her just to wake up.

There was so much that needed to be done.

I had to check on the foster homes and see how the girls were adjusting. It still killed me that two of them were lost to us.

I had been keeping tabs on the homes that the girls were placed in, making sure no foul play was coming to these poor souls. No parents were able to be found. I didn't understand how Marcie and one girl from the hospital had a home, but weeks went by, and still, two little girls had not been claimed. The foster system was the only choice. If I didn't practically live at the hospital now, I would have offered those little ones my own home.

"I understand you are angry," I said calmly, the mirror image of my Ivy stomping around and running his tattooed hands through his hair over and over.

"You don't fucking understand shit, you Zasranets!"

I didn't know a ton of Russian, but when I tutored Ivy, she often called me an asshole, so I did know that one.

"Mr. Vasiliev. Please..." I tried again, motioning the untrained dog to sit down.

"You talk like an old fuck. I am not sitting down, Gramps. I am going to find out who the fuck did this to my sister, and I will destroy them. If you want to put me in handcuffs after, so be it. I don't fucking care."

Now I scratched my beard, trying to figure out the right words not to evoke another fire under this man's ass. He was like a bomb. Any word about this woman in bed before us, and it blew the fuse and then some.

"I am aware of the culprit," I said slowly.

That stopped him, his lethal movements reminding me of the killer that got off scot-free. Eyeing me and walking to face me head-on, his height being a few inches under mine, did not make him any less able to square up to me.

"You speak now, pig, or lose your lying tongue."

I waved him off, stepping back and reminding my fists that this man-baby was my Little Ghost's brother and very important to her.

"Look, Lucius," I said, finally throwing up my hands in surrender, fearing I'd throttle him otherwise.

"Your father's men, Alyosha, took Ivy and me."

Before he spoke again, I cut him off. "I don't know where they are, but I have been tracking down possible locations for weeks now. I have no doubt I am close."

Lucius scoffed and rolled his green eyes. "Yeah, sorry, piggy, I am not sitting on my hands while you go run around and bully dumbasses for information for places that won't exist legally."

I thought about that. It was clear wherever Alyosha was, and the equipment, men, and tools at his disposal certainly weren't going to be police resource finds.

I couldn't place an ABP on a man not even known to be in the United States. The embassy wouldn't touch the fucking mafia, much less RPD.

"You need my help, big boy. Admit it so we can kiss and make up, for my sestra's sake. I really want to kill you, so trying to bench me on this isn't helping."

I sighed, eyeing the desk where the folder of my findings sat.

Maybe this hot head could offer intel in ways I couldn't. I certainly hadn't exactly gotten the best results with my means of interrogation. Still, my blood boiled when I even looked at him. The betrayal of Ella saving this shit hole was too raw...

"What did you do to Ella?" I said, my curiosity too much to bear any longer.

Lucius stared at me like I belonged in Hospital Thirteen, but so fucking what. He was going to tell me if he'd killed my partner because if he had, I would sooner fucking kill him than go anywhere with him...even for Ivy.

She may have killed, but from what I could tell, it was always about saving the girls. Her brother, on the other hand...

"Huh?" he said aloud, raising a brow and cracking his knuckles in boredom.

"What did you do to Ella?" I said again. "Ella fucking Fox."

Realization dawned on him, and that annoyed me. It annoyed me that he thought of her at all. I didn't love Ella. Nothing ever more than how I felt for my sister. Maybe that was why her betrayal had burned me deeply.

What I never expected was for Lucius to laugh at me.

His booming laughter rang in my head like a bell, startling me enough to shake my head. Was he really laughing at me?

Anger bloomed in my chest, and it melded with the burn of my partner's betrayal.

I swung. My fist had a mind of its own as it met with Lucius's jaw.

It was silent then. The man eyed me in stunned silence, but then he smiled—a dangerous smile.

"Okay, puppy. You wanna fight? Bring it on."

I tried to block him, but he instantly tore me off my feet. Our grunts and battle of strength were equal. When I got the upper hand and landed a blow, one of his followed. He was fast, and I was larger.

He went low, and I went high. There was no end to this fight and no beginning. We continued to block and tumble on the ground. I saw papers flying around us, the chair and folders knocked down in our tussle. Suddenly, a familiar voice stopped me in my tracks, and Lucius also froze.

That voice hit me like a slap across the face, and I wondered if Lucius had managed to knock me out after all because I was staring at Ella.

"Micah? Lucius? What the fuck are you idiots doing?"

Lucius got off the floor, cracking his neck and giving her a sly grin.

"Just playing with your boy-toy, baby."

She punched him in the shoulder, and as he feigned hurt with a pouty lip and kissy-face, she returned her gaze to me.

Those gray eyes looked hurt, and I could only guess they mirrored mine.

"Micah," she said again. Tears filled her eyes as she walked over to me.

Was this a fucking trick?

I didn't respond, just stared at her from the floor as she approached me. I felt like if I moved, she would vanish.

"He is going to faint if you don't explain it all, Little Shadow."

Ella wiped at her face, slowly sitting down beside me and picking up the papers that had all floated to the ground.

"Micah...I..."

She looked sad, confused, and embarrassed. That just made me angrier. I tamped down my happiness at even seeing her alive and allowed myself to feel that burn of her betrayal. Now, knowing she had been with my enemy all this time....

"Why?" I said, fighting the stinging tears I refused to let fall for her.

She played with the ends of her pale blonde hair, the sun making it seem even more blonde as she blocked the window of the room.

Halo or not, I knew better.

"Micah I...I don't know what to say."

I glared at her, my unease and anger growing. She felt so familiar yet so much like a stranger.

"Don't bother, Ella," I mumbled, trying to find my footing and leaving her on the ground.

Storming forward, I growled when Lucius shoved me backward.

"Oh no you don't, meathead. Stay here and listen to my woman. The amount of tears she's shed over your worthless ass is beyond me, but if you make her cry again, I'll gift her your pretty blue eyes for payment, ya got it?"

I glared, ignoring the tugging feeling in my gut and pushing past Lucius.

When I was outside the door, I could hear her crying, and Lucius, as much as a brute as he seemed, there was a gentleness reserved for her.

Sighing and feeling like a fucking dick, I turned around and walked back into the room. The curtain beside me was my anchor as I leaned against it. Ella caught my big ass form against the wall, and she smiled.

Lucius glared at me over his shoulder before picking up the blonde and walking her over to me. "Guess you like those pretty eyes in your head."

He sat her on her feet, and I felt instant regret at cornering my ass against the wall with no escape. Ella reached out her hand to me, and I stared at it like a fucking alien had sprouted wings from her green fingernail paint.

"First off..." she said awkwardly. "My name is Phoenix."

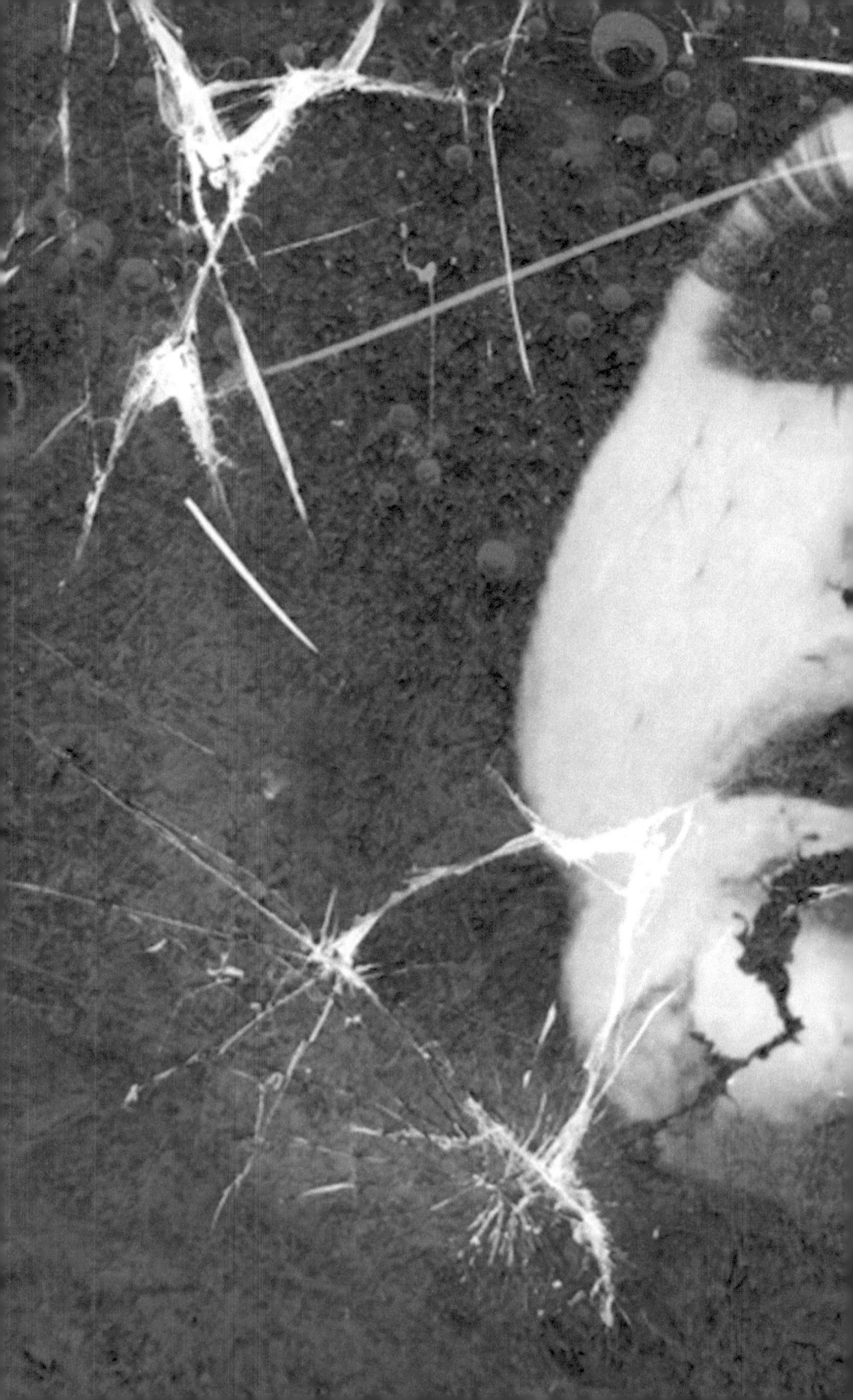

Lana

Chapter 36

I tossed and turned in the bed. Unsure if Quinn read my message or even opened my letter. I had no way of checking in with my son or my assets, and the knowledge was gnawing me alive.

My dear Micah and his little princess hadn't been back. For weeks, the news blaring on the TV had been about a fire that had claimed some minors' lives...

I still felt sick at the mention of those lives lost. It was my fault. Those girls died because I was a coward. Maybe they had started a fire trying to prevent themselves from starving to death. Such little girls were left in a dark apartment alone, struggling to survive for weeks, only to die from being desperate to eat.

I held my hand over my mouth, trying to curb my nausea. Alyosha was beside me. His naked chest and abs seemed to glow in the moonlight of the window. He turned to me, snaking his arm around my chest, making the fresh bruises on my skin tingle.

"Fuck, Ana. You are so warm. So wet for me."

I held back the tears. Even after all this time, I was only his ghost of Ana. Her life was over, but my actions forced me to take her place.

I thought about the words that got me into this hell. The fate I'd cemented for myself.

Years ago...

"LISTEN. I KNOW THE TWINS WILL BE THERE. HIS PRIZED POSSESSION, HIS son dancing on stage. An easy mark."

The gruff man looked into the bag, hesitant to accept the wealth he saw before him. All these idiots were cavemen. I swear they could never do anything.

Markus nodded at my side, his stoic posture uneasy tonight with the task at hand. I didn't understand why the dumbass couldn't use his position to do it himself. He could easily go into their home and end the perfect family with a well-lit match and some gasoline.

"Are you sure this girl's rat is the heir?" the gruff man said to Markus.

I hated my child being called anything but perfect. The moment I looked into his eyes, I knew he was my greatest gift. Every plan I had set in motion was ruined when I held him. I would never be able to give him up. Power be damned.

"The King and Queen will attend."Another confirmed clicking on their phone.

Later that night, I sat on the top balcony of the ballroom, and my view was clear. I watched Lucius and some girl twirling away on the stage. He grew to be a handsome boy. Even at age fifteen, you could see he *would be as beautiful as his father. There were many similarities in my son. They had the same dark midnight hair, but Kristiyan had my eyes.*

I watched on, the dancing coming to an end, and the little family in front standing tall to cheer for their talented child. It made me angry that my son would never be able to experience such things. His entire life only to be hidden away, like some animal.

I reminded myself it was for the best, trying to brush my tears away from my eyes.

The King and Queen had indeed attended. Alyosha stood tall with his arm lovingly wrapped around his beautiful, perfect wife, his daughter by their side, clapping excitedly with tears streaming down her happy face.

Not for long, little girl...

I thought about Penelope, wondering if she would have grown to cheer her big brother on like this.

Why think of the dead? It didn't bring them back. It only made their loss feel more suffocating.

How badly Alyosha and Ana will suffocate without their precious twins.

The grandfather clock in the hallway chimed, the symbol of an ending.

I leaned forward, forcing myself to watch every second of what would ensure my son would be the world's most powerful man someday.

I saw the shadows enter through the hall, a gun poised at the twins. Alyosha was beside Eilizaveta, and Ana was speaking with the female dancer.

The poor prince was all alone. His line of sight was the gunmen that would end his life.

Suddenly, Ana screamed and bolted toward her son. My assassin's bullet sank deep into her heart as she'd shielded the teenager.

Alyosha's roar deafened me, louder than the scream of the scattering people and bullets popping off one by one as my assassins were killed by Alyosha and his men standing outside.

I watched the twins from the shadows of my balcony. The girl was kneeling beside their mother, covered in her blood. The boy stood frozen, staring at the blood splatter on his white shirt, the blood of his deceased mother.

Alyosha screamed to the heavens, holding his wife and roaring in pain.

Ana-the queen was dead.

They say pain brings light to being alive, but the pain I'd witnessed unleashed a darkness. Alyosha took off his belt, walking over to his frozen son. Lucius had tears in his eyes but couldn't say a word.

"You fool! You coward! You are responsible for this. And you will pay."

I covered my mouth as the monster lashed the belt, the metal and clip side, down his son's back. The crack was louder than the screams and the bullets had been. The sound echoed around me.

Alyosha reared the belt back and whipped his son over and over. The boy's shirt ripped from the force, red streaks and flesh gaped from the tears.

The princess cried, trying to claw her way to her brother, but her father's men held her back.

The prince covered his mouth, his eyes filled with tears, and his face laced with pain, but he didn't make a sound, only stared over at his mother, who'd sacrificed her life for him.

I VOWED AT THAT VERY MOMENT NEVER TO LET ALYOSHA KNOW OF my son. Never would he lay a hand on my blood. I would protect my child with the very last breath I had, and I would do everything I had in my power to ensure others kept him safe long after my final breath was uttered.

My son would never be a king...but he would be alive.

The memories of that night plagued me like a nightmare. Every night, I saw Lucius being brutally beaten. I knew of Alyosha's cruelty. My own body had endured it time and time again, yet at no time had I seen that crazed man that Alyosha had been that night.

Lucius had fled to America, and Eilizaveta was held under lock and key. There had been no other time to end the twins, even if I had wanted to do it myself. I was forced to put all my efforts into hiding my son.

That was why I took my son to America, hiding him in the asylum from my home. Texas was a foreign place to me after being kidnapped so young, but I had to take the chance of going where Alyosha would never have dreamed me to go.

It was only after my travels that I found that my assets were not all lost.

It wasn't the life I wanted to live. It wasn't the life I wanted for my family, but it was the only thing I could offer.

Katerina kept her end of the bargain. We had become such good friends since she thought I grew up in Russia. With my knowledge of it, I guess I had, in a way. She was my closest friend while I worked my way into the force, and she always kept my secrets safe.

I always visited my son, but it wasn't safe a year ago. A serial killer had been murdering patients, and I knew that drawing attention to my secrets would only cause a dangerous situation.

Wasn't it just the ultimate smack in the face to realize the love of my life had not only fallen in love...but with the princess that I failed to murder?

Markus had gotten cocky, trying to buddy up to Lucius and become his best man. The moron didn't think that his new bestie would figure out his sister was in a cage, and that ended the sorry bastard.

It tied up loose ends for me, as Markus was the only living

person to know of my sins. Alyosha still saw me as his loyal mistress. His madame, and if I wanted to keep the only things that mattered to me alive…then, I had to realize I would always be this —Alyosha's toy. Until, at last, he finally broke me beyond repair.

Micah Quinn

Chapter 37

I could not wrap my head around the words that had been said. Ella was Ember. Both were Phoenixes, and both were the Snow White killers? Why did all the fucking women in my life have to be serial killers?

"I don't understand," I said out loud.

My brain had caught up a bit, but even now, after a week of adjustment, I couldn't look at Ella...Ember...Phoenix...Snow White the same way.

My brain fucking hurt.

"Quinn. Please," Phoenix said, shuffling through papers and clicking on her laptop.

We had gotten some new leads on possible locations for Alyosha by tracking new cases of missing girls. These were women. Ages ranged from late teens to early twenties. It looked like whoever was taking care of the little ones burned in the fire.

Alyosha must not want to play a parental role because he had not taken any younger girls since the tragedy.

My phone dinged, and I read the message, seeing it was one of the girls texting me from a phone I had bought for them in case they needed me. I knew it wasn't standard, but those sweet girls needed some people they felt safe to speak with.

I read the message again, trying to piece together what it meant.

> Little One 2: Hi! Mr. police, can you come see me? I need to talk to you. I saw the lady yesterday when I was in the market with my new mommy. I am scared.

> Quinn: On my way. Do not leave the house, and inform your foster family, please.

"I need to go take care of something," I said, grabbing my coat from Ivy's bedside and kissing her forehead.

Phoenix looked up from the laptop, concern in her eyes.

"Quinn? What's wrong?"

I ignored her rushing around and snatching a pair of pants from my bag by the window. I hadn't gotten a chance to do laundry in a few days, and some of this stuff was so singed from the fire that I had planned on chucking it into the garbage. As I continued to put on my winter coat and grab my keys, I realized I had grabbed the pants I had on the night of the fire. It still smelled like ass from being in the dumpster.

Oh well, I didn't have time to worry about it. All I cared about was getting to the little girl's side as fast as possible.

I shoulder-checked Lucius on my way out, knocking his feet off the desk and laughing with his curses as I exited, closing the door behind me.

Arriving at the house of the foster home, I turned off the car and made my way around the area, making sure there was no one looming in the vicinity. I did not see signs of tracking or anything to allude to someone staking out this house.

What woman did the little girl mean?

The foster mother opened the door and greeted me, her nose wrinkling a bit when she smelled my pants.

I really should have found different ones.

Sighing, I greeted the mother and stepped inside. The home looked comfy with all the nick-nacks you would expect, and I felt a sense of joy to see that the family had pictures of the little girl smiling and playing in their backyard. The images were hung by their TV and set on a table beside the door.

"Where is Veronica?" I asked, careful to say her name as the family had changed it. I hoped the little girl accepted and wanted the change.

"She is in her room. Thank you so much for coming here, Detective. Veronica says she has been having bad dreams lately, and I know you are a comfort."

It didn't escape my attention that the foster mother clearly did not know about the strange woman. Why would the little girl not tell her mother?

I walked the hallways of the tiny family home until I reached a door with a pink sign on the handle, butterflies in flight caressing the name "Veronica."

I was glad this little one had a chance. Transformation and healing were all I could give her.

"May I come in?" I tapped lightly on the door. "It is Detective Quinn."

Small hands opened the door, and the bright-eyed girl stood before me. Her recovery from the smoke had been a miracle. She had been so close to losing her life like the others, but somehow, she pulled through in the end.

"Hello, Detective," she greeted warmly. "What's wrong?"

More confused, I returned her smile and sat on the too-small teacup chair, worried my ass was going to get stuck on the plastic. The little girl smiled and ran to bring me a tea cake and a small cup with some liquid in it.

"Your text worried me, sweetheart," I took the offered items.

I began to take a hearty sip of the sour drink.

"Text?" she mumbled, chewing on her burnt cookie.

I tried to reach into my pants, but the damn chair was blocking my hands. Moving, I finally was able to finagle my phone out of my pocket along with a note. It fell on the ground, and I frowned.

Great. Two mysteries now for me to solve.

Setting the note to the side, I finally brought the screen over for her to see.

"Remember? What lady were you talking about? Did she speak to you?"

The little girl's eyes widened, and she shook her head, her cookie untouched now, as she picked at the edges nervously.

"Is something wrong, sweetheart?" I asked patiently. "What lady did you see?"

She fidgeted in her seat again, drinking the lemonade and dipping her cookie in the liquid. "Uh, well..."

I waited for her to continue, knowing that if I spooked her or rushed her, she would shut down.

"Do you know the lady?" I tried calmly, taking another bite of my burnt cookie and smiling with over-embellished "Mmmms."

She giggled and nodded. I put the cup back on the table, adjusting in this damn chair.

"Hmm. Is this woman your friend? Or has she not been nice to you?"

The little girl chewed on her lip.

"She isn't nice all the time. But she didn't let us get hurt by the bad men." Lana flashed in my mind. "But, the Madame took my phone, Detective. I am sorry."

I tried to school my features, hiding my face in my cup to process the information without startling the young child.

"The woman took your phone. So you didn't send this to me?" I showed my phone again, and the text lit up on the screen.

"No." The little girl had tears in her eyes. "The Madame told me to stop looking for them. I promised I wasn't trying to Mister Policeman. I promise I have been good. Please don't take me away from my new Mommy and Daddy. I don't want to lose them, too."

I forced a smile, patting the child's hand. "You are the very best little girl, Veronica. I would never dream of taking you from your new Mommy and Daddy. They need you, and you need them."

The child seemed to take a breath and settled down into her seat again, dipping her cookie and taking little bites through her giggles.

"What else did the Madame say?" I questioned, keeping my tone light and playful, poking the little one to ensure she was giggly and happy.

"She said to not look for them because they know where we are."

My blood ran cold. This little girl was being used as a messenger. The message was either a threat...or a warning. I couldn't be sure which one.

I swallowed, flipping to a picture of Lana on my phone, trying to feign that light attitude.

"Is this who you saw, sweet girl?"

The light faded from her smile and eyes. "Yes."

BACK AT THE HOSPITAL, PHOENIX AND LUCIUS WERE RAGING. THEIR hot-headed personalities were a hell of a duo.

"She has some fucking lady balls." Lucius spat, doing some weird tech thing on a headset.

They made this place look like an air traffic control center with all the computers, gadgets, and technology littering the rooms. We had to be upgraded a few times just to fit it all. Ivy was the center of this, and I'd be damned if they overcrowded her fucking space. No one was putting a cord anywhere near her.

"Lana is sending me a message," I stated. "She is letting me know that Alyosha and The Masks operations are well aware of our intel and progress."

Lucius cursed—a slew of Russian words coating his tongue.

"Well, if she wants to play that way. We can play back."

Phoenix got a dangerous look in her eye, making me realize she was two different people. Her personalities collided, and her personality was a mix of the two she used to be.

"I don't know if that is a good idea," I said, pondering the ramifications in my head.

Alyosha could have sent the message, for all we knew. The drugs had made me so hazy that I didn't even remember Lana being there. It was like when I tried to think about that area, a fire burned inside my skull and forced me away from the memories.

"I don't know," I repeated, staring at my phone.

"It isn't up to you! That's my fucking sestra on the bed. And my fucking father, who put her there!"

I waited for Phoenix to calm her bomb boyfriend down. My head was already pounding.

"What other options do we have?" She ran her hands through the Russian's hair.

I missed Ivy's touch. I missed her sweet hands and the softness in her voice. She was feisty and sweet. It was the most delicious combination of both.

I pushed at the memories, knowing my pain would not do me any good right now.

"We continue the path we started. We have more leads we have not followed up on."

Lucius rolled his eyes at my words.

"Fucking hell, pig. Chatting up strippers from my absolutely desecrated club is not going to help anyone."

Lucius was clearly still sore about the Black Mirrors Club being turned into Gya—the exotic dance club. The thought made me snort.

He glared at me and pointed to the sleeping beauty in the bed.

"Is that so funny, asshole? My sister is stuck in her head while you have the power to do something and choose the all-holy mighty way instead?"

His words stung, partly because I knew he was right.

I closed my eyes and breathed in deeply before typing in a message to the number I knew someone else had.

What do I even say...Should I tell them I know? Or play the game?

> Quinn: Hey, little one. I checked into that shop you gave me. There wasn't anything there, but I am going to head home now.

Bait sent.

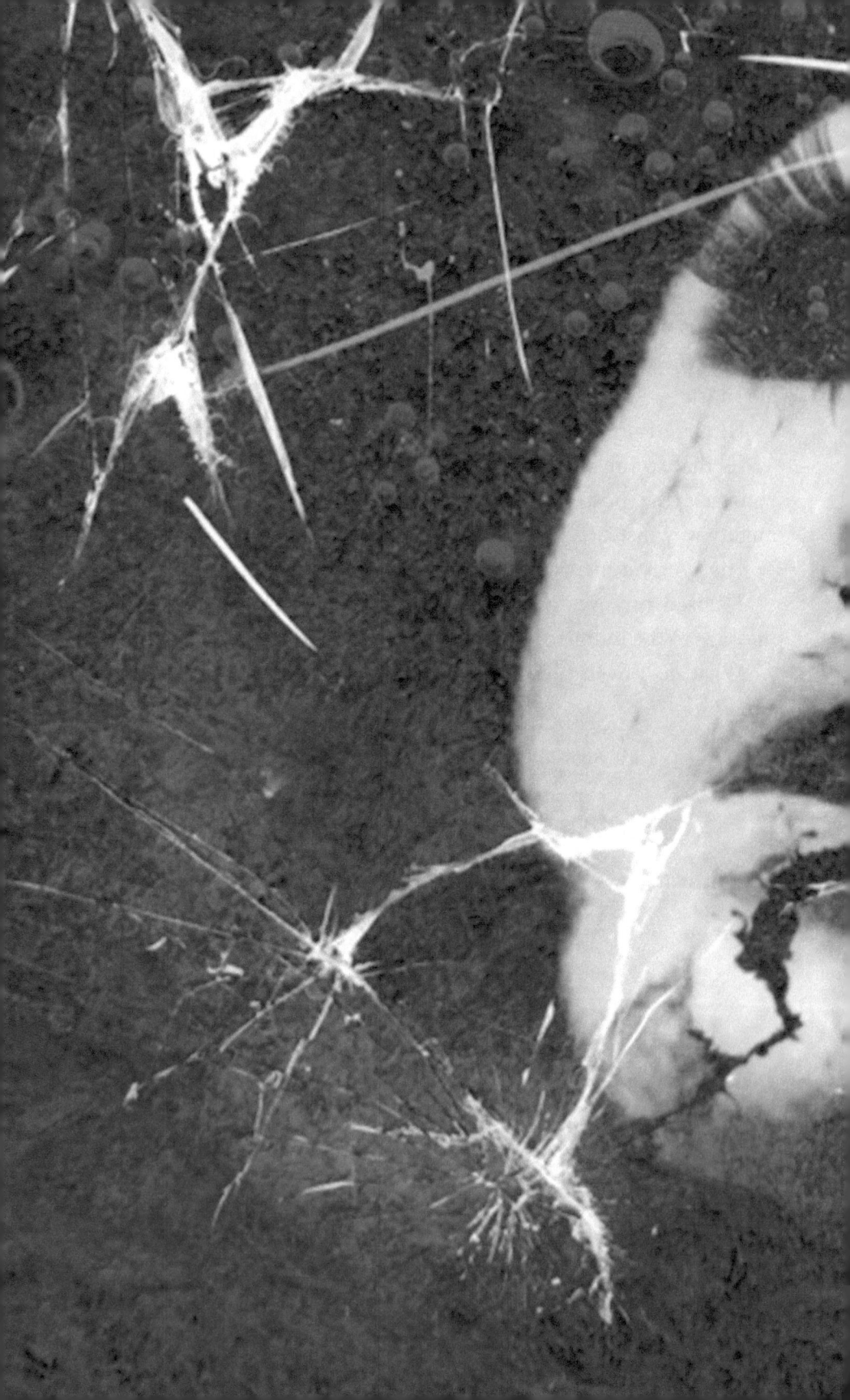

Lana

Chapter 38

I hid in the shadows of Quinn's apartment with my body flush against the wall by the kitchen counter. A door opened, and I stilled my movements, knowing Quinn was going to be here any moment now.

Taking a deep breath to center myself, I waited to see his face.

A sharp sting to the back of my head made me yelp, and green eyes bore hatred into me as I felt darkness take over.

I woke up in a dark room, my head throbbed, and I tested my hands only to find they were bound.

No! This wasn't Micah. If I couldn't tell Micah to free my son, he would be trapped his entire life and…

I couldn't die this way. Not by the goddamn hand of the son of a monster.

"Lucky you. You ambushed an unsuspecting woman. Your father would be proud."

Heat bloomed on my lips as a shadow smacked me so hard my head jerked to the side, and blood filled my mouth.

"Do not speak of my father. You whore."

I tried to wipe my mouth on my shoulder, trying to focus on the one light being pointed at me.

"You are trying to interrogate me? Lucius Vasiliev, I thought you were taught better. Or is it because you were self-taught in survival that you are stupid?"

Again, I was slapped, and again, my head jerked to the side, the feeling of vertigo and whiplash strengthening. If I could get him to make me pass out, he couldn't get information and, therefore, could not kill me.

I caught sight of those green eyes. He looked cautious, probably trying to understand how I knew his name and title.

"I know a lot. Which is obviously why you set up your little torture session," I spat, blood spewing from my mouth on the glass walls beside us.

"Where is he? Your master, your fucking dildo to power, bitch?"

I laughed at that. At least he didn't think I actually loved that monster.

"I do not know," I said calmly, gauging the rage flowing off of Lucius.

That was his problem—the reason why he would never defeat his father. Where calm and calculation were used for lethal precision with Alyosha, Lucius was fueled by rage, muscles, and dumb luck.

"Stop looking at me, you whore. I won't fucking touch you unless it's to break your fucking neck."

I smiled. Maybe not so much like his father after all. Word on the street anyway was that the prince found a stabby peasant to play with—the one his daddy had ordered him to kill.

"Are we not done playing house, Lucius?"

He narrowed his eyes at me, that gaze so much like my son's anger. It hurt seeing Lucius now, a man standing in front of me that mirrored my poor child.

I had to get out of this. I had to get back to him.

"You have secrets, and you will tell me one way or another, Svetlana Puriya."

Crafty He would dig up my name. My real name. The one that bared the same as his father. He must know of me, but not enough.

"If you had really thought you would get my secrets, your methods would not have been to torture me."

He growled, confirming that this was a 'cat and mouse game.' It was just a question of who would be the one chasing who.

"You think you have the upper hand? What would the big puppy Micah think of your little shenanigans?"

I paled at the realization that Lucius could hurt Micah.

"The cop loves your sister," I blabbered, my fear getting the best of me.

"Yes." He laughed. "I know the buffoon loves Eili. What I don't know is why *you* know that."

Fuck...

"I was his police partner," I stated, again fueled by fear.

Lucius tsked, dancing in my view in the shadow of the light, switching entirely to Russian. My ears caught every word.

"See, now that's another puzzle, isn't it? Why would a Russian woman who was not good at hiding her accent—and a true brethren of the homeland—know our little Quinny pea?"

I looked away, trying to feign confusion.

"Nice try," Lucius moved closer to me, the sly bastard. The moonlight behind me shone across his beautiful face, highlighting his ominous smile.

"Why don't we ask Mr. Handsome himself? Hmm?"

My blood ran cold. The door opened wide, illuminating Quinn being handled by a blonde woman. She walked over to the bound man and slammed him on his knees in front of me.

"This sweet little cop means something to you, doesn't he?"

Lucius dragged a dagger across Micah's throat. The sharpness of the blade nicked his skin, sending droplets of blood to bead.

"No. Please. Leave him alone," I begged.

My useless plan had gone to all hell with my only other weakness, who had access to my secrets in danger now. The female laughed, grabbing Micah's dirty blonde hair and yanking his head up to her.

"Definitely has the hots for you..." she sang.

Micah coughed and tried to pull away, growling at the dancing duo as they made kissy faces at us.

"Baby, we should give them some final goodbyes before we shove them out the window, yes?"

I swallowed hard. With the glass window behind me, I didn't know how strong the glass was, but I knew a human body flying through it wouldn't hold. I rocked the chair beneath me, struggling with the binds wound around my wrists and body.

Giggling, Lucius and his obvious lover waltzed out of the door after grabbing some sweets from the refrigerator.

"Lana? What is this?" Quinn said, looking into my eyes and begging me to make things make sense.

The poor man had been tortured, drugged, and forced to forget any information that would have answered that. He never read my note, and the pit in my stomach grew larger. I had to tell him about my son. I had to get him free of Lucius and his bat-shit girlfriend.

"Micah, please. Just listen. They don't need to kill you. It is me. You are innocent. I just need you to—"

The glass behind me exploded into a million pieces.

My chair flew forward, smashing me against the bar. Micah

rolled behind the couch from the blast, trying to search for me, as I fell off the bar onto my back in the chair.

Groaning, I tested my arms. The jolting around from the explosion allowed me to loosen my ties and wiggle free of the hold. I turned to the window, fear glazing over in my eyes. The eerie quiet was too much. No natural occurrence blew out the window.

The door was blocked from the inside by a table that had smashed into it, and I could hear the shouts and banging of Lucius and his lady trying to get in.

I ran over to pull Quinn away from the window.

"Quinn. You need to get to cover. This might be…"

A whizzing sound made me pause.

I felt weak all of a sudden, my body falling forward with a thud I barely felt.

"No! Lana!" Quinn ran to my side, flipping me over and holding me to his chest. He was covered in blood.

Was he hurt? No…looking down, I saw a hole in my side. The blood seeping out of the wound like Ana in the ballroom.

"Svetlana. Hold on! Just hold on. Lucius, Phoenix! There's a sniper!"

I tried to hold onto his words—blurry images of the two lethal people finally smashing into the door and rushing to my side.

How strange. They tricked me? Now, the joke was on me. He was nothing like his father, after all.

Maybe there was hope for Moya Kotva…

I held onto Quinn's hand, tears flooding my eyes as the world started to fade around me.

I would never see my son again. I would never be able to look into his eyes and tell him I was sorry. Never explain why I had to hide him and her all his life. Never be able to get the forgiveness I realized I desperately craved.

Was it cosmic fate that the man I loved, and who would never love me, held me and cried for me as I died in his arms?

I had to tell him. He had to know. But I could barely form words.

"My secrets…" I breathed, my lungs deflating and my eyes feeling heavy.

"I don't care. Lana, please, I just want you to be okay. I know you were under his command. I know he hurt you. Those girls told me everything. They told me you would take the punishments from the guys. That you would say you were teaching the girls everything so they wouldn't be touched. You are not a monster, Lana."

I let the tears fall. My soul had all but been born in a cage. I had taken too many lives, but I had ruined so many more. His sister…

"My secrets…" I said again, fighting the darkness to live out my final apology and protect the only one I loved. "My secrets…lie in…the…asylum."

His tears fell onto my cheeks as his confused blue eyes blurred to stars of black. I let out a sigh. My body was free of pain, my soul was cleansed of darkness, and my secrets were safely in his hands.

Finally, I could just…sleep.

Micah Quinn

Chapter 39

Two Weeks Later

I held the little necklace in my hand.

The ashes of Lana were sealed inside.

My old friend Goliath opened the door, his giant ass blocking all light like a shadow.

Lucius backed up and held up his hands. "Whoa, holy fuck, you didn't tell me you knew Goliath!"

Lith sniggered and held out his meaty palm. Lucius stared at it and scoffed.

"Aren't you a cuddly thing," he mused, walking over to me and mussing up my damn hair.

It was weird as hell not seeing Pharaoh. I still felt like I had failed that man, and I couldn't bring myself to face him since seeing him that night.

"Well, if it isn't the nosy piggy. We missed your weird aftershave, bro. Larry cried when he couldn't smell it lingering around here anymore."

I rolled my eyes but allowed Judas to clock me on the shoulder. All these fuckers were huge.

"Where is your 'picket fence,' Goliath?" It was weird not to see the fiery Latina attached to his hip.

He had a grin he couldn't hide at the mention of his love, and I smiled, trying to feign away the pain in my heart for the sweet Little Ghost still sleeping soundly in the hospital. Phoenix had spent two weeks convincing me to get my ass to this damn place and do right by Lana.

'My secrets lie in the asylum.'

The cryptic message had messed up my mind, but I couldn't leave my girl. Not after her insane fucking father took out Lana in my highrise. It wasn't right. Lana didn't deserve to die. She wasn't the monster, everyone thought.

"Whoa! Your name really is Goliath? No shit, all right," Lucius said.

Lucius and Goliath were like old frat boys meeting for the first time, hitting it off and making me feel like the old nerd in the corner.

"Ezello is getting the keys you so nicely asked us for."

I grimaced, feeling guilty for calling my friend in a huff.

I wasn't kind when I told him to find what was hidden at the damn place he was in charge of. For the last few weeks, he searched every drawer and crevice for anything that may have belonged to Lana. No paper trail was linked to her, and no item, no matter how buried, would have any significance to her.

We walked down the hallways, veering off to hallway B and making our way all the way down to where the special unit was.

Nothing could be found in the closets of the place, so why not speak to the ghosts that created them?

Joseph Derjerh was obviously dead from the debacle last year, but there were a few other patients in the special unit who may have some answers, and I was here to tear this place apart until I knew precisely what Lana was hiding here. How she even came to be anywhere near this place was a mystery, but I had to do one thing at a time.

Ezello stood at the end. Her brown curly hair bounced as she jumped in excitement to see me. "Micah, it's good to see you again."

"You as well, Officer Lavita." She giggled, twirling in her white-robed outfit.

I hadn't noticed before, but now I could see she definitely was not in the usual uniform.

Did she have another undercover assignment?

"I am studying to be a nurse. I am almost there."

I smiled, genuinely happy for her. Lucius didn't know a damn thing about any of them, so he just grinned and high-fived her. She laughed but returned the kind gesture.

"What are you hoping to find with this special unit?" she pondered aloud.

I shrugged, sighing and hoping this wasn't a lost cause.

"Honestly, I hope to get some damn answers. A friend led me here. And I want to know why."

Ezello politely smiled at my riddles, but instead of needling me further with a conversation I clearly didn't know how to have, she unlocked the heavy door and pushed it open.

The walls were lined with metal, not glass like the other areas. It was impossible to see anyone who might be inside.

"Uh…" I cleared my throat. "I need to speak with the prisoners that are able to form sentences. That may narrow it down."

Ezello laughed and shrugged her shoulders. "Well, that leaves two cells, Quinn. The ones at the very back."

I felt my hands get clammy, the realization that Lana's secrets could be told by the prisoners as long as I spoke the right words.

Ezello led all of us down to the end of the hallway and reached for a paper by the door. "This patient is named Kristiyan, aka Christian. He is a sadist and has ertophilia. Please be careful."

I swallowed a lump, hoping the sadist would speak to me about Lana. Ezello unlocked the door, and inside the room was… nothing. Ezello and Goliath looked around, confused and concerned.

On the walls, written over and over, was one word. "Mother."

Confused even further, Ezello left to figure out where the patient had been taken to while Goliath continued down the hall to the very last door.

"Uh, this one doesn't have a name," he said, confused. "It says, 'Thank you, Katerina. I owe you my happiness.' "

Katerina was a nurse who was killed in the massacre of Hospital Twelve. The poor nurse had been eaten alive.

Was she someone connected to Lana?

"What was the nurse? Who was her family? Where did she come from?"

Goliath held up his hands in surrender at my firing questions. I calmed my breath and tried to speak again, slower.

"Did Katerina know a Svetlana?" I waited, holding my breath while Goliath scratched his head and thought about what he knew.

"I don't know, man," he said finally. "I am sorry, Micah, but all I know is Katerina was Russian like this dude you brought."

"Who cares for this patient since Katerina died?" I asked.

Goliath looked at the sheet again. "Uh…Billy. But the man turned up dead a few days ago."

My eyes widened, "No one has cared for this patient for two days?"

Ezello looked upset. "I don't understand how that would

happen. I always do rotations. I mean...These cells were always taken care of, and I didn't think to—"

Goliath yanked his girl into his body, smoothing her face and telling her it wasn't her fault. It was still weird seeing the tallest fucker I had ever known in my life love someone that went up to his balls.

My blood chilled in my veins, the ash necklace practically burning in my hands.

"This is it," I said confidently, centering myself on knowing this patient would learn the secrets of Lana.

"Well then, without further ado..." Goliath leaned down and unlocked the door.

It was quiet, and I saw a small form kneeling by the bed. Her back was to us, and her hair was a beautiful orangish red. The hair my sister had...I felt a pit form in my stomach, the others staying behind as I walked forward, an eerie feeling growing with each step.

"Hello..." I said softly. "I'm sorry to bother you, I—"

The woman spun around. Her rosy, freckled cheeks and big blue eyes stared up into mine. I felt my throat close up.

"M-Micaiah?"

My mouth fell open. My knees hit the padded floor, and my brain fogged with disbelief.

No. It couldn't be.

"Penn..."

Penelope

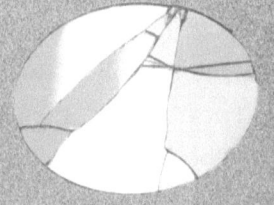

Chapter 40

My brother stared into my eyes—all these years, all this time trapped in these walls. And now he was here. Tears flooded my eyes, blurring my vision, and I ignored the gasps and chatter behind him of strangers to embrace my big brother. He held me so tight that I couldn't breathe, but I withstood it to feel his love.

I'd missed him so much.

I'd never dreamed I would see him again. I had been dragged across the world and then some, but now I was back in my brother's arms.

"I don't understand, Penelope," he said, pulling me backward from him to look at me. "How is this possible? How are you alive?"

The story of my life was painful—so much running, death, and pain. I didn't want to talk about that now. I wanted to talk about his life—what he grew up to be. I could see a lanyard around his neck, and his name next to the word 'detective' was a shock and also somehow not a surprise at all.

"Get her the fuck out of here. Now," Micah barked, his demanding tone snapping people into confused action.

An unnaturally tall man came to me, unlocking the chains that caged me for so long.

The weight of those chains falling to the floor felt like I was going to fall with them. They had become part of me.

Micah helped my wobbling form, and my legs felt like a newborn deer. I was never let out of here. I had been given meals for years, but Lana and Katerina were my only friends. Katerina had died trying to free me during the massacre. I hadn't seen Lana in so long, and Kristiyan...

I stared over at the dark-haired male by the door. He looked so much like Kristiyan that I nearly thought it was him when they arrived, but everyone called him Lucius.

I relied on spying and listening to gossip through the walls to gain knowledge. My only means of communication was speaking to the echoes of those voices. Maybe I had gone truly insane over the years of being imprisoned here.

"But wait...How do you know Lana? Do you know her secret?"

I chewed my lip, trying to figure out why Lana would have finally returned my brother to me, unless....

"Is she dead?" I said, my voice sounding weird to my ears.

I held my hands over my ears, the noise and sound overwhelming from all the people talking by the door.

"Guys! Please leave. You are making me...my sister anxious."

Maybe the words also sounded weird to him, too? He shook his head and looked at me again. The others mumbled apologies and left, leaving the door ajar.

Was I really free?

Was this some twisted dream?

"Is Lana okay?" I asked again, my fear and sadness heightened. I always felt for her. I couldn't hate my only friend. What happened hadn't been her fault. To blame a child for any of it was...barbaric.

Lana had found me. When I had escaped the fire, I had lived on the streets, hitchhiking my way back to America by giving deals to shady truck drivers. Once I got here, it took some time to find my old family home.

New families had grown and filled the void mine had left. Lana had lived next door, and it was after searching her home and family there that Lana took me off the streets in the middle of the night.

She had a job in the police then, and after forcing me to get clean and be off drugs and shaping me into a human being again, she locked me in here.

"I have to protect him," I said out loud, my thoughts and realities melding into one.

"Protect who? What do you know of Lana?"

"She's...I know her son," I said.

I knew my brother would protect him from his evil father... maybe he could protect me, too.

"Her...what?" Mickey was up and pacing. "Mickey? How do you know Lana?"

My brother shook his head. He had too much to say, too. I nodded my understanding, just so happy I was staring into my brother's eyes again, hearing his deep voice and feeling his warm hugs.

"I love you, Micah. I am so sorry."

My tears wet his shirt, and he hugged me tighter.

"Listen to me, Penn. I will never, ever let anything happen to you again. I am so sorry about what you have gone through...I will learn everything you have endured, and I hope I can help you heal with more time. I love you so much."

WE WERE SOMEWHERE IN THE COUNTRY, AND I HAD TO ADMIT I FELT like a child being babysat. Micah was taking me to stay with some friends of his. He said he didn't exactly have a place he stayed at long for now. It was so far into the country.

I knew what cars were, but the vibrations and the strange noises were giving me panic attacks. It took me a few hours to finally settle into the rhythm and accept wherever I was being taken.

Micah came to a gravel road, the crunching and bumping making me close my eyes and ears and wait for it to stop. After a few minutes, it was smooth, and my brother was gently squeezing my arm.

"We're here, Penn."

Here?

I looked out the window. A big, beautiful house was coated in white powdery snow. The chill of the cold made me think of those years on the streets, and I pulled my coat onto my body more—that feeling of sinking into my memories was going to swallow me whole.

"Okay..." I said, following his big feet to where we stood on a rug outside a porch.

The rug said: "Welcome! Ring the doorbell, and our cats are naked."

I found that odd and pondered the meaning when a sweet feminine voice rang out of the opening door.

"Hello! We are so excited to see you. Kojec is thrilled to meet his new roomie." I smiled, feeling odd, and looked at the tiny infant in the woman's arms.

I had never really seen babies except on TV or reading about them. They looked so breakable.

"Come on in out of the cold! Psy is grilling out back. The idiot never listens to weather channels."

Micah laughed in his warm, melodic tone and kindly took my

jacket and boots from me. I shifted my feet from side to side, not really knowing what to say. Micah saw a head bobbing from the patio door and took off in the direction where male laughter and jeering were heard behind the door.

The woman smiled warmly at me, her little baby yanking her hair to a point I assumed hurt, but the woman didn't seem to mind. She bounced the child in her arms and whispered sweet words to him.

"I am Lisa, by the way," she said. "You have had such a long journey, Hun. Why don't you take a seat?"

I looked at her gesture of the inviting couch behind me. A lit fireplace was beside it, and the warmth made me want to curl up on the rug in front of it.

"Very well. Nice to meet you, Lisa."

We sat in silence—the crackling of the fire, the only sound, and the muffled conversations of the men.

The baby made strange noises. From what end of its body, I wasn't sure. Lisa giggled, eyeing my scrutiny of her young.

"Want to hold him?" she preened, already getting up and plopping next to me.

My eyes bugged out of my head, and I swallowed. "Uh, I don't think that's a good idea."

My words were muted with her fussing as she adjusted the infant onto my lap in my arms.

It smelled like some kind of lotion, and the skin was so squishy.

"Aww... you're a natural," Lisa beamed.

I looked at her, fear coursing through my veins. It was cute, but I didn't want to accidentally drop it on the head.

"Kojec, do you have a new friend? Yes, you do have a new friend. Look at you, handsome boy!"

The volume of the mother made me cringe, and I tried to maintain my hold on her child as she cooed at it like a dog.

Micah and his friends emerged with steaks and hamburgers

from the back door, and when Micah spied my face, he sheepishly grinned, handing off the food tray to his friend and walking over to me.

"Let me get a turn with this cutie pie," he said, saving me by taking the babe from my shaking arms.

He was so good with it, making the baby squeal with laughter and pull his curls without fuss. It just looked at me like I was an alien. That was okay. I felt like one most days.

Even with it being a week after finally leaving that asylum, I didn't feel...normal.

Maybe I never would.

Micah Quinn

Chapter 41

As I walked out the door, knowing I left my sister with my dearest friend, I reminded myself she was going to be safe, and this was the best thing for her. It felt so hard because I just got her back after so many years, not even knowing she was alive.

I gripped the steering wheel, angry and hurting at all the fucked up shit that had happened in such a short time. I pressed the button on my car, dialing Phoenix on a video chat. She answered, and seeming to know what I needed, she smiled at me and switched the camera around to my sleeping Little Ghost.

I broke down, smashing the fucking steering wheel over and over again. My hands bled from the force, and the stupid material busted from the abuse. My badge fell in my lap from the front visor, my bleeding hands dripping onto the open leather. My name was smeared in blood.

"Fuck!" I screamed, hanging my head.

Phoenix didn't move the camera, but I knew she could see me. My Little Ghost watched my tantrum in her dreams.

I felt ashamed. So often, I lost control with her. Her beauty, wit, and annoying charm were always my catalyst.

"I am sorry, Phoenix. I…"

The camera switched to my old partner. She had tears in her eyes but didn't shame me for letting my tears fall or mention what she'd just witnessed. Instead, she smiled at me and made small talk about Penelope.

"She is okay. I think she likes Lisa. She doesn't know what to do with that baby."

It felt weird to laugh with my knuckles still bleeding from my outburst moments ago, but it was becoming clear that was a pattern in my fucking life.

"Does anyone know what to do with those little squishies? I mean, hey, they are cute, but they freak out over nothing and create toxic waste in their diapers."

I laughed harder. My old friend always had a way of cheering me up. I realized I missed working with her. It had been so long since I'd done something normal. A simple fucking case with a clear answer. Nothing had been simple since finding Ivy in that cage.

"Can I ask you something?" I didn't realize I even said anything aloud until she nodded.

"Do you ever miss working cases?"

Now, her eyes were brimming with tears again. "Honestly, I don't know. I feel like I have done so much. I have brought justice in so many different ways, too."

I ignored that, knowing she meant by taking it into her own hands. I wasn't so prideful that I would call her out on that.

"But I do miss being part of the team. You and Ally, mostly. How is she? Did Bleu have his baby?"

She looked beautiful when she was like this, expressive and giddy.

"Bleu had a little girl. I went to a picnic last fall with them. That little one has him wrapped around her finger. Ally is moving up in her career. She's still doing forensics, but I think she's going to be working with the FBI or CSI."

She nodded. We always partnered up, and things would work bigger and better. Her intelligence was well past what any paycheck from Rochester could offer. It still made me sad to know we would be losing her, though.

"I think I have some information from some calls made to the police." I stilled. The direction of the conversation veered hard and gave me whiplash.

"What did you hear?" I whispered, afraid I would go back into a fit if I spoke too loud.

She chewed on his pouty bottom lip, contemplating whether I was sane enough to take this on. I guessed.

"There is chatter surrounding the docks. A witness said some shady guys were going back and forth toward the old bridge…"

I completely blanked, her voice lulling in the background. "They are taking someone else."

She nodded hesitantly.

"I think so. They could be staking out the way to move the victim, but the pattern they've shown in the past is those tunnels were being used as if they were leading them somewhere."

My mind flashed to the last time I had been in those tunnels, and I shook my head, trying to dislodge those memories.

"I am on my way. When does it say the deputy will get there?" I asked.

Phoenix was silent, not meeting my eyes, as I was cleaning up and trying to wrap my knuckles with an old shirt in my gym bag. Starting up the car, I finally drove on gravel roads.

"They aren't sending anyone," she said finally, and I nearly crashed my car.

"Excuse me? Why the fuck not?" I didn't have to ask. I knew the answer.

No proof. I growled at hearing the confirmation. Such a broken fucking system.

AFTER LEAVING THE AIRPORT, I HAD TO TAKE A PRIVATE TAXI. I wasn't driving from Texas, and this was an urgent matter. Upon arrival, I tipped the driver and made my way down the steps into the darkness under King's Bridge.

This place used to be flooded with homeless individuals, but now, the space was littered with people with addictions and dangerous individuals waiting to rob and gut you for anything you had.

I kept my hand on my gun, watching the damp walls for any sign of movement. My other hand guided me with my flashlight. The tunnels were past the abandoned docks, but I wanted to search every part of this fucking place. If there was even one innocent girl here, I would find her.

I didn't hear or see anyone. The addicts were gone, their needles and baggies left abandoned like something or someone scared them away. Getting a feeling of unease, I continued to the spot where I had last felt Ivy's body. Her curves were trapped under me on this pipe, her delicate wrists handcuffed.

I shook my head. Thoughts like that were not going to be helpful in the slightest.

The tunnels were darker than usual. The moon was in a different phase tonight that didn't allow much light to stream in from the cracks above.

Echos of the dripping water moved about the space. I knew the tunnels went all over, including under the river by the docks. By the deep, earthy smell and my ears popping, I could tell I was lower than I had been previously.

I had to detour, not wanting to go to that specific tunnel where I was...

No good would come of me getting wrapped in my head. I didn't know If I could escape the prison of my memories, and time was of the essence. My cell phone light was flickering, and the signal was receiving zero to very little connection.

I stopped when I heard whispers from the tunnel ahead, killing the light and hiding behind a crevice of the rock wall.

"God, you moron. Now we got to find a new one! Alyosha is already fucking livid that we lost Lana. You were supposed to pop the cop, not his fucking mistress."

My blood ran cold.

I was the target, and Lana suffered.

"Listen, I didn't fucking mean to do it. It's hard as fuck to see out of those holes, and Lana blocked the pretty boy when I missed the first time. She asked for it!"

I heard a smack and wished it was my hands doing the action.

"Ow! What was that for?"

I heard a sigh in the darkness, which led to a small lamp-like light flickering ahead of me.

"I liked to fuck that one. She wasn't mousy and didn't fight me like the other bitches. She took all I gave to her. Her skin color was perfect for blackening, too. I had a game to see how purple I could make her. Fucking rainbow colors with all my marks."

I felt my teeth nearly crack. The knowledge of the mistreatment done to Lana being spoken about with laughter and pride...It made me see red, but I kept moving forward.

Two men...

Pulling my handcuffs out of my belt, I carefully gripped them and walked toward the two male assholes I could now see. Holding my hand over my mouth, I attempted to stifle the roar of anger begging to escape from my gut.

The lamp illuminated a woman. Her body was lying on the ground, her legs spread apart, and blood coated the ground below her. Her clothes were torn from her.

I was too late.

Fueled by anger at her fate, I charged forward, smashing one of the rapist-murderers into the cavern wall, knocking him out cold.

The other man gasped and dodged my blows, his fists blocking his face.

"Fucking scum bags," I spat, finding an opening and taking it, smashing the man in the ribs and bringing him down. Wrenching his arms behind him, I slammed my knee into the back of his, pinning his legs down.

"Fuck you!" he screeched, trying to break my grip.

I managed to click one cuff painfully tight. "Ow! Fuck off, you Svin'ya!"

The name hurt because only my Little Ghost would call me that—her Pig. Grabbing the other arm and smashing the man's face into the ground of the damp cave, I clicked the other cuff closed.

I reached for my phone to call this in.

Underneath my knee, the man spoke again, but his words made me freeze.

"Oh, you are the cop, our pretty princess fucked, aren't you? I heard she's a sleeping beauty now, right? Careful, big boy, we may follow you to go see her. We'll be sure to wake her up with our cocks, don't worry."

His sadistic smile broke something inside me.

The realization that these men threatened my Little Ghost while she was helpless in that fucking bed. They killed the woman lying on the cavern floor, and god only knows how many others there were. If I took them into the department, they would likely see bars for a few months, if that...and that was if Alyosha didn't bail them out before they even saw a court date.

"It's not enough," I said.

The sickening truth staring me in the face was that I was working for a different kind of evil—one that only cared about money, not justice. The department didn't care if murderers actually got what they deserved. All these sadists deserved was the death they brought.

"Say their names," I demanded to the man below me.

Confusion painted his features, and my anger spiked. I twisted his neck off the ground to face the dead female on the ground.

"Her. Say her fucking name." The man whimpered at the awkward angle of his frail neck and the pressure on his back from my knees.

"I don't know the bitch's name." He spat, his voice shaky from the pain and pressure.

Not. Good. Enough.

"Say her fucking name!" I roared at him, standing and dragging the man with me to the female on the ground.

There was a purse by her body, and I took one hand to pick it up and dump the contents on the ground. A shiny pink wallet fell out with lip gloss and other feminine nick-nacks.

Pulling the male up from the ground by his cuffed arms, I opened the wallet to her license. Her smiling face and vibrant eyes were going to be the last thing this fucking waste of space saw.

"Say her name," I repeated, smashing his face with the picture of the girl.

"Fuck! Okay..." he said, blinking and focusing on the picture in my hand. "Kirsten Romali."

That darkness settled in my blood, the image of the female's vacant eyes replacing her vibrant photo.

"Who else," I demanded, smashing the man with his bound arms against the wall, picking him up to my height.

"I don't fucking know all the bitches names that we kill. I don't fucking care!" I pulled him back and smashed harder, the crack in his bones causing him to scream.

"Good, then this makes it easier for me."

I enjoyed every single shriek of pain.

"Bianca! Ariel! Trixie…" He started to sob.

His eyes bounced around the caves. It was as if he was using the space to pull out the memories of the lives he took. I smashed him into the wall again, his head cracking on the stone behind him. He spilled off more names, all girls and women, young and old. He said their names. Each name he spoke was like a soul being freed. I recognized some of them. They were the little girls that died in that fire. Those children are no older than fucking toddlers.

I lost myself more to the darkness, letting it consume me. I welcomed its pull.

"Now hers," I said, watching the blood drip from the man down the wall.

"W-who? I don't know no one else, I swear. Please just take me in."

"Say her name," I said again, my body numb.

Realization dawned on the man that I meant Eilizaveta, and he whimpered his next words. " She ain't dead. Why do I have to say her name?"

"You put her there in the hospital!"

He cringed backward at my volume and opened his mouth, my Little Ghost's name leaving his cracked and bleeding lips.

"Now. Say mine."

Truly confused, he shook his head. "Fucking hell! I didn't do shit to you!"

I felt myself smile. A strange sensation overcame me.

This form of justice feels so…right.

"You will say my name. Because this day, with your cruelty, you have killed a part of me that fucking cared what happened to men like you."

The man paled, tears streaming down his face, mingling with the blood, his fate set in stone within my eyes.

"My name..." I roared, slamming the man down on the ground, walking over, and picking up the other man—the unconscious one. "Is Micaiah Fucking Quinn!"

I slammed the dead weight into the sobbing guy on the ground, their heads smashing together repeatedly. Blood coated my hands, my face, and my badge. Again and again, I said the names of the women and children lost to this world, the bodies under me starting to blur into broken, disfigured shapes.

At some point, I dropped to my knees, exhaustion, pain, and anger—all consuming me.

But, I freed those souls.

I let every single woman and child free from their cages of injustice—the cost...damning my soul to eternal darkness.

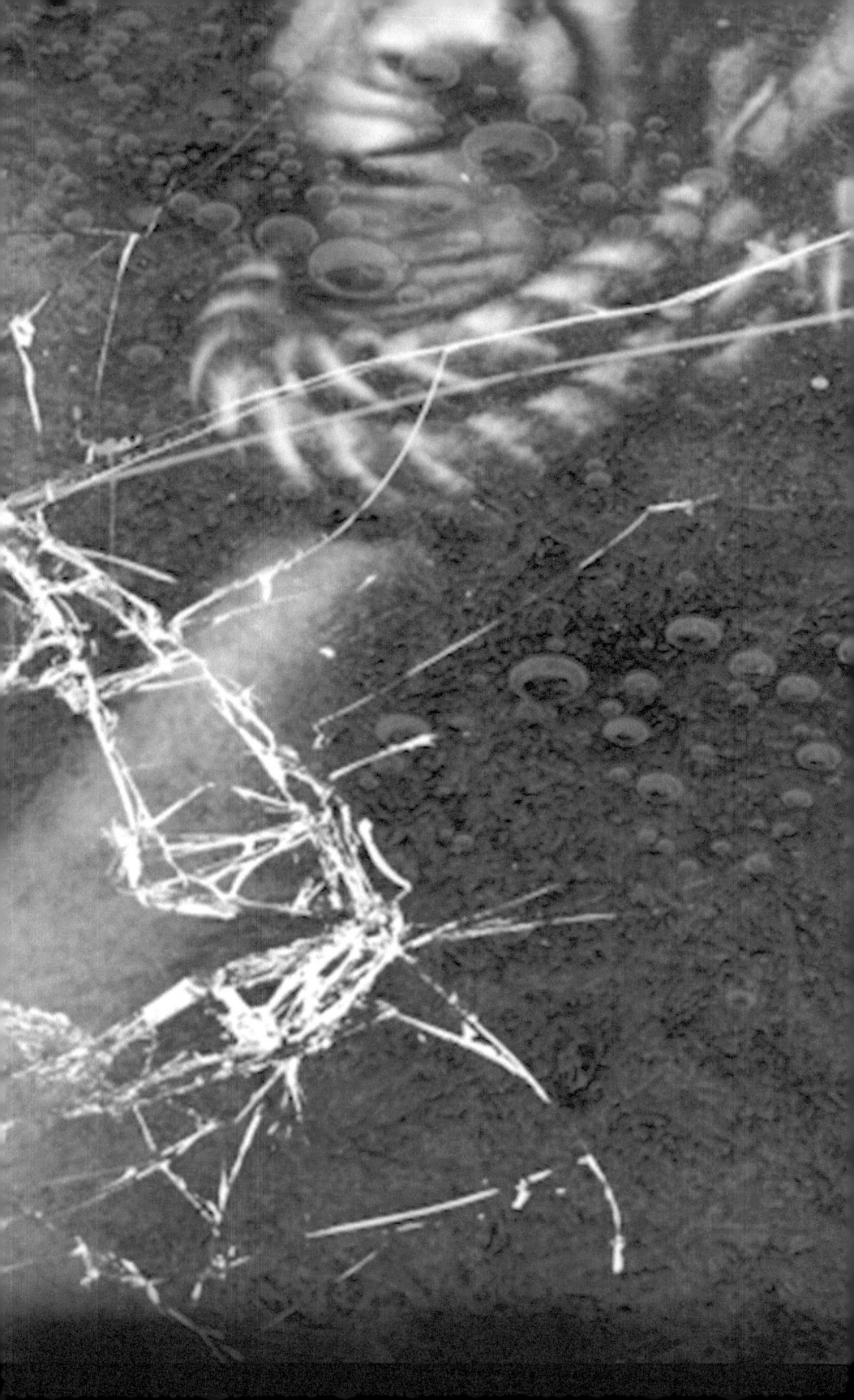

Ivy

Chapter 42

*D*arkness...

　　All I could see was darkness. It reminded me of when I was in that cage.

　　Sometimes, I was left for hours, sometimes weeks. It was okay. The light only brought rough hands and pain. I had come to love it when I was in the dark.

　　But now, I felt trapped. Worse than when I had been in the cage...maybe I never left, and my life was a cruel dream. Micah's voice filtered through the clouds of black, little ringlets of light peeking through with his words.

　　"They said your name, baby girl. I made them say it. They said each and every name of the souls they took. Hundreds of names. Hundreds of souls. I am so sorry, Little Ghost."

　　This voice felt different from Micah's. It was dark, ragged, and distorted. My knight felt...broken.

"They said them all, Little Ghost. Even mine. God help me, I am not savable any more than the ones lost to us."

He was crying. His words warbled with his pain and shook with anger.

What had happened to my knight?

"I don't fucking care anymore. I will use them now. You always said they only used me as a tool to do their bidding. Well, I am done. They can watch the killer they created to destroy them all."

Could he be talking about his career?

"I will use every fucking resource I can squeeze out of them to find every last bastard that hurt you and the others. I will take them all out. Justice. True justice will be met."

Could he mean...

"I always tried not to judge. I tried to see the redemption in people. Believed they fell into a path set out to fail and succumbed to temptation from desperation or pain."

He felt distant. His voice was moving farther and farther away from me, and the light it brought dimmed like a setting sun.

"Now I know it was all a fucking lie. People don't need a reason to be evil. They are sick. Sick in the goddamn brain and aren't wired correctly anymore. Some illnesses can not be cured, and the only way to keep it from spreading is to cull the whole fucking herd."

It hurt to hear my sweet Micah, my knight, talk about such destruction. It hurt to see his light fade so much. This was because of me. I always felt like Micah was blinding me with how bright he shone, but now I realize...

His light was what kept my world from being truly dark.

His voice was still fading, and the pull of darkness took hold of me so strongly that I began to suffocate.

I didn't want to leave him. I needed him to know I was here and would be the light and love he needed.

But all I could feel was him pulling further and further away.

Penelope

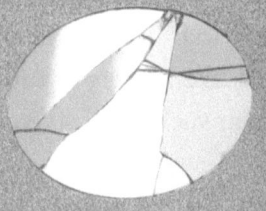

Chapter 43

I folded the sheet in front of me. I was starting to get the hang of these basic tasks, and though most people would hate them, it was fun to put my mind on something. I spent many years staring at blank walls, so using my hands for any task felt invigorating.

I heard the baby cry from afar in his room and waited for Lisa's cooing to come shortly after. She and that baby were so bonded. I never saw much of the father. I didn't even really know his name. He was always working at the bar they owned, and besides the back of his head, our introductions had not gone further than that.

Lisa had become somewhat of a friend. I never dreamed of calling other people friends again, but here I wanted to sneak into the hallway to listen to the beautiful lullaby she always sang to Kojec.

I tried humming the song and learning the lyrics and the

melody by looking it up online. Technology was still weird to me. Russia was not all that different than America, but in the asylum, we weren't even allowed shoelaces, so I barely knew how to tie my shoes, and I used the internet much less.

The baby continued to cry, and I looked at my door in confusion. Lisa never let that little thing sniffle longer than a few seconds, and it sounded like he was in full hiccupy wails. It made me uncomfortable to hear such shrill screams.

It reminded me of…

I shook my head, my painful memories of that fire needing to stay buried with the dead.

"Lisa?" I called out, cracking open my door a fraction and peeking my head out of the hallway.

No response, but that unnerving wailing. I covered my ears, the overstimulation quickly getting to me.

Fighting with my need to retreat and my nature to help, I pushed my way out of the door.

There wasn't noise in the house. The Brodens were likely asleep before their newborn woke them. It made sense…but why did I feel like I was going to puke?

I took slow steps forward, running my fingertips along the wall of the hallway, trying to steady my heart and my breathing as that screaming got louder and louder.

"Lisa?" I called again, reaching the door to the baby's nursery. "You okay?"

The room was dark, only moonlight showing from the open window. It was cold in here, and I wasn't an expert on babies, but I was sure cold weather wasn't good for them.

I walked over to Kojec's crib, and that awful sound was at an all-time high. I tripped over something in the darkness and went down to the ground. The crib rocked, and the startled baby cried even harder. I pushed myself from the ground, sitting on my knees and rubbing my foot from the ache.

The drapes from the window blew from a gust of wind, and the light from the moon altered its path, streaming in and landing at my feet.

I screamed.

Lisa lay at my feet. Her body contorted and crumpled in a heap.

"Oh god, Lisa..." I said over the wailing of the baby, flipping her over and squinting in the dim lighting.

My blood froze in my veins. Lisa's body felt cold, and I knew what death felt like. I had held too many dead bodies in my arms and was forced to say goodbye to souls that were taken way too soon, from little girls barely older than Kojec to people older than me.

My hands patted blindly on her body, looking for her chest or her neck to check her pulse, but when my hands moved forward to find her pulse, they fell to the floor into a pool of thick, cold liquid.

Her head...her head was missing.

I vomited. The steak dinner Lisa had made for me exited my body until nothing was left to heave.

That scream echoed in my head. I couldn't make out the words to say, the shock seizing my body. I crawled toward the crib, pulling myself up to shaky legs.

Little Kojec was lying in his crib, his wailing mouth open wide as he screamed for his fallen mother. Tears blurred my vision as I reached out for the little boy, my body sagging to the ground when he was in my arms.

I rocked him back and forth, trying to mimic his mother's lullaby. "Shhh. I am here, Kojec...I...I am trying. I don't know what to do. I am so sorry." I held that baby, rocking and rocking and rocking. I continued his mother's lullaby even long after his cries settled and his eyes closed again to dream.

I didn't let go of him even when the police arrived. I didn't know how they knew to come and find...Lisa.

"Miss? We need to take the body."

Lisa was nothing more than a body in a bag beside me—a headless body in a bag. I was covered in her blood. Her son in my arms was tainted with the dulling red, thick blood.

His father came back home at that moment, and his agony-filled roars were heard even outside the house as a police officer tried to soothe him.

He stormed forward, smashing into the room and waking the baby in my arms.

"What the fuck happened..." he screamed at me. I could see his arms shaking me, but I was overly numb and had been holding this little baby for hours. I couldn't feel anything anymore.

The baby cried, piercing my ears, and the flashing memories of blood and the moonlight shining on Lisa's cold body filled my mind.

I closed my eyes, rocking the baby again, singing the lullaby.

"What's wrong with her?" he barked, but I kept my eyes closed.

"We aren't sure, sir. She was in here when we got a call about screams from the neighborhood. No one has been able to question her."

Psy growled, smashing his hands against the crib I laid against.

I opened my eyes to see the man break. He fell to his knees, kneeling in the blood of his wife.

"No...you aren't supposed to leave me, Lis." He sobbed, his body shaking so much I could feel the vibrations.

"You promised you wouldn't leave my pathetic ass. You helped me find something to live for again...After so long of not wanting to wake up, you gave me a fucking reason to need to—and now... and now you leave me?"

I looked down at the mirror image of the woman taken away and the man beside me. The baby was chewing on his hand, watching his father break. There was love in his eyes. He didn't understand. He only knew he loved his dad.

I hugged the baby, giving his little cheek a nuzzle before looking at the guy beside me.

"Here. He needs you just as much as you need him." My words sounded weird to my ears, hoarse from the hours of singing and jittery with the fear I still felt.

Psy looked over to his smiling baby, reaching his arms wide for him...but stopped and turned away.

"No," he said, backing away from us and cowering in the corner of the room. "No. I can't. Lisa is the—" His voice broke. "Was...Lisa was the parent. I can't be anything but damaging to him."

I lowered the baby back down into my arms, trying to distract him with my finger as he continued to reach for his crying father.

"I can't, little doll. I can't be anything to him. I can't be anything to anyone. When Lisa died, she may as well have taken my soul with her."

Micah Quinn

Chapter 44

I grunted, pushing my back and arm muscles to the max with the weight. Sighing, I lifted it back onto the weight bench in my living room.

My phone rang, buzzing, and moving it across the chair it was sitting on, but I ignored it.

My sister was probably calling me to tell me she liked changing dirty diapers. It was the best decision to take her to Lisa and Psy's place.

Not only did I know she was safe there, but she was slowly starting to enjoy herself. The truth was that deep down, I was happy she wasn't near me. I missed my sister so much, but what I needed to do was not something I ever wanted her to witness.

I got up from the weight bench, wiping my brow with my towel.

The hospital here was a lot better. I appreciated that they

allowed me to move Ivy to Texas. It was much easier to keep an eye on Penn when I didn't need a plane ride to do it.

That being said, I needed a better gym at my apartment. I hated leaving Ivy. I knew that she was safe at the hospital, but I couldn't relax. I knew what I had to do, and boring a hole in the floor from pacing in Ivy's space was not going to help her wake up.

If anything ever would...

I shook my head, irritation and anger fueling my blood, as I made my way back to my bathroom. Stripping from the sweaty clothes, I turned on the shower. Once under the spray, I allowed the water to wash away my doubts and troubles. The heat unbound my used muscles.

A sound in the distance caught my attention: a thunking noise and then some creaking.

Did someone open my door?

I reached for my towel on the rack outside and let the shower continue to pour down the drain.

I always kept my gun near me, and I grabbed it off the sink's counter, ducking out of the bathroom door and using a tactile pose to make my way to the door unseen.

It was silent. The only sound I could hear was the shower, my TV low in the background, and the bubbler of the fish tank in the dining area.

"Hello?" I called out, feigning a disarmed approach.

I was in the kitchen, leaning against the wall. Behind it was the section that was the front door, living room, and gym.

I took a breath and flipped around the corner with my gun poised at the door.

I paused.

No one was around, but a box was at the foot of the door.

I stared at the box, a feeling of unease settling in my gut. It looked like a shoe box of some sort, and it was inside a plastic bag.

Had the teenagers of the building decided to play a trick on me?

This apartment complex was in the slums. I only rented it because it was a few minutes from the hospital, and the commute to see my Little Ghost was much easier.

I walked forward, not positioning my stance or my gun away from the door.

I was right in front of the box, and I looked down. The bag was holding a sagging cardboard shoebox. It was a red box with a picture of some white shoes on top.

There looked to be a note nailed to the box, written in red writing, "Detective."

Bile rose in my throat. Reaching down, I pulled the note free of the rusted nail. It smelled like iron.

Was that from the nail?

In scrawled black handwriting, I read the words.

DEAR DETECTIVE,

I AM A MAN OF FAIRNESS AND EQUALITY. SINCE YOU HAVE TAKEN NOT ONLY MY DAUGHTER AND LED TO THE DEMISE OF MY MISTRESS, I FOUND IT WAS TIME TO RETURN THE BALANCE BACK TO AN EQUAL PLAYING FIELD. ENJOY MY GIFT. I HAVE OTHER ENGAGEMENTS.

OR, I WOULD HAVE DELIVERED THIS PERSONALLY.

WILL THE SWEET-HEARTED COP CHOOSE HIS PAST...OR HIS PRESENT?

P.S. I WAS UNABLE TO DELIVER THIS...

MESSAGE TO HER FOR NOW, SO DO SAY HELLO FOR ME. TO MY DEAREST PENELOPE. HOW I MISS HER TASTE.

—AP

MY HANDS MOVED ON THEIR OWN, SHAKING WITH THE NOTE IN THEIR grip. Not knowing what I would find in this box was horrible, but the realization that whatever it was...it was my fault... that was torture.

The smell rose to me as I used the gun's muzzle to throw off the lid.

I coughed and covered my nose at the sight before me—Lisa's frozen terror, permanently printed into her eyes on her severed head, stared back at me.

I had known Lisa and Psy for years. They were my only friends.

My past...

I looked out the window, the hospital within eyesight from the apartment, and that sick feeling lurched inside my gut.

My present...

I took off in a sprint. My legs moved on their own as I ran with everything I had in me to reach the hospital. The blocks were a blur. The chattering and gasps flew by me as I ran toward my Little Ghost at breakneck speed.

I nearly took out a few nurses when I rounded the corner of the alley to the hospital. They were on a smoke break. Slamming into the front desk, the receptionist recognized me from my weeks here.

"Detective Quinn? Is everything okay?" she said, standing from her seat and dropping the phone from her hand to the receiver.

"No," I said, my voice ragged, completely out of breath and sweating all over the floor and desk.

Glancing down was when I realized I was still in a fucking towel. It didn't matter. Nothing did except getting to Ivy.

"Buzz..." I breathed. "Me up. Ivy. Floor. Now. please."

The startled woman fumbled with the switch, and when she hit the button, I took off again into a sprint through the door and up the staircase to the fifth-floor suites. I ignored everyone when I finally got to her floor, brushing past them and making my way straight for the room—five eight two.

As I reached the door to her room, I could have sworn I saw a hooded man heading for the elevator in the distance, some needle in his grip. Shaking my head, I walked inside the room. Lucius stood there—Phoenix at his side. I stepped forward, my heart beating out of my chest, my towel hanging on for dear life, and my soul shattering inside me.

A doctor was standing beside Ivy's bed, her hand shutting off the monitor by her side. A continuous tone sounded in my ears before the light on the screen turned black.

Lucius wasn't speaking. His eyes were open, not leaving his sister's bedside. Tears were cascading down his face as Phoenix cried into his shirt. My world became blurry, and everything looked like it was in slow motion. The doctor gave us all a sad smile and reached down to my Little Ghost's blanket.

I stared unblinking at her. Her chest wasn't moving. Her pouty lips looked pale, and her ivory skin looked...gray.

"Ivy? Baby?"

The doctor pulled the sheet slowly upward until my Little Ghost was covered with the material. I dropped to my knees, my entire world crashing around me. The disbelief and fear in my voice were all I could hear as the sobs began.

"Ivy...Little Ghost. No, you can't run from me anymore," I said, my sobs making my chest hurt, my heart feeling as though it was truly breaking inside my chest.

"You can't...run anymore. I...love you, Eilizaveta. I love you. I'm sorry. You didn't need to run from me. I would've accepted you."

Lucius approached me and reached out to me with his blood-symbol tattooed hand.

I stared at it, my numb body accepting the gesture and being hefted up into something I never dreamed of from my Little Ghost's lethal asshole of a brother—a hug.

The dangerous man held me up. My legs felt like they were going to give, and this man, her brother-her twin, kept me up on my feet, bearing the weight of my crushed soul.

Phoenix walked over, linking her arm under mine, taking some of my weight from her lover.

That's what partners are supposed to do...

I thought to myself, staring past them to that white sheet.

I should have let her lean on me, taken some weight off her shoulders.

My Little Ghost went through too much. She'd been torn apart body, mind, and soul. She took on the burden alone to give those girls the justice the system never did. She took on that darkness... and I shunned her for it.

I forced her to bear the weight of it alone.

She was gone because I...I couldn't accept her for who she was.

The realization shattered my heart more, and that weight brought me back to the ground, the couple's capacity to withstand my grief breaking me. This was my fault. Ivy was gone...because I wasn't there to be her prince. I wasn't there to be the hero she needed. I was too focused on saving everyone else, and the one person I would give up all the lives I rescued for, had needed saving.

"I...failed you, Little Ghost. You told me you didn't need a hero, that everyone was using me. You were right. You wanted me to embrace my darkness. Well, my love..." I dropped to the floor and crawled my way to her until I was cradling my Little Ghost in my arms.

"I feel nothing but darkness now. Without you...I'm...just a void. I don't see any light. I held onto my humanity because I wanted to make you proud...but now. I see only death. Darkness. I am going to find him, Eilizaveta. I am going to drain your father of all the blood he has spilled. I will nourish the flowers on your grave with his life's last drop. I am not a hero. Maybe I never was."

I looked down at my gun. The number of bullets in the magazine was only two.

"One of these is for that monster, baby girl. I will see to it he eats this fucking bullet."

I let the tears fall on her face as I rocked her, kissing her cold cheeks.

"The other one..." I said carefully, closing my eyes with my resolve. "Is for me."

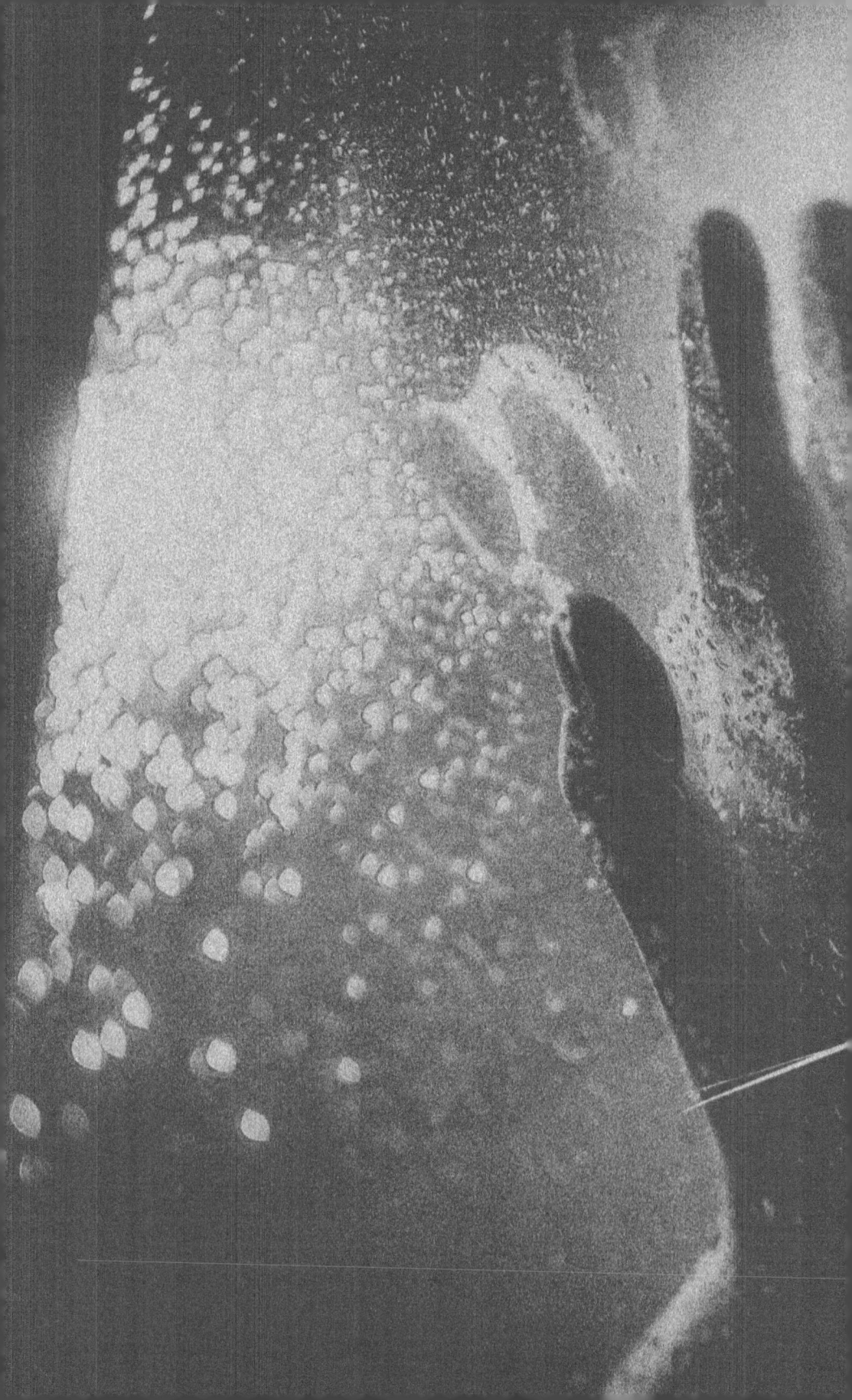

Penelope

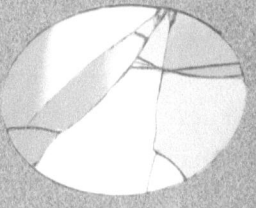

Chapter 45

I adjusted the baby in the carrier. His sleeping head was a wobbly accident waiting to happen. I held my hand over his bald head and rocked back and forth.

My brother stood beside me…well, the shell of my brother stood beside me. Mickey hadn't been the same since the woman he loved died. I didn't know how to help him.

I linked my arm to his, leaning onto his shoulder and trying to avoid the rain.

The priest spoke about loss and grief, and it broke my heart to see both men feel this so deeply.

Psy and Micah had been best friends for so long, and today, they held each other up while they stood in front of the people, standing by their lost loves' caskets.

The rain was relentless as it poured onto us. The dirt created a slippery mud that had everyone sinking. The priest continued over the thunder, and the men looked forward like there was nothing in the world but their loved ones.

A tear fell free from my eyes, and I turned my head to avoid the salty drop from slipping onto the sleeping child's head.

Lisa's picture was at the front, her smiling face and beautiful features shining bright. Beside her portrait was another woman's picture.

This woman looked ethereal and breathtaking.

She had dark, straight hair and pale white skin that contrasted her hard-edged golden eyes. The names looped on a sheet written on the adjoining frames. 'Lisa Broden and Eilizaveta Vasiliev.'

Both beautiful women, both taken way too soon.

I felt horrible that I felt so numb to death. My brother was mourning the woman he loved, and despite my best efforts, I couldn't offer the comfort I wanted. He quite literally found the deceased body of his best friend's wife beside him.

Psy's wife, Lisa, had been so kind to me. It was so...strange seeing a funeral. I couldn't help but wonder if they would want this in their next lives.

I know I sure didn't.

When I died, I didn't want people crying about me no longer being with them. Well, Micaiah had shed enough tears. I just wanted to see him smile.

He was all I really had.

"Now we ask the beloved of the dearly departed to speak their final words of goodbye," the priest said, stepping down from the platform. He offered a hand to the two strong men who looked so weak at this moment.

Psy cleared his throat and linked arms with Micah, the two friends leaning on one another as they mounted the steps one at a time.

Psy was first. He leaned down and kissed the coffin, where his wife's body lay...in pieces.

"Lis...I am truly lost. I don't know what to do without you and probably never will. You are truly my everything, and with your burial..., my happiness and purpose are buried, too. I love you."

Sniffling and active crying surrounded me, and I looked at the faces of everyone and the grief they showed for the deceased. I rocked the baby, whispering his lullaby softly to him.

My brother was next. He walked up to the woman in the casket. Her dark hair fanned out, and her body wrapped in a white dress that contrasted her hair.

Micah looked over his shoulder and waved to a man standing away from everyone by a tree.

The man walked forward, joining Micah on the stage. He looked dangerous, and every bit of the markings on his body told stories about his past.

I wondered how much this man had witnessed. He didn't act like the others here. His face was mostly covered in a hood, no umbrella, letting the rain soak his dark hair.

He looked so much like the woman in the casket, and it made me wonder if they were related.

"*Spokoynoy nochi, sestra*...Sleep well, sister," he said, a thick Russian accent coating his tongue.

With that, he dropped a rose on her body and walked away from the platform, seeming to disappear in the foggy night around us. Micah walked forward, his body visibly shaking as he reached for her hand.

"I won't say goodbye," he said softly, putting a folded paper heart in her hand. "I won't say goodnight." He pressed a kiss on her forehead. "I will only say one thing to you, my Little Ghost." I waited for his words, but he spoke so softly that it was impossible to hear. It sounded something like, "See you soon."

I waited for Mickey to walk back down to the rest of us, but he just stayed up there, staring at the unmoving chest of the woman he loved. Why did the world have to be so cruel? So much death and meaningless pain for nothing.

"Fuck you," I whispered out loud, getting some stares from the people beside me.

Awkwardness radiated throughout my body because of this poofy black dress, and it was making my legs itch. It was hard to keep Kojec asleep with the rumbling sounds of the thunder and rain overhead.

I must protect this baby at all costs.

I had a lot in common with Kojec. We were both new to the world around us. Everything sounded too loud, and all the senses God gave us felt like a cruel punishment. I refrained from putting my hands over my ears and sang the lullaby again, feeling the vibration in my chest as I softly hummed the words.

Psy walked down the steps, his boots sinking into the mud the minute he hit the ground. He was the only one of us here dressed comfortably. I admired that. I felt so weird like I wanted to scratch my skin off.

Lisa had told me leggings were a way to snatch a man, and as I was sheltered or…caged my whole life, I definitely didn't want to wear them now.

I was happy with the idea of no man ever touching me for the rest of my life. The proximity of being so close to family members and friends in suits felt like too much.

Dizziness hit me as my breathing picked up, and the vision in front of me looked like I was peering through a magnifying glass. Psy was near me, his tanned, rough features became completely blurred.

"Whoa!" My entire body had con-caved around the baby in my arms. The next thing I knew, I was staring up at multiplying clouds that refused to steady.

Thump, thump, thump.

At least my heartbeat meant I was alive.

"Little doll? Are you okay?" The words were weird, as if they were spoken to me while I was underwater.

Oh god, Kojec.

"B-Baby?" I stuttered, reaching for the little babe in my arms.

Kojec stirred under my exploration, annoyed at being disturbed. I sighed, and the fuzziness of the clouds and my heart beating lessened in my ears.

Psy's face came into full view, and I blinked rapidly, his features so close to my own. He must've caught me when I'd fallen. He had his strong arms wrapped around my torso, and the places his body had contact with mine felt...strange.

I had never looked at Psy, not really. It was passing glances the entire time I had been at their home, but now I could see the little flecks of purple color in his strange-colored eyes.

It appeared as if one eye was blue, but the other only had half of the color the other had and then completely turned to black.

"Penelope?"

I shook my head, pushing my feet firmly down and shrugging out of Psy's arms. My brother was standing beside me, calling my name and wiping at his tear-drenched face.

"I-I..." I stammered. "I'm okay, Mickey....a-are you?"

He let me give his arm a squeeze, and that turned into pulling me into a hug I feared would squish Kojec. I returned the embrace, turning my body over slightly to give the baby some space. It was what I could offer my poor brother.

"You take care of yourself, Penn." he scolded, tussling my red hair. "I can't be worried about you when I am gone."

I furrowed my brows. "What do you mean gone?"

He was cut off by that dark-haired man coming to his side. His presence was eerie. Something about him just shouted danger.

I could see a woman hiding by a tree not far off, and the way the man kept glancing back at her made me think they knew each other.

The darkness he carried with each step seemed to disappear with those stolen glances. Maybe it was love.

"Quinn," he said, and my brother and I looked at him.

Force of habit to respond to my last name. Quinn was what I'd been called most in my life.

We weren't allowed to give our names to the clients, so our last names were used as our first names. Sometimes, I thanked the heavens that my real name wasn't spoken in those rooms.

I could pretend the touching and pain were meant for someone else. Separate myself from the person they broke sometimes.

"Yes, Lucius? What do you need from me?"

I felt like I was listening to a private conversation, and I looked over toward Psy again, his sad smile masking any emotion. He thanked the guests, and people were starting to leave.

Were we leaving?

When would I see my brother again?

I frowned and chewed my fingernail, irritation causing me to chip the stupid nail bed.

I was not like Lisa. She loved fake plastic nails and a lot of different makeup.

I had makeup shoved on my face my entire life for appointments. But the minute I was free of their hands, I would wash it all away. To see my freckles again made me feel...alive.

"I love you, Mickey. So much. Come see me soon, okay?"

Micah didn't say anything, just pulled me into a hug again that felt broken somehow. I tried to move away to look at his face, but he wouldn't let me. I could see his friend's face. He looked at him with...understanding?

A feeling I couldn't shake in my gut made me nauseous. Awkwardly, I broke away from my brother and his friend and walked over to the bathrooms in the area.

My stupid shoes were sinking so much in this freaking mud like it was sand.

I started running, that fuzzy, tight feeling returning and stronger this time. I dropped the umbrella and held the baby's head as I threw off the useless shoes and continued to run to the bathrooms.

I leaned against the concrete divider that separated the men and women from one another, trying to catch my breath and calm my erratic heart.

The sounds of the crying, fake laughter, and the relentless rain were like a scream in my ears.

"Fuck," I breathed, ripping at the stupid leggings around my legs.

It truly felt like I was suffocating—this stupid dress and stupid leggings.

The garment was halfway off my body, plastered by the muddy terrain. As they disappeared, and I could see the smooth skin beneath them, I calmed a little.

"Fuck leggings. I don't need a man," I said, using my foot to unroll the thing off me the rest of the way, which proved difficult with Kojec waking in my arms.

After I finally got the ridiculous clothing off my body, I stood in the mud with no shoes or leg covering. I squeaked. Psy was standing at the other juncture of the divider, staring at me with curiosity and humor.

I huffed, glaring at the man. "Didn't think to help me?"

He smiled a wise smile that took me off guard.

"Doll, you didn't need any help then, and you don't need it now. Get in the car, Penelope. I will be waiting when you're done playing dress up."

I blinked, stunned. My unruly state hadn't bothered him. He just walked off.

Confused, I started walking back to the funeral area and heard a dispute coming from where everyone was gathered. My ears perked when I recognized familiar voices. My brother...and my parents!

Micah Quinn

Chapter 46

I rubbed my jaw, and my view was of the startled people. My father stood in front of me, his arrogance dripping off him as much as the disgust of my mother beside him.

"Micaiah!"

I ignored the fake fawning of my mother and spat blood at my father's suede shoes.

"Don't speak to me as if I am your child to scold. You abandoned that right a long time ago, Nancy."

My father's fist slammed into my jaw again, and this time, it took me down to the ground. I coughed and welcomed the buzzing in my ears. Maybe the one who forced me into this world could be the one to take me out.

"Micaiah," my mother said again.

Her worried looks were because of the scene being caused more than my well-being.

A FLASH OF BEING A LITTLE BOY RUNNING THROUGH THE HALLS OF our family home came into my mind. Penelope and I were playing a game of tag, and Mother's polished vase had fallen to the ground, busting into smithereens.

I had shoved Penn into a room away from the chaos and took the tongue-lashing of my father as well as my mother's words. They had burned as much as the glass gliding over my skin in my father's hand.

"You are only worth what you present, Micaiah. Now, your body reflects your mistake in lessening our worth."

My sister and I were always trophies to tote around for them. When my sister went missing, my family used it as a gateway into milking the assholes around them. They enjoyed depleting them of all their funds to increase their property values.

My sister...

I PUSHED MYSELF OFF THE GROUND. PENELOPE'S TELLTALE BRIGHT blue eyes and red hair were coming into view. She looked a bit disheveled, and her leggings and shoes were missing.

"Mickey?" she said, approaching and then stalling when her eyes locked on our mother's. God, they were an identical pair of each other.

My mother's plastic surgery-ridden mouth was gaping. Her eyes were wide as saucers, and my father held his fist paused in the air, his shock written all over him, too.

Penn was always the beloved daughter.

The good girl.

She went to their dumbass money parties and lived every fantasy my mother had cooked up. Their abuse had only gotten worse when Penn was presumed dead...maybe the relief sagging on their cruel features was real.

Nancy stepped forward. Her deadbeat son was forgotten as she continued to move closer.

"Oh dear heavens," she said, tears filling her eyes. "Is that really you, child? Has the lord brought my dearest girl back?"

Penn stood frozen, an array of emotions on her face. She looked embarrassed, scared, and sad—every single emotion displayed on her freckled face.

"Penn. Honey, you have returned to us." My father walked forward, shoulder-checking me as he passed me to approach my sister.

They were touching her face and hair, looking over her body, and discussing all the fake-ass ways they looked for years for her. I was the only one to use a fucking bicycle in the woods for hours. I was the one who took those stupid flyers to every single job I had, who bribed big rich assholes to broadcast her pictures, and the one who never forgot about her.

Me.

She will need someone when you're gone.

The realization had me stealing my posture and forcing myself to smile in return to Penn's inquisitive gaze.

"Mother? Father?" she said. Her voice was almost childlike.

They hugged her, tears welled in her eyes, relief and confusion making her lip quiver.

When they saw Kojec, they looked at her in horror.

"Oh god, child. Did you grow an abomination in your belly? Is that thing from one of them?"

Penn's face fell, and now, her tears reflected the pain in her eyes.

"That's my fucking son, you pompous dried-up cunt."

I smiled slightly at my best friend standing beside my sister. I wasn't leaving her without anyone. She would be safe with Psy.

"Oh my. Psy Broden? Is that you?"

Psy's face was hard as he shielded Penelope and his son from my evil parents' gaze.

"Fuck you," he said, spitting in their direction. "Get the fuck out of here and stop tormenting your son by trespassing from whatever gossip you heard. You aren't welcome."

"Get in the car, Penelope," he said, walking toward the car-park area after nodding to me with a look. His stare spoke volumes, like, 'I'm sorry for your asshole fucking dickweeds of a family.'

I captured his gaze, pleading with my eyes my hidden message that I needed him to keep my little sister safe, that I was sorry... and goodbye. My sister followed him, stunned, leaving our birthgivers behind her, hopefully for good.

I walked up to my parents. Their sputtering when I stood in front of them sounded mumbled. The meds I'd taken earlier to help me sleep were starting to kick my ass.

"Get the fuck out of here, or go bury yourselves in one of the graves before I fucking do."

My father's hand would never touch me again, nor would my mother's words. The cage they brought me up in was gone. I had freed myself from it the minute I realized I had a fucking mind of my own.

I didn't need their faces to be the last I would see.

The last of the partygoers had snuck out of the area, probably uncomfortable, to avoid the conflict unfolding before them. As my parents walked away with wobbly motions murmuring between each other, I realized it was just me and the grave digger.

Micah Quinn

Chapter 47

He had already lowered the coffins into their separate holes. Lisa was eternally resting in her finished grave—the gravestone was now cleaned, and fresh flowers were placed on top of it.

I swallowed the lump in my throat. The dirt on top of Ivy's grave made me sick, and the more the guy shoveled mud over her, the more I felt like I was suffocating. I could see little parts of the coffin. I had been thinking of this moment ever since I spoke to her at the funeral. I would be with her. Forever. The minute her life ended, so did mine. I needed to be inside the eternal bed with her before mud covered the hole.

"Hey, my man. I know this is unorthodox, but if you would allow me, I would really like to do this myself."

The kid looked like a teenager just trying to get some damn

335

extra money to make it through, so I hated myself already for my thoughts. If he disagreed...

"Well, I definitely have not heard that before." He chuckled, a sardonic tone underneath what should be a joyful sound.

Pausing, he wiped his brow with the back of his arm and leaned on the shovel. There was just a strip of color where the coffin peaked through now. The rain had begun pouring, making even that little visible piece of white look like muddied gray.

"Yeah," I said, trying my best to smile through the desperation filling my soul.

Fucking please, please, please just say yes. I really didn't want to knock out a kid, but as unhinged as I felt without my Little Ghost, I wouldn't put it past me tonight.

"Oh, all right, bro. It sounded like the standoff with your whacko parents was too much for you for one night. I'll let you take over. Just don't tell my boss, okay? I can't afford to get canned. I need the money to pay for my sister's ballet courses in the fall."

My smile instantly turned genuine. This kid reminded me of who I used to be. He was just a man who wanted to protect and do right for those he loved.

"You have my word, brother. Thank you."

The kid placed the shovel in my hand, and it felt like I was holding the weight of the world on my shoulders.

It was getting dark now, the rainwater creating a puddle at the bottom of the grave where Ivy's coffin lay.

I felt like I was drowning in it.

I waited until the sun faded below the trees completely. I couldn't see anyone around anymore. All the visitors said goodnight to their loved ones, and the smell of flowers and rain filled my nose. I smiled, a true peace coming over me before dropping into the grave with Ivy.

I pulled the heavy ass lid off the coffin, and my gorgeous Little Ghost never looked so pale. Rain fell on her face, making it look like tears were streaming down her cheeks. I leaned over her, trying to shield her from the cruel weather.

"I got you, Little Ghost," I promised while kissing her cold forehead.

I pushed my hands down into the crevice of the coffin and pulled my Glock from the cushion.

I lay down beside her, watching the rain fall from the clouds and wondering If Ivy's spirit would be waiting there for me.

I had two bullets.

Taking a deep breath, I wrapped my arm around the love of my life—the woman who gave her life to avenge the souls taken from this world so cruelly.

I felt their presence around me, like an unexplainable warmth...a beckoning.

"I am sorry," I told them. "I am sorry you didn't get a choice in so many things. I hope my Little Ghost was able to free your spirits to choose your path in your afterlives, whatever that may be."

The wind blew the trees around, and I felt its whispered touch even down this far in the ground.

"I will see you soon, Little Ghost," I assured, looking at her beautiful face one last time. "Whatever the next world has for me, I will not live without you. A world where you don't exist is meaningless. I will burn every universe to the ground until I find you again. If that means an eternity of torture for my sins, then so be it. I will find you, Little Ghost. I will always find you."

I put the cold, wet metal under my chin and closed my eyes, resting my finger on the trigger. Being ready to end this existence to begin my spiritual search for my Little Ghost was liberating.

Voices reached down to me—snide laughter, crunching, and the sliding sounds of boots in the sloshing mud.

I froze, the register of the tones recognizable...it was the men from the caves. I fought the memory burning through me of hands, bodies, and that laughter. The pain of that night rammed into my head and sped up my heart until there was a loud banging in my skull.

I blinked, my vision flashing to that damn cave, Ivy's face, and her cries as she saw the men surrounding me. I shook my head, trying to force myself back into my reality.

I blinked again. My body was thrown forward over and over again. My knees were weak and giving in to the unforgiving ground, the forces behind me unwilling to stop.

I growled, touching the face of my sweet Ivy. The chilling pelting of the rain reminded me of the blood that was dripping down my thighs.

Ivy's defeat in her eyes as I said her name over and over again to drown out their grunts and moans.

No...

Shaking my head, I tried to rip away from the cage trapping me in my mind.

I continued to struggle to get a grip on my here and now, to listen to the voices and decipher their meaning. I couldn't hear their words spoken now without hearing those of the past.

"Oh, you like that little prince? Give that princess of yours a show of how much you like this. Tell her how our cocks feel."

I gripped my heart, the pain of my memories making me feel like I was splitting in two.

"Please..." I whispered to myself.

Ivy's words flashed in my mind.

"You aren't a hero, Porthos. You are just a tool they use to get what they want. As soon as they are done with you, they won't need you anymore."

No...I am your hero, Little Ghost. Please.

So many voices were whispering into my mind, and their words were like a violent scream in my head.

'A person's worth is based on only what they possess.'

338

'You want more, big boy? I wonder if your girl is as much of a screamer as you are.'

'I don't want you to take away my darkness. I want you to embrace yours.'

I held my hands over my ears. The voices were loud, unrelenting.

"Well, well, well. Look who joined our sleeping Princess."

I froze. Those words sounded different, less of an echo, and more…real.

My eyes snapped open, and four cruel faces stared down at me. One of them grinned, and then a shovel was hurling toward me.

Everything went black.

Micah Quinn

Chapter 48

I tried to open my eyes, the feeling of throbbing and warmth flooding my head.

What the fuck?

I tried to recall my memory. I was lying in the coffin with Ivy, about to pull the trigger, and then…what?

The taste of mud and blood filled my mouth. My head throbbed in time with my heartbeat and the point of pain in my head. Strangely, warmth flowed out with each beat. Dizziness overwhelmed me, and I couldn't grasp my surroundings.

Why was I on the ground and not by the coffin?

I tried to open my eyes again. The pain of that simple task was mind-numbing.

Blinking from the rain falling on my face, I focused in front of me. Shadowy figures were in front of me, blurred and moving around a large black hole.

The grave.

"I...Iv..y," I reached my arm out that felt broken toward the figures.

"Iv-Ivy," I said again, my vision clearing slowly.

It was the men...two, maybe? They were pacing around the grave. The others must have left.

Were they trying to...steal her body?

"I don't get why boss can be cozy in his goddamned fleece pajamas, and we have to freeze our asses in the rain to collect this bitch." the gangly one moaned.

Good, they hadn't noticed me yet.

"Stop whining dumbfuck, before I turn you into fucking meat slabs to gift the boss. This is his madame, dumbass. You shot the last one, remember? I am going to make sure the little princess is good and fucking ready first."

The guy laughed nervously and continued shoveling dirt into the hole. "Yeah fuck Alyosha. Aleksia, you should be the King. Not him."

If they covered my Little Ghost, I wouldn't be near her in death.

No...

I pulled my useless, pained body toward the grave. Their squabble and the thunder above were the distraction I needed.

Please just let me get back to her, then I will let myself die with my Little Ghost.

"Damn, straight!" The gangly one forced out a snort. "Hah, maybe I should give him some fancy fucking slippers made out of the skin of your ass cheeks as my dethroning gift before I chop off the fucker's head?"

The bickering continued, and I waited for the timed strikes of thunder to pull my body forward again and again.

A loud shot rang out. The underling jolted with the shock of my gun and then fell into the hole below. The sound of his body hitting something below ended with a thump.

Had they closed her coffin?

There was so much mud that I felt like I was sinking into a hole, too. The grave was so close to my reach now.

That asshole stole my fucking gun, and now I had one bullet remaining. I'd needed two—one for his skull and the final for myself. But no, he had to take that choice away, too.

Fine. I would kill him with my bare hands then and save the bullet for myself.

The thug laughed and kicked mud into the hole after his fallen comrade.

"Sorry, Niko, but you'd go snitch to Daddy when you had the chance. I will be King one day, but I need to make Alyosha think he rules a little longer."

"Care to tuck me in, King asshole?" I said, coughing.

The pulsing in my head and the mud on my face only made breathing harder. The idiot finally noticed me. Jumping to the side and yelling his surprise, he leaned down, squinting at me.

"Well, aren't you a fucking zombie," he said. The amusement and sick cruelty of his tone at my drugged condition made me want to murder him even more. The meds I had taken were really kicking my ass.

But, if he shot me now, I would roll into the hole and be with my Little Ghost. It wasn't ideal, but fuck it. The evil dick looked at me, the hole, and then back at me again. The cogs in his fucked up brain were spinning.

Fuck...

"Oh, how sweet! Prince charming wants to sleep with his princess."

I averted my gaze, trying to get close enough to fall inside the grave. Fuck him. I wasn't giving him the satisfaction. He had taken enough from me.

The throb in my head was starting to dull from the drop in temperature, or the mud had made a makeshift bandage. Either way, the ringing in my skull had lessened enough so I could lift my head and put my knees under my body. My only hope was to try and push myself up.

"Agh!" All I could see was the skyline moving backward. I landed with a thump, and it felt like the wind had been knocked out of my lungs.

"No—nooo..." I wheezed, stammering, trying again to push my body up.

Okay...okay, that fucking monster had kicked me. He wanted to keep me farther from my goal. But fuck him.

The man stomped toward me, a hunger in his eyes that made my limbs stiffen. If he touched me, I would rip his arm off. Bending down and squatting in front of me, I watched as he stroked the barrel of my gun sensually.

"How many people have you fucked up with this beauty?" he said, licking the metal and cackling at me.

"I should return the favor back to all the people you screwed over with this beautiful weapon, shouldn't I? How would you love to be fucked right back by it? Will you scream for me so pretty again, big boy? Last more than a few minutes before you bust your thick load this time, okay?"

I growled, his eyes dipping to my pants. The memories of those very hands plagued my fucking memories again.

"You touch me, and I will make you dig your own fucking grave before burying your dick in it," I warned, locking my arm over my pants.

The man chuckled at me with such mockery in his tone that I almost retched. "That is big words for a man on his knees before me."

I glared up at him, the reality of his words kicking me in the ass to force myself to get up and move. Unfortunately, all my legs could manage was a quick stagger.

Fuck, I could barely keep my feet under me, and my body was not cooperating. It felt like my limbs were threatening to fall out from under me with every shuffle of my feet, but I wasn't close to her. I couldn't give up now.

I might be going to hell, but I would be damned if I didn't bring a demon down with me.

"I knew I liked you. That fire..." he crooned, circling me. I countered him, stumbling to keep him in front, and put the grave at my back.

"You like to dance, too? My, my... What a prince indeed."

I eyed my target and waited for his move. He was shorter than me, which meant he could bull-rush me and knock me off balance. I needed to be fast enough to move away and maneuver correctly.

As predicted, he stalked forward, and his movements were calculated. He used the weather as a distraction, making soundless movements with the booming of the thunder. Finally, when he was right in front of me, he lunged, his head down as to knock me over.

I sidestepped him, grabbing around his waist and using all the strength I could conjure to smash him into the ground. Taking advantage of his jostled state, I twisted his gun-wielding hand upward.

The fragile bone snapped under my fist, and I pressed down.

His scream was loud, rattling my brain at the closeness of his mouth to my ears. His mangled hand contorted uselessly. The gun dropped, falling into the grave, sliding on his pouring blood.

I got to a stand over the man sobbing on the ground. The man who took from me what I hadn't given him. The man who'd taken so many girls' lives and did the same unthinkable things to them that he'd done to my body.

"You're wrong," I said, my breath shaky with exertion. "You keep calling me a hero, saying I wanted to save my princess. I lived my entire fucking life being a knight for everyone—a tool to be used and disposed of," I continued, his wild eyes searching for an escape that wasn't there.

"There is no light in me anymore. No compassion or goodness. That was ripped out of me when her heart stopped."

I located the tears in his skin at his wrist, kneeling and holding him still with my body. I stuck my finger in the wound, and I twisted it around, widening the gap with careful movements.

The man screamed beneath me, begging for mercy he never granted.

"She's not...Ah!"

"I am not a hero," I repeated, ripping his flesh harder and using my knee to snap his bone. "All my Little Ghost wanted when she was finally free of your fucking cage was to free others with the same fate and to punish the ones who used her."

I used the bone ripped from his arm to stab him in the torso.

"Who's the screamer now, asshole?"

I laughed in his face, finally getting my hand inside the screaming man's torso. The muscle and tissue ripped, gushing his life's blood on my hands. It rolled down the mound where Ivy rested.

"I will put you in a cage like you did to her."

I felt his rib and gripped my fist around it, cracking the bone free and pulling it through the now gaping hole.

The man gurgled under me, his blood spurting out of his mouth with each faint beat of his heart. I raised the broken rib above his head and smashed it down with all the force I had left in my body. As it slammed into his eye socket, his thrashing stopped.

"Enjoy the fucking cage of hell, monster." Adrenaline leaked from my body, the energy I'd felt fading like a light as I sagged off the now very-dead bag of flesh.

I cradled the gun, and I allowed my body to slide down the river of blood of the enemies to my Little Ghost. Her coffin was open, mud, rain, and blood pooling around her body inside her cushion. She looked like she was floating on blood.

I pulled my broken, tired body into the coffin, her white dress now a crimson red. I wrapped my arm around her once more, grateful there was one fucking bullet left in the clip.

I sighed, a peace settling over me like a river.

"I love you, baby girl. Until we meet again." I kissed her bloody lips, taking in her beautiful face, holding the gun under my chin once more.

I took a deep breath, placing my hand on the trigger as two golden eyes opened beneath me.

"Por...thos?"

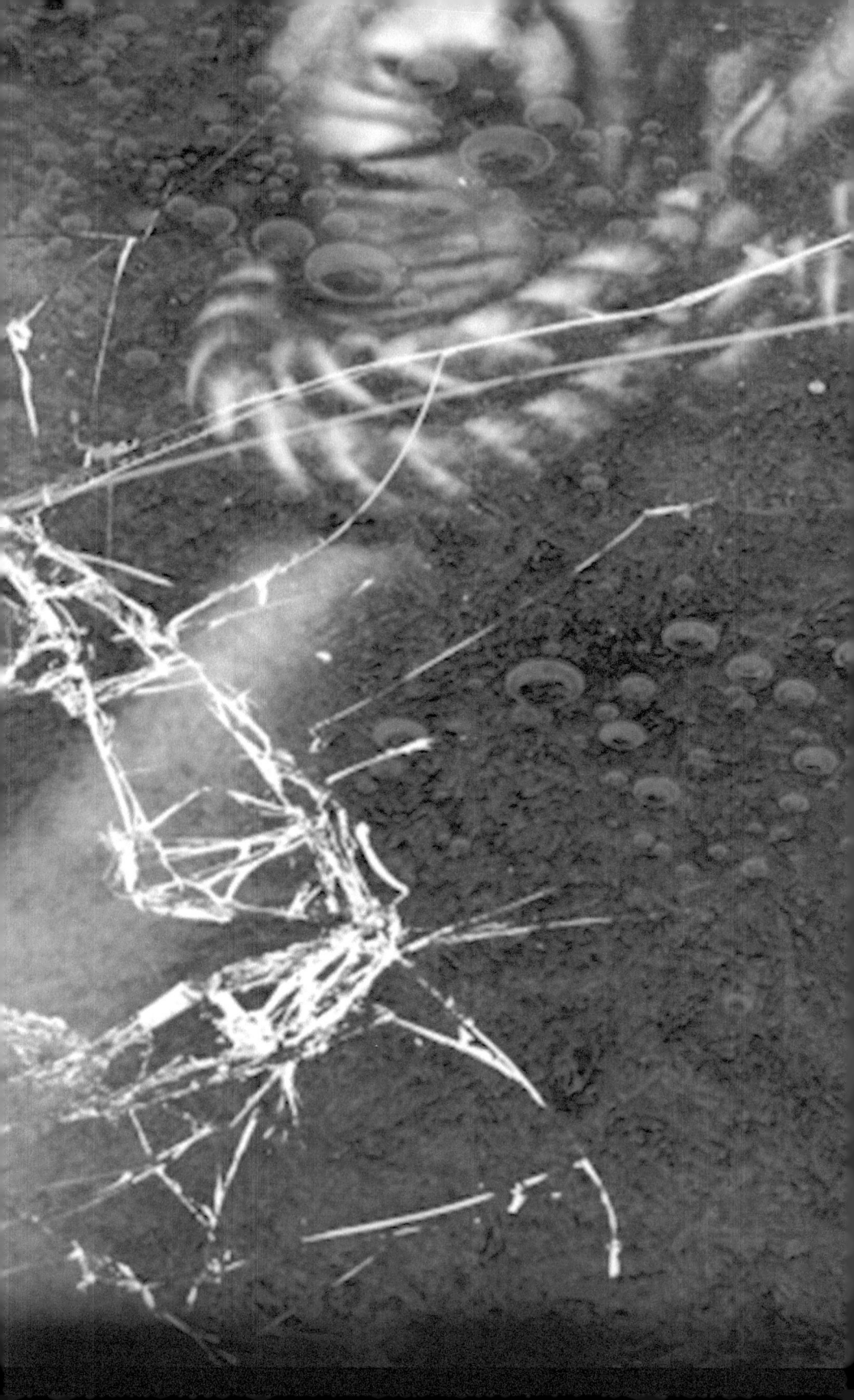

Ivy

Chapter 49

I stared up into tortured blue eyes.

My Porthos. He was here. He was…

I assessed my surroundings. Confusion and horror built in my gut. The man of my heart was covered in blood. From head to toe, he was saturated in it. The iron in the air singed my nostrils.

I was inside some kind of bed— no, I was inside a coffin. We were down inside a hole, and blood and mud surrounded us. There were two dead bodies, and we were lying in a pool of thick liquid…blood.

"Micah?" I said, uncertain of anything. "W-Where are we?"

Micah gripped me in a bone-crushing hug. His body was shaking so much that I felt as though he would break apart if I let go.

"Oh my god. Ivy. Oh, baby. Oh, Ivy. Oh my fucking god, my

Little Ghost." He was repeating himself over and over and kept smoothing my hair.

He looked like he was going to fall over. His face had bruises, and the top of his head had a different shade of red on it.

"Are you in pain?" I said, concerned, reaching for his head.

He seized my hands and kissed each of my fingers.

"No, my love. I have never felt so much happiness in my entire existence."

My confusion only grew as my surroundings cemented around me. "Micah, I don't understand. What...."

My Porthos simply shook his head and pulled my wrists toward him, kissing each inch of my flesh. The rain was pouring down onto us, and with each passing moment, I could see more of my beautiful man's face coming into view, the caked-on mud and blood washing away like tears from a god.

"Fuck Ivy, I am never letting you go. Ever. I will always follow you. I told you, you won't get away from me. I will follow you to the fucking grave."

I looked around. My god, we were in a coffin. He was definitely true to his words. The memories of the man came into my mind. There was a strange smell and the taste of almonds on my tongue. Did he put something in my IV line?

I was...dead?

"Micah," I said, wanting answers from him, but his blue eyes were low, and his kisses felt hotter on my skin as he reached my shoulder, moving the bloody garment out of his way.

"Your skin." He moaned, trailing those kisses to my collarbone. "You feel so warm again."

Again?

"Micah," I said, but his lips trailing over my chest made my breath catch, and the thoughts in my head completely dissipated like the wind around us.

"I have missed you so much, my love." He groaned, grinding his very alive cock into my thighs, pulling at the threads of the dress.

"The next time I see you in a white fucking dress will be our wedding day," he warned, a growl on my skin as he ripped the threads apart.

I felt my eyes go wide.

Wedding?

"Eilizaveta Vasiliev, my Ivy, my Little Ghost," he said softly, those hands traveling over my fevered skin, the chill of the icy raindrops creating a frenzy of sensations.

He slipped his fingers inside my waiting core, the feeling so distant but so amazing. He worked me expertly, making that rising wave go higher and higher, my stomach tightening with the need for release.

"Oh fuck. Porthos. Yes. Please, yes."

I couldn't help but moan and take all the emotions those fingers held—fear, sadness, anger, pain, love, and happiness.

"Little Ghost. My Little Ghost," he said, using his magical tongue to lick the juices his fingers created from me.

Moving lower, he found my wanting pussy and began licking and teasing my clit until I was at the point of insanity. If he kept this up, I would surely need to be admitted to the asylum he helped at....

"If you want to come, baby, then answer me a question first, please." He teased me more, sucking and lightly nibbling around every nerve ending I had.

I realized he was clothed, and that suddenly felt as maddening as the overstimulation I felt in my core.

"Yes. Yes. Yes." I moaned, not caring what he wanted. The answer was always yes for my Porthos.

He chuckled, allowing me to desperately claw off his shirt and yank down his pants, freeing that massive demanding weight at the junction of his thighs. He rubbed my thighs with the skin of his head, the overstimulation going into hyperdrive.

A delicious pain radiated everywhere, and I bucked my hips toward him. Our joining would be complete for a second time in the lethal dance we had only tested once in the tunnels.

"No more running," he warned, pushing just slightly in and retreating, causing me to whimper my response.

"No running!" I agreed, trying to impale myself on him.

He growled, his own need clearly getting the better of him.

"You are fucking mine," he said, biting my ribs hard. I shrieked and groaned, rolling my hips in agreement.

"I'm... yours..." I panted.

"Will you marry me, Ivy?"

I gasped, pushing him backward in shock. I searched his eyes for any humor or a flicker of teasing, but there was just need and... love.

"You...want to marry a killer?" Tears were starting to prick my eyelids.

He laughed out loud, leaning up to gesture around us. The blood still surrounded us, and the bodies were starting to be covered in the earth from the weather.

"I love every piece of your soul, Little Ghost. I love your past, your pain, your guilt, your grief," he said, laying back down on me. "I love your vengeance, your morality, your humanity," he continued, pushing into my heat.

The tears were blinding me. My disbelief at his words was something I had only dared to dream.

"I love your light," he said, inching deeper inside. "And I love your darkness."

Finally, he was further inside me, breaking all the boundaries of my heart and body I'd never freely given to another.

The bars around my soul started crumbling like a wall, and I finally felt the stone give to free the others.

"I love every part of you, Eilizaveta," he said, his tears falling as the need and hunger had him nearly filling me fully.

"I love every part of you because that is who you are, and I accept every burden you think you have. Don't fight your demons alone. I am here, and as you can see, I will live my life giving you the world. If that's the blood of your enemies, so be it."

His hips locked with mine, his hands smearing with the blood pooled around us. I felt like I would absolutely burst. I couldn't breathe and couldn't get enough at the same time.

This was a fire, but nothing like I'd felt in my past. It felt like my heart was burning away any doubts or fears I had. It left only happiness as pure as the love of my life as he thrust repeatedly inside me.

His body fit me so perfectly, even though I was small and he was big—even though he was light and I was darkness.

It didn't matter.

Nothing mattered but this.

Nothing mattered but the man I loved being inside my body, completing a puzzle I never knew I needed to complete.

I didn't feel caged anymore.

For the first time in a long time, I felt...free.

I brought his lips to mine, riding the waves his movements brought me. Over and over again, I emptied what felt like my soul into this man and his wicked body.

All I could see was him.

All I could hear was him.

All I wanted forever was...him.

Swallowing hard and, trying to catch my breath and holding him as tight as I could possibly hold him, I smiled and finally felt the cage disintegrate forever.

"My answer, Micaiah Quinn, is..."

I swallowed again and brought my lips up to his. Stealing his breath with my kiss and cementing my words, I whispered across his lips.

"Yes."

Two Weeks Later

I STARED AT THE FLOOR, TRYING TO STEADY MY BREATHING AND KEEP from puking on the doctor in front of me. Micah was by my side. His blue eyes were glassy, but his smile was determined. I knew my Porthos. He was worried, but I was, too.

I had been declared dead from the drugs put in my system, my body completely shutting down. Now, I'd been feeling these effects for a few weeks. Micah had been hovering over me, getting me crackers to nibble on the days I could eat and making sure I drank his water-electrolyte combinations.

Was my second lease on life really ending so fast?

"Ms. Vasiliev," the doctor said carefully, his old eyes hidden in the large round glasses. "The effects of the drugs given to you were most certainly a dangerous cocktail of potassium, opioids, and a few stimulants."

I waited with bated breath, squeezing Micah's hand in my own. He kissed my forehead and squeezed my hand tightly.

"Is that why she is so sick, Doc?" Micah urged, tapping his foot on the tiled ground.

"Patience, my love," I scolded, pulling his hand to my mouth and reassuringly kissing it.

"Possibly some aftereffects, yes." the old man continued. "But that won't affect the baby."

Micah continued to press the doctor, cutting his words off before he could finish.

"But will she be okay? Is there anything to get her to b—" he stopped suddenly, his big blue eyes blinking slowly while his mind worked.

"Di-Did you just say…baby?" he asked.

I thought I was hearing things, but a baby…

"Yes, Detective, I did. The fetus has remained unharmed by the aftereffects, and the experience of the vomiting, nausea, and dizziness is likely due to the pregnancy, not the drugs she was given."

My hand traveled to my stomach, my fingertips resting on my abdomen.

Baby…

Micah was quiet, his mouth opening and closing. I looked at my fiance, my concern written in my eyes in the reflection of the cabinet behind him.

"Porthos? A-Are you okay?"

My love, you are…you are okay." he said softly, tears flowing free from his eyes.

"We are okay, Micah," I said, my words feeling strange to even myself. "We are okay." I brought his hand to my stomach.

Our growing child was inside, safe, and alive.

"I-I…" he stammered. "I don't know what to say. Doctor, is there anything to help her sickness?"

The doctor laughed, hobbling over to a cabinet and grabbing something out of the wooden doors.

"It's called birth, Detective. Let this be one of the many times your child shows you no mercy."

I smiled, but Micah scowled.

"No. There must be something she can take in that wonderland of pill dispensaries. She is so sick."

The doctor sighed, scribbling random things on his notepad. Micah scoffed when he handed him the piece of paper.

"Doctor? What is this? Salty crackers and antiacids? Are you serious?"

I sighed and tried to de-escalate my well-meaning fiance.

"I am okay, darling. Please," I said. "Porthos. You are the best medicine." Micah grumbled but backed off the snickering health professional.

"I am so happy, Micah," I said suddenly, tears randomly welling in my eyes. "I am so happy!"

Micah seemed taken off guard by my outburst, but the doctor laughed harder.

"I will see you two in the next few weeks to check on the little one. Congratulations, mom and dad."

Micah had an exasperated look on his face, and I half expected him to chase the doctor out of the room. I squeezed his hand, making him remember that we were linked.

When we were alone, I let the tears fall more freely, and the cages around my heart slowly fell free even more. My fiancé, my beautiful husband-to-be, looked so scared.

I pulled him down to me on the medical bed, and the paper crinkled as it adjusted to his weight.

"Are you happy?" I snuggled into his side.

"Of course I am, Little Ghost," he said, but his eyes wouldn't meet mine.

"Micah," I said, and he finally looked at me.

"What's wrong? You fight injustices all the time, yet you can't smile at such a just occurrence now?"

Micah looked down.

"I am happy. Truly. I just…I am scared," he admitted. "My father is nothing short of horrible, and yours…" he trailed off.

I grimaced. My father was not going to go anywhere near our baby.

"My love, you are nothing like them!"

Tears streamed down his face. I kissed them away, one by one.

"You are extraordinary, and our child is lucky to be able to call you father."

He looked at me, his cage walls crumbling before my eyes with the freedom in his expression.

"I love you," he said. "I love you so much."

His hand traveled to my stomach. "And I love you, little one."

Micah Quinn

Chapter 50

A Few Weeks later...

Ivy was shaking, her body visibly vibrating as she walked forward to me.

"It's okay, Little Ghost," I assured her, rubbing her shoulder.

If I was being honest, I was scared. I didn't know how to do this, but I loved this woman so much. I wanted, needed her to heal.

I got to the end of the hall and flipped on the light, the room illuminating and glowing off the multitude of metal items in the room. Lucius and Phoenix certainly knew some...interesting toy shops.

I swallowed audibly and steadied my breath.

That was exactly what I had asked for: chains, knives, blindfolds, rope, and a number of other sex toys. It was all here and so foreign to me that it was a good thing I hadn't tried to find it all myself.

I ignored her gasp and walked all the way to the back, grabbing the chains that were linked to the wall. The handcuffs on the end were black and leather.

There was a multitude of different colored ropes and silks and a table lined with a blanket of all different colors, shapes, and sizes of sex toys. I could point out a vibrator in the lineup, but I was clueless about the rest. I should have asked for a lesson with this shit from the psychotic duo.

I started to deflate a bit. My fear and uncertainty that this was even going to be helpful was weighing heavy on my chest like the weird nipple clamp things on the table.

I reached for the blindfold. The simple velvet silk stood against all the rest of the daunting items. This felt safe. I wrapped it around my eyes, needing to put myself in the dark, willing to feel what she had all that time—the darkness and the fear of the unknown that lay in wait.

"Get the chains, Little Ghost," I said, positioning myself against the wall and holding the heavy weights out to her.

"Take that beautiful rage out on my body," I continued, listening to her breathing and her heartbeat.

"My very breath has always been yours."

"Micah. What are you doing? This is scary. I don't want to hurt you."

I smiled and shook the chains in front of me. "Then don't. Make what caused you pain into pleasure. Take control of what hurt you, and know it won't ever hurt you again."

Her breathing was so quick. It was a combination of fear and curiosity in her slow steps and unsteady speech. "I...don't know how."

"I've got you, baby girl. I am yours to do with whatever you please. I am at your mercy and your command."

She was at my wrists now, grabbing the chains in her delicate hands and hesitating before wrapping them around my wrists and twisting them around my waist.

"Tell me what to do, my love," I gently pressed, settling into the metal of the bands.

"Unbutton your shirt," she said, her voice stronger than before, her lust creating strength.

I could feel my dick grow with the knowledge that she wanted me like this.

I had never let any woman have control over me this way. I was always in control, always giving the demands, but this was Ivy. This was my beautiful bride. I would give her every part of me for the rest of my life. She owned my soul the day I saved her from that cage.

I listened to the demand, reaching my handcuffed and chained arms up to unbutton my suit shirt awkwardly.

I couldn't see her eyes, and that was killing me.

"Tell me what you see, Little Ghost."

Her warm touch startled me. The contrast between her heat and the cold chains made my skin tingle. I felt her caress my chest, her soft fingertips gliding over my collarbone, my pectorals, my nipples, and down my abdomen.

She kept going, dipping her hand into my pants and making me hiss from the contact.

"Fuck, my beautiful bride. Yes. Please touch me."

Her grip became more steady, her thumb brushing over my head and sending shivers down my spine.

I felt her breath on my stomach and her teeth on my hip.

"You bit me," I accused, utterly shocked.

She laughed in her husky, velvety tone and kissed the mark she had just nibbled.

"You are delicious, Svin'ya."

I smirked at her, my blind ass trying to maintain the cocky attitude. "Taste like bacon, huh?"

She didn't answer my question about my little pun, and instead, she pulled away from my bottom after unbuttoning my pants and letting them fall down my thighs to my feet. Now, I was anxious, but another darker part was wanting to feel her go further.

The table beside me rattled, and a switch sounded with a whirring sound, firing up afterward. I gulped, my body sweating with uncertainty. She walked back to me, the shadow of her dainty form barely visible behind the blindfold.

The vibrator wasn't small, but she grabbed something large enough to make my ribs shake when she brought it to my nipples and teased the hardening buds.

My cock danced for her with need as she dragged the toy down my torso.

She gripped me in her soft hands, my precome coating her fingers. I couldn't see a thing, but I felt a strange wrap being placed around the head of my dick.

"Are you ready, my husband?" she said sweetly, her innocence and kindness strange to hear with her little torment device in hand.

I opened my mouth to speak, but suddenly, I felt pulses of intense vibration on my cock, going from zero to a hundred, the vibration and stimuli so powerful I was unable to hold back my moans.

She grabbed my face and kissed my lips, her taste with those vibrations a current of unknown pleasures tipping me on the edge. She brought her hand down and grabbed my balls, sliding a smaller toy with a hum rather than intense shaking, now buzzing my special spot.

"Fuck Little Ghost. You are devilish after all, baby girl." I groaned, my moans a pathetic pant as she played with different speeds.

It was sending me close to the edge and then letting me down over and over. I felt so fucking unhinged that I was yanking on the chains and jerking my pelvis toward her.

A beast unleashed.

"Lay back, or it stops," she demanded, and I kept thrusting into the air.

The sensation halted. Her hand grabbed the device and pulled it free from my cock. I panted, trying to control myself. She was in control.

She. Was. In. Control.

My love for this tantalizing woman was all I could focus on to push my ass back on the cold wall and wait for her to come back to me.

Her shadow lingered around for a minute while I caught my breath, and finally, she returned.

"I am in control," she said, her soft voice strong and beautiful.

"You are in control," I repeated, my breath steadier.

"You will come when I want you to, Micah."

I whimpered despite biting my tongue. The edging was making me a pathetic mess.

"I will come when you want me to, my wife." I couldn't see it, but I could hear the smile in my voice.

"Good man." She walked back to me, a new item in her grip by the sound difference of how it moved in her hand. She dragged the item on my skin. This time, it was cold and sharp.

I felt her nick my skin, and a droplet of liquid dripped down my forearm.

She cut me.

"Does it feel good to make me bleed for you, Little Ghost?" I said as the endorphins and edging made me dizzy.

"Yes..." she said hesitantly.

I reached up with my chained hands and wrapped my fingers around hers, digging the blades deeper.

"Good, then do it again."

She gasped and followed suit, pressing the tip of the knife on my chest and pushing just a bit harder than the last.

God, she felt good.

She draped her silky thigh over my torso, her beautiful body facing mine as she straddled me, holding herself up on the chains that bound me.

I grunted at the force and held her beautiful, naked body up.

She poised herself around my thick cock and bounced herself onto it until she fully enveloped me.

"Fuck, my Little Ghost. Fuck."

I was so pent up from that damn toy and the blade. I began falling over the edge within a few minutes of her rocking and learning my body. As I came, the blindfold was pulled away, and I could see my gorgeous bride meeting her ride of pleasure. As soon as she finished, I pulled her to me.

After a good fifteen minutes of holding her, I glanced down. God, I was a bloody mess. My chest and arms were sliced with little cuts, and her naked porcelain skin was sporting my blood. That knowledge made my beast roar, claiming her harder and pumping into her deeper.

I lowered her body, flipping her against my dick and taking her from behind.

"My body has always been yours, Micah...my husband. Yes. Take me, I am yours."

Her words were a crescendo chant in my mind as I blasted my come so deep into her body. I could feel each pump being encouraged by her contracting walls. I may have been trapped in chains, but I no longer felt caged.

This woman and her beautiful strength and courage had freed me. I wasn't tormented by my mind and memories anymore. When I thought of rain, I thought of her lips as I kissed her and how her black hair tangled in my grip. My sister was safe, and all those years of pain and sadness would be filled with love and happiness.

Those monsters had tried to take her away from me, tried to give her a drug that made her dead to the world. If I hadn't been there that night determined to join my ghost in the afterlife, I wouldn't have found those assholes waiting like vultures to steal her away.

Her father wanted to use her, likely to replace Lana. But never again, I would never again let go of my beloved bride.

I looked down at my hand, my wedding ring shining bright, linked in the hand of my wife, Eilizaveta Quinn.

THE END

Micah Quinn

Epilogue

Nine Months Later

My sister ran into the room, linking her hand to my wife's, smoothing her hair, and whispering to her softly. I hated seeing my beautiful Russian beauty in so much pain. Her face was contorted in the most determined agony.

I felt responsible for this, and the anger that stirred in my gut made me feel sick. I swallowed, plastering an encouraging look on my face and glancing at the sheets taped behind her.

Picking one out, I read aloud, "Uh…great job, my love. You are opening. Blooming like a flower."

That clearly wasn't the right thing to say because the wrath of a thousand suns suddenly was on me as all three women glared daggers at me, and Ivy's dainty hand let go of the side of the tub long enough to smack the shit out of me.

I blinked in surprise, shaking my head as her scream turned into words. "I'll give you a fucking flower!"

Penelope gave me a sympathetic look.

Phoenix ran into the door, her wild, icy hair smacking Lucius in the face. She quickly kissed him and bolted to Ivy's other side.

A roar emerged from my sweet bride as another contraction hit. I walked over to Lucius, my once enemy and now my brother-in-law. He was just as annoying as a little brother.

"Your hand broken yet, puppy?" he snickered, dodging away from the demon's sounds coming from the doorway.

I laughed, but my hand felt completely broken from the amount of squeezing it had endured.

"I wouldn't razz me, Lucy," I warned. "Statistics prove that when women are involved in the birth of another, their hormones start craving one of their own."

Lucius turned as pale as his sister, and his laugh died off.

"Ha, yeah, right." He chuckled, but it didn't quite follow through with his earlier amusement.

The look on Phoenix's face was one of love. She loved Ivy. They all did. The girls were always together and could feel every little kick the baby made. Hell, Phi was practically bouncing on her toes the day we started to foster Marcie, and now another life was happening in her face.

"Porthos!" I jumped, Ivy's scream kicking my ass in gear.

Lucius still looked unsure of his entire existence when I ran back into the room. I nearly froze at the sight before me.

A human being coming out of the very thing I cherished so much.

I didn't think about anything at that moment. I simply acted. Jumping into the birthing pool, the blood and god knows what else soaked into my clothes. I kissed my wife, letting her use my body to scream as she brought the little human into the world, catching the little thing in my arms.

A mirror of my own blue eyes stared back at me, sparkling brightly, and all the sound in the world was gone. All I could hear was the sweet coos of...my child. Ivy looked breathtaking. Her body glistened with the sweat of her hard work, her eyes filled with love and complete abandonment.

My sisters were smiling, their love and adoration for the little bundle written all over their faces. I adjusted to sit beside my wife, bringing up our baby and placing her into my Little Ghost's waiting arms.

"I can't believe it," she said, tears spilling from her eyes as she looked down at the prize of her labors.

It was as if everything we ever endured was erased in this moment. All the pain and the fear became distant memories. The drugs given to Ivy to make her appear dead, her father trying to steal her to be the new mistress, the cave, the abuse, the cage—all of it was completely erased from time with one little look at this beautiful little life.

Lucius came inside, and Phoenix wrapped herself into his hold and sighed lovingly. Penn stepped back a little, allowing us some space and carefully watching from a distance.

Ivy gasped when the sex of the baby was revealed, and I smiled wide. My girls were together, held in my arms.

"What will you name her?" Phi asked, clapping excitedly.

Ivy looked at me, and I smiled, stealing a kiss from my gorgeous warrior.

"You always knew, Little Ghost." I reminded her that our conversations about the topic were known only to us.

Ivy had tears streaming down her face, and Lucius caught her gaze, the big brute shedding a few himself at the realization.

"Ana," she said, smiling down at our daughter warmly. "Anastasia."

Penelope

Hidden Reflections

Chapter 1

I thought back to the day my brother left me.

This was it. My brother was standing with the love of my life, and both were set to go back to New York and leave me here. It would be so weird losing my brother after all this time of missing him and just getting him back, but he and his creepy friends were right. I wasn't safe.

I had sat by the glass and waved out the window, my tears and heavy breath steaming up the texture.

Kojec was sitting in my lap, his little coos comforting me from my memories. He'd become my friend over the past few months. Honestly, we were all we had.

Psy was gone most days. He was throwing everything he had into that damn bar. I felt like I would have made friends at the asylum before he'd speak to me. We all had one conversation, and I think he was using me to look like he had his life together and not a sad widower with a baby.

He dragged me to this bar, where I met a sweet woman named Gardenia. She was selling the place she had built from the ground up because her daughter, about my age, died of cancer.

Life was so brutal that it didn't matter if you avoided sex traffickers, murderers, or mafia members in your life. You could still die from a disease that your body had. I felt like my life was a cancer. The act of simply living wasn't enough for my body.

No...it had to grow that tumor, or else it couldn't function.

I was too much of a coward to end it, and I was Kojec's only friend. His dad could barely look at him. I spent most of my days playing with the little guy, teaching him new things about the world around us, and honestly, learning it myself.

There was so much I wanted to know but wasn't brave enough to find out.

I loved the museums. It was amazing to see things preserved. For example, you weren't forgotten even when you were gone for so long.

The girls called me sometimes, mostly my new sister-in-law, asking me if I was okay and telling me updates about my niece. Her brother's girlfriend called me, too, but admittedly, she kind of scared me. I weirdly missed Kristiyan the most. We had been the only ones to talk to each other for so many years in that hole.

He'd often ignored me and insulted me most of the time, but I missed his voice. His poems. I wondered what happened to Kristiyan after the asylum was ripped apart.

Was he on the run?

Micah was so happy with his new little life that I didn't want to ruin it by asking what he knew of Lana's son. Maybe he didn't want to be found.

The door to the front beeped, and the seemingly harmless

doors hissed, allowing the safety mechanism to disengage and allow Psy into the door.

He swung a paper bag in his hand, tossed it over to the couch I sat on, and mumbled, "Got you food."

Absently, I thanked him and dug into the bag when I heard his bedroom door click shut.

I choked down the fries and burger. Weirdly, fast food made me miss the mystery concoctions at Hospital Twelve. Kojec woke up and sniped some fries, and I fed him the rest of my food and some fruits I cut up from the fridge.

"It's late, little dude. Let's get some sleep."

I took the babe to his room and sang him to him with his mother's song.

I missed Lisa. She was a nice person, and maybe friendship was one thing we had.

After Kojec was asleep, I went to my room silently, making sure I didn't make any noise while bumping around at night.

I had just about fallen asleep when my door creaked open, and a big shadow staggered inside. Blinking my eyes to focus, I readied a scream, but it was Psy. He was mumbling something, staggering around in no shirt and boxers.

"Psy?" I questioned, pulling my blanket over my nightgown to cover my breasts.

He didn't reply and instead laid down on my bed, looking up at the ceiling with a glazed look. I saw this at the hospital before—sleepwalking. He was stressed and sleepwalking.

I didn't know much about it, but I knew you weren't supposed to wake the person. Lying down slowly, I tried not to disturb the half-naked man on my bed. He rolled over and looked at me, his face oddly peaceful. His mismatched eyes were warm, shining brightly from the moon's light streaming in from my window beside us.

"You are beautiful," he said—a calm yet husky tone.

I didn't speak, and I was not sure what to say. Maybe he was seeing Lisa in a dream.

"So beautiful, Penelope."

I blinked, covering my mouth to hold onto the gasp.

Was he dreaming of...me?

"Like porcelain. My little doll. So beautiful."

He closed his eyes, murmuring those same words over and over until soft snores filled the room. I watched him sleep, contemplating what exactly to do. If I got up, it could startle him. He'd be confused if I had stayed here, but maybe that would be best. I snuggled into my blanket, Psy's big muscular body squished in the corners.

I watched the moonlight dance on his face and soon found myself sleeping peacefully for the first time in so long.

STALK THE AUTHOR

SK Pryntz loves writing gritty, thrilling, dark tales that will twist you into knots until you can't stand it. Her love of writing began at an early age, as well as singing and reading about fairytales. However, as she has grown older, the real versions of the fairytales are sincerely her favorites.

When she surfaces from her writing cave, she loves spending time with her husband and children.

ALSO BY SK PRYNTZ

Reflections Series

SHATTERED REFLECTIONS

CAGED REFLECTIONS

HIDDEN REFLECTIONS

The Asylum Devils Series

TWIST ME

Coming Soon...

BODY TOX

THANK YOU

Thank you to all those who decided to read my book. Only with your continued support can independent authors keep writing, which is why reviews mean so much.

If you enjoyed this book, please consider leaving me a review.

I hope you love my psychos as much as I do.

Sincerely,

SK Pryntz

TALK AWAY THE DARK

Remember you are seen.

If you or a loved one is in crisis, please reach out to the National Suicide Prevention Lifeline at 988, or the Crisis Text Line (Text TALK to 741741) to talk to someone who can help.

www.ingramcontent.com/pod-product-compliance
Lightning Source LLC
Chambersburg PA
CBHW022243020726
47496CB00004B/1039